STARS AND BONES BOOK III

Dreams in the Snow

BEATRICE B. MORGAN

AUTHORS 4 AUTHORS PUBLISHING
Marysville, WA, USA

Published by Authors 4 Authors Publishing
1214 6th St
Marysville, WA 98270
www.authors4authorspublishing.com

Library of Congress Control Number: 2021938847

E-book ISBN: 978-1-64477-097-9
Paperback ISBN: 978-1-64477-098-6
Audiobook ISBN: 978-1-64477-099-3

Edited by Rebecca Milkkelson
Line edited by Renee Frey
Copyedited by Brandi Spencer

Cover design ©2021 Brandi Spencer. All rights reserved.
Interior layout and artwork by Brandi Spencer.

Authors 4 Authors branding is set in Bavire. Book title is set in Allura and Bilbo Swash Caps. Series title and other headers are set in Cinzel. All other text is set in Garamond.

STARS AND BONES BOOK III

Dreams
in the
Snow

BEATRICE B. MORGAN

Authors 4 Authors Content Rating

This title has been rated 17+, appropriate for older teens and adults, and contains:

- Moderate sex
- Strong language
- Intense violence
- Attempted rape

Please, keep the following in mind when using our rating system:

1. A content rating is not a measure of quality.

Great stories can be found for every audience. One book with many content warnings and another with none at all may be of equal depth and sophistication. Our ratings can work both ways: to avoid content or to find it.

2. Ratings are merely a tool.

For our young adult (YA) and children's titles, age ratings are generalized suggestions. For parents, our descriptive ratings can help you make informed decisions, but at the end of the day, only you know what kinds of content are appropriate for your individual child. This is why we provide details in addition to the general age rating.

For more information on our rating system, please, visit our Content Guide at: www.authors4authorspublishing.com/books/ratings

DEDICATION

To Mom, who deserves all the Mother's Day cards, roses, and boxes of chocolate. You have been my biggest fan from day one, and words can't express how grateful I am to have you in my life.

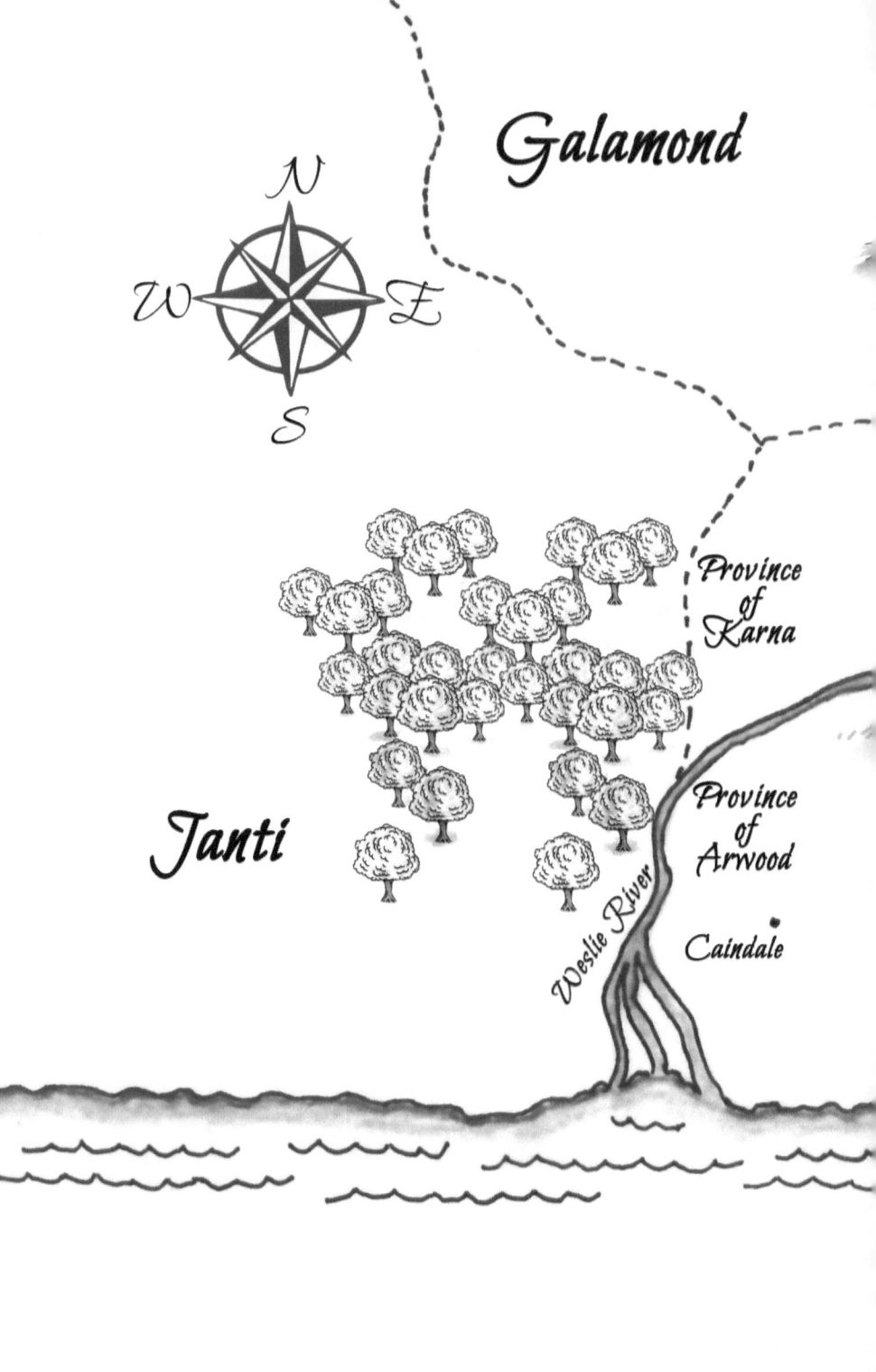

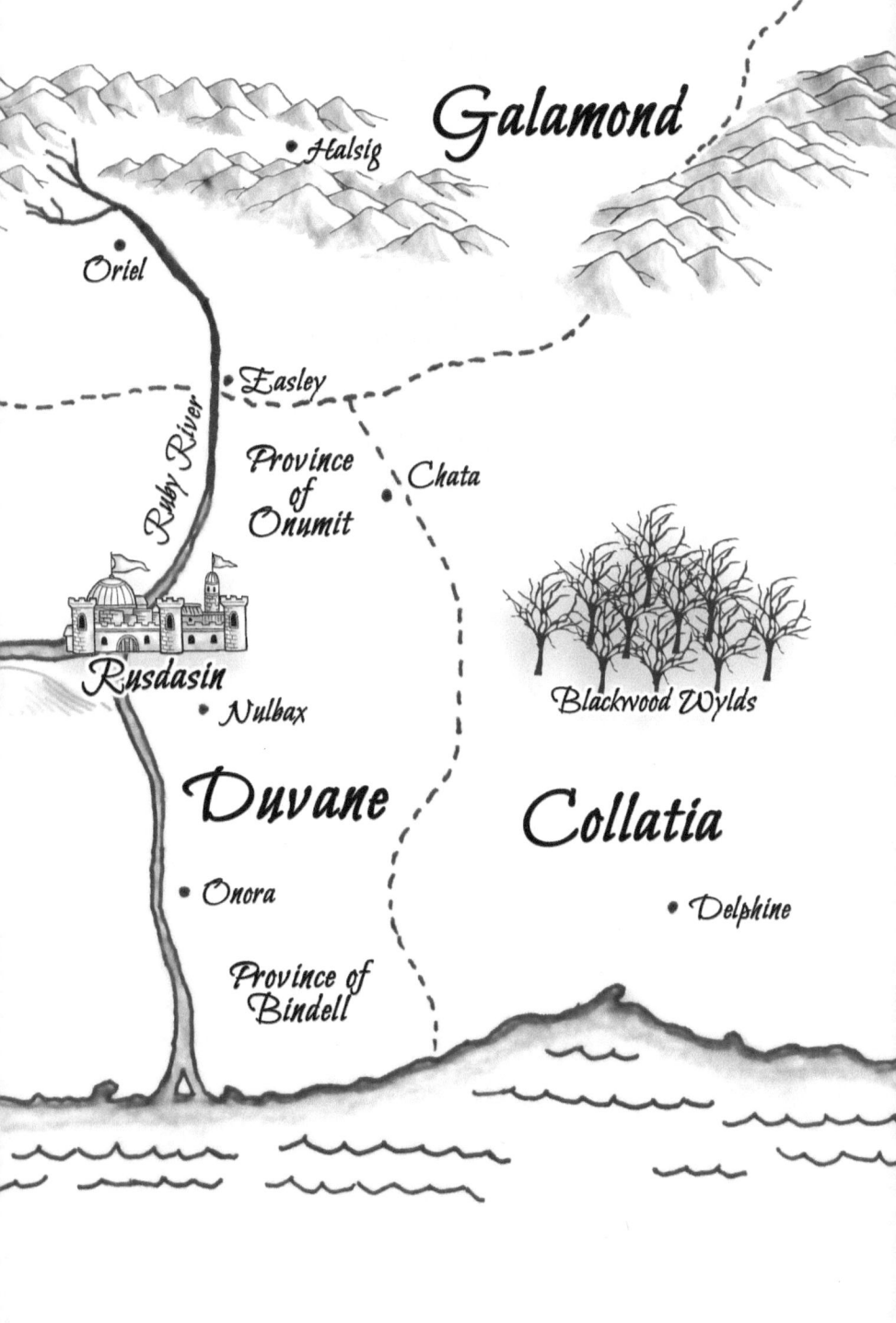

Works by Beatrice B. Morgan

Stars and Bones:
Thief in the Castle
Mage in the Undercity
Dreams in the Snow
Nightmares in the Ice (Summer 2023)

Hard as Stone:
Hard as Stone
Thick as Blood
Strong as Steel

TABLE OF CONTENTS

TABLE OF CONTENTS

CHAPTER ONE

Juniper Thimble slouched against the stern of the small boat as it gently made its way westward along the Weslie River. They had long since left the royal city of Rusdasin behind. They passed farmhouses, mills, and watersheds, but no one looked twice at the little boat or its two occupants. Farmers were too busy with their harvests, and she doubted word of her supposed death had reached this far.

Midmorning brightened into afternoon, then waned into evening. As the night overtook them, Juniper released a breath of relief. They had made it.

Her companion, Ison Rolin, yawned.

"Sleep." Juniper motioned to the floor of the boat. "I'll stay up on watch."

"Are you sure?"

Juniper nodded. She didn't feel remotely tired. Her nerves rattled far too much to sleep. Ison didn't object. He curled up on the floor of the boat underneath his cloak.

Her magic responded to the dark of night, awaking. She held her hand over the side of the boat and let a trail of snowflakes flutter behind it. The flakes dissolved quickly. Juniper didn't know if this little boat that smelled like mildew and fish had been worth selling out the Undercity. It didn't matter much now. She had left Rusdasin and the Undercity behind.

Still, the guilt stung.

She had sold out the Undercity. She had grown up on those underground streets, between the black market stalls, apostates, thieves, and assassins. Like it or not, the Undercity had been home.

And now she couldn't go back.

At least she'd warned her friends and allies of the inevitable invasion. They were plenty capable of handling themselves.

It hadn't been just her home. She'd condemned every person who called the Undercity home. She'd known that, too, when she'd offered the deal to Captain Tinnley. But, like usual, she had been thinking of herself, of what she wanted.

She told herself it had been for the good of the realm, to stop Nexon. The greater good. Still, those words felt hollow.

She couldn't worry about it now. She had her mission, and the Undercity would have to worry about itself.

All around, night bugs chittered and sang. She lost herself in the sound. Sooner than she expected, the east began to glow. The sky brightened; her magic waned. The forest sighed with a strange in-between silence. The night bugs had gone quiet, but the day-birds and bugs hadn't yet stirred, leaving the woods strangely, eerily silent.

The river pulled the boat along a bend, sloshing against the sides. She used her magic to smooth the turn. She could feel the water of the river, the power of it—she tried for a few heartbeats to command the water, to alter its course, but it proved too strong against her magic.

With the coming of morning, Juniper kept her ears and eyes alert—for beasts, for bandits, for any threats.

Ison let out a sigh. Gentle snores escaped his mouth. The days in the sunless Undercity had paled his ashy skin, but compared to when they'd fled the castle, he looked better. He had gained weight, his cheeks had filled, and his eyes no longer looked as haunted. His dark brown hair had grown out into curls. Sweat glued strands to his forehead and neck. It had done the same to her, and she felt remarkably dirty. They would have to stop somewhere to wash.

The boat drifted on. She could feel her ice magic waning with every minute, weakening as the sun rose and the moon fell.

If someone had told her a year ago that she would claim herself an ice mage, she would have laughed in their face. And likely punched them.

Yet here she was.

The Weslie River continued westward, but they needed to go north. She saw a small village ahead through the trees, built around half a dozen water wheels. By the smell, they raised pigs. As the boat came closer, Juniper scanned the forest. They could dock in the trees before anyone saw them. But with limited supplies and rations, and plenty of coin, she knew the logical thing would be to stop in the village. They could eat, collect what supplies they needed, trade what they didn't, and collect themselves for the journey ahead.

Juniper bent down and shook Ison's shoulder. He grumbled, inhaled, then opened his gray eyes. He blinked twice, his long lashes fluttering.

"Good morning," Juniper said sweetly.

"Good morning," Ison mumbled. He glanced around. "Why didn't you wake me up? Are you tired?"

She shrugged. Yes, but she wouldn't have been able to sleep. "I'll sleep tonight. There's a village ahead. We're going to dock and set out on foot."

Ison nodded and stretched. He pulled himself from his cramped sleeping position and sat. "Do you think they'll recognize us?"

She fingered the end of her auburn braid falling over her shoulder. She had thought to snag one of the wigs she'd used as a disguise, but in the chaos, she'd forgotten. "I don't know," she said. Trying to be hopeful, she added, "But, didn't you hear? Captain Tinnly killed Juniper Thimble when she tried to assassinate him. Hopefully, no one will be looking for her for a while."

Ison half laughed, a dry, bitter sound as he reached for one of the canteens in their supplies. Guilt tugged a little harder. Juniper hadn't forgotten the look on his face when he'd realized her death had been faked: relief, anger, and something darker she couldn't identify.

Using her magic, she guided the boat alongside the dock. Several other boats lined the rickety dock. Almost every boat held fishing baskets, nets, and poles. The reek of fish had seeped into the wood and sand. The town itself was still sleeping–windows were shuttered, porches were empty, and even the pigs and sheep snoozed in their little pens. It reminded Juniper of how little she had slept.

The town looked like any other riverside town. Signs indicated a general store, feed store, healer and apothecary, and seamstress. It held the essentials. A lantern flickered beside the door to a humble, weathered building whose hanging sign announced it as Bernard's Inn and Tavern, likely the only tavern in town. Juniper and Ison gathered their supplies from the boat, divided them evenly between their two packs, and started toward the tavern.

After being in the boat so long, it felt fantastic to walk. Juniper knew the feeling wouldn't last, not with all the walking they would be doing. Their plan included trekking north around Rusdasin and then heading east into the northern territory of Collatia.

There, they would hunt down Nexon's followers.

Juniper pushed open the tavern door. The old hinges squealed. A few travelers were drinking at a far table, and a group of farmers sat near the bar, playing a game of cards and dice. Wooden coins were piled in the middle. At the squeal of the door, most eyes turned their direction, gave them a quick once-over, and returned to whatever they'd been doing.

Except for one of the travelers sitting in the far corner, whose watery green eyes took in the two newcomers with a clinical, calculating stare—one Juniper had seen before. He was determining their worth.

She ignored him and guided Ison to the bar, where the bartender spoke in low tones to a woman in an apron. Their conversation ended before Juniper could hear. Their eyes took in the two new travelers, and Juniper put on her best weary, innocent girl expression.

"Can I get you something to drink?" asked the bartender in a deep, burly voice. "We've not got the finest ale, but it'll get the job done."

"Ale, please," Juniper said, tilting her voice in a southern accent.

Ison nodded and requested the same, in a similar accent.

They sat at a table near the window. The shutters didn't fit well, and water marks streaked the wall below the pane.

Two pints of ale appeared on their table, and Juniper gratefully took a drink. "Thank you." The ale wasn't the best, but it wasn't the worst. Better than the cheap ale of the Undercity. "What food do you have this morning?"

"Nothing fancy." He nodded toward the curtain the woman vanished through. "The real food won't be ready for a few hours yet. We've got the staples, though. Cheese and bread, maybe some fruit."

Juniper gave him a grateful smile. "All of that sounds delicious."

The bartender brought them a plate of hard cheese, leftover bread, and a bowl of blueberries.

"Thank you, kind sir," Juniper said.

He nodded and returned to the bar. His eyes darted over the travelers in the far corner, and a stout dislike passed over his face.

Juniper and Ison ate. She kept one eye on the other patrons. The farmers gave them no concern. Their pretend gambling gave them all the enjoyment they needed for the morning. But the five men on the far side whispered lowly, occasionally casting suspicious glances in her direction.

Obscenely obvious.

She held in her sigh. She didn't want to begin their journey with bloodshed, but she would if they started it.

A short while later, the five men got up, paid, and left the tavern. Juniper could feel their eyes on them as they departed, and when the door shut after the last man, Ison glanced warily at the door, then at her.

Even Ison, raised in the shelter of the Marca, had been able to spot them as bandits. She winked to reassure him, and he gave her a warm cautious smile in return.

Ison, unlike her, was not a fighter. The Marca had taught him about magic and history—book smarts, not street smarts. The Marca—the Order's school for mages—taught mages placid magic, not offensive magic. Though Xavier had been giving him lessons, Ison didn't have the fighting spirit, the drive to survive.

But that was all right. She wouldn't let anyone hurt Ison. Anyone wanting to harm him would have to go through her first, and—not to brag—she could pack one hell of a punch.

Their light but pleasant meal finished, Juniper paid the bartender and thanked him once again. Juniper heaved her pack onto her shoulder and took a step toward the door.

"Watch yourself," the bartender warned. He nodded toward the door. "Those men were looking at you like a wolf eyes a sheep. If they give you trouble, just give a holler. The men and I will come running. We don't like bandits in our woods."

Juniper gave him a coy smile. "Don't you worry about me, sir. We didn't make it this far without being able to hold our own." She nudged Ison.

The bartender laughed, but the worry didn't leave his eyes. "That's well. Remember, just holler."

Juniper and Ison left the tavern. The bandits weren't waiting outside or beside the tavern or in the narrow alley between the tavern and the general store. After trading what they didn't need and buying what they would likely would, Juniper and Ison started on the road north. It was nothing more than a stamped-dirt path through the woods, imprinted with recent hooves and wheel tracks.

All around them, the birds sang with maddening volume. Juniper had never been farther than the outskirts of Rusdasin, had never been this far into the forest, and she had never heard the sound so voluminous, so wild.

"Do you think they recognized you?" Ison whispered. "They kept looking at us."

She shrugged. "With these fat packs? Any bandit with half a brain would have been eyeing us."

Ison looked around the woods, eyes wide.

"Don't worry." She nudged him. "I'll be able to handle a few bandits."

She'd been practicing Bois's trick. She cast an invisible net of magic around them. She felt the blurry shapes of things: grass, bushes, and trees. Bois had been able to feel every blade on her person, but Juniper couldn't concentrate her magic that far. The more she focused, the more magic she used, and the faster she sapped her magic.

Juniper and Ison made their way along the winding forest road, up and down the rolling hills, around boulders, and across old stone bridges that arched over streams and rivers. They passed a few other travelers, most on horseback. No one paid them any mind. Her exhaustion slowly caught up with her, but she refused to acknowledge it. She would sleep when night came, when they made camp, when they could afford it.

No backwater bandits would get the jump on her.

CHAPTER TWO

Ison felt Juniper's magic net. She kept it light, or else she would exhaust herself. She hadn't slept all night, unless she'd caught a few hours when he'd been sleeping, but he doubted she had.

The sun had reached the midday point in the sky, shrinking shadows to puddles, sticking his shirt to his back, when Juniper threw a hand out to stop him. Then, he heard it—a hush of the birds.

Had Juniper's net felt something?

Then he heard footsteps in the forest. He brought air around him, an invisible shield—like Xavier had told him to. The air formed a bubble, pliable but strong. He could strike out at any threat with a whip of wind and deflect most blows.

"Ten," Juniper whispered, her lips barely moving.

Ison heard them coming closer. Ten sets of footsteps. Human.

"Look who we have here, boys," came a nasally male voice from the trees. "A pair of lost cats waiting to be skinned."

A horde of male laughter followed, and bandits stepped out of the woods. Five on either side, crossbows and swords at the ready. They wore tattered and patched leathers, their swords old and well-used. The leader of the bandits sauntered forward—the same man who had been eyeing them in the tavern. He stopped in the middle of the road, and his beady, watery green eyes roamed over Juniper with a hunger that made Ison want to hurl up his breakfast.

"We'll be taking your goods." He set his sword over his shoulder.

Juniper didn't move. She regarded the bandit with indifference.

The bandit frowned. "Your goods, bitch. Do you not understand?"

"Maybe they don't speak the common tongue," said another bandit.

"I heard her speaking this morning," said yet another.

"That don't mean she can't—"

"Shut up," snapped the leader. He turned his burning gaze to Juniper. "Well? Speak up, bitch."

"Oh, I understand," she said perfectly in the common tongue. "I'm just concerned that you don't understand."

He raised a brow at her. Ison tensed—they had magic, but they were surrounded by ruthless bandits. He'd heard stories of what bandits did to people. Horrible things, like heads on pikes and fingers in boxes. He suppressed a shiver.

Juniper continued, her voice even and cool, "I'm concerned that you're throwing yourself headfirst into danger for nothing. Surely, there is easier prey along this road."

"Your packs, now," he said through gritted teeth.

"Or what?" Juniper raised her brows. "You'll send your lackeys at me? I dare you to try it. See what happens."

The leader considered it. Then his brows furrowed in confusion. He took a step closer to Juniper. "Wait," he said, confusion clearing. He spat. "I thought you looked familiar."

Ison's heart thudded, but Juniper kept her expression calm. Ison tried to remain as calm.

The bandit leader took another step closer. Ison caught movement out of the corner of his eye—Juniper readying her magic. The soft scent of flowers followed, sweeter than any he'd smelled from the forest. Her magic had a bright blue hue, and a faint aura shimmered around her, so faint he doubted the bandits noticed.

The bandit leader's dirty face curled into a hideous smile. A dry laugh left his throat. "I don't know about you, boys," he said, "but I could use fifty thousand gold."

Juniper's breath came out in a quick huff; the bandits knew who she was.

"Where we gonna get that?" asked a rat-faced bandit, his face pinched in confusion.

"Don't you know who this is?" The leader pointed his sword at Juniper. "This is none other than Juniper Thimble, most wanted criminal in Duvane."

A ragged whisper of excitement and disbelief, tinted with uncertainty, rushed through the bandits. Ison didn't know if he was glad his name had been left out or not.

Juniper half laughed. "You're mistaken. Juniper Thimble is dead. Killed by Captain Tinnly not but a day or so ago. Even brought her head to the king."

"Heard that rumor," spat the bandit leader. He sneered. "Thought it was questionable then too. No, I remember you. I remember that face."

Juniper squinted at the bandit leader. He wasn't overly ugly, unless he grinned, nor was he excessively handsome. He was average in most ways.

"I apologize," she said casually. "I don't remember yours."

He whistled, and the bandits stepped closer. She nudged Ison, and at once, her magic lashed out: the barely-there bright blue formed into blunted spikes of ice, each shoving at a bandit's chest—the bandits on their left went up and into the trees. Crossbows went flying, the loaded bolts arching over the path and landing in the brush and sinking into trees. One lucky bolt struck a bandit with a meaty thwack.

A bandit from the right charged at Juniper, sword drawn. She spun and brought her magic up. His sword crashed into a shield of cloudy blue ice. Another bandit used her momentary pause to charge—Ison's wind soared behind Juniper, knocking the advancing bandit aside. The fallen bandits began to rise, and as Juniper turned to face the right, he faced the left. His wind knocked the bandits over as they rose, one by one, and yanked the weapons from their hands.

Bolts whistled through the air. His magic gave him a fraction of a moment's notice. Ison's entire being quivered. He'd never been in a fight like this. Xavier had tried to prepare him, but talking about fighting and actually fighting were very different. He kept his wind around him, shredding bolts as they came closer, wrenching swords from hands and pushing bandits back.

The leader and three bandits closed in. Juniper's ice shattered a bolt a hair's breadth before it could touch her cheek, feathering her skin with flakes of ice and wood. In the moment of hesitation, the bandit leader swung his sword down. Juniper dropped to the ground and rolled, avoiding the slash. She pushed him back with a chunk of ice to the chest, knocking the wind from his throat.

The rat-faced bandit threw himself at her, grabbing her shoulders, pulling the pack from her shoulders, grabbing her waist. Juniper let out a fearsome cry and grabbed the man's arm. The temperature around them dropped dramatically—Juniper's control on her ice magic waned. Ison's breath puffed. The rat-faced bandit screamed as he began to freeze, his skin turning red.

The bandit leader interrupted, swinging his sword at Juniper's neck. Ison and Juniper acted together, his wind knocking into the man's knees and her ice forming a shield. The sword sank into the ice—stopping barely an inch from her neck. If it frightened her at all, she held it in well. Her ice enclosed around the steel and yanked it from the bandit's hands.

Then his sword became her sword. Juniper used her ice like a third hand, brandishing the sword at the bandits. A tendril of bright blue ice forced around the hilt, as fluid as water yet solid as ice.

"Look around you," Juniper taunted, her exhaustion showing in her eyes but not her voice or posture. She held herself ready for more. "Your men have abandoned you."

The leader grimaced. Indeed, the eight remaining men were headed into the woods. "Cowards!" the leader shouted.

"You didn't say they was apostates," whined the rat-faced bandit.

The leader grimaced at her, then fled after his men. The rat-faced man staggered to his feet and started after his fellows, each step easier than the one before as the midday sun thawed him.

When they vanished, Ison let out an exasperated huff and doubled over. "Gods."

He wasn't cut out for that kind of excitement, yet a part of him loved it. Wouldn't Xavier be proud. His blue-gray eyes flashed in Ison's mind, along with a foreign pressure on his chest.

Juniper rolled her head over her shoulders. "Well, that was an invigorating exercise." This time, her voice reflected her exhaustion, dry and flat. She heaved her pack back onto her shoulders. She took a few steps along the road, and then put a hand to her waist.

She stopped cold.

"What is it?" Ison asked, quickly assessing her for injuries. He didn't see any.

She flattened her hand on the smooth leather of her belt. "Those bastards stole my dagger!"

Ison understood. Her dagger—Reid's dagger—the one the squire had given to her. Ison's gaze grew soft. "We're going after them, aren't we?"

"Of course we are!" Juniper stomped toward the woods where the bandits had fled. "I'm not going anywhere until I get my dagger back and skin the bastard who took it!"

With a sigh, Ison started into the forest after her.

CHAPTER THREE

Reid Sandpiper took a drink from his canteen. The water had warmed since their departure from Castle Bradburn, but water was water. A traveler could not be picky, and he knew his journey would only get worse. His horse snorted as if in agreement.

They traveled along the White Road. It had been aptly named. Whoever had built the ancient road had used white stone that had since been beaten into gravel by thousands of years of hooves, wagon wheels, and boots. The White Road stretched to the horizon, over the plains of central Duvane and along the rolling blue-green hills of northern Duvane. The hills gradually faded into steeper hills and would eventually become the thick pine forests of the kingdom of Galamond.

They had left the stables before dawn, and the world had since warmed and sprung with late summer's vibrant life. Birds chirped, and bugs chittered. The noise was incessant. Despite the tug of grief in his chest at Juniper's unfortunate death, the trek had started with the quiet thrill of adventure. But with every village they passed, that thrill had sunk into the reality of their quest. They rode through the outskirts of Rusdasin, and before them, the northern plains stretched to the horizon, spotted with ranches and farmland. They crested a hill, and Reid glanced behind him. Rusdasin, Royal City of Duvane, his home, was a stony blur on the southern horizon. He hadn't looked back since they left the stables. He didn't want to appear weak among his companions. But as they came to this particular viewpoint, he couldn't resist the urge for one last look. This quest would determine his future, their future, and the future of their kingdom. Its importance weighed on him, and the sight of his home so far behind him created a new kind of emptiness in his chest.

Beside him, riding on a bay, Squire Henry Julian let out a grievous sigh and pushed sandy hair out of his face. He, like Reid and the others, had forgone the official silver armor of the Order for less obvious traveling leathers. His shaggy hair would assist with the facade, Henry had reasoned.

"We're less than a day in, Henry," Reid said. "Best not tire so soon."

"I hate riding for so long." Henry slumped forward, his broad shoulders falling.

11

"You'd rather walk?" asked Sir Isaac Pinul, their knight chaperon for the quest. The knight was in his forties, and his tan skin showed signs of a life spent outdoors. He held himself straight in the saddle.

"Gods, no." Henry straightened.

A chuckle sounded from behind, where Squire Penet Berwick and their herbalist, Graison Alyun, rode. Neither had a natural affinity for the sun, and Graison had elected to wear a straw hat to keep the sun off his face.

Reid, Penet, and Henry were squires, knights-in-training. They had finally been given a king's quest, the success of which would grant them knighthood, and failure, death. To the kingdom, to the Order, and to Henry and Penet, their quest was to investigate and deal with an unruly apostate who had gone into hiding somewhere in the Dolomin Mountains of Galamond.

Only Reid, Isaac, Graison, and King Bentley Bradburn knew the true nature of their quest. They were to travel to the farthest reaches of the northern realm and find a mythical plant to heal Crown Prince Adrian from the poison in his blood. Should they fail, Adrian would not survive.

Reid would not fail his prince, his best friend.

He steadied himself in the saddle of his dark horse. He would succeed. He would save Adrian. He would become a knight.

Or he would die trying.

Their traveling party stopped for lunch, and Reid eagerly dismounted and stretched. He hadn't ridden a horse for so long before. They chose a spot in the shade of a towering oak a short distance from the White Road. While Reid and Penet sorted out rations, Graison and Isaac fetched clean water, and Henry watered the horses.

Reid welcomed the shade. Though his bronzed skin took the sun well, it felt nice to be out of it for a while. Henry flopped onto his back, closed his eyes, and let out a long calming sigh. He had inherited his mother's Jantian complexion, and his dark skin didn't balk at the sun. Reid rubbed his temples. He hadn't gotten much sleep the night before, and exhaustion tugged. Bristling, he felt eyes on him. He looked up and met Penet's stare. The other squire quickly looked away. Reid lifted his canteen to his lips.

"Something on your mind, Squire Berwick?" asked Isaac.

Penet's brows rose, and a blush warmed his ashy cheeks.

Reid swallowed his gulp of water with minor difficulty. Isaac hadn't even been looking at Penet, yet he'd sensed something amiss with the boy.

"I was only thinking," said Penet a bit sheepishly. "I find it strange that the king sent such a force to deal with one apostate."

Reid tore his dried venison in two. He clenched his fingers harder than he should have. He had anticipated questions, but not this soon. He hadn't been able to find a suitable, believable answer yet. Beside him, Graison paled.

"The reports were unclear," Isaac said, unfazed. "And you are free to return to the castle and explain your presence to His Majesty. I am sure he would understand."

Penet's entire face went red. Henry chuckled, earning him a glare from Penet. Henry didn't seem worried. If anything, he looked intrigued. Reid knew Henry to be clever—brash and childish at times, but clever. He had likely already guessed something else to be under the guise of their supposedly simple and vague quest.

Isaac glanced expectantly at Reid.

Reid held himself a little straighter. "As knights, we do not question the king's command. We follow. Obedience is a necessary trait of all soldiers, guards, and knights."

"Reid is correct," Isaac said.

Penet cleared his throat. "I apologize. I didn't mean to suggest myself ungrateful or disrespectful." He swallowed nervously. "I-I only find it strange that the king would send us away now, so many of us, while the prince is so ill and while there is uncertainty within the kingdom, to investigate a single apostate."

Penet exchanged a knowing glance with Henry. They'd had this conversation before. Reid felt a stone of worry settle into his stomach.

"It feels like a cover for something else." Henry glanced at Reid, as did Penet.

"Cover for something else?" Isaac raised a brow. He spoke in a lighthearted voice, a smile of interest on his lips. "Such as?"

Penet shifted uncomfortably, more on his mind than he'd said. His dark brown eyes flickered to Reid again, and Reid fought to keep his fingers from curling. Had the other two squires suspected something amiss with their quest? That they hadn't consulted him on those suspicions suggested they thought him in on it.

"I've been thinking that maybe the king wanted us out of the castle,"

Penet said, his voice low, hesitant. "You know those old rumors about there being a second heir? Well, I don't know...maybe..."

Reid released a slow breath of relief.

Henry leaned forward, elbows on his knees. "I agree with Penet." He pointed at Reid with a strip of dried meat. "I mean, let's think about it. Reid, you showed up at the castle when you were what, eight? Nine? Then you were raised by the captain of the Royal Guard. The king treated you like a son. He allowed you to attend the same lessons as Adrian." Penet drank in every word that Henry said, and Reid wanted to throw his canteen at the loudmouth. Henry shrugged, adding, "It's just a thought."

"My parents were murdered by apostates," Reid said as calmly as he could. "The knights who responded knew my uncle was the captain, and brought me back to the castle. The king treated me as he did because Adrian and I were close friends."

"Or maybe," Henry said, "You were sent away with Captain Sandpiper's brother to be hidden, because you are the secret heir. Then rebels found you. The knights knew about you and brought you back to the castle, or the knights thought you the captain's nephew, thus the ruse you live in today. Then this entire quest is the king's way of getting you, his second son, out of the castle."

Reid scoffed and tossed a bit of fat from his dried meat onto the ground. He stood. "I'm finished. We don't have time to dally."

Him, the king's secret heir. What a preposterous idea.

Still, the idea struck that fanciful part of his mind. He had been young when his parents and his brother were murdered. The king had treated him like a son throughout his childhood, from the first day he arrived at the castle.

Reid scoffed at himself for even considering the possibility. He looked nothing like the king or the queen or Adrian. He looked strikingly like Captain Sandpiper, who looked strikingly like his older brother.

Or maybe Henry was right. It would have been the perfect cover.

Nonsense, he told himself.

Somewhere in the back of his mind, a thought drifted—Juniper would have loved that story. Then, at the thought of her, his chest squeezed.

Dead. Juniper was dead.

He and the rest of the party returned to the White Road, and Reid focused his thoughts on his parents instead of the thief. But the more he thought about their faces, the blurrier they became, and the more disturbed he felt about it.

14

CHAPTER FOUR

Xavier Thimble had always kept himself separate from others. Free of attachment, safe from loss or grief. One bout of grief had been more than enough for him.

Being an assassin, he made a lot of enemies, and he wouldn't give them someone to use against him. Never again. And yet, lying on the couch in Josephine's parlor, listening to Bois, Nera, and Josephine talk strategy, he couldn't focus on them or the incoming raid Juniper had orchestrated. He found his mind going to that gray-eyed mage.

Ison. He couldn't keep the boy out of his thoughts. Xavier brushed a hand through his short brown hair.

"Where is Amery?" asked Bois, her soft feminine voice both grating and comforting.

It took Xavier a moment to realize she had asked him. He turned his head sideways. Tea and cookies sat on a low table in front of the couch, and a map of the Undercity was spread over the larger table, around which the girls stood. He was lying on his back, and from his angle, they stood sideways: Bois, with her pale blonde hair, fair skin, and faraway look; Nera and her short brown hair and tired eyes; and Josephine with her motherly scowl, whose silver-streaked black hair had been pulled back.

"Working," Xavier said. He assumed so, anyway. When he'd woken that morning, she'd been gone. Her and the young girl, Blythe.

"She needs to be in on these plans," Josephine said, her voice commanding and strong but also kind.

"I'll tell her," Xavier said.

Josephine straightened and set her one hand on her hip. Her other arm had been lost years before, and the sleeve hung empty. She regarded him coolly, her dark gaze not revealing anything of her thoughts. "How will you tell her if you're not paying attention?"

Caught.

Xavier let a short sigh through his nose and then twisted his body upright so that his feet touched the floor. He blinked and saw gray eyes, wide and looking at *him*. Like he deserved to be looked at. Like something other than the monster he was.

Nonsense. Xavier was a monster. A killer. A murderer. No one would look at him like that.

Yet Ison had.

"All right, what's the plan so far?" Xavier said.

"Our first priority is to safely evacuate our allies before the raid starts," Josephine said. "However, we don't know which entry the Watch will take, so we don't know which exits will be available to use."

Xavier leaned onto the table. Josephine motioned to their crudely drawn map of the Undercity. The exits were labeled with spare buttons.

"We don't know which entry points Juniper told Captain Tinnly about," Nera said. "But I think it's safe to assume that he would try one of the more obvious ones, not one that goes through the backroom of a shop or a fence."

"Or he will assume that we'd assume as much, and come through a lesser-known exit," Xavier suggested.

Nera shrugged.

Bois, being blind, didn't look at the map. Xavier hadn't known the girl long, but in the past few days, he'd spent enough time with her to know she mapped the world with her magic. She might be able to feel the ink on the paper, but he didn't know. He hadn't asked. He didn't really care enough to.

"And, our second priority," continued Josephine, "is to get our allies out of harm's way in an organized fashion. We don't want to cause panic."

"We will need to get out without alerting anyone that something is happening," said Nera, "and then we'll have to go somewhere without drawing suspicion."

"Where can so many go without being noticed?" asked Bois.

"That's something we will need to figure out eventually." Josephine scanned the map. "There are places topside that might suffice, but we might also have to split into several smaller groups."

"On the bright side, the Watch will be preoccupied and might leave us alone," said Nera.

"We should also plan for the worst-case scenario," Josephine said darkly. "If we should be trapped down here during the raid."

Silence fell.

"Juniper said the Watch would not attack us if we did not attack first," Xavier said. "But forgive me if I don't believe that."

"You think Juniper would lie?"

"Not Juniper, or the captain," Xavier said. "Not all watchmen are good men, and they won't care who they're slicing. They assume we're all scum worth killing down here. And, when the fighting starts, they might not be able to discern who is attacking and who is not." He had experienced that killing frenzy himself, where the instinct of survival kicked in, and anyone and everyone is a threat.

"I agree," said Bois, her voice small. Xavier felt the brush of her magic against him, mapping him, seeing him. "We need a plan to hide."

"Our earth mages can expand the safe rooms under the keep," Josephine said.

Xavier blinked once. "You have those?"

The older woman nodded. "They've been a secret. Most in my guild don't know about them, but it's the most logical solution. They could expand the rooms enough to hide most of our allies inside, even make tunnels connecting them."

"Our keep is not far," Bois added, "though we have few earth mages capable of moving so much at once."

"We can work together," Josephine said. "We must act in secret, keeping what we're doing from anyone else, even the guilds, until the time is right. If word gets out that the mages are building safe rooms, panic will spread."

They all agreed.

"If the earth mages are building safe rooms," started Nera, "why not make our own exit from the Undercity?"

Josephine's lips parted, and she looked at Nera with surprise that faded into pride. "And we can connect our safe rooms to the outside."

"The Watch won't know about it, so they won't use it." Xavier's charcoal energy magic formed a dagger in his hand, and he flipped it into the air. He caught it without looking.

"That is a plan." A smile curved on Bois's pale pink lips.

It annoyed Xavier how much she looked like a doll.

"And the only remaining piece is to find a place to stay topside," said Nera. "And if we split into groups, *places*."

"We'll need to be organized before we evacuate," Josephine said. "With team leaders and seconds, so everyone knows who they are supposed to follow once the evacuation starts."

Nera opened her mouth but closed it when the front door to the keep opened and closed. Two sets of footsteps sounded on the floor, both cat-soft. They started toward the parlor without hesitation.

Josephine's brows knitted, and at once, Xavier readied his energy dagger to strike. A second dagger appeared in his off-hand. Nera summoned flames on her fingertips, and a soft pink shimmer twirled about Bois.

"Oh, I can feel it out here," came Amery's voice from the other side of the parlor door.

Xavier let his guard fall. As he did, Bois and Nera followed his lead. The parlor door opened, and Amery leaned against the doorframe.

"Feel that, Blythe? That sizzle in the air? That's the feeling the air gets when a mage is about to turn you into pudding," said Amery.

Blythe, a girl of ten years, nodded. She stood at Amery's side like a shadow.

Amery sauntered into the room. Pale red blush touched her olive cheeks, kohl lined her onyx eyes, and her red lips curved in a seductive smile. She wore a noblewoman's gown of lilac and indigo, and soft-soled leather shoes. She sat on the couch beside Xavier, her posture stiff—a corset. Blythe wore the puffy clothes of a noble girl, and she looked less like the thief Amery was training her to be and more like a little girl. Her black hair was pulled into pigtails, and rouge graced her dark brown cheeks.

"So, what did I miss?" Amery pulled out a pearl-encrusted fan from her sleeve and began to delicately fan herself.

Xavier chuckled darkly. "Maybe if you would have been here, you'd know."

"You were here," Josephine said. "And I don't recall you having much part in it either."

He shrugged.

They quickly told Amery of their plan to build safe rooms and a tunnel to the surface.

"The biggest problem is having a place topside to go once we're out of sight," Nera said, finishing the recap.

Amery slapped her fan closed against her palm, looking like a real lady. "Well, aren't you lucky I came when I did. I just happen to have a place."

"You have a place?" Xavier asked. "That will fit us all?"

Amery grinned at him, coy and secretive and clever. "It just so happens that I bought a house this morning," she said as if discussing it over tea with topside ladies. "I signed the paperwork not an hour ago. It's a lovely little manor by the Weslie. Tucked away from the road, facing the river." She glanced at the ceiling. "It's not too far from here."

Josephine laughed, and Amery gave Xavier a knowing grin.

"You knew that would work?" he asked.

"I knew we needed a place to hide topside, and I've had my eye on it since the previous owner fell ill," she said sweetly, mock tragedy on her tongue. "Lovely little garden too."

Xavier laughed. He didn't want to know how Amery knew the owner, nor whether the illness had been natural or on purpose. He wouldn't put it past her.

"Then it is settled," Josephine said. "We start construction immediately."

CHAPTER FIVE

Unseasonable heat glued Reid's tunic against his chest and back. It would seem Bala would end the summer with a heat wave before allowing Boxel to bring the harvest. With the rising temperature, the conversation among the party remained light. They traveled on, passing through small towns and settlements, most of which Reid had memorized as part of his training. A knight could navigate his kingdom blindfolded.

They passed farmers readying for the harvest. The wind whistled through the golden fields of wheat and turning beans, creating a haunting whisper. They passed several other travelers and small caravans. No one paid them any more mind than they would common travelers. The king had worked secrecy into their quest well—the fewer people who knew about their quest, the better. Their supposed apostate might have spies who could warn him of their approach.

In reality, the fewer people who knew about their quest, the fewer people to question it.

The sun gradually sank to the west. With the first streaks of golden twilight, they came upon a small roadside inn. A few houses were scattered within the woods around it, and a few farms dotted the hills. The inn was nothing grand. The wooden walls were weathered and gray, but a new sign of hammered iron welcomed travelers and advertised food, drink, and beds. After a long day of riding, Reid had never seen such a lovely sight.

"Would it be better to rest here or camp out of sight?" Reid asked Isaac quietly, as to not bother the others with the question.

"I see no harm in this place," Isaac said. He added lowly, "There will be a time in our future where inns are not an option."

They guided the horses to the sparse stable. A few other horses occupied the straw-strewn stalls, watching the newcomers. The inn had several rooms, and they paid for two.

"Heading north, sirs?" asked the plump innkeeper. She cast her bright brown eyes to them all in turn.

"Yes, ma'am," said Reid.

"Well, you best watch yourselves." She pointed to Reid with a short finger. "There's been rumors of bandits and apostates in the northern woods."

Reid exchanged a glance with Isaac. Bandits had always been a problem on the roads, but apostates too? Something about the warning didn't settle well.

"Don't you worry, ma'am." Isaac patted the pommel of his plain steel—he kept his Mage's Bane sword hidden under his cloak. It would give away his title as a knight. "The boys and I have trained for bandits."

The woman nodded, though her worry remained.

Reid, Henry, and Penet went into one room, while Isaac and Graison shared the second. The rooms were nothing special. The beds were simple wooden frames with feather mattresses and course linens.

Henry looked at it all with complaint written on his face. Penet, however, didn't have such qualms. He set his pack on the floor and reclined on the bed with an easy sigh. Reid did the same. It felt fantastic to be rid of his pack and to recline after the long day of riding. He understood the weariness of travelers coming to the castle now.

On the little wooden table in the corner of the room stood a miniature statue of Blugo, god of winter, patron of lost and weary souls. It was a common symbol for inns and waystations.

Juniper had been born under Blugo's stars.

Again, Reid cursed himself for thinking of her. It would do him no good.

"There are a lot of people staying here," said Henry.

Reid glanced at his fellow squire. Henry remained standing, though he had lost his forlorn expression for one of curiosity.

Reid sat up to listen. Indeed, he could hear the murmuring of several people, dozens of people.

"But there were so few horses in the stables." Penet sat up.

"They didn't come on horseback, then." Henry met Reid's gaze, thinking the same—why were so many people traveling on foot?

※

Dinner turned out to be a simple stew of chicken and root vegetables. Reid, Isaac, Graison, Henry, and Penet sat at one of the long tables on the inn's first floor. Fourteen other people joined them, several families by how they clumped together at the tables. A middle-aged couple sat beside Isaac, and their son and daughter-in-law sat beside Reid.

The talk revolved around bandits and apostates. The couple explained how they had fled their village, a few days' north, after apostates attacked.

"They killed everyone," said the older man, his beard several days old.

"They killed everyone who didn't hold magic." The son's voice was stronger than the father's. "Which was most of the village. We only escaped because we lived on the outskirts. We heard the commotion and had time to leave. Most others...didn't."

"Why would they do such a thing?" Penet asked, a shocked breathlessness in his words.

"Apostates don't always operate on logic or reason." Though Reid's parents' faces might have blurred, he could see the faces of their murderers clearly.

"They didn't ask for anything," said the father. "I-I would have paid them, but they weren't after anything but destruction."

The sudden solemnness of the inn settled onto their party. Penet swallowed, and Henry wore no humor. Reid allowed worry into his expression. While he hated to hear that such an attack had happened and that people had died, this incident did further their ruse—apostates to the north.

Reid knew these people would never gain back what they had lost. They could rebuild a house, a farm, buy more livestock, but the shredding of peace would take time to heal. What the people lost would never be replaced.

"What will you do now?" Penet asked.

"My sister runs a bakery in Rusdasin," said the father. "She and her daughter. We will help them where we can and work our way back to our livelihood."

"I worked with the blacksmith," said the son, more to his father than the others. "I could find work at a smithy in the city too."

His father nodded numbly.

"I know a few low-ranking knights in Rusdasin," said Isaac. "I will send word to them of this first thing tomorrow morning. This will be heard."

"Thank you, stranger," said the father.

Reid wanted to do something more for the man, but he knew nothing could be done. He had likely grown up in that small town, knowing every single person that lived there. Now, most were dead. Gone in a single night.

As night fell, the candles burned low, and the travelers trudged up the stairs to the rooms. Reid didn't think he would be able to sleep, not as thoughts of loss and his impossible quest churned together in a ball of anxiety. But as he rolled onto the strange bed, his weariness pulled him down into a deep, rejuvenating slumber.

✺

Reid dreamed of a crackling hearth fire, warm and welcoming. He sat before it, the warmth on his face, and beside him sat a beautiful girl with auburn hair, fair skin, and midnight blue eyes. She held her hands to the fire, warming them. She wore a dress of dark blue silk, the skirt puddling around her folded legs. Her hair cascaded over her shoulders.

"You worry too much," she said, her voice clear but distant. She shifted, and her hair fell over her shoulder, exposing her slender neck. The neckline of her dress left her collarbone exposed, and he could see the beginning of the scar that snaked down her front.

"The quest is too important," he argued. "The most important thing I've done. It might be the most important thing I ever do."

"Saving a kingdom is important," she agreed. "Saving a friend is also important."

"Exactly. I must succeed. In order to succeed, I need to keep the quest a secret from Henry and Penet."

She smiled at him, carefree and arrogant. "Are you worried they'll take the glory?"

"Of course not."

"Then don't worry so much. As long as Adrian is saved, the quest is a success, right?"

He didn't answer.

"See? You are worried about Adrian, but you're worried about your reputation too. What, do you think the king will just knight one of you?" One of her brows rose, and her eyes were smiling. She knew him too well. When he didn't answer, she laughed. "Don't worry. If you mess up, I'll swoop in and save Adrian myself."

"How?" Reid laughed. "You're dead, remember?"

She shrugged, the movement elegant and smooth. "I have my ways, Squire."

A log in the hearth broke, and embers shot into the air. Reid brought his hands up to cover his face.

"Reid!" Juniper called from far away. "Wake up!"

Reid snapped awake and knew something was wrong. The crackling of the hearth, the stench of smoke—he bolted upright, and his heart fell into his groin.

Thirsty flames licked the dry wood of the window pane, inching up the moth-eaten curtains.

"Fire," Reid breathed. He stumbled out of his bed and thrust his feet into his boots. His blanket landed too close to the window; flames eagerly seethed through the threads. *"Fire!"*

Henry and Penet jumped out of their bed, stumbling for their boots.

"Fire!" Reid screamed.

Smoke billowed toward the ceiling, puddling against the roof. Reid pulled his tunic over his nose. The fire quickly took his blanket. A moment more, and he might not have woken up at all. His shouting spread—others were waking up. The three squires dressed as quickly as possible and ran into the hall. Panic spread out of the rooms, screams and shouts to hurry.

"Out! Out! Out!" shrieked the innkeeper, standing at the end of the hallway in her nightdress. Her hair was sticking out of her nightcap.

The guests rushed through the narrow hall in nightclothes and cloaks, their pitiful belongings clutched in their arms. Reid slung his pack over his shoulder and raced out of the burning inn after Henry. He ran through the main room and into the night just in time to hear the thwack of a crossbow—then a scream of pain.

In an instant, he took in the scene. Fire raged over the inn, painting the darkness of the forest with flickering shades of yellow and red. The terrified guests stood before it, and armed bandits edged toward them.

Without thinking, Reid dropped his pack and unsheathed his sword. A bandit came at him, and Reid attacked. The bandit was out cold before he hit the ground, but the next wasn't so lucky. He didn't live long enough to feel the ground. Reid yanked his sword free of the bandit's chest and knocked his elbow into the nose of another. Bones crunched.

The third bandit stumbled back, gripping his bleeding nose.

One of the guests shrieked, "Bandits!"

With an extra breath to spare, Reid took in his attackers. They wore mismatched leathers, but their steel looked to be of good quality. Several bandits stood back with torches in their hands.

Then he realized *they* had set fire to the inn.

They had meant to burn them all alive.

Reid's rage burned. The bandit with the bleeding nose charged at him. Reid easily maneuvered and parried the thrust, and as the bandit reeled back and fought to regain his balance, Reid buried his sword in the bandit's gut. He twisted the blade—pulling a scream from the bandit—and yanked the blade free. The bandit collapsed.

With a knight and three squires, the bandits didn't stand a chance. A few of the other guests joined, and although they lacked the same training, they held their own. The bandits fell quickly, and those remaining dropped their torches and fled into the darkness of the forest.

Reid breathed in and out. The blood rushing through his ears slowed with each breath, each heartbeat. His rage calmed and faded into a dulled anger. The fire crackled as it ate the inn and everything left inside. It looked as though everyone had made it out—they all stood gazing upon the fire, the flames reflected in their eyes.

Reid cleaned his blade on a dead bandit's sleeve, then sheathed it.

This was why he had become a squire. This was why he wanted to become a knight. To stop senseless violence from happening, to make sure that apostates and bandits didn't harm innocent people.

"It won't kill him," came Graison's soft voice.

The herbalist knelt beside the young man who had sat beside Reid at dinner. He had taken a bolt to the thigh.

Graison dug into his slightly singed satchel and produced a few herbs and ointments. As the flames consumed the inn, he crushed herbs into the ointment, dislodged the bolt, and applied a thick layer of ointment to the wound. The man's wife tore a piece of linen into strips for a bandage.

"It feels better already." The son's face had gone terribly pale.

"That is the willow bark. It numbs the pain. It will hurt worse come morning," said Graison. "I would stay off this leg as much as possible for as long as you can."

"You can ride the horse," said the man's mother.

"But what about you?"

She gave him a motherly grin and patted his shoulder. "We will have to move slower, but I can walk for a while."

Reid strode to where Isaac knelt, cleaning his bloodied blade on the shirt of a dead bandit. Isaac stood and sheathed his blade.

"Those bandits were surprisingly well-armed," Isaac whispered.

"You think they weren't simple bandits?" asked Reid.

Isaac glanced at Reid. "They didn't want to steal anything. If they had, they wouldn't have set fire to the inn. They used fire to flush everyone out."

"Or kill us all," Reid said. "Do you think they were mercenaries?"

Isaac didn't nod or deny the claim, and Reid took that to mean that the knight thought it possible.

A section of the inn collapsed, sending fiery embers rushing into the sky. A figment of his dream returned, but he shoved it away. He could not dwell on dreams.

"Well, I had mold growing in the storeroom anyway." The innkeeper looked at the burning inn with remorse, resting her chin on her hand. "And I won't have to worry about those squeaky stairs."

Penet and Henry came to stand beside Reid and Isaac. Wood creaked and cracked. Another part of the roof and a wall collapsed and spit feathery embers into the inky, smoky sky.

"You think they followed us here?" Penet asked, his voice low.

"Our quest was no secret," added Henry. "Everyone in the Order knew, and so anyone in the city could have found out. Clearly, someone doesn't want us to go after this apostate."

"It is possible," Reid said. Or, more likely, someone didn't want them to go after this plant.

"Or," Henry said, lowering his voice and glancing at Reid with deathly seriousness, "someone wants to get rid of the second heir."

Reid groaned, and Isaac released a controlled sigh.

"What now?" asked Penet.

"We camp nearby," Isaac said to the entire group, including the refugees. The few who had been talking amongst themselves hushed. "We will have someone on watch at all times. We rest tonight, and tomorrow we head out."

No one objected. They found a quiet spot among the trees, and everyone who could helped. No fire was needed, not with the mild night, not with the inn still burning. It would likely burn for several hours, maybe a few days.

Isaac took the first watch, but Reid couldn't sleep. He lay awake, listening to the inn burn, watching the light lessen, and wondered how many of the others did the same. His mind went back to his dream, the dream in which Juniper had been there with him. It had been her voice commanding him to wake up.

Had she somehow gotten into his dream from the void? Warned him? Saved them all? He had heard stories of dead loved ones returning in dreams, bringing warnings and messages. Until now, he hadn't believed it. An old memory surfaced, one he had long forgotten—his mother tucking him in at night. She had told him stories of dead loved ones visiting in dreams. She had used a word for the phenomenon, but Reid had long forgotten it. Still...the memory had a blurriness. He could almost see his mother sitting on the edge of his bed, her hair pulled back, but her face was blurry.

Reid took the second watch, and when he could stay awake no longer, he allowed Henry to take over.

When dawn finally came, smoke still billowed from the smoldering inn. Several farmers came to make sure everyone was all right, and promised the innkeeper that it would be rebuilt before the next summer. The refugees packed what little they had, and most headed south, toward Rusdasin.

Reid and the others headed north. They rode for several hours; then Isaac brought them to a halt. On either side of them, the forest chittered and sang. The trees had started to turn, the green faded with late summer's exhaustion.

"We should split up." His eyes focused south.

"You think we're being followed?" asked Penet.

Isaac didn't answer. Penet and Henry exchanged knowing glances, and Reid felt a strange sensation of guilt. They didn't understand the importance of their quest. They couldn't, not until the secret could no longer remain hidden.

"Henry and I will continue along the White Road," Isaac commanded. "Reid, Penet, and Graison will go west through the forest to the Fox Road, then head north. We will reconvene in Easley. It's a town just inside the Galamond border."

No one argued. Reid pulled out the spare map and marked the location in his mind. The Fox Road was due west, maybe a half a day's ride. They would reach Easley within a few days of each other, if all went right. He eyed the winding Fox Road to the border of Galamond. If Boxel ushered in a gentle autumn, the trek would not be a problem. The weather would be mild until they reached the northern parts of Galamond and the Dolomin Mountains. That far north, the snow and ice never melted.

After studying the map for a moment, Reid led Graison and Penet west—straight into the forest—leaving Isaac and Henry to continue north along the White Road. As Reid left the road, the thick canopy took the worst of the heat off his skin.

Reid heard Isaac speak. Henry's loud voice responded, "I know, it's to draw attention away from Reid."

Reid huffed his annoyance.

"He's joking, right?" Penet looked pale.

"Yes," Reid said.

It was to keep attention from Graison and him, because only the herbalist knew how to identify and handle the damn plant, should it even exist. And this way, Isaac and Reid would have to both be slain for the quest to entirely fail. Twice as hard for anyone following them.

He steered his horse through the forest, keeping his eyes ahead of him and his ears on all sides. Thankfully, Penet did the same.

CHAPTER SIX

Juniper and Ison trekked through the forest after the bandits. Though the bandits kept quiet, they didn't mind their footsteps as they plowed their way through the foliage. They would have made horrible thieves. The Undercity would have eaten them alive or forced them to adapt and get better, like it had her.

And she had gotten better, stronger.

By some grace of Blugo—Juniper's patron god—the bandits were going northeast, the same direction Juniper and Ison had intended to go. The bandits were not in a hurry, and Juniper and Ison easily caught up with them. She felt a predatory amusement in stalking them and picking off the stragglers one by one. She delighted in the confusion after every disappearance, of watching the others search the nearby woods, asking who had seen Baret last, where Short had gone, and why Gull hadn't returned from the stream. Unfortunately, none of the lackeys she'd plucked had been carrying her dagger.

The sun began to sink, and the bandits set up camp in a clearing. They lit a fire and lounged around it, cooking the germs out of the water, roasting a few rabbits, and sipping from canteens. Juniper and Ison waited just far enough away, hidden in the thick boughs of an oak, watching and listening as the bandits' laughter grew louder and more slurred.

"I'd say those canteens don't hold water," murmured Ison.

"Agreed," Juniper said. "I'm sure we could snag one or two if you'd like."

"No thanks."

A beat passed. Did she imagine the heaviness in the silence? Juniper shifted her eyes from the bandit camp to Ison. The pale moonlight illuminated the serious face he had worn since they started after the bandits.

"Are you all right?"

He caught her eye, but his expression softened only slightly. "Yes. I've just been thinking about what we're going to do once we get over there, rather than..."

There—Baxion, the mysterious settlement of rebel mages in the north of Collatia.

"Rather than wasting time playing with bandits?" she asked.

Ison bit his lip. "I wouldn't call this playing, but...bandits prey off the innocent. They deserve justice."

"And they are getting that justice," she said. "I'm just going about it in a way that pleases me."

Ison let out a gentle laugh, his lips curling upward ever so slightly.

"And a drunk bandit is an easier target than a sober one." Juniper nodded to the bandits. Two of them were singing a song about a woman of the south, golden skin and dark hair and other things.

At the thought of golden skin, Reid surfaced in her mind, his bronzed skin and short dark hair, his honey-brown eyes.

In the past, she reminded herself. And getting blurrier every day.

One day, it wouldn't hurt so badly to think about him.

Juniper and Ison fell into comfortable silence. The sun sank lower and drifted onto the other side of the world. Above, the stars twinkled between the inky clouds. Juniper's magic responded to the night, growing and flowing like she had turned on a tap. Juniper flexed her magic between her fingertips.

"Is it that much different?" Ison eyed the little icicles forming and vanishing between her fingers. "Day and night?"

"Yes." Ice grew along the top of her hand and down her wrist, mimicking an iron gauntlet like the City Watch wore. She even formed the little indention for the smith's stamp. "It's easier to make ice at night. I feel...stronger at night, like I can do more."

Her magic felt bottomless.

Ison nodded, eyes tracing the ice.

"I wish I still had that book about water magic you let me borrow," Juniper said. That book, along with everything else in her room in the castle, had likely been burned. Or returned to the court magician's personal library.

"They will be easy to find outside of Duvane," Ison said. "I'm sure the mages in Collatia know more about magic than you or I, and half the teachers in the Marca."

The mages outside the Marca taught themselves how to use their magic and often ended up proficient in natural magic—the magic that came from within themselves. The Marca taught mages to use unnatural magic, the magic that existed in the world, for spells and other such simple things. Natural magic had more power than unnatural magic, and the Marca and the Order looked down on mages who used it.

"Jun," Ison whispered, his voice urgent, "look."

One of the bandits lumbered toward them. Jun released her magic, and her ice gauntlet vanished. They readied themselves for quiet, deadly assault, but the bandit lumbered just out of immediate range from where they were perched in the trees. Juniper slunk to the ground, Ison behind her, and stalked after the drunken bandit. They needed to be far enough away that the scuffle wouldn't alert the others. The bandit wound his way through the forest to a small stream. With his back unknowingly to his pursuers, he untied the front of his pants and relieved himself into the stream.

Juniper shot Ison a glance saying, *This is why I clean the water we drink.*

But should she take down a man so exposed? A part of her wanted to, but the other part of her wanted to give him the time to tie his pants.

When had she become so thoughtful? Maybe Reid's sense of duty and honor had rubbed off on her more than she'd thought.

The bandit rolled his neck over his shoulder. A breeze picked up—the bandit sniffed. A heartbeat later, Juniper caught the scent—smoke. The worst kind of smoke that came with the stench of singed flesh and burnt hair.

Ison gasped softly; he met her eye.

Something had been burned.

The bandit tied up his pants and headed south, toward the source of the odor. Curious, Juniper and Ison followed safety behind.

The scent grew stronger with every step. The breeze whispered through the foliage, against the thousands of leaves and through the brush, the scent heavy and strange in the forest. The bandit stepped around a thick wall of brush and spat a curse. Juniper found out why.

They had come to a village, or what remained of one. A dozen log homes had been burned to the ground, roofs collapsed, walls fallen in, the dirt between homes charred. Ashes littered the ground. The bandit stopped halfway between the first two homes, scratching his neck.

Juniper risked a closer look. A few embers still glowed within the first house, deep in the ashes. Fire had engulfed this village a few days ago, maybe. But she had never seen a fire burn so much in such a concentrated area. The trees surrounding the village were untouched, the leaves not even parched from the heat.

Ison crept beside her, suspicion on his features. He thought the same.

And the final evidence came on the breeze that whisked through the ashes. Underneath the stench of burnt flesh and hair was the subtle floral tang of natural magic.

The bandit started to turn back, a feverish panic on his face—Juniper wrapped a tendril of ice around his ankles and yanked his feet out from under him. The bandit let out a high-pitched yelp. Hanging upside down, he flailed until he spotted Juniper and Ison. The fear on his face turned into terror.

"I-I wasn't doing nothing, I swear! I was only just looking! Let me go, I'll leave!"

"What happened here?" Juniper kept her voice low. She took a step closer. Just out of spitting range. She wouldn't make that mistake again.

The bandit looked at her, then at Ison, confused. "You don't know?"

"No," Juniper said. "That's why I'm asking you."

The bandit blinked.

"You think we did this?" Ison asked.

"Well, you is mages, and this place got burned." The bandit motioned to them with his dangling hands as if he weren't hanging by his ankles.

"Just because we're mages doesn't mean we burn things to the ground," Ison spat back.

"My apologies." The bandit raised his hands in submission.

"What do you know about this village?" Juniper tightened her ice around his ankles.

"I-I don't know what it is," he said. "I only smelled it and come to look, you know. We've been hearing stories about mages burning villages that don't agree with them, you know."

"Mages have been burning villages?" Ison's eyes widened, then narrowed. "Where?"

"To the north," the bandit said. "That's why we's not going that way no more. Too dangerous for normal folk like us, you see. Them mages is starting something, and we don't want none of it."

Juniper glanced at Ison, and a silent agreement passed. Mages were burning villages that didn't agree with them? It sounded like something Nexon's mad mages would do. It sounded like something Clive would have agreed to.

She caught the subtle movement—the bandit reached for a dagger at his waist. To what end, she didn't know. She didn't find out. She wrapped her magic around his hand, tight enough to force him to drop the dagger.

"Bitch," snarled the bandit. "Let me go!"

"After you insult me?" Juniper let out a pitiless laugh. Her magic found his neck and, in the time between two heartbeats, snapped it. She released his body and let it fall to the ground. A quick death. She took no joy in torture.

A quick search of his body yielded nothing. He did not have her dagger.

"Jun," Ison said, eyeing the glowing embers of the nearest house. "This place was burned with magic."

"I know," she said. "That means we might run into apostates along the way. We'll have to be careful from now on."

"It's things like this that justify the Marca's dislike of mages and the Order's desire to keep mages under control." Ison's voice was flat, his eyes hard. "Living in the Marca, we heard stories of mages burning fields and breaking the earth to swallow entire homes and blowing buildings apart, and it was because of those mages that the mages in the Marca were so..."

"Punished," Juniper said.

Ison bit his lip.

"This isn't the work of ordinary apostates," Juniper said. "I'd bet gold these apostates are listening to Nexon or one of his commanders. Bois said he was gathering followers all over the kingdom."

Ison nodded. "We have to stop this."

"And we will," she said. Or die trying.

How many mages would cling to Nexon's promise of safety and power? How many apostates would flee to him in order to save themselves from the Marca? Too many. They knew the Marca was an oppressor, a prison, and Nexon promised the opposite of that. If she'd grown up like any other apostate, she would have gone to him too.

Juniper and Ison searched the ruined village. They did not find as many human remains as there could have been. A small consolation. The more she saw, the more convinced she felt that the village had been burned just to be burned. To frighten people. To make the presence of magic known. To make Nexon's power known.

A warning to the kingdom, to the king.

She didn't like it.

The two of them made their way back to the trees where they could see the remaining bandits. None of them had wandered off, and most had passed out. A few had stayed up on watch, but they paid little attention—they were playing a game of dice over a stump. Juniper and Ison found a cozy spot in the fork of a massive oak. Ison rested first, and Juniper stayed up on watch.

She wouldn't be able to fight Nexon one-on-one with him hiding in the castle's walls or wherever he was. He had a thousand years on her magic. She wouldn't stand a chance. No, their best bet would be to wedge Nexon's power the sneaky way, to dismantle his empire, to disrupt his followers, to rattle his grip of power.

And to do that... She didn't know where to start. She'd rattled Clive's little horde of mages well enough, but that had been more of an accident.

A hand on her shoulder made her jump. Ison had crawled onto her branch and knelt precariously above her. "Jun, get some sleep."

How long had it been? She blinked—the bandits had all fallen asleep, even their lookouts. The fire burned low.

She conceded, pulling her cloak tighter around her. She closed her eyes, though it did little.

CHAPTER SEVEN

Reid, Penet, and Graison made their way single file through the forest, up and down hillsides, through thickets and groves, across streams and shallow rivers. They couldn't travel as fast as they could have on a road, not with the uneven terrain. They couldn't afford an injured horse. They moved steadily northwest. Near midday, Reid halted their trek for a drink and to rest the horses. Though Reid stayed alert, he found no sign they had been followed.

The ground gradually leveled, and they rode in closer ranks. Graison rode between the two squires. He hadn't said much since the fire. A darkened, faraway look had taken residence in the herbalist's gaze. Reid knew that gaze. It belonged to someone who had witnessed horrible things. A piece of innocence had been shattered. Reid and Penet had been trained for combat, to expect the worst, but Graison hadn't. He had grown up in the safety and shelter of the city.

"Was that your first battle?" Reid asked.

Graison nodded. "I saw a few fistfights in the taverns, but...no one died. No one set things on fire."

Reid understood. To hear about the horrible things people were capable of was one thing, but to witness firsthand was another entirely.

"I remember the first fight I saw that resulted in bloodshed," Penet said quietly. His eyes continued to scan the forest for threats. "I was eleven, working the front of my uncle's smithy in Rusdasin. These two men started shouting at one another in the street. One pulled a sword on the other." Penet paused and glanced at Graison. "He ran the other man through."

Graison's somber gaze widened, hands tightening on the reins.

Penet continued, "The first time I took a life, I was with Sir Hogarth. I was just a pledge in the Order. We went south to speak with a possible apostate and to do a routine check of the villages along the border of Janti known to harbor mages. We were ambushed by apostates—three of them. Sir Hogarth took care of two, and I fought and killed the third. I still remember that day. Partly cloudy. A bit chilly. I remember the feeling that went through the steel, the sound it made as it met flesh and bone."

Reid wondered if Penet expected Reid to share his first kill. Reid didn't volunteer the information. He remembered the day as clearly as Penet remembered his own. That sort of memory didn't leave a person, and it shouldn't.

"Death is always a serious matter," Sir Darvel had said when Reid had been a pledge. "Taking a life should never be your first action. Violence should be your last resort."

The memory had faded at the edges, but he could still hear the knight's words, see his stare, both filled with honor and dignity. Sir Darvel had solidified Reid's decision to join the Order rather than following his uncle's footsteps in the Royal Guard.

"You are not wrong for feeling disheartened after a battle." Reid echoed the words Darvel had long ago said to him.

Graison stared at Reid. Though the herbalist had a few years on Reid, he looked younger.

He steeled his will, mimicking the knight from his memory. "A death is no easy matter for any decent man. A man who can look upon death without feeling remorse is no man at all."

"I like those words," Graison said, his voice small. "But it bothers me... Who would want to burn down the inn? Who would want to kill so many people in such a horrible way? What kind of person thinks that way?"

Penet glanced at Reid. They both had an answer. Of course, Reid's answer differed from the other squire's.

"The worst kind of human being," Penet said. "The type who doesn't care about laws or justice or his fellow humans. The type who seeks violence for entertainment, for power, for a rush. The type of man who joins bandit gangs and seeks lawlessness."

"The type of man the Order seeks to rid the world of," Reid added.

"Someone doesn't want us to fulfill this quest." Graison's voice was barely audible over the sounds of birds filling the forest. His hand, the one closest to Reid, shifted toward his satchel, where the book he borrowed from Mason Hobbs rested. It gave one of the few descriptions of the mythical plant they were to retrieve.

Luckily, Penet had been looking ahead, not at the herbalist.

Reid returned his attention to the forest. He had his doubts about the so-called bandits. They were likely mercenaries. Bandits attacked with chaos and poor skill. The attack at the inn had been organized. No threats were made. Reid had never heard of bandits being so well-armed either. Instead of a mismatch of stolen steel, they had well-made steel. Graison was right—someone did not want them to go where they were going.

Or—argued the innocent sliver of his brain—they might have stopped at the wrong place at the wrong time. Those bandits could have been following someone else who stopped at the inn.

Still, Reid's gut suggested otherwise. The timing had been too suspicious.

❉

Fox Road came into view. The sun tilted downward, a few hours from the western horizon, and the forest glowed a strange hazy gold. It wound through the northwestern forest of Duvane and was not as well-traveled as the White Road since it was narrower and steep in some places. Oaks and birch grew close to the roadside and shaded the road from the direct sunlight. Grass grew in the center of the road, where the wagon wheels had not trampled it.

The sound of rushing water rose and rose, and as they came around the bend, Reid saw the source: a wide river flowing south. Where the river intersected Fox Road, an old stone bridge arched over the rushing waters. Its thick supports, slick with algae, vanished into the water.

Someone stood on the bridge.

Reid let out a soft groan. Graison inhaled sharply. Penet alone held in his displeasure.

Bandits, judging by their mismatched leather armor, blocked the bridge. Several of them. Reid quickly took in the river. They could ford it, but it would leave them vulnerable to attack. It would take too long to go around and find another part of the river to cross. Best to fight the bandits and move on, and leave their bodies as a warning to anyone else that sought a life of lawlessness.

Penet set his hand on the pommel of his sword and gave Reid a quick nod—he had come to the same conclusion. Determination hardened Penet's expression. They would fight if they had to. Reid guided his horse to the front as they approached the bridge.

"Toll's fifty gold," said the bandit standing in the middle of the bridge. He uncrossed his arms and set his hand on the hilt of his sword.

"That's a steep price for a river that's not very deep," said Penet.

Graison gripped the reins with white knuckles.

"Move aside." Reid wanted to tell them they were interfering with the business of the Order, but he didn't want to give them away. If he had worn his silver armor, they would have thought twice about their toll.

The bandit laughed and unsheathed a dagger. He pointed the gleaming steel at Reid. "Pay the toll, or we take it off your corpse."

Penet inhaled to speak, but Reid cut him off. "Where did you get that dagger?"

The bandit blinked, then lowered his gaze to the dagger. "It's mine. I found it."

Reid climbed down from his horse, hand on his hilt. He knew that dagger. It was his dagger—the one he had given to Juniper.

Had this scum taken it from her corpse? Someone had and then sold it on the black market.

His blood boiled.

The bandit stepped closer, and his men closed in. Penet dismounted and pulled his sword from his side. Graison stayed back, his face pale as death.

"Fifty gold," demanded the bandit.

"Try to take it," Reid spat at the bandit.

The bandit came at him.

A fight, then.

CHAPTER EIGHT

Juniper and Ison crouched just out of sight from the bandits' new post, a foolish toll on a stone bridge. They were close enough to hear the bandits arguing—the disappearance of Clemen, the bandit she had left in the ruined village, had shaken the group. Some said they were being hunted, others said it was a monster that lurked at night, and others voted to stop at a shrine to pray for forgiveness from Bera, goddess of shadows.

Their chittering about a monster had given her a strange satisfaction. Ison, however, didn't approve.

And, to her dismay, the bandits had taken a turn toward the south. She and Ison needed to keep heading northeast. So, this would be their last haunting of the bandits. They lurked out of sight, within range to hear them arguing about what toll—or tax, depending—to exact on the travelers.

"Shut up, all you," snapped the leader, commanding his men with her dagger in his grubby hand. "Don't worry about it. I can judge a person's coin purse by looking at 'em." He waggled her dagger at the closest bandit.

Juniper inhaled slowly and exhaled. Bastard. He wouldn't survive another encounter with her. She'd make sure the monster devoured them all.

"What's the plan?" Ison pushed a loose strand of hair behind his ear. He had conceded that morning to let her tie back his hair—his curls had been hanging in his eyes. A piece of leather secured most of his unruly locks behind his head, but a few shorter strands framed his face.

"We kill them all," Juniper said plainly. "No survivors to go tell the world that we're here or that they saw Juniper Thimble alive. I'll take the big ugly one in the middle and the one on his left. You throw the one on the right into the river. Once he's covered in water, it will be easy to just freeze him solid."

Ison nodded, though his eyes darkened at the prospect of killing. He'd argued several times the day before to steal the dagger when they slept. She would be doing the killing, to save his hands from any more of it.

"These aren't normal people," she said. "There's no diplomatic solution with bandits. You know the old saying: you live by the sword, you die by the sword."

"You're getting ruthless." Ison gave a tight-lipped smile.

"It's a ruthless world," she said. "One that has tried multiple times to kill me. I'm alive because I fight back, and I'm going to keep fighting back until it finally kills me."

Ison huffed at her logic. He opened his mouth to say something, but his gray eyes drifted over her shoulder. His frown deepened. He whispered, "Look."

She looked, and as she did so, she heard the clopping of hooves. She bent her neck to the side to see around the brush. Three horses approached the bridge from the opposite side. More refugees? The forest didn't give her a clear view of the riders, other than browns of leather. The travelers hesitated to approach the bridge.

Juniper sighed dramatically. "And those bandits are about to descend upon those poor, unsuspecting travelers, who probably have loved ones waiting on their swift return."

Ison groaned. He knew she was right, but he didn't want to admit it.

"I should have finished them off leagues ago," she said, conceding.

"Let's just get on with it," Ison said, exasperated.

Juniper started to creep through the brush, keeping close to the river. Ison followed. He hadn't wanted to follow the bandits at all, but he knew how much that dagger meant to her. She'd have to make it up to him somehow.

She paused as close to the water as she could without risking being spotted. The travelers and the bandit leader were talking. She could hear a mumble of male voices over the rushing of the water. She pointed to a shadow on the forest floor. Unlike the dark green shadows of the canopy, this shadow did not undulate. She looked up, and Ison followed her eyes.

Sitting in the trees, hidden under the canopy in pale leathers and leaves, was a bandit archer. He was watching the bandit leader intently, still as stone. As Juniper and Ison watched, the archer pulled an arrow from his quiver and slowly notched it.

"I don't think the travelers are faring too well," Ison said.

"Time to help them out." Juniper called on her magic, and it responded with a rush—she would never tire of the feeling. She gathered her bright blue magic between her fingers. A ribbon of ice soared around her palm.

"To help out strangers?" Ison asked. "Are you feeling all right?"

"By helping these poor souls and ridding the world of these ruffians, we are doing everyone a favor." She cocked her head at him. "*And* that bastard still has my dagger."

The archer began to pull back the bow, and Juniper formed an arrow of her own of glittering clear blue ice.

She heard swords unsheathed on the bridge, a fight starting. The archer readied, but before he could pull the bowstring taut, she let her ice arrow fly.

Her arrow struck true—right through the archer's neck. He didn't have time to shriek. His arrow limply shot forward and clattered into the brush. He tumbled from his perch, struck a rock, and his body—thanks to a push of her magic—rolled into the river. A round of curses spat from the bridge, and the fight began in earnest.

She started toward the bridge, keeping to the river. Ison's wind slashed across the bridge, knocking two of the bandits off their feet. One fell into the river; the other hung on the bridge's side. Juniper brought the water up and latched it around his body with icy claws, yanking him into the water. She felt the two bandits struggle to rise to the surface, to swim to safety, but her magic held them under.

With a thought, their necks snapped in unison. An easier and quicker way to go. The current pulled the bodies downriver.

Juniper skipped across the river on stepping stones of ice. She paid no mind to the two men in unremarkable leather armor—she went for the bandit brandishing her dagger like a trophy.

The bandit leader's eyes met hers. In a heartbeat, those eyes widened in recognition. His remaining men fought the travelers, steel clashing against steel. The traveler who had attempted to engage the bandit leader in combat let out a huff of frustration as Juniper jumped into the middle of the fight. She ignored him. The bandit leader was hers.

"Bitch," spat the bandit leader. He flourished her dagger. "I shoulda killed you when I had the chance."

"I was thinking something very similar." Juniper pulled water from the river. Tendrils snaked up the shore, glistening in the later afternoon sunlight. "Only I would have done the killing, and your body would be rotting."

The bandit leader took a step toward her, face twisted in hatred. Her tendrils of water latched onto his back leg, forcing him to stumble. He glanced down—her water encased his leg, then the other, then his waist. The ice started at his ankles, slowly snaking along the surface of the water. It inched up his back, his chest, his arms—his breath fogged from his lips. She could have formed ice faster, but this was about dramatics, not efficiency.

A shadow appeared behind her—a bandit. Juniper had been too focused on the leader. She tried to worm a tendril of ice away from the leader, but the bandit moved too quickly. Her heart thudded, and her grip on her magic faltered. The traveler appeared between her and the second bandit, and steel struck steel with an ear-splitting crack.

The bandit stumbled back several steps. The traveler did not relent. He fought with surprising skill. These were not simple travelers, then.

"Gods," gasped a baby-faced man in a green cloak. He stood beside his horse, but the horse wanted nothing of the battle. It backed up, trying to pull its reins from the man's shaking grip. The horse shrieked and reared up. The young man dove out of the way of its hooves and into the sand—the horse galloped into the forest. The baby-faced man scrambled to his feet, unhurt and shocked, clutching his satchel to his chest.

A bandit saw it too.

What was in the satchel worth guarding? Worth paying for hired help?

The bandit leader tried to move, and Juniper brought her ice all the way over his body and left him.

A bandit launched toward the baby-faced man, whose first defense was to shield his face with his bare hands. Juniper shot arrows of ice at the bandit, but she had shot too quick to aim—all but one missed. The one ice arrow struck the bandit's shoulder with a wet thwack that reverberated through her magic.

The bandit continued toward the man and his satchel, despite his bleeding shoulder. Juniper started toward the bandit. The young man looked between Juniper and the bandit, fear bright in his eyes. He trembled. Juniper threw herself between him and the bandit. If the bandit recognized her, he didn't give notice.

He came at her with a sword of cheap steel, and she met his thrust with daggers of blue ice. Her skill outmatched his, and the fight didn't last long. She parried, knocking him back, and sent one of her ice daggers into his heart. Letting it melt, she had another ice dagger in hand in less than a heartbeat.

The bandit gasped, ashen-faced, and collapsed. Dead.

"T-thank you." The other man grasped the satchel with white-knuckles. He noticed her stare, and his grip tightened.

A third traveler shouted—three bandits surrounded him. Juniper summoned daggers of ice. She could already feel the strain, but she kept going. She sent one dagger flying like an arrow into the throat of the bandit about to slice through the traveler's back. At the same time, the traveler thrust his sword through the cheap leather of another bandit's chest.

Juniper tried to summon a second ice dagger, but her ice wobbled—it squeezed in her chest. The traveler spun and plunged his sword into the third bandit.

The traveler straightened and turned toward Juniper. Their eyes met.

Her heart skipped a beat, and then another, for she looked into the eyes of no simple traveler. She looked into the eyes of Squire Penet Berwick.

And he recognized her. His lips slowly whispered her name.

In their hesitation, a thwack and a grunt of pain—the young man fell to the ground beside her, an arrow sticking through his neck.

Her next breath tumbled from her lips.

In a rush of panic, she cast her magic around her—an archer sat hidden in the forest. An arrow came flying at her throat—it sank into a shield of ice. She molded her ice around the arrow and sent it flying back at the archer.

A shriek and a thunk followed.

Her magic squeezed, pulsing with use. She had used too much too fast.

And just like that, all the bandits were dead—except for one. She sauntered to the bandit leader. He remained in an ice cast, holding her dagger. As much as she wanted to freeze him solid, she didn't have the magic left. The ice had already started to melt. Using the dregs of her magic, she snapped his neck. Her ice melted, and the bandit collapsed to the wet dirt. Her dagger clattered to the ground.

"This is mine," she said haughtily, as if the dead bandit could hear her.

She eyed the dagger. He had used it. She'd need to sharpen it. Bastard. Nevertheless, she slid the dagger into her empty sheath.

"Yours?"

That voice—Juniper froze. A shiver traveled down her spine and made her bones feel like iron. Footsteps approached. A sword was sheathed.

She turned, stomach quivering and full of stones, and found herself looking into Reid Sandpiper's honey-brown eyes.

CHAPTER NINE

Juniper couldn't move. Her thoughts slammed to a halt. Reid looked her up and down, disbelief obvious. Juniper felt the uncertainty leaking into her own features. No one moved. Ison and Penet stood silent in her peripheral—she couldn't take her eyes off Reid. She never thought she would see him again, let alone be under his gaze.

He stepped closer, but she couldn't find the strength in her legs to move. He stopped just outside of dagger range. Not that it mattered—her arms no longer worked either.

"Juniper?" he whispered. His eyes searched hers. "You're alive."

She didn't have the words.

Ison shifted, drawing her attention, and she remembered. "Your friend," she whispered to Reid, her voice small and unsure. "He's dead."

Reid blinked, a beat passed, and then his eyes widened. He rushed to where the young man lay. Blood formed a pool around his body. Juniper watched as Reid put a hand to the young man's chest, then his wrist.

"Dead," Reid confirmed.

Penet and Reid shared a glum look.

Ison appeared beside Juniper, hand on her elbow. His gray eyes met hers, concerned and uncertain. He mouthed, *Are you all right?*

She didn't give him an audible answer. In truth, she didn't know. She hadn't anticipated this meeting. Not in a thousand years.

"There's nothing we can do," came Penet's kind voice.

Reid heaved a sigh, then stood. His expressionless eyes took in Ison, then Juniper. For a terrible heartbeat, she held that gaze. Felt it needle into her skull. Reid stole his eyes from her and looked to the golden streaks in the sky. It would soon be night. The sky told her so, and her magic confirmed it.

"We will bury him along the roadside," Reid said. "It is the best we can do right now. Then, we camp. It's nearly dark."

"Let me help," Juniper said, a question not a command.

Reid and Penet shared a glance. Penet nodded to Reid, letting him decide.

"It is the least we can do," Ison said.

Penet stepped closer to Reid. "I would feel safer at night having two mages around."

"Apostates," Reid corrected, the word bitter.

Juniper met Reid's honeyed glare. She and Ison, two wanted apostates, stood before two squires. By law, Reid had the right to execute them for their supposed crimes, for their wild magic. But he didn't move. He didn't reach for his blade.

"Does that matter right now?" Penet motioned to the dead bandits. "Did you see the way they fought? They took care of those bandits in a fraction of the time we could have." Penet met her gaze. "And, if not for Juniper, I might be on the other side of the veil with Graison, or close to it."

Reid didn't look enthused.

"We can take care of camp while you..." Juniper nodded to the body. "Take care of your friend."

A beat passed, then another.

"Fine," Reid said at last.

Juniper and Ison brought the horses into a clearing a short walk from the river and out of sight from the road. Ison found Graison's horse in the forest and, by some miracle, was able to calm it enough to lead it to the others.

"Animals like you more than me," Juniper said, mostly because the silence was irritating.

"I helped in the Marca stables a lot," Ison said. "Animals were better company than some people."

Juniper had trouble summoning a flame—she had nearly depleted her magic in the fight—but she managed a small one, enough to light the dry leaves and logs. Night had fully fallen when Reid and Penet appeared, dirt-spotted and sullen. Juniper and Ison were sitting by the fire, watching fish cook over a spit that they'd constructed from sticks and stones. Penet sat opposite them, and after a moment, Reid did too.

For a long, tense moment, none of them spoke. Juniper kept her eyes on the fire, afraid that if she met Reid's gaze, she would freeze again.

"I didn't think you the fishing type," said Penet, motioning to the four fish, one for each of them. "You caught them quick."

Juniper glanced up at Penet. Reid sat beside him, the flames turning his eyes amber. He was looking at her. Her chest clenched, and she fought to keep her eyes on Penet as she said, "I cheated with magic."

She had formed a bubble of water around the fish, trapping it, then lifted it from the water. It had taken several attempts to keep the fish from wriggling out, but she'd done it.

"Makes dinner easier, regardless." A gentle laugh rolled off Penet's tongue. That laugh vanished; his face became serious. "Thank you, Juniper. Do you...do you mind if I ask you something?"

She shook her head.

"We all heard you were dead," Penet said. "Killed by Captain Tinnly."

"Yes." No sense in trying to pretend otherwise. Reid and Penet both fixed a curious stare on her, one more intent than the other. "It's a complicated story, but I asked him to help me fake my death in order to get out of Rusdasin. I thought it would be easier for a dead girl."

"And he agreed?" Reid asked, skeptical.

She met his gaze. A fire raged through her middle and into her fingertips and toes. "I traded information for the favor." She picked at the dirt under her nails. "I told him how to get into the Undercity without killing half of his men."

Reid's brows rose. "You betrayed your own?"

"Only those who deserve it," she said. "I warned those who didn't. If the captain is a man of his word, which I believe he is, then only the thugs and scum will be dead."

Reid's gaze burned into her, and she stole hers away and looked at the fire instead. She felt the fire and her magic react—her magic shied away from the fire. It yearned for darkness and cold.

"Why are you two out here?" Juniper tried to sound casual, but it came out nervous.

"We've been sent to deal with an unruly apostate in the north," Reid said. "It is our king's quest that will grant us both knighthood."

Her chest squeezed in delight for him. "Congratulations."

Reid nodded his head in thanks. Penet mirrored the action.

"They sent two squires to deal with one apostate?" Ison asked.

"See?" said Penet, nodding toward Ison. "I questioned that too."

"There are rumors of other apostates with him," Reid said quickly, his tone dismissive. Penet didn't seem to catch it, but Juniper had heard that tone before—he was hiding something. Reid caught Juniper's stare. "We know few other details."

She caught that tone too. *Don't question it. Not here, not now.* Not in front of Penet or not in front of Ison?

"Your friend didn't seem like a squire," Ison said.

Juniper agreed. By the way the young man—Graison—had cowered from the fight, he'd had little stomach or skill for it. By his chubby cheeks, he hadn't lived a life that required him to.

"He was an herbalist," Penet said. "There are rare herbs in the north that we can't grow easily down here. That's why the king sent him."

Ison nodded. Juniper had no doubt he could name those herbs without a second thought. He had pointed out herbs in the forest as they'd stalked the bandits—herbs that could cure nausea, herbs that became hallucinogenic when boiled in a copper pot, and herbs that warded off infection. She felt much safer eating berries that Ison approved.

The fire died down, and no one spoke while they ate. Juniper was ravenous after expending so much magic, but she had only caught four fish. She could have eaten three, but she kept that to herself.

Fishbones thrown into the dwindling fire, the four of them set up three tents.

"Graison won't have need of his tent," Penet said. "Consider it yours."

Penet retired into his tent, and Ison went into Graison's tent. And then only Juniper and Reid sat by the fire. Their eyes met.

"Of all the people in the kingdom," she said casually, quietly to avoid bothering the others.

"Indeed," he said.

Her throat suddenly felt dry. Standing, she fumbled with her canteen. She made her way through the forest to the river, the firelight dimming with each step, her magic growing in the moonlight. At the river's edge, the firelight no longer touched her. She uncapped her canteen, drank the rest of it, and bent down to gather clean water.

Footsteps approached, calm and controlled. She didn't need to look up to see his face.

Holding her canteen with one hand, she worked her magic through the river. She brought a snake of water upward, pulling pure water from the grime and dirt, and fed the snake of clear water into her canteen.

Reid held his canteen out. "Please."

She brought a snake of clean water up and out of the river and into his canteen.

"Thank you." He stood close enough he only had to whisper. He capped his canteen as she capped hers.

"It's better than taking your chances with the cleanliness of the water," she said awkwardly. She dared to meet his eyes and felt a thud in her chest as his moonlit eyes met hers. "For all we know, a village upstream empties their chamber pots into the river."

She found it hard to breathe with his eyes so close to hers.

A heartbeat passed. Then another.

"You honestly sold out the Undercity?" Reid asked.

She nodded. "I wanted to get out of Rusdasin, but Maddox didn't want me to go. He said I had to do one last job before he'd let me go. He wanted me to assassinate Captain Tinnly."

"Tinnly is a good man," Reid whispered.

"I know." She met his gaze once more, and her knees felt stronger and weaker all at once. "I was going to kill him at first, but then I saw how he handled his men and crime. I knew I couldn't kill him without feeling guilty for the rest of my life. Maddox had never sent me after an honest person before. It was always someone who'd cheated him, or who'd cheated someone with enough coin to hire an assassin. Liars, cheaters, and your typical scumbags. I've no problem killing someone the world would be better off without, and Tinnly is not one of those people." Her voice softened. "The world needs more people like him."

Like you.

Reid studied her face for a long moment, his own unreadable. "I got your letter the same day I heard about your death." He looked out to the river. "*After* I heard about your death."

She bit her lip. She knew she should have sent that damned letter sooner. "I'm sorry. I tried to write it a dozen different ways, but it never sounded right."

"It sounded fine."

She gawked at him, at the implication—did he mean...? Her knees weakened. She had told him that she loved him in that letter. Told him he had her heart and always would. Those had been the very words she wrote over and over.

With every passing moment, her cheeks warmed, her heart trembled, and she felt as though her knees would give out.

"Juniper," Reid said, urgency on his tongue. "I told you a half truth when I explained why Penet and I are out here." He swallowed, and his nervousness magnified her own. "Adrian was poisoned, and it will kill him. The king sent Isaac, Henry, Penet, Graison, and myself to retrieve a healing plant from the far reaches of the realm. It might be Adrian's only chance at surviving. Someone doesn't want us to find it. We were attacked, and we split up. Isaac and Henry continued along White Road. Penet, Graison, and

I continued north on Fox Road. Only Isaac, Graison, and I were told about the truth of our quest. Henry and Penet both believe we are hunting an apostate."

She took it in. She'd heard of such a plant, able to cure any disease or illness, but as folklore and in adventure novels.

"The herbalist was going to find it," she concluded.

Reid nodded grimly.

A jolt of shame shot through her chest. "I'm sorry."

"You didn't kill Graison."

"I could have protected him better."

"And then Penet would be dead or seriously injured," Reid countered. He wore no blame for her in his eyes.

An idea blossomed. "Reid"—she paused at the sound of his name on her lips—"Ison is great with plants."

He frowned but didn't argue. "That he is."

"Let us come with you. We could help you in case more bandits show up, or worse."

His brow furrowed.

"We heard rumors of apostates in the north burning villages. You could use two on your side."

Reid's eyes bore into hers, and she anticipated his firm no. It didn't come. He stared at her, considering, his face a stoic mask. "I agree. You and Ison make a formidable pair in a fight." His frown deepened. "What are you and Ison doing this far north? Chasing bandits for the hell of it?"

"Following the bastard bandit who stole my favorite dagger," she said.

He frowned, but a light blush warmed his cheeks. He glanced down to the dagger at her waist. The dagger he'd given her.

She took a deep breath and said, "We found out some things in the Undercity that made our escape necessary. Those rumored rebel mages were there. We met them. They believe they are following Nexon, the Iluvin archmage—the same apostate who made those monsters we thought were demons."

Reid's breath left his throat in a guttural spat of disbelief and surprise. He shook his head. "That's impossible. There's no such thing as an archmage, and even if that were true, it would make him—"

"More than a thousand years old." She looked back toward camp. She thought of how Nexon had possessed Ison, those icy blue eyes that looked at her with ancient hatred and malice. A thousand years' worth.

"Do you believe them?"

"Yes." She met Reid's gaze. It became easier each time. "Not necessarily that it is Nexon, but that it is an apostate powerful enough to exist within the castle without alerting the knights to his presence, to assert his will over others, and to send his thoughts into their minds. Iluvin, for certain. And, if I am right, which I'm fairly certain I am, he is still in the castle."

"You think Nexon is still lurking in the castle?" Reid breathed the words, taking a small step closer to her.

"I do." She gauged his reaction.

He shook his head and ran a hand through his short chestnut hair. It had grown out since the last time she had seen him.

"I didn't want to believe it either, but I've seen too much evidence otherwise. Ison and I...gathered some intelligence that Nexon's followers are hiding in the north of Collatia, plotting his return to power."

"That's where you were going?" Reid rubbed his temple. He dropped his hand to his side. His gaze became accusative. "To join them?"

She frowned. "To *stop* them or burn their hold to the ground or something."

He chuckled darkly. "You think two apostates could make a dent in a camp of apostates?"

"It's the only lead we have. It was either that or do absolutely nothing and let that bastard continue his dark plans." She put her hand over her heart. "And I for one would like to break a few of his bones for all he put me through. I'm sure Ison would like to get a few hits in too."

"What did he do to Ison?" Reid's brows came together, and he looked toward camp.

Juniper sucked in her next breath. She'd said too much.

Reid brought his gaze back toward her. At her silence, he asked again.

"It's not for me to tell," she finally said.

Reid frowned at her avoidance, but he didn't push her for an answer. He turned his attention back to the moonlit river. For a long moment, they stood there, the cicadas singing.

"Juniper," he whispered, "I...I am glad you're alive." He turned toward her, and she felt his words before he spoke them, written in his grave expression. "But there can be nothing more between us."

She nodded. She knew. She *knew*. Yet it hurt. "I understand," she whispered. "Not only am I an apostate, a thief, and a murderer, I'm also dead. That itself is a crime."

His lips turned upward slightly, his only reaction.

She fought hard to steel herself. "You are a knight, or you will be soon, and you've got a future ahead of you. Glory and honor." A future that would be marred with someone like her.

And now the words of her letter felt beyond foolish.

She took the first step back to camp.

"What will you do after this?" he asked, stepping with her.

"Ison and I will continue into Collatia," she said, "to see what we can do about the rebel mages there. Maybe we could find information to relay back to the king. Gods only know. Or we very well might be walking to our deaths. It's hard to say."

Reid inhaled like he had something else to say, but he didn't. They walked back to camp in silence. The fire had burned to embers. Reid paused outside his tent. His eyes briefly landed on Juniper, and then to his tent. Her heart thudded, and before he could say anything, she ducked into Ison's tent. She lingered on the other side of the flaps, listening. Reid stood for a heartbeat longer, then climbed into his own tent.

Had he been about to invite her into his? How dare he even consider inviting her into his tent when he had just said could be nothing more between them!

Ison took up half as much space as Reid did anyway, and the two of them could easily fit into the narrow tent. Besides, compared to the trees they had been camping in, this tent was luxurious. She pulled the weapons from her person and laid them on the far side of the tent, and curled underneath the blanket beside Ison. His eyes fluttered open, glossy with sleep, and he rolled onto his side to make more room for her. He slung his arm around her, for comfort, not affection.

Was Reid lying awake in his tent? Thinking of her? Of her sleeping in Ison's tent instead of his? A selfish part of her considered climbing on top of Ison, if only for Reid to hear them, but she didn't move. She didn't need to prove anything to him, and it wouldn't be fair to Ison.

And what would Xavier think? If they ever saw him again.

And what would poor Penet think? No, for Penet, she could be civil, because he had never been anything but civil toward her.

CHAPTER TEN

Just after dawn, Juniper woke to Reid's voice urging them to get up. While the squires readied the horses and struck the camp, Juniper whispered to Ison about the change of plans. He heaved a sigh through his nose but didn't complain. She wanted to find Nexon, but she also wanted to help Adrian. Helping Adrian seemed infinitely easier than defeating Nexon.

They set out. Juniper and Ison rode the dead herbalist's horse—which responded better to Ison than Juniper. After traveling through the forests, it felt nice to keep to a road. Fox Road was narrow and weedy. It wound north through the countryside, shaded by the thick canopy.

"And," Juniper whispered in Ison's ear, "if we save Adrian, the king might look at us with favor."

"Is that important?" Ison whispered back.

Juniper kept an eye on Reid and Penet. They rode slightly ahead but out of earshot.

"The king has an army of soldiers and a foot in the door with the Order," Juniper reminded him. "We are but two apostates against an untold number of apostates and fanatics. We could use the king's favor and his aid. It would be in his best interest to get rid of Nexon and his uprising."

Ison looked doubtful. "Do you think he'd even listen to us?"

"After we save his son from the brink of death?" Juniper arched a brow.

Ison didn't look enthused about the endeavor. "I can't argue that his aid would be invaluable."

She saw the question in his gaze: *But is it worth the time?*

Juniper opened her mouth to argue. Yes, it was worth their time to save Adrian, but someone cleared their throat. She and Ison jumped. Reid and Penet were both looking back at them, at the small space between them, knowing a whispered conversation had been interrupted.

She straightened, stealing her lips from Ison's ear.

"We are to convene with Isaac and Henry just inside the Galamond border," Reid said, his words professional. "That is where we are headed first."

"We split up after mercenaries attacked us," Penet added, not knowing Reid had told Juniper the night before.

"Mercenaries?" Ison asked.

"We met a large number of refugees." Penet proceeded to tell them about the night they had stayed at the inn and how mercenaries had tried to burn it to the ground with them inside.

She met Reid's skeptic gaze. He had been right to split up. Someone did not want them to succeed. Someone did not want them to save Adrian. She would bet all the gold in the Undercity that someone was connected to Nexon. At the same time, her chest squeezed. She thought of the village they'd found, burned to the ground with magic.

"One of the bandits told us of apostates in the north, burning villages and scaring people," Juniper said. "The bandit said they hadn't gone north because of it."

Reid and Penet shared a deep frown.

Penet's didn't last as long. "But I'm sure our apostates are better." He smiled at Juniper. "I've seen apostates in the wild fight, but they don't fight like you."

Juniper smiled back at his compliment. "I had training. In fighting and swordplay, not just in magic."

"Speaking of," Reid said, "Your skill in magic has greatly improved."

Warmth rose in her cheeks. "I'm not sure if that's a compliment or an accusation."

Reid glanced back at her with a roguish look—the squire she had teased and accidentally fallen in love with.

"Improved?" Penet's brows rose. "You knew?"

Reid's roguish look evaporated. "Yes, I did."

Penet glanced back at Juniper. "I thought I detected magic in your room, and it never made sense."

"It was a secret," Juniper added. "And you can see how I didn't want to admit to being an apostate to a squire."

Penet nodded, though he looked betrayed. "Yes, I understand."

"I've been training with magic since I left," Juniper said. "Ison has too. I doubt a few measly backwood apostates will stand a chance against the four of us."

Penet grinned with pride, and though Reid tried not to, his agreement reflected in his eyes. He knew, despite his reluctance to it, that having Juniper and Ison on their side would play in their favor. Hers too, hopefully.

They rode on, shaded from the sun by the thick forest. Ison kept their horse behind the squires, and Juniper sat behind Ison. She kept her magic in the air behind and above her, for arrows and bird droppings alike. No bandits barred their path. They met a few other travelers, including a courier with no time to waste and a small caravan of refugees. Their village had been burned and blown away—they did not offer more explanation.

As the refugees passed, Juniper caught Reid's eye. Apostates attacking villages. Mercenaries attacking inns. Adrian's poisoning. The gathering of apostates in the east. It was all connected. Nexon, or whoever the hell he was, had likely orchestrated it. His rising gave apostates the gall to attack, to flaunt the freedom Nexon had promised them.

And for someone to have known of this secret quest, there had to be someone with an insider's knowledge—someone within the castle, within the king's inner circle.

She met Reid's uncertain gaze with confidence. They would find the plant, save Adrian, and deal with Nexon.

They would.

※

They continued steadily north. Fox Road narrowed and widened, but never widened enough for the three of them to ride abreast. Penet took the lead, and Reid fell behind Juniper and Ison. Trapped between two squires. She had no doubt Reid intended to monitor them.

Midmorning, the blue sky faded behind wispy gray clouds. Those gray clouds thickened quickly into a storm. Within the hour, bruised thunderheads rolled overhead. The humidity rose, and the air cooled. Stories told of these battles between Bala and Boxel: the thunderous fight for seasonal dominance, the winds that blew the trees barren, and the rains that flooded fields. The first clap of thunder shook the sky. She felt the rain before it started, an urge that ripened the air around her, charged it. The first drops struck the leaves, a gentle whisper that rose into a roar as the rain overtook them. Cool drops soaked into her hair, her tunic, her cloak. Soon she was soaked.

Oh, her magic danced within her! She felt the rain as it fell, felt it on her person, felt it on the others as if she had cast her own magic around them. She felt her magic in Ison's hair, on his skin, and she felt it on Reid's and Penet's. The rain made her a bit reckless, and she focused on the rain that coated Reid's face and neck, the taut muscles of his chest and back.

The rain continued into the afternoon, shifting from a downpour to a mist that turned the world into a blurry dream. The heat-exhausted trees became vibrant shades of green and chartreuse, the sky a steely gray illuminated by the sun on the other side.

She'd always loved storms. They made her feel energized. As a child, she would leave the Undercity and find a rooftop to feel the storm. Back then, she'd pretended not to be a mage. She'd shoved her magic down deep. Now she realized that pull came from her magic.

How powerful of a mage would she be now if she hadn't shoved her magic down? If she had taught herself to use it sooner?

Would she have been able to command the rain? Move lakes?

One day, she would.

✳

Reid did not mind the rain, but he did mind wet clothing. Particularly wet shoes. As much as he wanted to stop and find shelter, they didn't have the time. He didn't know how long the storm would last, and they had limited rations, time, and patience. He had the feeling he would need as much of the later as possible.

Were the gods laughing at him? Sending him a king's quest and then sending Juniper to his rescue. And Ison. The two of them had shared a tent. A *small* tent too.

A drop of rain hit his temple and slid down over his eye. Reid wiped it away on his sleeve. The rain soaked Juniper's hair, making it several shades darker. Her hands were on Ison's waist, and though he told himself she held on for balance, he still wanted to push Ison off the horse.

His thoughts went to the couple at the royal greenhouses, the lavender and honeysuckle, and the juniper tree planted aside from the garden. If he was right, they were Juniper's parents, the ones she barely remembered, the ones she had been taken from.

He knew he should tell her, but how? What would it accomplish? He had his mission, and she had hers. Telling her of her parents would only give her a reason not to risk her life to protect her kingdom and prince.

Maybe it would be better not to tell her.

Especially not in front of Ison or Penet.

Not when her motives were still unclear.

CHAPTER ELEVEN

When night fell, they found a clearing off the roadside, shaded by a grove of oaks and birches, shielded from sight of the road. Through silent teamwork, they built a fire, found dry logs to sit on, watered and fed the horses, and roasted fish over the fire.

While the fish cooked, Juniper used her magic to pull the water from her clothes. Ison held his arms out, and she performed the same trick. "Anyone else?" Juniper wiggled her fingers.

"Yes, please," Penet said, weariness pulling at his eyes.

Juniper obliged. Penet heaved a sigh of relief at his dry clothes.

"Reid?" Juniper asked, feeling his name on her tongue.

Reid hesitated, looking at her fingers like she might stab him instead.

"Oh, come on," Juniper said. "You'd rather be soaking wet?"

He huffed a sigh. "Fine."

As her magic reached for the water in his clothes, Reid tensed. She fought to keep her mind on the water, not on the strong body it touched. Reid held his scowl, and a part of her wanted to freeze droplets in places he couldn't ignore. She didn't. She pulled the water from his clothes, leathers, and gear. It hit the ground with a wet *splat*.

Ison gathered a few herbs from the forest and added them to an herbal drink he cooked over the fire. He added more to the satchel he'd taken from the herbalist. "Wards against head colds and other things lingering in the rain might cause," Ison explained.

When the others hesitated, he drank his tonic first. Juniper followed, and the squires reluctantly drank. It tasted like weeds, like she had bitten off the top of a dandelion.

After dinner, Juniper took their canteens and refilled them with clean water from a nearby lake. The forest sang with cicadas, but not as strongly as it had the nights past. Soon, autumn would silence the summer bugs. The lake remained still as glass. The moon reflected perfectly on the surface, the crescent speckled with grays. The lake, the moon, the water—it called to her. It needed her. She needed it—to be submerged in the water, surrounded by it. Her magic stirred and danced like a flame, tugging under her skin, urging her to the lake.

It made her feel like she could lift the whole lake if she wanted to.

She didn't want to, so she didn't try. Her magic hadn't fully replenished from the battle with the bandits. Their sparse diet and quick pace hadn't allowed her the time. But she could do other things.

She returned the canteens to camp. "I'm going back to the lake to bathe."

No one argued. It wouldn't have mattered. She would have gone anyway. She turned on her heel and started away.

The lake remained still, the moon and stars reflected in its glassy surface. She glanced behind her to make sure none of the others had followed. Seeing none had, she undressed. Naked, she waded into the cool lake water until it reached her navel.

She magicked water through her hair, washing out the grime, sweat, and dust. Oh, she felt infinitely better! She dove under the surface, through the cooling, familiar water. It welcomed her like a friend, like it knew she belonged. With her night eyes, she could see shapes under the water: fish, plants, rocks. She felt the water, felt the precious air within it, and brought it to her face, right into her nose. It took effort to breathe, but after a few breaths, she got the hang of it.

She swam through the deepest part of the lake. Her magic traveled easier and farther through the water, and as she swam toward the depths, she could sense the remains of what felt like a boat at the bottom. She didn't detect any monsters that might eat her alive or other threats, but she did feel something of life—tiny creatures that kept to the edges of her magic sight, like they knew. As she moved, they moved.

She swam downward, and stilled.

Resting at the bottom of the lake was what looked like an ancient stone house, the weeds and algae having reclaimed it ages ago. Who would have built a house at the bottom of a lake? Or, as her logic added, the house had sunken into the lake ages ago.

Slowly, the ruins began to glow. Not the ruins, she realized, but tiny creatures within.

The creatures emerged one by one until their bluish-green glow illuminated the ruins. She saw not one house but many. A village.

She swam closer, slowly. Most of the little creatures scattered for the shadowed corners of the underwater ruins, but a few of them stayed. A few brave creatures swam closer to her. She stopped moving and let them come closer on their own to let them see she posed no threat. Three little creatures swam closer to her. They looked like fish but also birds.

The bluish-green glow of their bodies revealed little scales, large white eyes, and claw-like hands and tiny talons. Feathery fins lined their torsos. Their bodies were no bigger than her smallest finger.

Water sprites.

One swam closer. Its large milky eyes blinked. It looked at Juniper in awe, wonder, and fear.

Sprites were supposed to be magical creatures, so she sent a gentle nudge of her magic to the closest sprite in greeting. The sprite let out a faint high-pitched note, muffled by the water. At the sound, sprites emerged from the ruins below—hundreds of them. They began to glow, shades of bluish green and yellow, bright as daylight. They echoed the note sang by the first, a haunting melody.

A greeting, she realized.

A dozen sprites made easy laps around her, their glow following a heartbeat behind in the water. Those sprites started to swim toward the ruins, their little talon-tipped hands beckoning her to follow. They called to her in their strange underwater chime, like those infernal things that hung from porches in the city.

Their call pulled on her magic deep within her, and she gave in to the urge to follow. They guided her down, down, down, into the depths of the ruins, through the age-old and forgotten village, through what must have been a square. A fountain lay at the center, the carved statue covered in algae and unrecognizable. So much of the village looked untouched, yet some places looked as though the streets had cracked open and walls had collapsed. She couldn't imagine what type of cataclysm had sunk the village.

Magic, her gut suggested.

Then the ruins ended abruptly—jagged rocks lined the edge. Something had indeed sunk the village. Her gut twisted at the notion.

The sprites reached the edge of the ruins and then guided her up—she spotted moonlight reflecting on the calm surface of the water. The sprites led her up to the moonlight, and they hesitated a few inches below the water's surface.

Go, they seemed to say.

She broke through the water's glassy surface. The sprites had led her to a moonlit clearing. Not all of the ruins had sunken into the lake. An old temple lay half on the shore, its walls covered in climbing ivy and moss. Within it, crickets sang. Tree roots had grown through the temple's walls and floor, twisting the stones. Moonlight draped through the towering, ageless oaks and maples.

What had the sprites led her to? What was here they wanted her to see?

She felt something but couldn't tell what.

She swam to the bank sheltered by a willow. Climbing out, the warm air kissed the cool water on her skin. In a heartbeat, she whisked the water out of her hair and off her skin. She could feel something tugging on her magic, urging, needing. She stepped through the willow branches and crept through the ruins, eyes open and ears alert. She came to the far side of the temple, where the wall had been toppled over in several places and taken over by vines and tree roots.

In a patch of moonlight, she saw what the sprites needed her to see.

In the shade of the silver maples lay a dire wolf.

CHAPTER TWELVE

Her breath caught in her throat. The beast was the size of a horse, its thick fur shimmering shades of white and gray. It lifted its head and blinked its black eyes at her. It didn't move.

It took her a heartbeat to realize why—one of its back paws had been caught in a bear trap.

It exhaled and let out a whiny growl, like it knew. She met its dark eyes. She did not see fear—she saw frightening intelligence. Within the wolf's gaze, her nakedness felt more apparent.

Not much she could do about that now.

Her eyes moved to the bear trap. A regular trap wouldn't have been able to hold a dire wolf. It would have to be enchanted. That meant a hunter had set an enchanted bear trap to catch this dire wolf.

Judging by the fresh blood around the wolf's paw, it still bled. Judging by the dried blood, the poor beast had been trapped a while.

The wolf let out a quick snarl, impatient. Its ears twitched upward, and its nostrils flared to catch her scent. It could likely smell far more than a regular wolf—what did it smell on her?

Juniper swallowed. "You're trapped, though I suppose you know that. I can help you, but you have to promise not to bite my hand off when I do."

The wolf blinked, tilted its head, blinked again, then snorted agreeably.

She took careful, purposeful steps toward the dire wolf. It didn't take its eyes off her, and she kept her hands where it could see them. Not that she had anywhere to hide a weapon. She got close enough to feel the heat radiating off the wolf's powerful body. It twisted his head to watch her as she bent down to the bear trap. The jagged edges had cut into the wolf's leg but not deep. It would survive.

Using her magic, she closed icy hands around the jaws of the trap. She sent icy tendrils underneath to the mechanism and, in a few quick turns, took it apart. The jaws loosened, and the wolf stepped out.

"There you go." She let the useless trap collapse in a pile of parts.

The wolf stood several heads taller than her, and it tilted its head down to look at her. Its jaw could bite her head right off her shoulders. It snorted.

"You're welcome," she said.

The wolf considered her, blinked once, and then strolled into the shadows of the forest with barely a limp.

She found the sprites waiting for her at the pool, just below the surface. They guided her back through the inky depths and ruins to where she had first met them at the bottom of the lake. She wanted to explore the ruins, but the sprites gesture toward the surface, their chirps and chimes an indication: *Go that way.* There was something else to see?

She bid the sprites farewell and swam toward the surface with a strange sense of apprehension and satisfaction. How many people could boast of having met water sprites? She had little time to dwell on it, however. As she broke the surface of the lake, an exasperated man's voice said, "Thank the gods."

Juniper gasped and sank deeper into the water, up to her chin. She readied her magic in defense but quickly released it—Reid stood on the bank beside her clothes, eyes wide. He wore something similar to worry on his moonlit features.

"What are you doing out here?" Juniper swam closer. She stopped when the water reached her shoulders. "I said I was going to bathe."

"And you've been gone nearly an hour," Reid said shortly. "And I arrived at a silent lake and a pile of clothes. I thought you'd either been taken or drowned." He glanced around the shore for possible threats.

"It would be hard for me to drown in water." She used her magic to snake a tendril of water toward him.

He smacked it with the back of his hand, and it tumbled to the shore. He glanced at her clothes, then at her, and her cheeks reddened.

"Yes," she said sharply. "You can see I'm not dead."

"I also wanted to speak with you." He cleared his throat and straightened his shoulders, ever the professional squire. "I have something I wanted to ask of you."

"Right now?"

He looked again at her clothes. "It can wait a few moments while you get dressed."

"Fine, then." She started toward the shore. With the first step, the water receded down her chest.

Reid stepped back. His heel hit a rock, and he stumbled. He caught his balance before he fell, but not before a smirk twisted her lips. He turned his back on her. Biting back a laugh, she climbed out of the lake. She magicked the water from her skin and hair and dressed quickly. She kept one eye on him, but he didn't peek. He didn't even try to. It irked her, though she supposed he had already seen her naked. It would seem it hadn't been enough for him to want another look.

"I'm decent." She pulled her clean and dry hair over her shoulder and began to braid it. "Now what is it that you want?"

Reid turned. His eyes snagged on her hair. He started to speak, then stopped. He cleared his throat, and the subtle expression on his face fell into his stoic mask. "I came to ask you a favor."

She dropped her braided hair on her shoulder and set her hands on her hips. "Which is?"

"I want you to train with me."

She lifted a brow. Chuckling, she said, "Just like old times?" Even as she said the words, her chest tightened at the memories.

His cheeks reddened. "I want to gain experience fighting someone trained in both combat and magic."

Juniper blinked once. "Training?" she repeated. "With magic? With me?"

Reid persisted. "If there are apostates waiting to ambush us along this road, then I will need all the training I can get, and one area the Order doesn't put much effort into is practical experience against magic."

He held her gaze, and a prickle started at the base of her spine and zapped upward like lightning.

"Why not ask Ison?" she asked, though the thought of Reid training with him irked her.

"You have the combat experience," he said calmly. "But, if you would rather me not—" He took a step back, toward camp.

"No," she said quickly, and he stopped.

His brows rose. Damn him—he'd drawn her into his trap. And she fell for it. Still, she had his full attention. Both of his honey-brown eyes focused on her. She wanted to be selfish. She wanted his time for herself. Her head told her to say no, but everything else told her to say yes.

Reid waited for her answer.

"Let's train," she said.

CHAPTER THIRTEEN

Juniper followed Reid to a clearing he'd found while looking for her. She tried not to think about it, but his looking for her tugged at her heart. She brought a tendril of the lake's water with her, snaking it around her fingers as they walked. "I hope you realize I'm more powerful at night," she taunted.

He harrumphed.

The clearing was far enough away from camp that they wouldn't disturb Ison and Penet, but close enough to the lake that she could draw from the water if she wished. Reid stalked to one side, and she stood on the other. He rolled his head over his shoulders, faced her, and drew his sword. The steel glinted in the moonlight.

"Ready?" he asked.

She divided the lake water into twin daggers of clear blue ice. The moonlight went through them like ghostly diamonds. Reid's studious gaze shifted, then returned to his stoic indifference.

She came at him first, and her ice clanged onto his steel. Back and forth they traded blows, dancing around the clearing. Neither landed a blow on the other. Suddenly, they were back in the castle, training in front of the hearth in her room. Juniper laughed as they simultaneously blocked each other. Chips of her ice daggers flew into the air with each thrust, shattering into bits of shimmering dust, feathering in the moonlight.

She hadn't fought someone with this much skill since she'd started fighting with magic. She found that as Reid's steel chipped her daggers, she had to reform each dent and ding—and it was draining. Her magic still felt strong, but she knew she wouldn't be able to keep up this pace for too long. Not as long as Reid.

But still they danced around the clearing.

Reid took a step back, disengaging the fight.

Juniper brought her daggers to her sides, then let them go. They took a breathless moment to look at one another, letting their breaths catch up. Damn it if Reid didn't have a smile on his face.

"What?" Juniper asked. "You thought I'd be rusty?"

He shrugged. He had something on his tongue—his lips started to form words—but he pulled them back. His smile faded. He cleared his throat, sheathed his sword. "Send your magic at me."

She blinked. She gathered the lake water she'd dropped on the ground.

"No, send your raw magic at me." He flexed his hand, stretching his fingers out and in. "I want to see how well I stand up against raw magic."

She hesitated, then let the water fall. Not wanting him to think her weak, she summoned the raw energy of her magic. Rather than ice, bright blue magic formed in her hands. She shaped it into an arrow. It took more effort than commanding water.

Reid extended his hand in front of him, pulled his fingers in, took a deep inhale, and as he exhaled extended his fingers out. A shimmering shield formed from his palm—a ward.

She understood then. She thrust her magic toward his ward. Her magic crashed into the shimmer, the front of the arrow bursting apart on contact. Then Reid's eyes widened, the ward dissolved, and the remainder of her magic hit him in the chest. He let out an *oomph*, and she recalled her magic.

"Are you okay?" she asked.

He put a hand over his chest where the magic had hit him. "Not unlike a fist." He let out a breathless chuckle. "Don't tell me you've not wanted to punch me."

She tried to chuckle with him, but it felt hollow. "Well, I suppose I have."

Reid shook out his hand. "Again."

She obliged. She readied her magic arrow and sent it into his shimmering ward. Again, his ward deflected the arrowhead but quickly shattered. This time, Juniper recalled her magic before it hit him.

"Again," he barked.

Again, his ward shattered.

Reid spat a curse as he shook out his hand. Frustration, she realized. He flexed his fingers—the same motion she'd seen him doing in her room back at the castle while he studied at her bedside.

"Again."

She sent an arrow of magic into his ward, shattering it again and again and again until sweat beaded on his forehead. Frustration and irritation burned in his eyes. Her own exhaustion caught up with her, and each arrow felt like squeezing life out of her chest.

"Maybe we should quit for the night," Juniper said after her arrow sent him stumbling back a step.

"No," Reid said. "Again." An order, spoken like a knight.

She sighed, knowing what would happen. So stubborn. She summoned her magic, but as she predicted, she had depleted herself. Her magic flickered in and out, and then she felt the tightening in her chest that radiated along her nerves. She gasped, her magic vanished, and she fell forward onto one knee. She caught herself on the soft ground, panting for breath.

Reid didn't speak. Juniper pushed herself back onto her feet. Reid regarded her coolly, his stoic expression not betraying his thoughts.

"I'm exhausted," Juniper said firmly. "We're done for tonight."

Reid opened his mouth, presumably to argue, and she cut him off, "We both need our rest. We have a long ride ahead of us, and if you intend on exhausting yourself here, you're only letting Adrian suffer longer."

That shut him up. He stood, shook out his hand, and nodded. "You're right."

She started toward camp. Reid followed a step behind. Penet and Ison were sitting on opposite sides of the fire, and at the sight of Juniper and Reid, their conversation ended.

"There you are." Ison quickly looked her over. Looking for what, she didn't know. "If you weren't back soon, we were going to come looking for you."

"We would have gone sooner," Penet said, "but I didn't want to stumble on something I couldn't unsee." His cheeks warmed, and his smile turned mischievous.

She felt her own cheeks redden with the implication, which she hoped Reid didn't notice.

"Juniper was helping me with my wards," Reid said at once.

Ison glanced at her for confirmation, and she nodded.

Penet yawned, and few words were spoken while they headed into their tents. Juniper didn't look at Reid as she ducked into the same tent as Ison. She watched the flames of the dying fire flicker shadows against the canvas. It didn't take long for her exhaustion and need for replenishing rest to pull her under.

CHAPTER FOURTEEN

They woke the next morning, struck camp, and set off for another long day of traveling. The clouds rolled overhead, parting just long enough for the sun to burn off the morning fog and warm the world. The cooler air of the morning whispered of the autumn to come, and Juniper welcomed it. They didn't speak until midday, when they stopped to let the horses rest and drink from a stream and to let their riders share a meal of dried meat and fresh water. Juniper took their canteens to the stream to refill, and as she snaked water into the first, Ison appeared at her side.

"Are you all right?" he whispered.

"Yes. Why, what are you thinking?"

"I think it was a strange coincidence we ran into them."

"I agree." She snaked water into the second. Silence returned as she pulled grime and dirt from the water. "We're helping them in hopes that the king will help us." And because she wanted Adrian to be all right.

"And how are you in other regards?" Ison asked even lower, so much that she almost didn't hear his words.

"What do you mean?"

He gave her a knowing look. "Working on wards?"

She blushed at the implication. "We were," she said, her voice steady. "I went for a swim, met some water sprites, saved a dire wolf from a bear trap, and then when I came back to the shore, Reid was there. He'd come looking for me and wanted me to fling magic at him so he could test his wards in a real fight." She snaked water into the third canteen.

Ison's mouth fell open, and his eyes widened. He tried several times to speak, but words fumbled on his lips. "*What?* I don't know what part of that to pick apart first."

She chuckled and then told him in better detail about her moonlit swim with the sprites.

"And the wolf didn't try to bite your hand off?"

"I asked him not to."

Ison shook his head in disbelief. "The Marca taught us that dire wolves were smart and cunning and devious with a taste for human flesh. I guess that was inflated?"

"He seemed smart and cunning." Smart enough to understand her. She snaked water into the fourth and final canteen.

"It makes me wonder what other kinds of creatures are lurking in these woods." He glanced at the shadowed forest, thick with weeds and brambles.

All of them, she wanted to believe. "Do you think the wolf let me close because of my magic?" she asked.

"I don't know." He shrugged. "That's not something the Marca taught. We didn't learn about magical creatures beyond what we needed to, like unicorns and pixies, and they never wanted to talk about the old creatures like dragons or dire wolves. They only said they probably didn't exist anymore. I admit, I'm glad to know they do. Doesn't mean I want to meet one though."

"He was beautiful." Juniper capped the canteens. Ison took two, and she took two, and they started toward where Reid and Penet readied the packs. "And I'm glad to be learning these things through experience, not just through stories and books."

Ison smirked. "I don't know how much truth there is in your smutty books."

She had long stopped blushing at the mention of those books. She searched for something else to say, and her eyes fell on Reid's back. He was saying something to Penet too low for her to hear. The sun brought out the gold tones in his bronze skin. A shadow darkened the lower half of his face.

"I'm not sure how real the fighting was, though," Juniper whispered. "We were fighting with steel and ice, not wooden staves."

"Because neither of you are fighting to kill."

She hummed her agreement, and as she handed Reid his canteen, a plan started to form.

❊

That night, they camped in a grove. After their dinner of roasted rabbit, Juniper suggested Reid try his wards again. He didn't object. They left Ison and Penet to talk to one another and followed a stream to a clearing. Juniper strolled to the far side of the clearing, and before Reid was ready, she shot an arrow of magic toward him.

He didn't summon a ward—he dodged to the side. The arrow grazed his sleeve, as she'd intended.

"What was that?" he demanded.

"I'm keeping you on your toes," she said playfully.

He frowned.

"What?" She shrugged dramatically. "You said you wanted practice. You think some angry apostate is going to wait for you to adjust your stance?"

She shot out another arrow of magic. This time, he summoned his ward—but her magic crashed into and shattered it. Again, she shot her magic at him. This time, she watched him—in the moment before the magic struck, his eyes widened in uncertainty. He lacked the fierceness in his eyes, the drive to win, to survive. Ison was right. This wasn't real for Reid—his heart wasn't in it.

She shot another arrow before he was ready. It hit the ward, shattered it, and rather than let it dissolve, it skimmed past his cheek. He put a hand to his cheek and glared, but she didn't give him the chance to balk—she shot another arrow at him, and another right after. His ward slowed the first down considerably, but as the second hit, the ward broke apart.

"You've gotten a little rusty," she drawled. "You've spent too much time brooding, haven't you?"

His frown became a shade angrier. "My best friend is dying, and we might be the only ones capable of saving him," he spat.

She shot another arrow. He dodged.

"I hear you were with him when it happened," Juniper taunted.

Penet had told her about Adrian's poisoning. She braced herself for the effect her words would have and added, "Why didn't you stop him? Why didn't you do something? You could have saved him."

There. Something in Reid's eyes snapped and burned. He unsheathed his sword and came at her, a growl on his tongue.

She blocked his thrust with an ice shield and met his attack with a sword of ice. "Maybe you *are* losing your touch." She tried to keep her voice light despite their fight.

They danced around the clearing, trading blows. He fought hard, but not hard enough.

"Do you still think I did it?" Juniper asked. "Because if I wanted him dead, he would have been dead months ago."

His sword chipped into her ice. "You were too busy playing a lady to do anyone harm," Reid spat at her.

"That might be a little true. But be honest, Reid," she purred his name, "I made a fantastic lady."

He snarled and spat a curse.

"Oh, come on, everyone loved me!" she said playfully. She saw the tiny cringe in his face.

His attacks came harder.

She played with fire, and she knew it. "I had you, Adrian, and Ison under my fingers. I could have robbed the king blind, and no one would have known."

His blade slammed into her ice hard enough to knock her back a step. Almost.

"Tell me," she crooned, going for blood, "Would you have kept me in your closet?"

The burning became rage, rage that came from hurt—he angled for a thrust, she angled her shield to block, and then he moved so quickly she didn't have time to counter. He thrust his pommel into her ice shield. It shattered, and she fell backward onto the dewy ground.

Her back hit first, knocking the breath from her chest. In the next moment, Reid was coming at her, and something inside of her took over. She gathered her magic into an arrow and sent it hurtling toward his chest.

Reid pulled his fingers toward his palm and thrust them out, and with the motion, his shimmering ward appeared like cloudy glass. Her magic crashed into the ward.

And it held.

Juniper jumped to her feet, but Reid thrust his ward forward, against her magic—and as he did so, something surged through her magic, her bones, her blood, her muscles—a blinding pain. Her vision blackened, she collapsed, and in that moment, her magic vanished.

Gone.

After the pain came fear. A terrible fear that she'd never known rose within her—her magic, gone.

Someone called her name from far away.

No, her magic wasn't gone. She felt it in her blood, depleted but there. Slowly coming back. Slowly rejuvenating.

Reid appeared in her hazy sight. She could barely focus on him. He knelt beside her. He didn't look happy.

"You did it," she said, her voice weak. "Don't say I never did anything for you."

He blinked. His anger dulled into realization, and he let out an exhausted sigh. "I could have done you serious harm."

"What did you do?" she said, her voice a little stronger.

"Wards are not only defensive, but they can be used offensively," he explained. "I used the ward to rebound your magic on you, and by doing so, disabled it. I've been told it's like having your magic ripped out of you."

"Yes." She'd only heard of knights using combat magic, reserved for fighting apostates.

"Can you stand?"

She tried to shift her numb legs, but they did not respond.

In a swift motion, Reid lifted her limp body into his arms. She tried not to think about the strong shoulder she leaned against, even as her heart fluttered into her throat. They started toward camp, and she caught the smell of him. Leather, sweat, and that woodsy scent that belonged to him. Admittedly, the woodsy scent was not as strong as the others.

He didn't walk fast, and slowly her magic returned enough for her to feel her limbs.

"Do you feel better prepared for when you face a real apostate?" A part of her still didn't accept that she was an apostate.

"I do," he said. "Thank you, even though your methods were harsh."

"Sometimes you need to be harsh. Especially when dealing with someone as stubborn as you."

His lips flickered upward, and the subtle smile reached his eyes. He continued toward camp, and for a while, neither of them spoke.

Halfway to camp, she stopped him. "I don't want the others to see you carrying me back." She wriggled her feet. "I can walk."

He lifted a brow. "Self-conscious about appearing weak?"

Her face heated. "Maybe. Or maybe I don't want them to assume anything more than they already have."

He chuckled but obeyed. He set her feet on the ground, hovering his hands behind her while she gathered her footing.

"See?" She stood strong. For the moment.

"That's impressive," he said. "I've heard that when magic is rebounded, it could take hours or days for a mage to regain their full strength."

"Well," she said haughtily, "I'm not just any mage."

"That you're not."

She caught his honey-brown eyes in the moonlight, dark as ink drops.

An owl hooted overhead, low and lazy. Somewhere, in the deepest parts of the forest, a dire wolf hunted for his dinner. The stream trickled along, gently splashing against the rocks and the grassy shore.

"That will be an impressive attack when you encounter an apostate."

She focused on the texture of his leather cuirass. "You know, I didn't mean those things back there. I was trying to piss you off."

A beat passed.

"And it worked," he said, nodding. "Thank you, again."

She smirked. "It's not every day I get thanked for pissing someone off."

"In that situation, it worked."

Juniper glanced up at his face and found him looking back. And it was only them and the forest, no one else. No sick prince, no ancient mage bent on destroying the realm, no time limit, no rush. Just them. The familiarity in his eyes struck something she hadn't felt in a long while, something she had dearly missed, something she had told herself over and over that she would never feel again.

Reid moved first, stepping slightly closer to her. Her heart jumped into her throat as his eyes dipped to her lips. She should have stepped back, but her treacherous body stepped toward him.

She lost her breath, lost all other thought, as Reid's lips pressed against hers. She wanted more. She wanted to grab him and push him to the forest floor and take what she had missed—but she didn't. She couldn't.

They parted, and she met his honey-brown eyes. He leaned in for a second kiss, but she intercepted him. She placed a trembling finger against his lips.

"Reid," she breathed, her words trembling. "We can't."

He pulled away. Regret pulled on his features, but understanding quickly replaced it.

"You are a squire," she whispered. "You will be a knight, the best of the Order. There's no place for someone like me there."

It was the same reasoning she'd used since she first thought of his lips against her own.

Emotions fought behind his eyes. After a long moment, he nodded. "You're right," he said, his voice weak. "You're right," he said again, firmly. He shifted his eyes elsewhere.

As much as it pained her, she held her fists at her sides. She wanted to reach out to him, to touch him, to tell him that she still felt for him despite her reasoning, but she didn't. It would only hurt her, and him, and make his quest for knighthood more difficult. No, for his sake and her own, she would keep her thoughts to herself.

And, before her eyes, the emotions vanished from Reid's face. His stoic mask returned, the face of a royal guard, of a soldier, of a knight. He shielded himself behind a knight's scowl. She had a thought to tease him about it, but she couldn't form the words.

"We should get back to camp," he said. "Can you walk?"

"Of course." She started away from him at a clipped pace.

He followed a step behind.

Penet and Ison remained by the fire. They both looked amused.

"I was just telling Ison about the secret heir," Penet said to Reid.

"Not that again." Reid sat down by the fire.

Juniper sat on the opposite side. She shouldn't feel jilted, but she did. Not wanting to pout, she asked, "What about the secret heir?"

"That it's actually Reid." Penet nodded toward the other squire, who looked like he might strangle Penet.

"Is that true?" Juniper asked.

"Of course not," Reid said firmly, clearly not fond of the talk.

Penet recapped the theory that Reid might be the lost heir, taken out of the castle to live with Captain Sandpiper's brother. But then, rebels found them and he was brought back to the castle where the king treated him like a son. And their quest's real purpose was to get Reid out of the castle.

By the fury in Reid's eyes, he thought the whole thing rubbish.

"That's an interesting tale," said Ison.

"And a tale is all it is," said Reid, ending the discussion. "Now, unless you'd like to start telling ghost stories, I suggest we get some sleep."

Reid stormed to his tent, leaving the other three looking after him.

❋

Reid lay awake in his tent, watching the light of the fire die slowly against the thick canvas.

What the hell was wrong with him? He had thought he had put Juniper behind him, pushed his feelings for her aside. Yet tonight, something had just...felt right. The sounds of the forest, the way the moonlight shone in her hair and gleamed in her eyes and turned her pale skin to porcelain. And then she had looked at him with those eyes, and he just...needed her.

The news of her death had hit him hard, but it had enabled him to put his feelings for her aside. It made it easier to forget her. But seeing her again, being so close to her, hearing her voice, touching her—all those feelings came crashing back like an uppercut.

He could still feel her lips against his. Of all the girls he'd kissed, none had struck him like she had. None had stained the front of his mind like she had.

But Juniper was right—there could be nothing between them. It would only bring trouble for both of them. When this quest was over, he would ride into Rusdasin and become a knight. Juniper would vanish into the shadows. He couldn't afford an affair with an apostate or a wanted criminal, dead or not. It would ruin his chances for knighthood.

He couldn't risk it.

And Juniper knew that.

He hadn't been thinking clearly, but she had. She knew what would happen if they pursued something more. He would have to let her go, and he didn't know if he had the willpower to survive losing her a third time.

And if she was right about Nexon, gods... What did that even mean?

Reid had no answer. He didn't know what to do or tell her to do. A knight was supposed to have the answers, the strength to make hard decisions, and the will of steel to follow those decisions through. Even though he didn't want to let her go again, he would. He had to.

Penet snorted in his sleep. The fire had burned lower still.

He'd wanted to punch Penet for telling Ison and Juniper the nonsense about him being the secret heir. Did Penet enjoy the story, or was he serious? Penet had never been the jokester.

Yet, as Reid tried to pull his father's face from his memory, the face that surfaced was his uncle's.

Had he forgotten his father's face?

Panic struck his chest like a thousand pins, and he went back into every memory he had of his life before—there, his father's face. He had green eyes, like Reid's uncle, and the same chestnut hair and bronze skin as Reid. The panic subsided. And his mother—Reid had inherited her eyes. He never knew where she was from. His uncle didn't know exactly either. A small village to the east.

He looked far too much like his parents to be the secret heir, if a secret heir even existed. But still, that impossible what-if sounded—could he be Adrian's brother? The king had been kind to him, more so than any other children who lived in the castle.

And by the little things his uncle and aunt had said over the years, Reid had surmised they thought his father might not have left the castle on his own will. His uncle had once said that Reid's mother had wanted to go to the country. His aunt once said Reid's father had wanted to return. Conflicting stories. Reid had never given them a second thought until now.

✳

"Do you think Penet's story has any credibility to it?" Juniper asked Ison when they had arranged themselves for sleep.

"I doubt it." Ison's breath was hot on the back of her neck. "But it's a fun story to think about."

"It is," Juniper said.

She knew things about Reid that Ison didn't, and she knew that apostates had attacked his home and murdered his family. He had been spared because his mother had told him to hide. Had those apostates been rebels looking for the secret heir? It was possible. What if Reid knew, or suspected, and wanted to keep it secret? That would explain his dislike of the subject.

Indeed, it was a fun story to think about. As she fell asleep, she wove her own story of Prince Reid.

She woke with the dregs of her magic stirring.

Ison's warm breath hit her neck, his lips a hair's breadth above her skin. The fire had died out. Dawn had not yet broken. In that daze between sleep and waking, she wanted Ison's breath to be Reid's. For a moment, it was. But, she soon realized it was not. It would never be.

Her magic stirred again, a gentle nudge—a warning. Had she been fully awake and thinking, she might not have noticed the uncanny feeling in her stomach. But in the awareness that came from waking up in a strange place, she felt it.

Something moved in the forest. *Somethings.*

She cast her fragile magic out as far as she could without feeling a strain. She found strangers moving toward them, slow and cautious. Humans.

Drawing her magic back, she rolled over. She covered Ison's mouth and shook him awake, a finger to her lips. He jumped, instantly awake. Footsteps sounded against the grass. She heard the swish of steel against leather—a sword unsheathing. She rose from her sleeping position. Steel cut through air a heartbeat before an ax sliced through the canvas.

The blade sank into the ground, right where her neck would have been.

Chapter Fifteen

Juniper screamed and threw an ice-fist into the chest of her attacker. He stumbled back, and before he could react, she sent a dagger of ice through his throat. In her panic and rage, her ice smothered him, freezing him solid. He shattered into a million bits of ice and flesh. His ax clattered to the ground.

Her scream had stirred the others. Penet and Reid jumped from their tents, swords ready. Steel flashed in the moonlight. Bandits surrounded them, at least a dozen that she could see. Ison swept three of them into the air with a gale. They landed with bone-breaking thuds.

She felt the night empower her dwindling magic, and she used it. Juniper fought with frozen daggers, commanding them without touching their handles. She sliced through the throat of one, then another, and another, and as it neared the fourth, Reid's blade beat her to it.

But the bandits kept coming. They wore dark leathers and painted steel armor that deflected her ice arrows and daggers with *pings* and *dings*. Still she fought. She couldn't send her ice fast or hard enough to pierce armor. She had to get her aim just right—through the throat, the shoulder joint, the buckles on the sides—and every bandit wore different armor than the one before, making each a new search for the weak spot.

Steel crashed against steel, ice, and wind. Juniper pulled her magic into daggers, arrows, and shields, but for every throat she sliced, for every bone Ison shattered, another bandit appeared.

Had she woke to some nightmare?

Her magic stores hadn't fully rejuvenated. It squeezed and tugged inward like a muscle about to seize. This couldn't go on much longer.

She slashed her ice at a bandit, knocking him off balance, enough that she slammed the ice blade underneath his helmet, slicing deep into his flesh. She knocked his body into another when she heard a guttural gasp of pain from behind her, and she knew immediately who had been hurt. She whirled around, magic first, and gripped her icy claws into the bandit whose blade glistened with Reid's blood.

A blind rage took over. Her ice consumed the bandit. Shattered him.

Reid fell to his knees, blood seeping from a wound that reached from his side to his navel. If he had been wearing his armor, he wouldn't have been hurt.

Ison shouted, and his magic sent five bandits cresting into the air. They hit the ground with sickening thumps. None rose. Three bandits came at Penet, regardless of the slaughter of their friends, and while he parried one thrust, Ison deflected the other with a vicious wind, the third struck his back. Penet cried out in anger and pain as his sword sliced through the bandit. Ison's wind sliced the other nearly in two.

Juniper gathered what magic she had left and cast it out. The moisture in the air settled on the bandits. She needled her magic between seams and through buckles. The moisture became ice, and that ice became dozens of tiny blades that pierced whatever flesh they touched. A collective scream of sudden agony rose from the remaining bandits. In their distraction, Ison whisked them up and slammed them back down.

And then the battle was over.

Penet sank to his knees, blood seeping from his back. Reid collapsed. Pain twisted his features. Blood poured from his side.

Juniper felt her magic collapse in on itself, squeezing on her insides and pulling inward. Everything inside felt like it was imploding.

Ison stumbled to her side. "Are you hurt?"

"I'm fine," she gasped.

"Your magic," Ison explained. "Deep breaths." He stumbled to Reid's side. "I-I might be able to staunch the worst of the bleeding." He held his hand over the wound, and a faint gray-green glow formed under his palms.

Reid's barely conscious gaze slid to Ison, but he said nothing.

Again, his life rested in the hands of a mage. Juniper wanted to help, but with her magic depleted, there was nothing she could do. Even if she had magic, she didn't know the first thing about healing. Useless.

She took deep breaths like Ison had said, focusing on that pinching seed of magic inside of her. It grew, the magic slowly rejuvenating, but not nearly as fast as she wanted. She needed sleep and something to eat, neither of which she had time for right now.

While Ison had staunched the bleeding on Reid and Penet, sweat beaded his brow, and he looked a few breaths from collapsing himself.

"Well," gasped Juniper as Penet managed to stand, using his sword for balance, "we're alive, at least."

"But we can't stay here," Penet said between pants.

"They might send more." Juniper nodded. "But you two need to heal."

Neither of them argued.

Juniper and Ison packed the camp as quickly and efficiently as they could. Reid and Penet were in no shape for travel, and Juniper led the slow, careful trek to a cave she had spotted when she and Reid had trained. The mouth was narrow and partially hidden by hanging moss and climbing vines. They tied off the horses on towering stalagmites, and neither Reid nor Penet waited for a bedroll before they collapsed on the stone ground.

Ison summoned a forever flame and set it on a lower rock, enough that it illuminated the four of them in its bluish glow.

"Those bandits," Reid gasped between uneven breaths, "were too well-armed."

"And numerous." Juniper's voice was stronger than it had been before. She saved anyone else from speaking by saying, "I doubt they were simple bandits. They attacked first, were too many, and not a single one of them said a word during the fight. Not even as they met their deaths or saw their fellows slain. Bandits are generally foulmouthed and stupid."

Reid didn't respond, but he wore agreement on his features.

They fell into silence. Juniper leaned against the cavern wall, taking each breath as it came. Her insides felt knotted up and twisted. Reid and Penet fell asleep, and Ison followed their lead from his slumped position against the wall. Juniper needed rest. Her body screamed for it, but her mind refused.

Juniper stood, intent on fetching blankets for them, but Ison stirred. His sleepy gray eyes found her. She tiptoed closer.

"A rune... A rune to hide the door," he breathed. His cheeks were pale.

"Show me," she said.

Ison drew a rune in the dirt on the cavern floor. "Draw one on either side of the door, directly across from each other."

She slipped a dagger from her pack, and slowly carved the complicated rune into the stone. She carved the second rune, and as she finished the last mark, she felt the runes connect, felt the magic shared between them—it felt different than her own. A faint scent of metal filled her nose, there and gone. The air between the two runes distorted. The distortion reached to the cavern's ceiling and to the floor.

She turned around to tell Ison she'd done it, but he'd already gone back to sleep. On the floor this time.

Juniper reached out to the distorted light. It hummed under her palm. She touched it—warm, gentle magic flowed between the runes. Taking a breath, she stepped through it. Nothing happened. But, where the cavern mouth had been now stood a very solid-looking wall of stone, identical to the stone around it. It blended in perfectly with the surrounding rock. Had she not known where to go, she would have missed it.

Which meant that anyone who came looking wouldn't see it either.

Juniper memorized the location, the trees, the rocks, and then headed back toward their camp. The bodies of the bandits remained. She went to the first and yanked the hardened leather helmet from his head. While dead and glassy eyed, the man looked no different than a man should. His dark eyes stared upward listlessly.

In her looting, she found a few daggers of medium quality, silver and bronze coins, and odds and ends. Nothing abnormal for bandits to have on their person. Still, it bugged her. Why had they attacked? Why so many?

A shuddering gasp shook her out of her thoughts.

One of the bandits had not yet died. His dark eyes stared upward but blinked. As Juniper walked into his view, his eyes shifted slowly to her. He had sustained a slash to the neck, but it hadn't been deep enough. No, the wound that had brought him down was on his side, deep and freshly bleeding.

"Who are you?" Juniper asked.

Confusion came over the man's face. "Why?"

"Why indeed."

"What happened?" His voice sounded rough, dry and raspy.

"What do you mean what happened?" Juniper bent down. "You attacked us."

Confusion looked back at her. "No," he breathed. "I didn't."

Juniper stood above him as the light left his eyes, and he was dead. His eyes drifted as his spirit left, giving him the same glassy expression as the rest. She pushed him from her mind and looted what she could.

By the time Juniper returned to the hidden cave, her bones felt like sand, and her blood felt like lead. She deposited everything she had taken off the strange bandits in a pile near her pack. She'd look through it later.

The cave smelled like blood, warm, sticky, and coppery. Juniper sat with the others. She held her eyes on Reid until she saw his chest rise and fall several times, and did the same to Penet.

Someone did not want them to survive this quest. Meeting bandits along the road was not uncommon, but being surprised by well-armed bandits in the middle of the night? This was twice someone had tried to intervene with the quest. Three times, counting the actual bandits.

Someone wanted Adrian to die and knew Reid and Penet were after the only thing that might save him. Or, a little voice in her mind said, someone believed the story about Reid being the secret heir.

Nexon had been trying to get rid of Adrian for months. Nexon was in the castle. He could have heard about the quest. If he had, he would have his people looking for them, trying to ruin the quest.

Juniper let out a slow sigh. Why did the world have to rest on her shoulders? She looked to the saddlebags, hastily packed, and their supplies. They had done well with rations, with her and Ison to catch wild game and fish and clean river water for drinking.

Right now, in this cave, they were safe.

And that safety allowed her to close her eyes, just for a moment.

❄

Juniper woke to a loud hoot from outside the cave. Her body craved more sleep, deeper sleep, but she forced herself to sit up. On the other side of the rune's protection, the forest glowed with the blue-gray mist of early dawn. The others were still sleeping. She managed to stand, using the wall for support, and once on her feet, released a sigh—she felt better than she had before her nap, but she still didn't feel good.

She ate from the rations. Her appetite mirrored her mood—she didn't eat much.

Juniper went through the satchel that had belonged to the herbalist. What was his name? Graison. Inside, she found vials and notebooks and quills and ink bottles, and a curious leather book with no discernable title. But a thump in her chest responded to the book—something about books stirred that sense of adventure. Between the covers of a book, anything could happen. What sort of book did the herbalist think important enough to bring along?

Juniper sat close to the forever flame and set the book in her lap. To her dismay, though she should have expected it, the book contained information on plants. Each page held two pictures of plants and short descriptions of each, including its smell, color, location in the world, desirable growing habits, and its uses and cautions.

The leather had worn on the edge, and the pages had faded. Juniper had held enough books to know the difference between old and ancient. This book was ancient. She carefully flipped through its brittle pages. She hadn't heard of some of the plants—Jester's Hat, Curling Wisp, Poke Pods. The plants themselves looked like something out of a children's storybook, mad and only something from the wilds of imagination. According to the book, Jester's Hat only grew between rocks in the full sun, and its petals turned bright red during the hottest days of the year. Curling Wisp grew in the shade in cool climates but didn't like snow. Poke Pods grew in the tropics and produced a poison so potent, the smell could render a man unconscious.

She turned page after page. Strange, curious plants with odd habits and particular growing needs. And then she came to a beautifully drawn flower with a long elegant stem and white petals. The petals started as pale blue and grew out to a stunning white. According to the delicate script of the author, the flower was called Boxel's Grace.

> Said to heal any ailment, disease, ill condition, or unwanted parasite. Planted in the Garden of the Gods by Boxel in the beginning. Extremely rare, possibly extinct. Thought to be a myth by many. Grows only in the most extreme climates on the ends of the realm.

Ends of the realm.

Reid let out a shuddering breath, and her heart jumped into her throat. Her eyes went to his wound. It had stopped bleeding, as had Penet's, but it didn't look good. She shut the book and set it aside. They needed her more right now.

She looked to Ison, but he slept deeply. He had taught her a few of the common healing herbs—she rooted through the herbalist's satchel. She found a few of those herbs but not enough. Using what little power she could muster, she formed a ball of water. She added the herbs to the water, crushing them as it went, and removed the excess water until she formed a paste. She divided it between Reid and Penet, though she gave more to Reid—his injury looked worse.

The herbal paste ran out too fast. She would need more. Surely, she could find them in the forest. A few herbs, fresh air, and they would heal properly...right? Yes, they had to. But if she didn't find any... She wouldn't be able to live with herself if she returned to find either squire gone or, gods forbid, both. Reid had paled considerably with pain and blood loss. As had Penet. She had to do something.

Looking at the two of them, labored breathing and painful expressions even in their sleep... A desperate plan formed.

She looked inside herself, for her dwindling seed of magic. Her magic gave her a healing advantage. As she looked inside, somehow she knew it was possible. She reached for that seed of magic and divided it into four. Two of those seeds traveled along her blood, her bones, and appeared in her hand as two tiny orbs of blueish silver.

She knelt beside Reid and dropped one seed over his wounded abdomen. It floated down to his bloodied skin and vanished, a drop of water into blood. Reid shuddered but did not wake. A soft sigh eased from his lips.

She felt the loss of her magic, the dividing. She felt the pitiful amount of magic she had slowly replenished shatter. But she knew he would be all right. Her magic would heal him.

She did the same to Penet; only, her seed of magic hesitated before touching his skin. It lingered against his wound, and at Juniper's behest, entered his body to heal.

Juniper sat between them, watching. Their breathing evened. A small amount of color returned to their cheeks. And as she sat there, the wound on Reid's side stitched itself together the slightest bit.

The third seed she gave to Ison because her magic seemed to regenerate faster than his. It sank through his ashen skin easily and merged with his own dwindling magic. She would lend her magic to them for the day or maybe the next, however long it would take to heal, and then she would take it back. Simple.

They would be all right.

Despite the hollowness in the place her magic had been, she knew she would be all right too. While they healed, she would see about more healing herbs. She emptied the herbalist's satchel of everything but what she needed to safely gather and carry herbs, and started into the early morning outside the cave. Her knees were shaky, her body called for rest, but for the three sleeping men in the cave, she would endure.

CHAPTER SIXTEEN

Juniper wandered through the sunlit forest, between the bushes and weeds, over the brambles and treacherous tree roots, and around the towering oaks, maples, and birch. She didn't move fast. She couldn't. What magic she had left shrank in the sunlight. Too much movement made her dizzy.

Why did she think it was a good idea to take a walk through the woods with no magic?

Somewhere around midday, she found the first of the healing herbs. She carefully picked as many as she could and stored them in one of the vials. She then followed the sound of rushing water to a stream for a much needed drink. Her magic could barely clean a sip of water at a time.

She sat on a rock beside the stream. This close to the river, her magic responded. She didn't feel as bad.

What if Boxel's Grace was nothing more than a legend? What if they got to the end of the realm and found nothing? Then again, archmages were supposed to be legends. Legends had one foot in the truth, it seemed. Still, so many things could go wrong. The book said nothing about what part of the plant did the healing. What if they took the petals and they really needed the stem or the roots?

A few whiskered fish swam by, glittering as they glided through the water.

Would Reid be angry that she'd given him a bit of her magic? She didn't know. She would like to think that saving his life counted for something, but she couldn't know for sure until he woke.

She could remove the seeds before any of them woke up to discover it. That way, she wouldn't have to worry about it.

There. Plan done.

Still...she could feel those three seeds. They tied her to each one of them, and she felt their being on the other side. She felt the magic guiding her back to the cave. Tugging.

If Reid woke up and felt that, he would be furious.

She would risk his fury for his life. Again.

The whiskered fish turned a certain way, and the sunlight shimmered off their pale scales. Almost silver. Silver catfish, said a voice somewhere in the back of her mind. She had seen the fish at the market. They were rare and pricey fish. And three swam in front of her.

Like a flash of lightning, the shimmering silver scales vanished into the depths of the water.

Juniper stood up straight, and the world shifted under her feet. She caught herself on a tree before she fell into the river. Sleep, her body screamed—deep, dreamless, rejuvenating sleep.

She stepped away from the river. Her magic dwindled, her attention wavered, and the edges of her vision blurred. Leaning against an oak, she took deep breaths until the feeling went away.

A footstep sounded in the forest behind her.

Ison, she hoped, come to chide her for leaving in her state and to drag her back to the cave to rest. She opened her eyes and turned to greet him with relief—but it was not Ison. A man walked toward her, a few years older than she, with an unruly beard and brown eyes.

She opened her mouth, but within the inhale to form the words, two hands grabbed her arms, and someone else thrust a bag over her head.

And she had no magic.

So she screamed. The shrill sound echoed through the forest, silencing birds, but it ended when a fist collided with her chest. She gasped to regain her breath.

"Think twice before you open your mouth," spat a man.

She struggled, but stronger arms forced her to the ground. A rope tightened around her hands and then her ankles. Her heart hammered faster and faster.

"Tie her good," grumbled a man to her left. "We can't have another wander off in the night."

Ropes secured her arms to her body, and a broad someone hoisted her into the air and over a thick shoulder. Already dizzy, they moved her too fast for her to know which way was up. The movement churned her stomach, and she thought she might upchuck her pitiful meal into the hood. She shut her eyes and tried to breathe deeply, forcing her nausea and panic down.

Her attackers walked for a while. There were at least two of them, maybe three. She couldn't tell a direction—they could have been walking straight into the sky for all she knew. The forest protested this unruly kidnapping with angry chirps and manic chittering and low growls, but the men did not balk. If anything, they moved faster.

She tried to think of a way out, some clever maneuver, but her exhaustion threatened to take her. It weakened her limbs and fogged her brain. A few times, she thought she fell asleep, because the man carrying her would jostle, and she would slam back into her bones.

"Hakle, she dead?" asked a nasally man somewhere behind her.

"Nah, she's breathing," said Hakle, the man carrying her.

"She's not moving," said the nasally man. "Boss said this one can't die."

"Shut up, Lace, I know breathing when I feel it."

The man named Lace huffed.

This one. How many others had these men stolen from the forest?

They walked for what felt like hours. Juniper came and went between barely awake and unconsciousness. Then Hakle moved, and she fell onto something hard and wooden. A gate snapped, an iron lock clicked, and a horse whinnied. Juniper rolled onto her side and sat up but could see nothing but filtered sunlight through the bag.

"What is this?" Juniper demanded. When no one answered, she asked, "Where are you taking me?"

Something smacked against metal terrifyingly close to her face.

"Shut up," spat Lace.

"Quit lollygagging, and get this cart moving," said the first man. He spoke with a northern accent and mild education, unlike Lace or Hakle. By the command on each word, he led the other two.

The cart they'd thrown her into started to move, and she lurched backward. She inched around the tiny space. A gate kept her from getting out. Two windows of iron bars mirrored each other. Not that it mattered. She couldn't get far with bound hands and feet. She leaned against the wall of the cart.

The men rode above her, their conversation too muffled by the wheels, the horse, the forest. Her heart hammered despite her exhaustion.

For the second time in her life, she had been thrown into a kidnapper's wagon. Where would these fools take her? The Undercity? Laughable. The joke would be on them.

The wagon hit a bump and jostled her against the side.

Bound, hooded, and depleted, she could do nothing but wait for her magic to regenerate. When it did, the fools who thought her easy prey would be sorry.

They would die slowly.

*

Juniper spent a terrifying day in the back of the cart. Her stomach growled only once. Still, her appetite hadn't returned. Had giving her magic to the others affected her that much?

The cart jostled through the forest. Birds chirped and sang and cawed. She couldn't tell which direction they were headed. The unevenness of the trail suggested they followed no road, but she didn't know the winding country paths and trails of Duvane enough to know.

Reid might have known.

At the thought of her friends, her chest squeezed. What would they think when they woke up to find her gone? Would they look for her? Would they find her?

They paused once to rest and relieve themselves, for which the bag was mercilessly ripped from her head.

Hakle, an ugly man with a scar lining the side of his face and grungy brown hair, cut the ropes binding her ankles. He held a sword at her. "Take care of business," he said. "Don't try nothing, or I'll run you through."

As she limped toward a modestly secluded spot, Hakle followed. She ran through every possible escape tactic. Hakle, who seemed to suspect her thoughts, pressed the sword against her back. As she relieved herself, she forced herself to meet his stare, to make sure he looked at her face. All the while, he grinned.

Oh, she would kill him slowly. She imagined his death a dozen different ways before she finished.

Then Hakle threw her back into the cart without the hood—a small consolation. He threw a few strips of dried beef through the iron window, and she tried her best to eat. She got through one, and her stomach coiled at the thought of more. He pushed the mouth of a canteen through the bars and held it while she drank.

Hakle drank from the canteen next, and the idea of his mouth anywhere near where hers had been threatened to bring her meager meal back up.

Footsteps approached through the brush, two sets, and Hakle turned. "Hey, Boss, how much you think we'll get for this one?"

"It depends on the others on the block," said the leader of their little group. "I'll head down to the square once we get there to spy the other stock."

"I heard that they is trying to cut down on the trade," said Lace, his nasally voice irritating. She would rip out his tongue before she killed him. "That Bradburn was putting pressure on old Devlin about it."

Devlin? The only Delvin Juniper knew of was the King of Janti, Devlin de Caroel. And Janti just happened to be big in the slave trade.

Great.

"Bradburn don't have power in Janti," snapped Hakle.

"But he's a king, right?" asked Lace.

"He is a king in Duvane," said Boss. "Every Bradburn king for the last five hundred years has been pressuring Janti about their slave trade. Nothing's happened yet. Nothing is going to happen. Devlin's got too much gold in it."

They climbed back onto the cart, and they started off through the forest. This time, without the hood, she watched the trees pass. Watched the shadows gradually lengthen as the sun sank.

A coldness sank into her bones. Janti. They were taking her to Janti, intent on selling her at the slave markets. She reached inside for the seed of magic, the sliver of what she had left. It dwindled. Hadn't it been long enough to replenish? Even enough to get her out of the cart? Even now, she wasn't sure how far they'd traveled, but according to the shadows, they headed northwest.

To the border over the Gallas Mountains, where the patrols didn't pass. Where they would cross into Janti without notice.

Juniper sighed and lay flat on the bottom of the cart.

What would the others think? Her heart clenched at the thought of them waking up to find her gone, assuming the worst. Would they think her a deserter? Dead? Drowned? Would they even attempt to find her? How would they find clean drinking water without her?

The cart jostled over a large bump, sending her rocking to one side and then the other.

"Careful, Lace, you'll bruise the goods," said Hakle.

The cart traveled further northwest. Maybe by the time they reached Janti, her magic would replenish. Janti favored magic. She might be able to get passage back to Duvane. Unless someone realized who she was.

What a mess.

Juniper passed between periods of rest and unrest, not knowing how long she slept each time, until at last the cart came to a halt. The sun had set, and the forest beyond had filled with shadows. Hoots and low growls emitted from the darkness. She remained inside while the slavers started a fire and erected tents. Footsteps approached the cart. The lock clanked open, and the gate swung outward. Hands grabbed her ankles, then her arms, and hauled her out.

Hakle sat her down on a log. A fire blazed in the center of a camp. Two men sat around the fire. She knew Lace instantly, for his rat-like face matched the sound of his voice. The other, the leader, had a stronger presence. He had broad shoulders and a wild beard but sharp eyes.

She quickly took in her surroundings. They were still in the forest, but the trees grew cramped together, roots sprawling over the forest floor like a tangle of snakes. Twisted vegetation grew around the thick trees, shading the moonlight in a grayish green.

Hakle thrust a canteen into her hands. "Drink."

Juniper grasped the canteen with her bound wrists. Awkward, but it worked. She drank the stale water greedily.

Hakle sat beside her, sword across his lap.

A day. A day had passed. They had taken her a day's ride away from Reid, Ison, and Penet, and the magic she'd gifted them to heal. She didn't know if the distance would affect their healing, but it affected her. Her magic hadn't replenished. It yearned for what she'd given to them. It cried out for it. It made her limbs feel like sand, stole her appetite, and blurred her thoughts.

Even if she managed to get free of these slavers, she wouldn't make it very far.

Why had she left the cave?

The slavers ate and drank around the fire, speaking little. Then, the leader appeared before her, a strip of dried meat in his hands. "Eat," he said. "Thin girls don't sell for nearly as much. You need meat on those bones."

She hesitated. Not only did her stomach not feel like eating, she didn't care how much gold these fools thought they could get for her.

"Eat it yourself, or I will force it down your throat," the leader said, each word a threat.

Juniper grasped the dried meat in both hands and bit off the end. The leader stood before her, watching, a smug look on his face. She swallowed despite her nausea, bit off another chunk, and as she lifted her chin to meet his eye, she noticed his eyes had dipped down to the collar of her shirt.

Looking down her shirt. Bastard.

He noticed her stare, and he sneered.

Oh, she would kill him first.

CHAPTER SEVENTEEN

Amery stood in the doorway to the root cellar of her manor as the earth mages broke through. The solid dirt moved effortlessly, creating hardly any mess, and vanished down the tunnel. Through the hole, one of Josephine's earth mages appeared. He had dirt smudged on his nose and his forehead, and when he saw Amery, a wide smile stretched across his face.

"Gerald!" Amery threw her arms open in delight. "How wonderful it is to see you again!"

Gerald climbed into the root cellar, admiring his handiwork. He and a handful of earth mages had been put in charge of making the tunnel between Amery's manor and Josephine's keep. It had taken a few trial-and-errors for the right location, but they'd done it with minimal mess.

And the best part? No one had found out. They had supported their tunnel with wooden beams and scrap metal no one would miss. The project had been gradual but efficient. Amery had loved watching the progress, even though she hadn't done much of it herself.

She kept her new Mage's Bane dagger at her hip, though Josephine's mages had never given her reason to feel threatened. Bois's friends were different. They had fallen for Clive's fantastical nonsense. Amery liked the security of Mage's Bane. She'd chosen a simple leather sheath so no one would know its real power until she unsheathed the blade.

"I've got to go tell Josephine it's finished." Gerald vanished into the dark tunnel. His footsteps quickened into a run.

Gerald had explained how earth mages didn't need light to see. They could feel the earth and anything on it, which helped them to see underground. She'd called him a mole, and he'd frowned. That's what she had taken to calling the earth mages: moles.

Amery shut the root cellar's finely crafted wooden door and made her way through the larder, then the kitchen, into the spacious manor. The silence of it thrilled her. The smell of linseed oil and silver polish suffused the air. The crystal and brass chandelier that hung in the foyer glistened in the late evening light.

Her heels clicked on the tile as she made a slow lap of her new house. She'd kept her purchases to a minimum to avoid suspicion, but she'd bought what she needed, like silk sheets, a few day dresses, food, and a marvelous deep blue housecoat, which she currently wore. Through the window, boats traveled along the canal, carrying goods, people, and musicians.

She could get used to living in this.

She made her way to the second floor and into her spacious bedroom. Two windows overlooked the canal, outfitted with deep blue curtains. She strolled to the window and casually pulled her Mage's Bane dagger from her hip.

It was such a lovely blade. The dark steel feathered with red like blood. As she turned the blade, sunlight caught the particles within the steel, whatever Mage's Bane was made of. The hilt was elaborate but functional—her favorite.

"That's not a toy, you know," came a drawl from the doorway.

"I'm well aware." Amery flashed Xavier a sly grin.

His blue-gray eyes stared at the blade in her hand. He remained in the doorway. She loved the terror the blade caused in a mage's face, though she understood why Xavier wouldn't like it. One cut from this blade, and his magic would devour him from the inside. A torturous death for a mage. Which was why she kept it. If any of their new allies turned on them, she'd end them. She'd told Bois and Josephine as much. Neither had looked enthused, but neither had objected.

But, because she liked Xavier, she sheathed the blade and draped her arms over her chest.

"I hear the tunnel's finished." He sauntered into the room.

"It is. We're that much closer," she said. "Once the raid starts, we have our easy exit. The only problem is making sure we're all within range of the tunnel."

Xavier nodded. "Any word from your spy?"

She shook her head. "Blythe will be back by sundown."

"That's basically now."

"Give or take half an hour." Amery waved off his concern. Blythe was no fool. The girl had sharp wits and clever eyes. She wouldn't get caught. If she did, she'd get out. The girl had promise.

Xavier whipped his head to the doorway, perking up at something Amery hadn't heard. His magic, likely. "Speaking of," Xavier drawled, "that sounds like her."

Indeed, Amery found Blythe in the bedroom on the far side of the house that overlooked the street—the room Blythe had chosen for her own. The walls were sage, and the ceiling had the same copper tile as the rest of the second floor. Blythe's growing assortment of daggers, throwing knives, and poison vials were scattered on the surface of the cherrywood dresser.

Blythe, even at ten years old, stood with the posture of a lady. Her narrow shoulders were straight, her spine an arrow, and her body still as marble. Rather than her typical dark purples and grays, Blythe wore whites and pale blues, perfect for sneaking around during a sunny day. The only part of her small frame visible was a sliver of her dark face and her glinting black eyes.

"Glad to see you made it back in one piece," Amery said. She looked into those black eyes, but she found no inkling of emotion behind them. Yes, the girl had promise.

"Easy work," Blythe chimed, her girlish voice dry and somber. She pulled the blue scarf from her mouth and the hood from her short dark curls.

"News?"

"The City Watch isn't making any obvious moves," Blythe reported. "Or subtle ones. I didn't hear a word about it from the watchmen I followed, even when they were alone. I gather either they are true in keeping it a secret, or they don't know about their captain's plans."

"That is a safe assumption," said Xavier. "Many of the Watch are blabbermouths. Trust me, I've gotten more than my share of intelligence from squealers."

A voice came from the first floor, near the kitchens. Blythe's fingers twitched toward the daggers at her side. Xavier mirrored the action.

"Sounds like Nera." Amery calmly strode into the hall. She glided to the grand staircase, running her fingers along the polished rail.

A few moments later, Nera came from the direction of the kitchens, a smudge of dirt on the fire mage's nose. "Ah, there you are," Nera said. "Sorry about walking into your house uninvited, but I called from the cellar, and no one came."

Amery brushed the offense away. "You'll soon be staying here too. Might as well get familiar with it."

Blythe snuck in from her bedroom, her footsteps quiet as a shadow's. She came to stand beside Amery and leaned against the railing. "You know," Blythe said sweetly, "I might not have gathered much, but you might ask Nera."

Amery glanced at Blythe, who held her stare on Nera. There—a spark in those dark eyes. She knew something. Amery turned her attention back to Nera as Blythe added, "She's been seeing the captain more than I have."

Nera's face blanched a deathly white. Amery's calm smile faded, and Xavier appeared on Blythe's other side.

Nera looked between the three of them, outnumbered and outmatched, and she fisted her hands on her skirt. "It's not what you think," she said quickly.

Amery started down the stairs. Her hand closed around her Mage's Bane dagger, a motion that did not go unnoticed by Nera. Amery stopped just outside of dagger range. Nera, to her credit, didn't move.

"You've got one minute to explain." Amery's hand tightened on her dagger.

"The captain promised me gold for information," Nera said. "It was too good a deal to pass up, so I obliged."

"How long?" asked Xavier, his tone seething.

"A week and a few days," Nera said in a single breath. "He asked me if he could trust Juniper's deal, and I said yes."

Xavier spat a curse.

"What else have you told him?" Amery demanded.

"I-I told him where the smaller entrances are," Nera said, talking faster with every word. "He asked about the guild masters and the child market. He knows Juniper told her friends about the invasion and that we're planning to escape before it happens. I-I'm supposed to tell him when we're ready, so he'll attack. That's why he hasn't attacked. He's giving us time to get the innocent out."

Xavier rolled his eyes. "Yes, because we are so innocent."

"And he believed you?" Amery asked.

"I don't know." Nera's hands shook.

"Captain Tinnly is a decent man," Blythe said. "Far better than most in the city."

Nera nodded. "He will keep his word."

"And when we're finished and safely out of the Undercity, you'll run off and tell him to attack?" Amery asked skeptically.

"Yes." Nera swallowed and straightened her shoulders.

Xavier harrumphed. "Well, I suppose that solves that problem."

"I'm sorry I kept it from you," Nera said, sincerity dripping. "I couldn't risk being found out. I'd be killed before I could explain."

"You would have," Xavier said.

"But this way, it works out in our favor." Amery nudged Xavier, a meaningful expression in her eyes. "We won't be anxiously waiting for an invasion. We can take our time."

Nera nodded.

"Who else knows?" Amery slid her dagger an inch out of the sheath so that Nera could see the feathered red.

"No one," Nera said, her voice tight. "I-I swear it on Rappa as my patron."

"We should tell Josephine." Amery released her dagger and started toward her room. "Wait for me, I'll change into something more appropriate."

"I'm sure no one would mind," Xavier drawled.

"I would mind," Amery started. "I don't want to spend tomorrow getting dirt out of velvet."

❄

Xavier walked back to Maddox's keep in a foul mood. All this time, Nera had been a spy. A damn spy. And he hadn't seen it, hadn't sensed it. He stormed through the alleys rather than the streets, hoping some unlucky fool would try to jump him. He needed someone to take his aggression out on.

Unfortunately for him, and fortunately for everyone else, no one dared cross his path. The thugs and scum he passed skittered out of his way like rats. Usually, it gave him a sense of satisfaction, but today, it only made him want to hit something more.

Halfway to the keep, he forced himself to relax. He didn't want to alert anyone that something was amiss, certainly not Maddox.

The thought of leaving the bastard down here lifted his spirits and pulled them apart at the same time. Despite all Maddox had done, all he forced Xavier to do, the man had become something of a father. He would never replace Xavier's real father, the man whose face had blurred with time. Xavier couldn't see the face clearly, but he could hear his father's hearty laugh, the chime of his mother singing as she cleaned their small house, the smell of the farm.

A lifetime ago. A different world entirely.

At the keep, Xavier was reaching for the gate when two girls, courtesans by their tight bodices and low necklines, and smart by the daggers they wore, walked by.

"...monsters, I'm telling you," said the blonde with lips the color of blood.

"Nonsense, you're losing it," said her companion, a brunette with lips like plums.

"I know what I heard! I've heard all sorts of sounds in this forsaken place, and I've not heard something like that, like growls underfoot."

"Some people like growling," said the brunette.

"Not like that." The blonde playfully smacked her friend's arm. "This sounded like something was digging up under the ground to eat me. It was bloodthirsty."

The brunette laughed. She said something else, but Xavier wasn't listening. He was strolling in the direction the girls had come from.

Growls from underfoot? He thought of their tunnel—but it was on the other side of the Undercity.

He slowed to a leisurely stroll, listening. This time of evening, the magelights glowed low, mimicking the twilight above. Their light slowly turned molten, paler and paler, until he walked through a moonlit street. He didn't know how long he walked, but he was about to give up when he heard it—a growl. Low, guttural, primal. Angry.

The blonde had been right. No human could make such a sound.

He paused where he stood, listening to the never-silent Undercity. He sent his shadow magic out before him, searching the world like Bois did, but he found nothing but the stone floor, the buildings, the alleys, and mice fighting over leftovers.

He heard the growl again, to his left. Xavier turned down a narrow alley full of barrels and crates. He heard a short growl and what sounded like claws upon stone. He'd raked his daggers across stone enough to know the sound steel made, but the resonance of metal and organic material was different—whatever grated on the stone was not made of steel.

His heart thumped. Who, or what, prowled underneath the Undercity?

Following the scraping of the stone and occasional low growl, he arrived at a dead end alley. Beside him, rundown houses stood dark for the night. Xavier closed his hand around his dagger. He had a horrible feeling about this.

The skittering claws came from his right, and he let himself into a rundown house.

To his amazement, no squatters had made this place home. He spotted evidence of life, but that life had long since stopped coming here.

The skittering sounded closer than ever.

He unsheathed his dagger. Light as a ghost, he crept through the stone house. He searched each empty room. The last room, the backroom, the room furthest from the entrance, held a single woven rug. The fibrous material looked stiff and new.

And horrendously out of place.

Xavier gripped the edge of the rug and pulled it up. He swore.

Underneath the rug was a hole. It went straight into the stony ground, angled for easy movement. Far below, the darkness swelled so thick, he couldn't see through it. From within the hole, the guttural growl sounded. Farther away.

Someone else had made a tunnel into the Undercity.

Xavier returned the rug where he'd found it and got the hell out before whatever lurked underneath decided to come up for some air. He knew how to pick his fights, and he knew when to come back with reinforcements.

CHAPTER EIGHTEEN

Juniper rattled around in the back of the slavers' cart. Her magic had replenished to a fraction of what she needed it to be. She would endure this, though, if it meant Reid and the others would heal and survive. She had gone through worse. If she could heal them with this strange journey as the cost, she would pay it.

They traveled steadily north for days, and still her magic dwindled. Her appetite never returned. Nausea threatened to send what she forced down her throat back up.

At times, usually at night, she would wake from strange dreams and feel a powerful need for her magic, to claw her way back to that cave to get it back. In those terrifying moments, all she knew was the need. Those fits passed and gave way to panic, dread, and shame. If the slavers heard any of it, none mentioned it.

The slavers let her out of the cart twice a day to relieve herself and drink stale water and eat whatever they felt like giving her. Sometimes dried meat. Sometimes cooked fish. Sometimes roasted rabbit. One evening, they struggled to catch fish in a nearby stream, and her own misery kept her from taking delight in their struggle.

The others would have woken up by now. What did Reid think? Ison would be frantic. Ison knew she wouldn't have left without saying something to him. Would they feel the magic inside of them and know what she had done?

Would they look for her? Or would they count her life lost, like the herbalist, and continue on?

With every gray dawn, the air grew colder. Ageless trees covered the rolling hills, their leaves parched shades of green, chartreuse, and lime. A few weeks, and the hills would be a blaze of autumn orange and crimson. Where would she be in a few weeks? The hills grew steadily steeper. Beyond them, she glimpsed small mountains. Strange shadows moved through the forest. Stranger sounds called: caws, bleats, and guttural whines. She imagined the worst monsters lurking through the shadows, bigger than a dire wolf, meaner than a demon.

At night, the air cooled. The slavers tossed her an old cloak, and she wrapped the smelly fabric around herself. The cold didn't bother her as much as it once had. Her magic's doing, no doubt.

The cart stopped for the night, and Juniper didn't know how long it had been. A week? Two? The lock clicked, and the door opened. Hakle hauled her out of the cart and escorted her to a log by the fire. Gods, the flames felt good on her skin.

"Cold?" Hakle fingered the buttons on his wool jacket.

"A little," she said.

Lace chuckled. He racked his eyes over her body. "We'll take turns keeping you warm."

She wanted to spit at him, but she feared it might cost her supper. Or worse, her cloak.

"We'll keep you warm all night." Hakle pulled the canteen from his side and put it to her lips.

She took a greedy drink. As she drank, Hakle grabbed the ties of her tunic and yanked the collar of her shirt down. Her panic flared, and without thinking of the repercussions, she spit water into his face.

"Bitch!" Hakle staggered backward.

"Stop it, both of you," snapped Boss, his voice calm and steady. Juniper had heard the others call him Kane, but mostly Boss. He stood on the other side of the fire, his furs warm and clean compared to the other two. He eyed her with indifference, a butcher sizing a cow. "We'll get more money for a virgin than a used whore. Keep your hands to yourselves, or you'll not get a coin of the profit."

Hakle's jaw jutted like he might argue, but he didn't. He sat down next to Juniper and pouted like a child. Lace sat on her other side, eyeing her as he sharpened his daggers. She adjusted her tunic back, a feat with bound wrists. She didn't want them to get an eyeful, and the cold air against her skin gave her the worst of chills.

After her meager rations—smaller than usual—they threw her back into the cart to sleep. They erected tents for themselves, covered in furs and leathers. The threadbare blanket they'd tossed her did little. The fire died, the night settled, and the air turned bitter cold.

If not the cold, she would starve. Already her body showed signs of it. Her hand bones protruded, and her trousers were looser.

Juniper let out a shuddering breath. Fog emitted from her lips. Of all the ways she imagined her death, in the back of a slavers' cart had never been one of them. A bit lackluster for her.

Her mind kept returning to the three men she'd left in the cave with her magic. Without her, would they find Boxel's Grace in time, or would the bandits pick them off before they even made it to Galamond?

A chill ran through her, and she shuddered as she curled into herself.

And she prayed—the first prayer to leave her lips in a long while. A prayer of desperation. She prayed not only for her life, but for her friends' lives—Reid, Ison, Penet, and Adrian. Amery, Xavier, Blythe, and all the others in the Undercity. She didn't know if they had made it out or even if Captain Tinnly had invaded. They might all be dead.

That thought pushed her to the brink of her desperation and helplessness, and her prayer became a plea.

Help, she begged. *Help me, please.*

The silence of the forest came as her only answer.

❋

Another day passed. The sun didn't warm the forest as much as before. The slavers trekked farther north, farther from her friends, farther from the only kingdom she knew.

Another dawn, another supper. Another night thinking she would freeze to death before dawn.

Help did not come that night. Or the following day. Evening fell, and while the slavers erected their fur- and leather-lined tents, they let her sit by the fire. They had donned furs and wools while her bones felt numb from cold. She held her bound wrists to the fire, marveling in the warmth. The fire soaked into her skin, and she would rather sleep outside on the hard ground by the fire than in the cart.

She looked into the flames, barely listening to the slavers' talk of an early snow or of the wolves that roamed this side of the mountains or the bears that would tear canvas tents into threads. She focused on the warmth on her front, the blood slowly pulsing through her veins, the dwindling magic creeping through her.

Had she broken something when she'd given her magic away, and it couldn't return?

She still felt the tug south, toward where those magic seeds were. If she could get away from the slavers, she might be able to follow it and find them. If the northern weather didn't kill her first.

What irony, she thought with a bitter laugh, that she should freeze to death.

The sky, unlike the nights before, was clear. Millions of stars twinkled in the inky darkness, and though she felt a tingle of her magic, it was not enough for her to use. Maddox had made his wards learn astronomy, and according to the stars, the slavers had gone farther north than they had west.

The stars are the original map. The map of the gods, Maddox had told her. *Learn them, and you'll never need a paper map.*

Juniper found Blugo in the stars. She traced his cloaked figure with her eyes, the lantern at his feet. *Help*, she begged his starry self. He had helped her escape his temple. He had listened—unless it had been a terrible coincidence.

Why bother with temples and gods? Xavier had asked Amery when she had gone to give an offering on her birthday to her patron, Espone, goddess of merriment.

Why bother? Amery had said in reply. *Why bother to breathe? Why bother to blink? The gods do more in your life than you realize. You want to think everything that happens is by your own hand, don't you?*

Xavier had started to answer, but held his tongue.

Juniper stared at Blugo. She was shivering, starving, thirsty, and—though she hated to admit it—afraid. She feared for her life. She feared the ending that these slavers had in mind for her. She feared for her friends.

Help me, she begged Blugo once more. *And I promise to end the slave trade in Janti. How can I end Nexon while I'm dead?*

A foolish promise, she told herself. What could one girl do about a trade that covered an entire kingdom and had claws in others?

Hakle told a joke that sent both Boss and Lace laughing. She kept her stare on Blugo, looking for something, anything. A rustle came from the forest, jostling the low branches of the pines. It sounded remarkably like laughter—even the forest laughed at her.

"See something up there?"

Juniper dropped her gaze and found Hakle staring at her. She didn't answer.

Boss stood with a groan, one hand on his absurdly ornate belt buckle. "I'm going to take care of nature's business." He stomped into the woods, out of sight.

Hakle watched Boss's back until it vanished. Then he nudged Lace with a wicked grin on his ugly face.

Lace squinted to understand. "What?"

Hakle nodded toward Juniper, and his smirk made her skin crawl.

Lace frowned. "Boss said no."

"Boss's not here right now." Hakle stomped over to Juniper and grabbed her by the arm, yanking her to her feet. "Want to stay warm tonight, little bitch?"

Yes, but not in the way he wanted. Juniper kept her lips closed.

Laughing, Hakle pulled her to his tent and unceremoniously threw her inside. The tent, while bigger than the one she had shared with Ison, was not tall enough to stand in. The ground had been padded with furs. Luxury compared to the cart. Hakle crawled inside, sneering as he closed the distance between them.

Every instinct told her to fight back, to kill him, to rip him to shreds, but her body refused to move. Her mind shut down. Her already shivering bones began to tremble as he pushed her down onto his bedroll.

Admittedly, the tent was warmer—not worth it.

Hakle closed one hand around her throat and pushed her into the bedroll while his other hand fumbled with her trousers. She tried to kick, she tried to pull his hand off her, but her limp arms and legs barely acknowledged her commands.

His fingers tightened on her throat—

A low, guttural growl came from deep within the forest.

Hakle froze, as did she. The sound came again, unlike anything she'd ever heard. In the dim light, she saw Hakle's eyes widen.

Movement outside the tent—Lace getting to his feet.

"What's that?" Hakle called to Lace.

"Maybe a bear," muttered the other slaver, loading a bolt into a crossbow.

"I've never heard a bear like that," Juniper whispered.

Hakle grimaced at her, but the fear brightened in his eyes. "It could be a wolf," he argued.

She pounced on his fear. "Wolves hunt in packs."

Hakle swallowed. Truthfully, she didn't know what a bear sounded like or how many wolves constituted a pack. But, as she contorted her features with fear, Hakle mirrored that fear.

"Lace, go check it out," Hakle demanded.

"But—"

"Boss's not here, so I'm in charge," Hakle said. "Go check it out."

Lace muttered his objections colorfully but stomped toward the edge of camp. His booted steps were cautious, one after the other, crunching frozen grass and pine needles.

And then—

"Bala's Breath," Lace gasped.

A growl, and then something large moved swiftly through the brush, coming closer. The crossbow fired. Lace screamed—a fierce growl sounded, deep and menacing. Lace's scream ended abruptly with a meaty *thwack*.

Stumbling, then a crash of canvas and wood. Lace had fallen into the other tent.

Hakle's hand on her throat loosened. He was trembling.

Lace groaned, rolled, and screamed again. Something large lunged, crunching the wooden posts of the tent. Hakle cringed at the unmistakable sound of flesh tearing. Lace's scream went higher, higher, then silent.

"Shit," Hakle gasped. "What's that?" He scrambled off her and toward the tent's flap.

He unsheathed his sword as the beast started to eat Lace—the sound of teeth and wet flesh brought bubbling bile to her throat. Hakle left the tent, sword-first. At once, Juniper threw her feet under her and rolled onto her knees. Something in her bones clicked. Her hunger no longer mattered. Her dwindling magic no longer mattered.

Survival mattered.

If Lace's corpse and Hakle's stupidity distracted the beast long enough, she could untie the horse, grab a pack, and head south. She started with grabbing a dagger out of Hackle's satchel, left by the tent flap. Maddox had made sure his thieves knew how to use a knife while bound, and she held the hilt between her feet and started on the ropes binding her wrists.

"Gods above," Hakle gasped.

The smacking sounds of eating stopped. She put more pressure on the ropes.

Hakle spat a curse, his voice trembling—a plea.

The ropes snapped free. Juniper rolled through the tent's flap and jumped into a run toward where the horse had been tied... The horse was gone. Of course. These buffoons hadn't secured it, and it had likely fled at the first sign of the trouble.

She stopped dead in her tracks.

The beast stood over Lace's half-eaten corpse—a mass of white and gray fur, blood dripping from its jaw. Its teeth crunched through Lace's bones like twigs, ripping meat like paper.

A dire wolf.

CHAPTER NINETEEN

Every fiber in Juniper's body went numb. The wolf shifted its intelligent brown eyes to her, black nose sniffing. She had seen those eyes before, looked into them once.

The same dire wolf she had freed from the bear trap. And it knew her too.

Hakle whimpered, drawing the wolf's attention. The wolf licked its lips, smearing the blood through his fur and whiskers. Its wide nostrils flared in Hakle's direction, and a low growl emitted from its throat. It started toward Hakle with the tense gait of a predator.

"Stay back, beast!" Hakle's voice shook as he swung his blade at it, a child swatting at flies.

Juniper stumbled away from Hakle. Her ankle struck the edge of his tent, and as she fell backward, the wolf pounced. She hit the ground. Hakle's bloodcurdling scream ended with the ripping of skin and meat, the crunching of bone, the splattering of blood on the cold ground. She closed her eyes tight and stayed on the ground.

When the gory sounds ended, Juniper struggled to her feet.

The wolf spat broken bones and sinew onto the ground beside the fire, then shook its head. It snorted at Hakle's body.

Had she had anything in her stomach, she would have emptied it onto the ground.

The wolf turned its eyes to her. It blinked, and that look of familiarity returned. The wolf cocked his head to one side, studying her. In that moment, it looked more like a dog than a wolf. This close, she could see a patch of tawny fur along its belly. One of its eyes closed slightly faster than the other.

It snorted, circled her once, twice, all the while sniffing her. Then, it came to stand in front of her, blocking her view of the two dead slavers. She had a suspicion Boss wouldn't be coming back to camp either.

The wolf tilted its head and let out a whine, a warm sound from the back of its throat—a question.

"I'm all right," she said. "All things considered."

The wolf seemed satisfied with that answer. It nodded, its ears flopping, and she had the urge to reach out and touch it, to see if its fur felt as soft as it looked. No sooner had that thought entered her mind, then the wolf bent down and nuzzled its forehead against her cheek—it kept its bloodied maw away.

Yes, it felt as soft, if not a bit dirty. She ran her hands along its shoulder. Thick downy fur cushioned her touch. She closed her arms around the wolf's powerful neck, not tight, but enough to be considered an embrace, and said into his fur, "Thank you, friend."

The wolf let out a snort that she took to mean, *You're welcome, but let's stop meeting like this.*

The wolf gave her a nod of farewell and headed into the woods. She stood still, watching, until she couldn't see its white body any longer.

Blugo had sent help after all. No other answer explained why the wolf had appeared, other than the chance it had been following her since she'd freed it, but that seemed...impractical. Nature was too cruel and unbiased. Blugo had intervened.

She glanced up at his stars. "I suppose this means I have to find a way to dismantle Janti's slave trade."

No one answered.

She sighed. That was a problem for another day.

Juniper ransacked the slaver's camp for supplies, taking as much clothing as she could from their packs. Much of the best stuff had been on their persons and now lay torn and bloodied. She did find two cloaks, which she fastened over her shoulders, a thicker jacket, another pair of socks, and a few weapons. She stuffed all the food and supplies into a well-used satchel. She didn't bother with much water. She could clean her own.

Satchel slung over her shoulder, a scarf around her throat and mouth, two hoods over her hair, three pairs of socks between her boots and the frozen ground, and a god above her, Juniper trekked north. She followed Blugo's stars—they pointed her toward Galamond. From there, she would try to send word to the others. Maybe she would meet them there. Reid had intended to meet back up with Isaac and Henry in Easley.

Despite her weariness, her dwindling magic, and low supplies in an unknown forest, she could still be useful to Reid and his quest. She could find the plant first, or find it if they failed. She could get it back to Adrian and save him.

Deep down, somewhere deeper than her magic, a spark of hope reignited.

❄

That spark of hope dwindled as she walked and walked and walked through endless pines and between rocky cliffs and bluffs and crystalline streams. Still, she walked, only pausing to eat and drink and rest her feet.

The pines grew taller and thicker. Brown pine needles softened her steps.

And she walked. She had no path or road or trail. The land grew wild and colder. Rocks jutted from the ground, cold and gray and blue, like teeth.

Every night, Blugo's stars twinkled. *Keep going,* he seemed to say. *You're almost there. Don't give up.* She imagined his voice: deep, rich with mirth, and strong—one that could command armies yet speak gently to a child.

With that voice in her ear, she walked on.

Her feet hurt. She shivered, despite her thick cloak and jacket. Her fingers trembled, her dwindling seed of magic quivered for its sisters, and her thoughts blurred at the edges. The sun sank. She knew she should find something of shelter to wait out the night's coldest hours. Yet she kept walking.

Finally, after full dark had fallen, she came to a shallow cave within the rocks. She tumbled inside, numb from cold and exhaustion. While not warm, the cave shielded her from the worst of the wind. She tried to spark a flame on her thumb, but her magic squeezed with the slightest effort. She would have to do it the old-fashioned way.

Leaving her pack in the shallow cave, she scourged the dark forest for branches and dry wood. Using the flint she'd taken from the slavers, she managed to start a small fire.

Small, but better than nothing.

She sat beside it, thawing herself, her mind too tired to think. She drifted into an uneasy sleep.

❄

The sun warmed the east, gilding the tallest pines and the tops of the jutting stones. Mist hovered above a glassy lake. Juniper cleaned lake water to drink, a slow process with her dwindling magic, and ate a small ration of dried venison. She gathered her pack and set out for a long day of travel. She didn't stop to think about her odds, her exhaustion, or a warm bed in a city.

She thought of her own survival, getting to wherever she was going, and not stopping for anything.

The sun lightened the shadows of the forest but not all of them. The pines left large patches of dark green between them.

She spotted elk in the distance, their sheer size and antlers enough to give her pause. She spotted more than a few brown bears, of which she stayed clear. She heard the howling of wolves, real wolves, not the friendly dire wolf. Fuzzy white rabbits bounced through the brush, fast as the wind.

The air grew drier, and her breath heaved as she climbed the rocky incline of a small mountain. Resilient pines grew out of craggy rocks, bending upward and shading little nesting sites for an unknown creature.

Still, Juniper walked, climbed, whatever she had to do to keep going northward.

She came to a clearing on a hillside. A tall berry bush grew in the middle, the only place where the sun beamed down. The dark green branches were spotted with bluish-gray berries. Juniper glanced for any wild animals. Seeing none, she tiptoed to the bush.

Oh, the sunlight on her face felt marvelous.

She picked a berry and rolled it between her fingers. She popped through the skin with her fingernail and lightly rubbed the juice on her wrist. She waited, but no skin irritation followed. Tossing the berry to the ground, she carefully walked around the bush until she found nibbled-on branches. Something had been eating them, and no carcass lay on the ground. She picked one berry and plopped it into her mouth.

At once, she recognized the bittersweet flavor—frost berries. Maddox's favorite wine was made from them. They grew only in the cool northern air.

That bubble of doubt vanished in her chest. She picked a large handful and continued northward.

❄

The sun vanished behind thickening gray clouds midway through the afternoon. The pines grew further apart yet taller. The smallest rocks jutted thrice her height. A few crows and blackbirds cawed. Soon, as the clouds thickened, the wolves silenced, the birds hushed, and the forest became deathly quiet. She had entered an ancient part of the forest.

She came upon a stream that tumbled from one rock face into another, cascading down the smooth stones into a deep pool with thick ice at its edges. She drank from the waterfall, the chilly water easing her dry throat.

Her body begged for rest and something warm to eat, desperately yearned for it, but she couldn't. She had to keep moving.

When she slowed, when she paused, she could feel it—the need. The urgent need for those seeds of magic. Her own cried out for them, clawed against her insides, begging and whining. When she paused, she could feel those distant seeds, and she knew the others were alive. She didn't dwell on it. She had to keep moving to keep the need away, to hush the starvation in her magic, to keep the exhaustion at bay.

Keep moving.

❊

The snow started as a light glitter, but with every breath, every step, it came down a little harder. It gathered on the ground, on the rocks, in the pines. Soon, the forest floor between the pines was covered in white. Had she traveled far enough to encounter snow? She had lost track of the days. Without a breeze, the snow fluttered straight to the ground. It muffled all other sound, save for her breath, and quickly accumulated. Thicker and thicker it snowed, until the world turned into a white and gray blur.

Juniper slowed but kept walking.

She had to keep walking.

The storm swirled into a blinding whiteout. She couldn't see beyond a hand's reach in front of her face, making the distance between each pine seem endless. She wouldn't be able to keep up her trek in a blizzard. A shivering hopelessness found root in her chest. After nearly walking into a low bough heavy with snow, she ducked underneath an ageless pine and collapsed into the snow-free needles underneath. Snow rapidly drifted beyond the low boughs. Just a break. She would wait out the storm.

Juniper pulled her cloaks tighter, curled in on herself, and waited.

❊

Juniper had strange dreams of snow and ice with her at its center. Ice so cold, it burned. Her ice. In her blood, her bones, her hair—ice. She ruled a kingdom of ice from a palace of cold blue stone. Bits of ice clung to her eyelashes, hair, and cloak like diamonds. Dire wolves prowled her kingdom, her best spies.

She woke to find the dream planted in reality. Snow had found its way underneath the boughs. Wind swirled the snow mercilessly and whistled violently through the pines, a haunting song of death. Snow clung to her eyelashes, the loose strands of her hair that had come free of her braid, and the fur-lined hood of her cloak.

So cold.

So full of ice, her ice. Unforgiving and unbiased.

She curled inward, stealing away into that frozen darkness within herself. It offered only slight protection.

She'd always liked the darkness best.

❄

Juniper thought she had died. The world blurred, but it glowed. The glow moved through the snowstorm, a ball of yellow light.

The otherworld? Her afterlife come to take her away?

Through the blurry white, a figure approached. It wore dark furs and leathers. It held the light. It loomed closer.

Juniper couldn't think straight. Hiada had sent a caller to bring her to the other side. Her own ice had claimed her.

The shadow came closer, closer, closer—it ducked underneath the pine. The furs became bits of dark brown and gray, the pale leathers well-worn and padded with wool, the torso lined with pockets, pouches, and daggers. Between the hood and the thick scarf, in the place where eyes should have been, were two glass orbs. As the figure came closer, and as the light shifted, Juniper saw behind those orbs—brown eyes. Human eyes. Blinking and wide. The figure said something, a feminine chime lost on the wind.

Juniper shook her head. Words wouldn't come.

The figure reached out, a leather-clad hand on Juniper's shoulder. She gave her a little shake. She said something else, but her voice sounded farther away than it had before.

And then Juniper saw nothing more—the world went black.

CHAPTER TWENTY

Reid came and went between the dark comforting abyss of sleep and painful reality. In those moments of waking, he listened to his heart. He'd never listened to it before. It felt...warm. A pulse within him, keeping him alive. Reminding him he was alive, he had not yet died, and he might still live.

In those moments of waking, he found himself staring at a stony ceiling. A fire flickered bluish light. Warmth seeped through his tunic, into his skin, into his bones. A horse snorted. Cool water dripped onto his tongue. He heard footsteps and a voice, but he couldn't bring himself to investigate.

He thought he saw auburn hair and pale skin, but he didn't know if he'd fallen asleep or remained awake. She dotted his dreams too.

Each time he woke, he found himself a little more aware than before.

Residual pain stung every part of his body. Wounds from the battle. Another surprise attack when they had been vulnerable—a well-planned attack. Had he been fully armored, his injuries would have been minor.

They would not be so vulnerable again. Someone would stand watch at night.

Maybe Juniper or Ison knew a spell to guard their perimeter.

The thought sent a gnarl of surprise and disgust through him—how could he even think such a thing? To ally with apostates...

Still, he knew Juniper and Ison. Neither would attack him in his sleep.

And for Adrian, he would ally himself with mages. With apostates. Juniper wanted to help Adrian, and he would let her.

Reid cracked an eye but saw only the blueish white flame throwing shadows across the ceiling. He heard breathing other than his own—the others remained nearby.

He thought of the letter tucked safely inside his tunic. *I love you.* He thought of his future as a knight. *Sir Sandpiper.* He thought of his best friend, lying near death, waiting on him to succeed.

He would heal. He would succeed. He would save Adrian. He would become a knight.

❄

At last, Reid came to. Unlike before, the powerful drowsiness did not pull him downward. He felt the hard floor beneath him, the warmth of the fire on his face, and the pain in his body from lying in one position for far too long. His body felt like stone itself, though when he tried to move his arms, they listened.

He inhaled deeply and held it, stretching his lungs, then exhaled. His tongue felt like sand, and the feeling continued down his throat. Inside, his heart beat. Steady and warm—pulsing.

No...that was not his heart. Reid lifted a hand to his chest, over the heart beating as it always had. What he felt, what he had mistaken for his heart during his slumber, felt different. Strange but comforting. Familiar yet foreign.

Above him, the shadows of the flame flickered over the cavernous ceiling. He turned his head toward the fire. Blueish white flames sat on a stone. Forever flame—a mage's doing.

"He's awake," came Penet's voice. At once, the other squire appeared above him. He knelt, a grin of greeting on his unshaven face. "Reid? How are you feeling?"

Ison appeared on his other side, brow furrowed and lips angled into a frown. His gray eyes scanned Reid's middle. "Your wound is gone."

Penet reached a hand toward Reid and helped him stand. He wobbled, but his legs held. Ison handed him a canteen. Reid drank greedily.

"You've been out for almost two weeks," Ison said flatly.

Reid nearly spat out the water. "Two weeks?"

"Twelve days." Penet looked better than the last time Reid had seen him. He'd been wounded too.

Reid glanced to the cave's mouth. Beyond, sunlight dazzled across the forest floor. The wind tossed loose leaves around the ground. It took a moment to see the distortion—magic hid the cave.

"Twelve days?" Reid put a hand to where that blade had nearly gutted him. Not a scratch. He would be sore for a while, but his skin had healed. He glanced at Ison. "I suppose we have you to thank for the healing?"

Ison's frown deepened. "No."

Reid mirrored Ison's frown. "What do you mean?"

"I healed you as much as I could before Jun and I hauled you both here," Ison said. "I expelled my magic doing so, but it wasn't enough. I collapsed. When I woke up, your wounds were healing on their own."

Reid glanced around the cave. It indeed looked like someone had been living inside. All their equipment had been brought from their disturbed campsite, plants and herbs were drying from the ceiling, and it smelled like a garden. Ison's doing. Both Ison and Penet watched him.

"Where is Juniper?" Reid asked.

Neither of them answered.

"Where is she?" he asked again.

"She was gone when I woke." Ison nodded toward the supplies. "As was a satchel and a few of the vials for herb-gathering your friend had. I suspect she went out to gather healing herbs. You both had evidence of a salve on your wounds, but I knew how much we had. It would not have been enough. We would have needed more. Jun knew how to find what we needed."

"And?" Reid glanced toward the cave mouth with a terrible feeling in his stomach.

"I haven't seen her," Ison said.

Reid took a few steps toward the mouth. He stopped just inside the rune's shield. The thing inside him, whatever it was, seemed to be tugging on him. It seemed to be pointing him to the forest. He had never felt anything like it, such a need, a desire.

"She's been missing for twelve days," Penet added softly.

He didn't need to say it—for one to be missing that long generally meant they were dead.

"Juniper is resourceful," Ison countered.

Reid steeled himself. He focused on his quest, on saving Adrian. He turned to the other two. "This doesn't change anything," he said firmly. "If she left that long ago and hasn't returned, it's safe to assume she's not coming back."

Ison cringed, and Reid understood—as much as he didn't want to believe it, as much as he wanted to search the woods for her until they found her, he had more important things to do.

"We have a quest to complete." Reid turned to Ison. "Do you still wish to accompany us?"

Ison looked like he might be sick. "I don't have much choice," he said quietly. "I'm not equipped to survive out here on my own."

In truth, they would need him for the plant's retrieval. "An herbalist and a mage will be useful for this quest's completion," Reid said.

Ison nodded. Whether Juniper had told him the truth, Reid didn't know. If not, he would have to.

"Do you think she's just run off?" Penet glanced outside.

Ison met Reid's stare, and they both knew the answer. No. Juniper would not have run off and left Ison with two squires. Something else had happened to her. In Ison's gaze, Reid saw worry. Deep worry. Ison had been awake for twelve days, waiting for her return. Reid couldn't imagine the anxiety the mage felt.

"Strike camp," Reid ordered. "We leave as soon as possible. We've got half a day's light yet."

He had spent twelve days in this cave—they had lost twelve days of travel.

They readied in silence. The horses were more than ready to leave the cave behind. As they worked, apprehension sank deeper and deeper into Reid's bones. The thought of leaving Juniper in the woods by herself sickened him. The thought of her wandering back to the cave, starving and weary, only to find it empty made it worse. Despite the worry he felt, he kept his shoulders straight. He needed to appear strong and confident in front of the others.

It had not been an easy decision to leave without her, but he made it. Knights sometimes needed to make the hard choices. It did not matter, he told himself. He and Juniper could not be together.

As they steered the horses out of the disguised cavern mouth, Reid couldn't help the guilt settling on his shoulders. Had he been the reason she'd left? If he hadn't pushed her away, would she have stayed? Would she still be here? Would she be riding on his horse instead of with Ison?

As they rode out, Penet took the lead.

Reid rode behind Ison. "Juniper knows how to navigate by the stars." He met Ison's gray eyes. "She knows where we are going to meet the others. She is intelligent and clever enough to know where to go and stubborn enough to get there. We have a mission to complete, and we will put our mission first."

Ison nodded, though his shoulders remained slumped and his brow furrowed. He cast his gaze around the forest, as if expecting her to come running toward them with some harrowing story of bears or ghosts or wood nymphs to explain her delay.

But she didn't.

Reid thought to the auburn hair he had seen in his dazed sleep. Had that been her leaving? Or a dream of her? He too scanned the forest as they made their way back to Fox Road. Juniper did not appear.

Gone. She was gone, again.

Guilt weighed on his heart. He thought of Juniper out in the forest alone. He wanted to spend however many days it took to find her, yet he knew he couldn't waste anymore time. Adrian was dying, and Juniper was the strongest girl he had ever met. She could handle anything. Still, leaving her tore his heart in two. He focused on that strange pulsing within him that pulled north, toward his quest's end, knighthood, and his future. He followed it.

CHAPTER TWENTY-ONE

No other bandits or marauders appeared along Fox Road. Reid kept his eyes open nonetheless. When they camped, Ison carved runes into the trees like the ones in the cave so that a web of magic made it look as though their camp was nothing but wild brush and weeds. They were not attacked at night.

The air grew cooler with each day they traveled. The animals appeared furrier, the trees reached taller and broader, and the air turned drier. The rolling hills steepened, and in a few days, pines outnumbered oaks. Rocks jutted from the ground, wolves howled, and bears prowled in the distance.

They stopped at a small village, well-armed and protected by an iron-enforced wooden wall, and stocked up on supplies and cold-weather gear. Reid did not miss the worn wanted posters hammered to the wall. He didn't look close enough to see if he knew any of the faces. Beside him, Ison tensed. The shopkeeper greeted them with suspicion until Ried admitted they had been dispatched to deal with an apostate.

"Finally, the Order sends someone to deal with them," breathed the woman at the trading post who had sold them fur-lined cloaks, gloves, and extra-thick socks. "Those mages have been causing trouble all over the place."

In the small tavern, the three of them—Ison in disguise—listened as the townsfolk told stories of mages destroying villages and taking captives. They killed anyone they deemed unworthy, the too young or too old, or anyone who fought back.

"Where are they taking them?" Reid asked.

"No one knows," said a bearded man with shoulders wider than the doorway. A mace hung from his hip. "No one comes back from wherever it is."

"Nothing good," said another. "Gods only know what those apostates do with people. I've heard they sacrifice them to tainted gods for unholy powers."

"I've heard they eat them," said another.

Ison cringed.

"Don't you worry," Penet assured them. "We will take care of it."

They left the village the next morning to a grand farewell. Hopeful faces lined the narrow street to the gate, waving and cheering them on. Reid forced himself to wave back. All those people thought they had come for them, to save them, to protect them. Guilt pulled heavier on his shoulders.

Penet waved to the people, sitting up straight and proud. Relief settled on Reid's shoulders as the gates closed behind them and they continued north. He would have to explain the truth to Penet sooner or later, just not right now.

※

Gradually, a little more with each league, the weather turned from the late summer of Duvane to autumn of Galamond. And finally, after days of traveling through pine forests and fields, they arrived at the walled village of Easley. That meant they had arrived in Galamond.

Easley was a sturdy village of log homes and burning hearths, as signified by the smoke puffing from every chimney. The air smelled of woodsmoke and something sweet, though Reid couldn't identify it.

The inn had been built in traditional Galamond style: one main room with a vaulted ceiling with one side designating as a sitting space, the other for cooking and eating. Twin hearths of sturdy gray stone burned on opposite ends of the room. Exposed wooden beams along the ceiling held up racks of drying herbs, and the inn smelled like thyme and wood smoke. After so many days of traveling, it was a welcome sight.

Voices filled the hearth room. Two dozen or so people lounged about the space, talking and drinking. Most wore furs and were armed with axes or maces.

At the sound of the main door, several heads turned toward them. It didn't take long for Reid to spot two familiar faces among the strangers.

Henry jumped from his place by the hearth and ran to meet Reid and Penet.

"Thank the gods," Henry breathed. "I thought you two were long dead."

"We ran into some trouble," Reid explained as Isaac, who had been sitting on the far side of the room, joined them. "I'm surprised you're still waiting."

"We had bandits following us," Henry said. "They thought we didn't know they were stalking. Then the Hawley Bridge was out, conveniently, and it took five days to go around it. Then we ran into a village ransacked by..." Henry glanced around. He added in a low whisper, "Magic. We stayed several days to help the survivors."

"Nothing you couldn't handle?" Isaac looked at the hooded figure standing behind Reid.

Ison glanced up at Isaac, and the knight at once grabbed the hilt of his Mage's Bane sword.

Reid flung his hand out between Isaac and Ison, saying, "We've got a story for you."

"What is this?" Isaac whispered.

Henry looked between Ison and Reid, confused and worried. "Where's Graison?"

"Dead." Reid glanced between Isaac and Henry. "Ison is with us."

"Where—" Henry started.

"We will explain everything," Reid said.

"After something warm to eat," Penet added on the heels of his words. "Please."

Isaac glared at Ison, then released his sword. "Fine. We've a room here."

They retreated to the suite that Isaac and Henry had been staying in, a comfortable space with two beds, a wolf skin rug, and thick wooden walls. Isaac and Henry sat in silence as Reid explained what had happened since they had split up.

"I am surprised Juniper Thimble"—Isaac lowered his voice at her name—"not only came to your rescue, but agreed to help you in your quest." He glanced at Ison, who didn't speak. "Ison, as well."

"She cares." Reid met Isaac's gaze. "She didn't like the sound of apostates terrorizing innocent people."

Isaac hummed his understanding.

"But why?" asked Henry. "She's an apostate, right? So wouldn't she be trying to stop you from stopping them?"

Reid looked to Isaac. The knight nodded. The time to reveal the truth had come.

"Henry, Penet," Isaac started, his tone grave, "there is something about this quest you must know." Neither squire seemed to breathe. "We were not sent to hunt down apostates. We were sent to find a mythical plant that will cure Prince Adrian's sickness."

Henry narrowed his eyes, glaring at Ried. "Did you know?"

"I did," Reid nodded.

Penet took it all in, face ashen. "You didn't trust us enough to tell us?"

"The fewer who knew the truth, the better," Reid said. "We were going to tell you when we could."

"This quest is too important," Isaac added.

"We're chasing a plant that might not even exist?" Henry rubbed his face, messing his dirty hair. "Are you kidding me, Reid? We were sent to find a *plant*? Is this a joke?"

"No." Reid held his friend's gaze. "And you've seen that someone does not want us to finish this quest. Someone does not want us to save Adrian."

"Whoever poisoned him." Penet frowned. "Which means that whoever poisoned Prince Adrian also knew the truth of the quest."

"Which implies," Henry said, irritated, "that the king doesn't know who he can trust and who he can't. And Penet and I were unknowns."

"Until now," said Reid. "He knew we would tell you eventually, and he trusted you to send you on this quest."

"Does Juniper know?" Isaac asked.

"I told her," Reid said, and Henry groaned. "That is why she agreed to help. She cares about Adrian and about stopping whoever is behind it."

"And she is good in a fight," Penet added.

Henry stood and threw his arms into the air. "How is no one else worried about this? Of all the people in the kingdom, why did Juniper Thimble save you and then agree to help? Obviously, she planned the whole thing. She poisoned Adrian, and now she's trying to finish the job by stopping your quest to save him. Why in Bala's Garden did you tell her about it, Reid?"

Reid blinked, glanced at Isaac and Penet's confusion, and a heartbeat later, he understood. Henry knew nothing about Juniper's involvement in the Demon Crisis or her role pretending to be Lady Roslyn that spring. Henry, unlike Penet, had never met her.

"Henry," Isaac said, exasperation on his tongue.

"And am I the only one concerned with accepting help from an apostate?" Henry motioned to Ison.

"Henry," Isaac said firmly, gaining the boy's attention. "It seems you've missed out on some very important information. Sit down."

✳

Reid thought Henry took the information well. He sat on the bed, mouth open, eyes wide as Isaac and Reid took turns relaying what had happened since the night Juniper had tried to steal the king's crown and been conscripted as Adrian's royal protector. Reid left out the steamier bits that Henry didn't need to know.

Ison remained quiet, taking in the story with gloomy eyes. Juniper's disappearance had hit him hard, and the mage had said barely a word these past several days.

There was also the matter of Ison's role in the Demon Crisis. Juniper had mentioned Ison had the right to revenge on Nexon too. That would be something to discuss later, without an audience.

Henry's brows furrowed as Reid concluded the story. Then he snapped his mouth shut.

Penet smirked. "I don't think I've ever seen Henry speechless."

Isaac chuckled and set his hand on Reid's shoulder. "Congratulations, Reid. Another feat few have accomplished."

"But—" Henry started.

"It doesn't matter now," Reid said before anyone else could. He glanced at Ison, then Isaac. "Juniper isn't here."

At the admission, his chest squeezed, and that little kernel of strangeness tugged. West this time.

"Juniper was worried about Adrian," Reid said. "He never treated her as anything but a friend. She wanted to help, to save him."

Henry chuckled darkly. "Or she's come along to help finish the job."

"She can't do that very well now," Penet added bitterly.

No one had any response to that.

"We rest tonight," Isaac ordered. "I'll see about getting another room. We leave at first light."

Reid told himself again as he and Penet followed Henry down to the main room for something warm to eat that he could not have changed things. Juniper had gone out on her own, and whatever had happened to her hadn't been his fault. He could not have stopped it in his condition. Still, the heaviness of guilt pushed down on him.

He would have to do something to honor her memory once they returned to Rusdasin, once Adrian was well. He should have told her about her parents when he'd had the chance. Now, Juniper would never know, and her parents would never see their daughter again.

CHAPTER TWENTY-TWO

Isaac procured a second room, and for the first time in weeks, Reid slept in a bed. He didn't think he would sleep soundly, but Ison assured him that the rune carved discreetly into the back of the door would deter all ill-intentioned visitors.

Reid hated relying on magic, especially from an apostate, but he didn't argue or scold Ison—knowing the rune was there indeed helped him shut his eyes.

Reid, Ison, and Penet shared a room, and when Reid blew out the candle for the night, none of them spoke. Sleep did not feel that far away. His thoughts churned over his quest. He had reconvened with Isaac and Henry. They had arrived in Galamond. They still had a chance to find the plant and get home to save Adrian.

Still, unknowns nagged at him. And with the silence, the little thing tugging at his chest refused to rest. It became incessant, pulsing and beating like a second heart. He put a hand over it but realized he didn't know quite where it was. It felt...deep within him, somewhere he'd never noticed before.

He distracted himself with thoughts of riding into Rusdasin, victorious, and being greeted by the king. The royal healer would take the plant, Adrian would recover by dinner, and a feast would be thrown in honor of Adrian's good health and Reid's heroism. That night, in front of the castle, Reid would be knighted.

Sir Sandpiper.

Those thoughts lulled him into a deep rest.

❋

First light came too soon.

Penet woke Reid. "I'm heading down to find something warm to eat," Penet said to Reid and Ison, who sat up in his bed with a mess of hair and drowsy eyes. "You're both to meet us down there as soon as you're ready."

"Yes, yes," Reid said.

Penet left, and Reid stood and stretched. He hadn't slept so well in a long while. He moved to the single narrow window that let in sunlight through the thick foggy glass. It made the world beyond look like a glowing white nothingness. Galamond had many threats, from sudden snowstorms to wolves and bears. The farther north they traveled, the more dangerous the trek.

By the time Reid washed his hands and face in the basin and changed into fresh clothes, clouds had taken over the sky. He stood, buckling on his gear as Ison washed up and fought his unruly head of brown curls.

"Is something wrong?" Ison's soft voice came. He motioned to Reid's hand—Reid absently held it over his chest, over that strange something he felt.

"Oh, it's nothing." Reid returned his hand to his side.

Ison pinned his eyes on Reid's chest, where his hand had been, as if he could see straight through his leather cuirass, skin, and bones to whatever it was. "Can you feel it?" Ison whispered. Then he put his hand to the same spot on his own chest.

A certain familiar rage burned under Reid's skin. "Feel what? What did you do to me?"

Ison shook his head, his eyes the same color as the overcast Galamond sky. "I did nothing. Juniper did it. She would have had to. She must have done it when we were all passed out."

Reid closed the distance between him and the mage. "What did she do?"

Ison held his hand over his own chest, expression unsure. His fingers tightened in his shirt. Whatever Juniper had done, she had done it to Ison too. "She..." Ison started. He heaved a breath, and his eyes unfocused. "It's magic I feel. But it's not mine."

"What is it?" Reid insisted.

"It's her magic," Ison whispered, fear in his voice but also confusion. "It's the only thing that makes sense. You and Penet were gravely injured. My healing wouldn't have been enough, yet when I woke, you were both miraculously healed." Ison met Reid's eye. "She gave us each a portion of her magic."

"Magic?" Reid gasped. He flattened his hand over the strange something in his chest. It was magic inside of him?

"Can't you feel it there?" Ison's voice was quiet and misty. "It's what healed you so fast. It's why my magic regenerated so fast. And...it's alive. Feel it? I think it means Juniper is alive. It...wants to go back to her. Can you feel that? It's pulling. It wants her, not us."

Reid indeed felt that. He glanced again to the window. That gentle tug... "Juniper is to the west."

"I think so," Ison said.

Reid took a small comfort in knowing the magic kernel within him had come from Juniper. She would not have done it with malicious intent. If what Ison said about his injuries were true, then she had done it to save him and Penet from death. Still, the idea of having magic in his body felt worse than having a disease.

"What does this mean?" Reid asked Ison. "How do I remove it?"

"I don't know if you can," Ison said. "I think only Juniper can do that."

"Can you remove it?"

Ison paled. "I've never met a mage who has tried something like it. To take a portion of one's own magic and bring it outside of oneself, let alone give it to another...most mages can't do that. She..." Ison pulled his bottom lip between his teeth.

"She what?" Reid asked, stepping toward Ison.

Ison swallowed. Fear twisted his features. No doubt being an apostate among three squires and a knight took a toll on his mind. "Jun's learned so much in such a short time. Her base magic is stronger than most. It's...remarkable."

"You sound uncertain," Reid said.

Footsteps sounded in the hall, but the owner passed their room without hesitation. Soon the others would come looking for them.

"I don't know what it means for her to be able to do it," Ison said. "I've met and trained with a good number of well-learned mages, squire. Juniper's well of magic is abnormally deep, especially for a mage who has only been using her magic a few months."

Reid had noticed that too, but he had equated it with all the training she had been doing, by herself and with the court magician. Gods only knew what she had learned with the Undercity apostates.

"Do you think she will get stronger?" Reid pulled his cloak around his shoulders.

"It is a possibility," Ison said carefully. Graison's cloak, which Ison had taken, didn't fit his narrow shoulders.

The idea that Juniper might still get stronger sent a cold wind through his knees, threatening to tremble. He had seen her fight with and without magic, and both were a sight to behold. Even without her magic, Juniper was a force. Magic added to her deadliness and prowess.

"After this," said Ison as Reid reached the door, "I am going to find her."

"I will not stand in your way." Reid might go with him, if only to get rid of this thing in this chest. And to make sure Juniper was all right.

The two of them joined the others in the hearth room for one last warm meal before they set out across Galamond.

Reid's mind kept returning to the kernel of magic within him. Juniper's magic—a piece of herself she had given in order for him to heal. Without it, he might have died of his injuries. If he focused, he could almost feel her. A thread tugging him westward.

As they headed to the stables after breakfast, Reid not only caught Ison glancing westward, but Penet too. She had given him a kernel of her magic for his life.

Three kernels of magic?

A brutal wind blew down from the mountains, and it would only get worse. They did not wear all of their cold-weather gear, and Reid dreaded the weight of it. They trotted along the road that would take them north, to a village whose name even Reid did not know. Isaac now led the party.

The clouds looked like snow, heavy and steely. Reid did not want to worry about snow any sooner than he had to. Galamond had a nasty reputation for dangerous winters, and despite not being the snowy season, the farther north they traveled, the higher risk of snow and ice. By midday, the clouds had thinned enough for slivers of blue to appear between them.

They rode steadily north, winding through pines, between boulders, and alongside crystalline rivers. Reid pressed a hand where that strange sensation of magic beat, alive and pulsing. It didn't feel dangerous. It felt warm but cool. Like Juniper's ice magic.

He slowed his horse to ride beside Ison, leaving Penet far enough behind and Henry and Isaac far enough ahead they wouldn't overhear. "Ison," said Reid, "how common is it for a mage to take out three kernels?"

Ison blinked.

Reid motioned to Penet with his eyes.

"Gods," Ison breathed. "Not very, if at all."

"There is something else I wish to ask of you," Reid said. More of a command. "This quest matters greatly to the future of Duvane. I must ask if you—"

"I'm not here to cast the kingdom into ruin, if that's what you're asking," Ison said, exasperation in his words. "Juniper told me exactly what you were doing. That's why I'm still here. I don't trust any of you sword-throwing buffoons to know this plant from a dandelion."

Reid straightened in the saddle. Ison cast one bitter look in Reid's direction, one the mage often saved just for him—one Reid remembered from the days after the Demon Crisis, when Ison and Juniper had gotten so close. Reid held in what he wanted to say to the mage, what he wanted to accuse Ison of—the nights the mage had spent in Juniper's chambers, slept in her bed, and shared a tent.

Reid forced himself calm and said through gritted teeth, "I am glad you decided to join us. I agree, your skills with herbs are invaluable."

"And it's what Jun would be doing if she could," Ison said. "And, if it were me lying near death, I know Jun would do it for me."

Reid nodded, and the two men stared at one another a heartbeat longer, each glaring daggers.

CHAPTER TWENTY-THREE

Ison had never been fond of horseback riding. He preferred traveling by wagon or on foot. He liked horses well enough—they were good listeners and never judged—but they were nothing to their magical cousins, unicorns. Horses held blank expressions, while unicorns wore their intelligence proudly.

He found Galamond's harsh weather disagreeable. The cool air seeped into his clothes and pinched his skin. The wind found its way into invisible seams in the cloak, in the little stitches between the fingers of his gloves, and into his boots. He had trouble imagining it would get even colder.

Steely clouds swirled above, as if waiting to unleash a blizzard. Every once in a while, Ison glimpsed the pale blue sky on the other side. It bore a striking resemblance to the blue-gray eyes of an assassin, one Ison hadn't allowed himself to think about. He didn't know how to think about it, let alone what to think about it.

The path wound through towering, ageless pines, between ancient archways of gray and white stone, the engravings long gone from the weathered rock. The wind whistled through the pines, singing a haunting tune, foreboding and beautiful—just like Galamond. The people had learned to live in the harsh land and had become as sturdy as the stone. Something about the land suggested a far older age than even the pines could imagine, a land and people long forgotten.

Somewhere—Ison couldn't remember exactly where, but likely in the Marca—he had heard of Galamond as the motherland, where all had come from. Ice giants had come from the mountains and chased the humans south, where they had stayed. Ison didn't know if those stories had any truth, but looking at the ghostly blue-gray mountains in the far distance, he could imagine ice giants. He thought of those legendary creatures lingering in the forgotten wilderness of the mountains, surviving the worst of the winter, if only to prevent himself from thinking of Xavier, or of Juniper and her divided magic.

He didn't know what to think about that either.

Slowly, the path became more mountainous and narrowed, forcing them to walk single file. The narrow trail wound up steep mountains of gray stone and crumbling edges, hardy bushes of jagged branches, and steely-eyed goats with thick fur coats and curving horns. Their bleats echoed off the stone.

They reached a fork in the path. Penet scouted one way, and Henry scouted the other. It left Ison in a strained silence between Isaac and Reid. Henry came back first—his path was clear. A few moments later, Penet returned—his path had been blocked by a landslide. Impassible.

So they took the path Henry had scouted. It wound up into the mountains and soon turned treacherous. Isaac led them along winding ledges that looked down over sheer drops, ending in certain death for unlucky travelers. Up and up they climbed, then down, then up, and with every glimpse off the mountainside, Ison felt his breakfast threaten to reappear. Instead, he focused on his horse's braided mane and the stitching of the specially designed outerwear to keep the horse from freezing.

Heights were another thing Ison didn't care for. Lucky for him, as a mage raised in the confines of the Marca, he had never had to deal with them.

Higher and higher they climbed until clouds gathered in patches below them, hiding the true distance to the ground. Reid's horse, walking behind Ison, whinnied.

"Easy, girl," Reid said soothingly to the horse.

Ison had noticed when they'd fallen into single file, Reid had automatically guided his horse behind Ison, blocking any easy exit. The other squire, Henry, rode in front of him. It hadn't taken long for Ison to prefer Henry's joking personality to Reid's hard one. Still, Henry wore the stoic face of a squire well.

The path led them to a long, narrow ledge on the side of the mountain. Below, the mountainside held rocks sharp enough to rip a man and horse to shreds long before they hit the valley below.

Ison felt Reid's stare on the back of his hood. No doubt wishing for Ison to fall from the ledge, saving him the trouble of dealing with an apostate. But if Ison fell, who would find this damned plant for them?

It gave him a strange sense of satisfaction to know Reid needed his help in order to complete this king's quest, and if Ison changed his mind, Adrian would die. Reid wouldn't become a knight, and Duvane would enter a state of chaos over the next king. A part of him wanted to cause all that trouble just because he could, because of all the trouble Duvane had given him.

Then Ison would surely become the most wanted apostate on the continent, and no corner of the realm would be safe against the squire's wrath.

Adrian had never given Ison a reason to wish him ill. No, Adrian had always been friendly. He had looked Ison in the eye the few times they had spoken and looked at him without hatred or suspiciousness or indifference. Like he was a person, not just a mage.

A vicious wind came in from the north, blinding Ison. It seethed through the seams in his clothes, a preview of the ice and snow that lay at the realm's end. He squeezed his eyes shut and looked down. The wind died down, but not entirely.

"Is there no other way through these mountains?" Henry called. Though he rode a few feet from Ison, the wind carried his voice far away.

"This is the shortest, most direct route," Isaac shouted. "By avoiding the main roads and the towns, we avoid being spotted and recognized."

"And if we're attacked out here?" Penet asked.

"Then we leave their bodies behind as a warning to anyone who might be following," Isaac said a bit tersely.

Henry grumbled something Ison couldn't make out.

They came around a bend, and the path narrowed more. Ison's insides quivered at the sight—ahead, the rocks beside the path looked ready for a landslide. He dared to glance down the steep mountainside. He swallowed, but it felt like something had gotten caught.

As Isaac's horse started over the narrowest part of the ledge, small rocks loosened and tumbled down the mountainside, straight to the rocky ground leagues below. Ison never heard or saw them hit the bottom. Penet followed, giving his horse an encouraging pat. He didn't look thrilled about the crossing either.

As Penet crossed, more rocks loosened and tumbled down. Some were small, but some were large as fists. The path held.

Ison followed one rock as it clattered down the mountainside, clanking and banging, until he couldn't see it anymore.

"Long way down." Henry scanned the drop with a straight face.

Ison's horse walked behind Henry's. As Henry started across, a few more rocks came loose. With them, the remaining rocks rattled. The sound rattled against Ison's mind and bones, shaking him along with it.

Henry made it across, but as Ison's horse started across, his magic trembled. It lashed out in warning. Ison felt it then, something...wrong. He gathered his magic in reflex. Even if he didn't need it, having it close gave him peace of mind. Halfway across the narrow ledge, he felt it again. He couldn't identify the feeling, but he knew it came from magic. Magic had been used here, and recently. Did the squires not feel that?

A few rocks loosened and tumbled.

Reid started across the ledge behind him.

Ison looked at the rocks. The magic had...changed something. Tampered. He turned to warn Reid, but before the breath left his throat, a vicious *crack* sounded. And then Ison felt it—the ground falling from underneath him.

The horses whinnied and stumbled. The entire ledge gave way, crumbling. Henry's horse kicked and jumped beyond the crumbling stone, but Ison and Reid were not as lucky. They started to fall.

Isaac shouted, but the roar of cracking rock drowned out the sound. All around, rocks and stone and white-hot panic. Ison came out of the saddle. His horse whined and cried, as did Reid's. The squire fell through the air, his usual stoic expression one of true fear. The ground raced up faster and faster, and something in Ison snapped—his magic lashed out at the air as the ground raced up to meet them.

CHAPTER TWENTY-FOUR

Xavier had slowly, piece-by-piece, taken his favorite things from Maddox's keep to Amery's manor. He didn't want Maddox to notice. Maddox, thankfully, had been busy these past few weeks. Xavier had hardly seen him in the keep. With all his connections, Xavier wouldn't be surprised if Maddox already knew about the invasion. He'd likely planned his own escape, or he was spending as much time topside as possible to avoid it.

Either way, Xavier would be long gone. Along with anyone he remotely cared for.

To be honest, he felt torn. He'd always looked out for himself. All his life, or most of it, he had worked against the City Watch, and now he had stooped to helping them invade his home.

Or not really his home. A home forced upon him. No, while he felt some sort of attachment, that attachment came from familiarity, not love. The Undercity could burn for all he cared, along with the scum inside it.

And yet Xavier belonged in the Undercity. He did not consider himself a topsider. He belonged among those who would burn, yet he had somehow been invited to survive. He wanted to. He wanted to see what happened after the invasion. He wanted the guild to thrive despite the Undercity's fall. He wanted to see Ison again.

"That's how change works," Amery had said with a dreamy sigh the night before, over tea on her new balcony that overlooked her garden. She wore one of her billowing day dresses, all silk and ribbons. "People invade other people. Land changes hands. Kingdoms change names. Things change, and people move on. Maybe the world will be better after; maybe it won't. There's just one way to find out."

Blythe had appeared between them, a shadow of a girl. "She's here to see you."

"Ah, yes." Amery had swung her long legs over the side of her chair like a lady about to see a guest. "Let's not keep her waiting."

Nera had returned from her meeting with Captain Tinnly. The invasion would happen at sunrise in two days' time.

And they had less than a day left.

Xavier remained in the Undercity to make sure no whispers of the invasion or the escape had gotten out. Amery was at Josephine's, guiding everyone into the tunnel. Josephine had gone to Amery's the day before and helped everyone settle.

Soon—things would change soon. By this time tomorrow, the Undercity would be gone. Compromised. He would be a topsider, like it or not.

Maybe he could find the time to track down his parents, if they were still alive.

He headed toward Maddox's one last time. On the way, he passed Blythe. The little girl didn't give him a breath of attention, yet her eyes were focused and alert. The little thief reminded him of Juniper, careful and crafty. A dangerous combination.

Maddox was out. The guild members lounged about the first floor, a few trained in the basement, but Xavier passed them all. He'd ignored them for a good part of his life, and he didn't want to start seeing their faces now. It would only make their deaths worse. He went straight to his room, passing Amery and Juniper's shared room. Amery had taken most of her things to the manor weeks ago.

Amery couldn't have kept something as big as a manor secret from Maddox. Their guild master definitely knew about it.

He took what he wanted from his room, slung the pack over his shoulders, and sighed at the light weight of it. He'd never been one for things either. He lingered in his little room. How many hours had he spent up here, staring at the stone ceiling, praying to be returned to his family? Too many. But that was a long time ago.

No one came to save him. He had saved himself. He would do it again too.

Xavier headed out of the keep, ignoring his fellow thieves and assassins. He turned toward Josephine's without looking back.

He made it to the market.

Then the screams started.

Xavier turned in the direction of the screams and fighting, swords and steel clashing and clanking, echoing off the stony walls. Xavier stood frozen as the sounds grew louder. Then he spotted the bits of iron through the crowd, the magelight glinting off armor.

The City Watch had not waited until sunrise. They had lied.

And Xavier and his friends were out of time.

Xavier started running, hands empty, and hoped no watchman thought him a threat. He heard the slaughter, scum and thugs fighting for their lives and falling. Xavier stumbled down an alley to avoid the Watch, and another, climbed through a house, and into the alley on the other side. Xavier peeked around the corner. The Watch had poured into the Undercity by the market, between him and Josephine's. Getting to Josephine's would be impossible! At least most of the others would have made it into the tunnels by now.

He crouched and started to the alley's other end. He'd have to avoid the dense fighting and skirt the other side of the Undercity, around the fountain, and maybe he could get into the tunnels through the Dual Fangs' keep.

He had to try. Like hell if he was going to sit here and cower and wait to be found and killed.

He started along the far side, skirting the streets, avoiding the fight. Plenty of scum needed to be killed. He made it to the far streets when he heard something underneath the fighting, a rumbling roar of a sound, coming from below.

And it settled somewhere deep in his gut, a tremble of fear.

The roar grew louder, came closer, and Xavier froze where he stood—he could see the abandoned house where he had heard those strange sounds, where a hole led somewhere he did not want to go.

A crash and clatter, and a roar sounded from above the ground. Xavier started the other way. He did not want to meet whatever that was. Two watchmen came around the corner, swords bloody. Their eyes fell on him.

Xavier didn't move to pull out a weapon, though he gathered his magic. The two watchmen started closer. He'd kill them if he had to. He could, easily, with a flick of his magic around their necks.

And then a crash came from behind him.

Both watchmens' gaze darted over his shoulder and grew wide with fear. "What is that?" asked one of the watchmen, his voice trembling.

Xavier dared to look, then stumbled back a step. Climbing out of the abandoned house was possibly the most horrible thing he had ever seen. It walked on four legs, paws the size of dinner plates, talons as long as a grown man's finger. Leathery skin pulled taut over corded muscle. Patchy, matted brown hair gave it a rabid look. Black eyes settled on Xavier. It looked like a sick wolf but not like a wolf at all.

A monster.

"Can't be," gasped the other watchman.

Now Xavier pulled one dagger of steel and summoned one of magic. "Look lively, boys," he said to the watchmen as he backed away from the beast. "You've got a challenger."

The monster stalked toward them, growling and baring yellowed fangs.

"It's a demon." The watchman's hand shook on his sword.

"It's not a demon," corrected Xavier. "It's just a monster, and it needs killing." Xavier held his ground. Juniper had told him about the not-demons she had encountered in the castle, the things that had done the evil apostate's bidding. This monstrosity would certainly fit the description.

The monster came at them, bounding on its powerful legs. Xavier launched himself at it first. He thrust his dagger at the monster's throat. The monster twisted to dodge. The steel nicked the beast's leather skin. The creature swatted him—Xavier used his momentum to swing himself over the monster's head, slicing a shadow-dagger of his magic across the side of its neck. Blood splattered, black in the magelight. The monster howled and threw Xavier off. He hit the ground and rolled onto his feet.

The two watchmen took his lead and engaged the beast. One landed a blow to its hip; the other managed a scratch on the front leg. The monster kicked one watchman and swatted the other out of its way. Xavier changed his approach. His steel hadn't done near what his shadows had, so he sheathed his steel and summoned a second dagger of his charcoal magic. The monster noticed and lunged, teeth and talons ready to crush and rip.

Xavier tried the same maneuver on the monster—hitting it once so it would dodge and help him onto its back—only the monster had learned. As Xavier's first hit sliced the skin on its thick neck, the monster did not dodge—it lashed at his side. Xavier felt the sting of teeth against his side, and he had less than a heartbeat to respond. He twisted and kicked the monster's jaw and sliced his dagger at the monster's shoulder.

The monster stumbled backward, and Xavier stumbled to the ground. He rolled back to his feet—pain lanced through his side. The monster had got him. He felt for the wound—skin deep but already a burning rushed through his blood. Poison.

Damn it. He hated smart animals.

The monster recovered and swatted at one of the watchmen, knocking him into the side of a building. He did not get up. Xavier lunged at the beast again, careful not to use the same move twice.

Xavier managed to dodge its talons and teeth, but he felt the sluggishness of the poison working its way through his blood, slowing his reactions. The beast came at him—Xavier thought he moved in time, but the sudden pain in his leg proved him wrong.

He went down, his shadow daggers flickering in and out of existence. The beast seemed to laugh, like it knew that it had won. Xavier met its woeful brown eyes, and the monster licked its teeth, each longer than his fingers.

So stupid for him to die like this, to some magical monster.

The monster howled—a shadow appeared from above. Amery landed on the monster's back, Mage's Bane dagger in hand. She plunged the dagger into the monster's back, to the hilt, and it let out a painful howl. Amery yanked the dagger free and held on as the monster wriggled and bucked. She plunged the dagger down a second time.

The monster's breaths gurgled—blood in the lungs.

Xavier stumbled to his feet. He saw his chance. He summoned his magic and sent a bolt into the monster's exposed neck. At his command, his magic flattened and grew, severing the monster's head from its shoulders. Amery jumped off the monster as it collapsed, Mage's Bane bloodied and dripping.

Dark blood splattered the ground and Amery's face. More seeped from the monster's corpse. And then the body burst into black ash, scattering over the blood.

The world wobbled. Amery appeared in front of him. His lunch started to burn its way back up his throat, and his skin went clammy.

"That doesn't look good." She studied the wound on his side.

And he was out.

CHAPTER TWENTY-FIVE

Amery wanted to throw things at Nera, but she somehow managed to uphold the posture of a lady. She paced, a small concession to her agitation. She paced in her bedroom, the only room she hadn't allowed others to sleep in. This was her room. And, as the only room free of refugees, it had become the command center.

"How could you lie to us?" Amery snapped, seething every word at Nera.

Nera sat on the bed, her beige skin pale and her hands shaking. "I-I didn't. The captain said sunrise."

"He came in the middle of the night," Blythe added, her voice wispy.

"You're lucky no one was hurt in the skirmish." Amery's thoughts went immediately to Xavier, who had been carted off to the sick room when they'd arrived. Josephine promised he'd be all right.

"I swear it, he said sunrise."

Amery inhaled, retort on her tongue, when a cool voice cut in, "And that only proves the captain didn't trust you like you trusted him."

The air in the room intensified. Amery saw the change come over Blythe and Nera, though Nera showed it much more openly. Amery turned to the window, where Maddox climbed in, spotless boots first.

"You know, some would think it rude to enter a lady's bedchamber without knocking." Amery set her hands on her hips. "Didn't I lock those?"

"You did." Maddox slid the window back into the pane and locked it back with a sharp click. She would never understand how he did such tricks.

"You could have used the door," Amery said.

"And miss the look of surprise on your face?" Maddox offered her a humored smile.

Nera blinked at Maddox. Blythe held her surprise in much better. It would seem Amery alone did not feel surprised at Maddox's presence. She was, however, surprised he'd come in through the window.

Maddox strolled into the room and paused at the sideboard and poured himself a drink. He glanced at Nera then Blythe. "What? You honestly think I wouldn't hear about the invasion? You wound me."

A swift knock sounded on the door.

"Enter," Amery said.

A little boy from Josephine's guild opened the door. The knob barely reached his chin. "Xavier's awake. Josephine wants to talk to you," he said and set off again down the hall.

Amery went at once, Nera and Blythe behind her. She didn't know if Maddox followed. His presence wasn't important for the next conversation.

They found Xavier lying on a mattress in the sick room—it had been a lounge, but it worked better as a sick room. His wounds had been patched up, though he looked exhausted and pale.

"Bad news?" Amery noticed the look on Josephine's face.

"Yes, unfortunately."

Amery sighed, though she had expected bad news. She sat down beside Xavier's bed.

"I'm afraid our troubles may only get worse." Josephine told them what Xavier had told her about the monster he'd fought. "And this monster's appearance proves Nexon is still making them."

Xavier cringed. Amery didn't need to wonder why—Ison had been used like a puppet the last time those monsters had been created. That meant someone else was being used.

"What do we do?" Amery asked. "There might be more of those things."

"It came from underneath the Undercity," Xavier said. "From those ruins."

"The ruins Juniper and Ison slipped into from the castle to get into the Undercity." Amery rolled her eyes. "Of course those things would be in the ruins. It's dark and creepy and a maze. It also suggests Nexon is still in the castle."

"There's not much we can do from here." Josephine cast her motherly stare on them all. "The Watch is crawling all over the Undercity, and they will be suspicious of the beasts too. Let them investigate it for now. We can use the time to recover. We've all undergone a change."

Amery agreed. She needed a rest. She headed up to her room. A din of voices filled the house, a constant mumble, like a lord's afternoon party. Amery had attended plenty. Bedrolls lined nearly every room, some wall to wall, and even in the halls. Some had even taken to the cramped attic space. She released a pent-up breath in the quiet, empty space of her bedroom.

Maddox stared at one of the paintings, a large scenery of a beach during a half moon. He'd poured himself another drink. She didn't mind—he'd bought most of the liquor anyway. She shut the bedroom door loud enough to gain his attention, though he kept his gaze on the painting.

"This place is more fitting," Maddox said after a pause. "My guild always did need a better place, somewhere fitting of our status. We are practically neighbors to the Watch up here."

Amery steeled herself. "Maddox, we need to talk. I need to elaborate on why I asked you here."

His brows furrowed at that, but he gave her his full attention.

She proceeded to tell him all about Nexon, the monsters, what Juniper and Ison had gone to do, and why she hadn't given him many details as to why he shouldn't be in the Undercity come sunrise. All the while, he remained quiet.

"Ah," he said at last, looking down into his drink. "I won't lie, her betrayal hit below the belt."

"If Nexon has his way, if he wins, he'll enslave or kill anyone without magic," Amery told him. "Which includes the two of us."

Maddox pressed a warm kiss to her temple. He sat at her writing desk and gracefully crossed his ankles. "I can't say I like the sound of that. I suppose I could do something to help her out. She would be in my debt again. Excuse me, love, I've letters to write."

CHAPTER TWENTY-SIX

Reid thought he had died. It took him a moment to remember why. The fall. The crumbling mountain path.

Above him, gray clouds drifted across the gray sky. Snow floated through the crisp air, dotting his face. He could feel the snow melting as it kissed his skin. He felt the hard ground beneath him.

Alive. He had lived.

He took a breath, then another. His lungs worked harder than they should have.

Someone panted to his right. Reid rolled onto his side. He felt bruises starting all over his body, and he vaguely remembered the rocks they'd fallen with. Ison wheezed, on his hands and knees, sweat shimmering on his face and neck. His arms shook.

Reid looked again at the cliff where they'd fallen. Clouds drifted between them and it.

They should not have survived.

Reid pushed himself into a sitting position. The rocks scattered around them in a perfect circle, leaving the ground where they had landed free of debris. The horses had not fared as well. Dead, he could see. Crushed by rocks or killed by the fall—he didn't know which.

Ison coughed, his breath ragged.

"We're alive," Reid gasped, his own voice raw. From shouting? He didn't remember.

Ison sat back on his knees, ashen cheeks flushed, gasping for breath. With a shaky hand, he pushed his curly hair out of his face and took in the scene around them.

There, the faint floral scent of natural magic twinged with the metallic scent of unnatural.

Reid looked up at the impossibly high cliff again. Then he shifted his gaze to Ison's. "You used magic."

A fierceness chilled Ison's stare. "I saved our lives," he stammered, his breath fleeting. That fierceness faded. "It was all I could do." He glanced at the horses, unspoken apology on his face.

And without Ison's wind magic, they would have been crushed by debris or by the fall.

As much as Reid didn't want to, he said, "Thank you."

Again magic had saved him.

Ison staggered to his feet. How much of his magic had been expelled to save them? Reid stood and took stock of himself. Nothing felt broken, just a few scrapes.

On either side of them, the gray stone of the valley wound out of sight. Mountains trapped them within.

"We're on foot from here." Reid glanced once more at the steep cliff. He couldn't see the path they'd fallen from, but they had been heading north-northwest. They weren't terribly lost. Not yet. "The others will have gone on. If we keep going, we might find a path up and meet them."

"Without horses?" Doubt filled Ison's face.

Reid started walking north. "Man has walked on his own two feet for thousands of years. Unless you would rather wait out your death here. I choose to at least try to survive."

Reluctantly, Ison started after him. "It's a bit ruthless," he said after a few steps. "To assume us dead and move on."

Like they had done to Juniper.

"It's a part of the quest," Reid said. "The quest must come first. No matter what."

Ison grunted his disagreement, though he didn't argue.

They salvaged what supplies they could carry from the saddlebags and started north. The valley wound on, cold and unforgiving mountains on either side, without sign of a way up. Bluffs stuck out of the rockface, small caves opened, leaving plentiful shadows for predators to lurk, unseen. They kept walking through the whistling wind that whipped snow against their cheeks.

Reid didn't have high hopes for their survival. The cold already needled into the seams of his fur-lined clothes. Beyond the dwindling supplies, the harsh weather that could turn into a snowstorm in a moment's notice, wolves, bears, and whatever else lurked in the mountains, two humans stood little chance. As much as he didn't want to think it, they would need Ison's magic.

Reid led the way. Ison walked a step behind, his breath ragged. To have saved them from that fall, he would have expended a great deal of magic.

"We can rest if you need to," Reid said.

"No," Ison said. "I'm fine."

"You'll need your magic."

"It's regenerating." Ison coughed and pulled his cloak tighter. "Jun's magic is helping."

"And if you didn't have her magic?" Reid could feel that seed of magic too, resting there in his chest, beating like a second heart.

"I suppose you'd have to carry me." Ison's tone carried a hint of humor. "Or, most likely, we'd be lying on the ground with several broken bones."

"Was that the first time you've done that?"

"I slowed our fall and kept the rocks away," Ison explained. "The Marca doesn't teach us how to use raw magic or how to control our element to such an extent. I've controlled air to move smaller things, but never a human, let alone two."

"I don't know what lurks deep in the mountains," Reid said. "Anything that can thrive here isn't something I want to meet."

"You think wind could be a weapon against a bear the size of a house?"

"Better than letting it rip out your throat." Reid felt much better about their slim odds with having a mage, even if it was Ison.

Two had a better chance than one.

❅

They walked through the mountains until the sun began to decline, suggested by the fading gray light on the other side of the thickening gray clouds. Reid did not want to see what came out at night, and at the next cave, he ducked inside. He could see the back of the cave—no threats. It didn't look as though anything had been using it as a home either.

"We've no wood for a fire," Reid said. They hadn't passed any trees or anything that looked burnable, minus a few scraggly bushes.

"We don't need a fire." Ison closed his hand, and a moment later, a bluish white flame appeared.

Forever flame. The brightness of it made Reid realize just how dark it had been. He blinked the sting from his eyes. Ison set his flame on the floor. He proceeded to carve runes at the cave's mouth, similar to those carved on the forest cave.

"What do those do?" Reid asked.

"It's a combination of three runes." Ison carved the mirroring rune across from the first, his voice wispy in concentration. "The first is to shield the entrance from unwanted visitors. The second keeps the wind from coming inside. The third prevents odors from passing through. No wolves will catch our scent. Our heat will also stay inside."

Ison finished the rune, and Reid felt the air in the cave calm, like someone had shut a window. The air on the other side became distorted, like he looked through a shallow puddle. Ison retreated to the forever flame and slumped on the floor. The flame highlighted the angles of his face and turned his gray eyes the same haunting bluish white.

Reid sat on the opposite side of the flame. Trapped in a cave on a godforsaken mountain with few supplies and a mage—a knight's test, indeed.

Still, Ison had secured a campsite, set up a perimeter, and started a fire within a few minutes. Reid would have spent hours doing all of that, and without those runes, the cavern would have remained vulnerable.

Part of him was glad to have Ison there, but underneath it, something yearned to throw him through the rune's distorted light and into the unforgiving night. Damn him for his useful magic.

"Did they teach that rune in the Marca?" Reid asked casually.

Ison looked up over the flame. "No. That one I learned on my own from the books the court magician had."

Reid held his stoic expression. He knew that old man had books no mage should have. Still, at the same time, those runes had most likely saved their lives tonight.

"Not every mage outside the Marca dabbles in dark magic," Ison said. "Most of them do not."

"I suppose you have firsthand knowledge," Reid agreed.

Ison nodded. "I didn't until recently. I thought most of them monsters too, because the Marca told me they were. I imagine the Order does the same to its squires."

Reid tightened his fist but held it where Ison couldn't see. They did emphasize that any mage outside the Marca practiced dark magic, for why else would a mage resist the Order's law?

"If it makes you feel more confident about the Marca, they only teach the safe magic and punish those they think might turn to dark magic." Ison laughed bitterly. "They teach us to heat water, heal minor cuts and bruises, things that could be used in households by servants. They teach mages to be slaves to non-mages. They don't want us to learn anything that could be considered a threat against them."

"That is understandable," Reid said.

Ison glared.

"Not teaching you something that could be a threat to them."

"Magic itself is a threat to them," Ison said. "It is a threat by nature, and there is nothing that can be done about it. It is what it is." He met Reid's glare with one of his own, but softer. "Wouldn't it be to the king's advantage to have mages among his soldiers? Think of the benefits of a rune like this one on the battlefield, behind enemy lines, for his spies. Magic could save lives, if only the Order didn't see us only as a threat to their power, something to squash, something to lock away and pretend doesn't exist."

Ison reminded him of Juniper then, defending magic with logic and possible benefits.

"Magic is dangerous," Reid protested. The Marca needed to exist, to protect the mages from themselves, to teach them how to properly use their magic and be safe about it.

"If a boy was learning how to smith blades, would you only allow him to make dull, useless blades for his own safety?"

Reid frowned. "A sword could only kill one at a time. Magic can kill dozens."

"Anything can be used to kill," Ison said. "Rocks, sticks, silverware, scarves. It's not the tool, but the mind that intends to kill. The blacksmith apprentice would forge blades until he was making blades that people feared, expensive blades of impeccable quality. Why not treat magic the same? Mages should learn the basics of control, history, and what any student would learn, but their learning should not be stunted because of what they *might* do."

Reid found himself agreeing, but he couldn't bring himself to say it. "Magic is as much a danger as it is a blessing," he said instead. "People are slaughtered by mages every year, by mages who only want to prove their strength, like the apostate hiding in the castle. My own family was murdered by apostates fleeing from the Marca." Or whatever the hell they were doing.

Ison's face didn't change. "If the Marca wasn't such a horrible place, mages would not flee from it."

Reid clenched his fists, and he didn't bother to hide his dislike of Ison. "You defend murderers?"

"No. The Marca's problems don't justify murder. If the Order made the Marca a place where mages could learn without worrying about being punished for existing, or treated like animals or slaves, or thrown into the dark rooms for nothing more than a childish remark..." Ison clenched his fists, then released them. "The Marca is more prison than school."

Reid's anger flared, but he held it in. "What's to stop mages from learning dark magic?"

"The same thing that stops a man from learning how to dissect another human being or how to build explosives. Common decency," Ison said. "Just because a man has a sword doesn't mean he will carve out his wife's heart. Just because a man has magic doesn't mean he will set fields on fire or learn dark magic."

The conversation fell into a stiff, angry silence. The mage and the squire stared at each other a heartbeat longer over the fire; then Ison turned his gaze elsewhere. Reid leaned back against the cavern wall, watching the sky beyond the distortion fade from dark gray to black. The snow started as flurries, and within a time that Reid thought far too short, the valley floor was covered in white. Unseasonable snow. Of course. They hadn't anticipated snowfall for several days' north. Ison had saved them from the plummet, but Reid doubted he could do anything against a snowstorm. He noticed, with a spiteful relief, that the snow did not pass the rune's protection.

They ate small portions of the rations, for neither knew when they might find wild game or vegetation. Or the others.

They were in quite the predicament. Snow piled higher and higher against the distortion, inch-by-inch, the large snowflakes tumbling faster and faster. The world beyond turned a dark snowy gray. Hopefully, the others had found shelter for the night.

"You don't think we'll make it," Ison said plainly.

"I haven't been in a situation this dire before," Reid said.

Ison glared at him over the fire, hatred burning in his eyes.

Reid let out a small sigh. It would not help to be angry when they depended on each other. "Thank you. For the fire. It has helped."

Ison's gray eyes shifted to the fire, then to Reid. The bluish white reflected eerily in his eyes. "You're welcome."

Reid reclined on the hard ground. "I can't imagine this being easy for you. Traveling with three squires and a knight as an apostate."

"A well-known apostate," Ison corrected.

Reid didn't disagree.

A low grumble came from outside the cave, guttural and thunderous. It seemed to come from the mountain itself.

Ison and Reid sat up in unison. The snow came down harder, blurring the other side in gray. Through the storm, Reid saw nothing.

"Thunder?" Ison whispered.

"I've never heard thunder like that." Reid tightened his grip around his hilt. Like it could do anything against a beast of the mountain.

"Nothing should be able to see the barrier or pass through it." Ison didn't look convinced by his own words.

Another growl sounded, closer, again seeming to come from the mountain. All around them.

"I've heard abominable monsters lurk in the mountains," Ison whispered. "Bigger than a bear, hungrier than a wolf, and smarter than most humans."

Reid had too. Over campfires, hearths, and in the barracks. Some of those beasts supposedly had magic. Terrible, frightening magic. He reminded himself that those were just stories. If only his heart believed it.

Ison settled to the cavern floor and pulled his cloak around himself. Reid tried his best to relax. He would need his sleep.

Knowing something unknown and deadly lurked outside did not bode well for the night's rest.

CHAPTER TWENTY-SEVEN

Juniper woke to a blazing hearth. Shadows danced across the vaulted ceiling, pooling between the thick wooden beams. Heat, glorious heat, surrounded her body and sank into her bones. She closed her eyes and breathed slowly, deeply. The warm air smelled of cloves, pine needles, and wood smoke. Something bubbled. Juniper opened her eyes and turned her head to the side—her neck was stiff, and her body fared no better.

An iron pot hung over the hearth, and whatever cooked within had filled the room with a hearty aroma. It made her mouth water. On the wall above the hearth, massive antlers hung. Someone had tied little bundles of herbs to three of its prongs.

With each breath, each blink, she woke up a little more. She was underneath a mound of woolen blankets, quilts, and furs. She wasn't in a bed, but on the floor in front of the hearth. She turned her head to the other side, a feat with the thick furs cradling her neck. The spacious room held a bed, a desk, wide bookshelves, and a sitting area. Steam rose from a mug on the table, and one of the chairs was pushed back—someone had been sitting there recently.

Voices came from somewhere in another room, muffled by the walls.

Juniper tried to sit up, but her body and the heavy blankets protested. What little strength she had was smothered under the blankets.

What had— Oh. She remembered. The slavers, the dire wolf, the woods, the snowstorm, the mountains...and the stranger. That stranger had rescued her. Unless this was some slaver outpost and they were warming her so they could haul her off to market.

She exhaled, the breath weak and dry against her throat.

The voices came closer. Something moved across the wooden floor. Someone laughed, a feminine chime.

"Hello?" Juniper called to the empty room. Her voice scraped against her throat.

The voices in the other room halted, and footsteps approached. A door on the other side of the room opened with a heavy creak.

Two women walked in. One was older, with pale wrinkled skin and silver hair tied in two braids that nearly reached her waist. She wore a thick set of dark gray robes. The other woman was younger, closer to Juniper's age, maybe a few years older. Her raven hair fell down her back in a thick braid, save for a few strands that fell about her heart-shaped face. She wore well-made fur-lined leathers.

The younger woman gracefully knelt beside Juniper. She was beautiful. Her olive skin had paled with the dreary Galamond weather. She had soulful, clever brown eyes. She was not heavyset, but she wasn't skinny. She had a warrior's strength of muscle on her curvy figure.

"The daredevil is awake." The older woman walked to the cooking pot. "I had half a thought she wouldn't wake up."

The raven-haired girl gave Juniper a friendly smile. "Yet you live," she said in a voice as warm as the hearth. The girl's leathers were finely made for adventure and warmth, not for looks. She wore smaller throwing knives on both arms, a dagger on each thigh, and pockets hidden throughout the middle.

"You saved me," Juniper said.

The raven-haired girl nodded. "Lucky for you, I was tracking a bear out in those woods, or you'd be long dead in the snow. You're safe now, traveler. You're in Oriel."

Juniper blinked. She'd never heard of Oriel. "Galamond?" she croaked.

The raven-haired girl considered her, then nodded. "Of course you're in Galamond." She tilted her head. "What were you doing all the way out there by yourself? Only a fool would think themselves capable of surviving in the basin."

"Basin?" Juniper asked.

The girl blinked but did not show pity. "The Yulun Basin, the land between the edge of the Dolomin Mountains of Galamond and the Gallas Mountains of Janti. It's a treacherous place, full of wolves and bears and steep cliffs."

Juniper had heard of such a place, but she had never had use for the information.

The raven-haired girl started to say something, but the older woman interrupted, asking, "Roslyn, did you bring the bergamot? I'd say this stew is ready."

"You'd think I'd forget it? You only mentioned it about a dozen times." The raven-haired girl pulled a small leather pouch from one of her many pockets and tossed it to the older woman, who caught it without looking.

"Thank you, dear." The older woman poured dried leaves from the pouch into her hand, crunched them into dust, and sprinkled it over the pot. The white steam turned a pale purple, then returned to white.

It took a moment for the words to register in Juniper's sleepy, near-frozen mind.

"Roslyn," Juniper croaked, the name falling from her lips in desperation as the reality settled.

The girl in question raised her finely plucked brows. "Yes?"

Roslyn. A wild woman of the north, beautiful as she was clever, who knew the woods of her homeland better than anyone, who had found her way home after being blindfolded and left in the woods with nothing but a knife and her wits.

Juniper laughed—what were the odds?

Roslyn's curious expression fell into a frown. "Is my name funny? I've always been rather fond of it. I was named after—"

"Your mother's grandmother, who claimed she skinned a bear alive with nothing by her garden shears," Juniper finished.

Roslyn sat in silence, her mouth hanging open. Even the old woman glanced over her shoulder in surprise.

Roslyn blinked once, then narrowed her eyes at Juniper. "Yes, actually, I was. But how in Blugo's Blizzard do you know that? Who are you?"

Juniper laughed again at the impossible coincidence. Blugo had sent the dire wolf to her rescue and now Roslyn Derean? He must have taken her promise to end the slave trade seriously.

"Adrian Bradburn told me about you," Juniper said.

Roslyn's brows rose, but her skepticism remained. The hearth warmed her face and highlighted her hair with yellows and golds. "Interesting," she said after a long moment. "Then answer me this, stranger: what brings you this far north?"

"Juniper," she corrected. "My name is Juniper."

Roslyn nodded her acknowledgment.

"Here." The older woman handed Roslyn a canteen, which Roslyn then handed to Juniper. "Drink up, or you'll worsen the damage the cold did to your throat."

Juniper took a long drink. It tasted like honeyed water, only warmer and spiced. It coated the dry sides of her throat and stayed there. Juniper didn't know if it was just an herbal drink or something magic.

"I met Adrian earlier this year." Juniper told Roslyn everything. From the night Captain Sandpiper captured her, the binding spell she and Adrian shared, to her impersonation of Lady Derean and the accusation of attempted assassination. She told her about the quest for Boxel's Grace, the slavers, the dire wolf—everything.

During the tale, Roslyn and the older woman remained stone still and deathly silent. Roslyn's face shifted between interested and skeptical to curious to frightfully worried. Juniper's story ended with the mysterious figure lurking out of the snowstorm, and her throat felt as though she'd swallowed hot coals.

"The stew is ready," said the older woman.

"Can you stand?" Roslyn asked Juniper. She maneuvered her legs into a squat and held her hands out for Juniper's.

Juniper pulled her arms from the heavy blankets, and Roslyn pulled her effortlessly to her feet. Without the warmth of the blankets, a chill raked over Juniper's skin. Someone had removed her filthy traveling clothes, leaving her in just her undershorts. Roslyn pulled the top blanket off, which turned out to be a fur-lined cloak, not a blanket. Juniper hugged the cloak around herself while Roslyn gathered trousers and a long-sleeved tunic from another room. With Roslyn's assistance, Juniper pushed her sleepy limbs into the warm clothes. Roslyn then set Juniper's leather boots and woolen socks by the hearth.

They'd gone to such lengths for her, for a stranger.

Juniper sat at the table, and the old woman set an earthenware bowl in front of her. The steam carried the scent of herbs and seasonings—with her first bite, Juniper felt the warmth soak her mouth, her throat, and down into her chest. She couldn't help giving a grateful hum.

How long had it been since she'd eaten? She hadn't had an appetite since she'd divided her magic, but her stomach yearned for another bite. She hoped it signaled the regeneration of her magic. She felt inward. Her sliver of magic no longer quivered. It had grown imperceptibly.

"Fynilli is one of the best cooks around," Roslyn said, nodding toward the older woman.

"Thank you." Juniper took another bite and then added, "Both of you."

"Eat all of it," said Fynilli. "Two bowls ought to do the trick. Easier to get the bergamot and ginger in by stew than by potion or tea. Gets more of the good effects."

Juniper didn't question what bergamot was or what it did. She didn't care. She had heard Ison mention the herb before—he drank it in his tea, so it must be good.

For a while, the only sounds came from the fire and Juniper. Halfway through her bowl, Fynilli filled it back up. Juniper did not complain.

"I admit," Roslyn said, fingers playing with the end of her braid, her voice almost girlish. "I find it strange that Adrian was parading around someone disguised as me."

"It wasn't romantic," Juniper said. "We only saw each other when he stopped by my prison cell of a chamber or when I was pretending to be you for the pleasure of other people."

"And he told you who I was?"

"He couldn't stop talking about you." Juniper looked up from her soup to find Roslyn's eyes pinned on the end of her braid. "How brave you are, how beautiful you are, how much he thought about you, how much he missed you."

Roslyn's cheeks flushed pink. "He said those things?"

Juniper nodded. "He worries that someone else will sweep you off your feet before he gets the chance," she said. "Or that you've forgotten him."

Roslyn let out a girlish laugh. "He's jealous of the wild men up here? Absurd! I'd sooner wed a bear, though it wouldn't be much different. They're both covered in hair and share a temperament."

"At least the bear might smell better," added Fynilli.

Roslyn laughed. Her grin shrank, and she said, "I was worried Adrian would move on. He's surrounded by court girls crowding for his attention, with all their manners and dresses and time, while I'm stuck up here in the woods." Roslyn let out a short sigh.

Juniper started to speak, but Fynilli tapped the edge of her bowl. "Eat, child."

Roslyn leaned onto the table. "Are you planning to return to Rusdasin after you find Boxel's Grace?"

Juniper nodded. "We have to take the plant to the royal healer."

Sitting up straight, Roslyn declared, "I'm going with you." Not a question—a command.

Roslyn looked at Juniper with the regal air of a ruler. Juniper decided then she would be happy with a girl like Roslyn sitting on the throne. Adrian had been right. She did like Roslyn.

Roslyn sat waiting, her eyes pinned on Juniper. It took a moment to realize she waited for an answer—despite the command.

"I would be delighted for your company," Juniper said, and she meant it. Then she thought of the quest, and her smile faded.

"What is it?" Roslyn asked.

"The others." She had no idea where they were or what they were doing. "They wouldn't have stayed to look for me. They would have gone on."

"Well," said Fynilli, "if they are coming for Boxel's Grace, they will most likely pass through Halsig. It is the last village on this side of Galamond, save for a few bandit camps and ratholes on the far-flung edges."

"How far is that from here?"

"With good weather, about three days," Roslyn answered. "With the snow, maybe four."

"I can't say for sure if that's where they're going," Juniper said. "I was never told the details after journeying to Galamond."

Roslyn shrugged. "Don't worry, we'll get there."

"We?"

Roslyn grinned. "Of course, *we*. You think I'd throw you out into snow with just a friendly pat on the ass? No. I'm going with you as far as I can. I want Adrian to live too."

"Well then, you're going to need a helping hand." Fynilli set a bowl of stew in front of Roslyn, who didn't hesitate to tilt the entire bowl to her lips.

❋

After the warm meal, Roslyn guided Juniper to one of the bedrooms. The room had a burning hearth, a bed piled with quilts, and a small washing basin and earthenware pitcher of clean water. Roslyn explained that the house belonged to the king. Every town and city had a house for the king or his dignitaries when they visited. Being the king's relative, even by marriage, Roslyn was entitled to its rooms. Most included staff. The house in Oriel held minimal extravagances beyond what one needed to survive in the harsh winter.

Even with the warm meal and ample rest, Juniper felt stiff and achy. Every step had given her back some sense of strength, but she still felt the lack of her magic. It felt like she had three holes in her chest, leaking her magic, preventing it from rejuvenating.

"That's what nearly freezing to death will do to a body." Roslyn helped Juniper to the bed while a servant stirred the fire and added another log. "You'll need more rest if you intend to travel."

Juniper didn't argue. Her exhaustion craved the warmth of the bed.

"Amylia will be outside, should you need anything." Roslyn nodded toward the servant girl.

Amylia bowed her head and took up a guard's position in the hall.

"Fynilli mentioned wanting to talk to you, but she decided to wait until you were of better mind, her words."

"I look forward to it." Juniper's spirits rose as she wiggled her tired limbs underneath the furs and quilts. Oh, she could sleep for days in this bed! It reminded her of her bed in Castle Bradburn, soft beyond reason. Already, she could feel the herbal mixture of the stew worming through her body, pushing her magic to regenerate, pushing her strength to return.

Roslyn made sure Juniper was tucked in, then left. With the hearth burning, the room didn't feel as large. It felt cozy. Juniper closed her eyes, and she could picture her chambers in Castle Bradburn, her bed, the hearth, the desk—only the smells were different. Castle Bradburn had been a mixture of dust, polish, and linseed oil. This house smelled of woodsmoke, spices, and snow.

Safe—Juniper had been saved, and she could still save Adrian.

Juniper didn't care what Fynilli wanted to talk about, where she was, or what she had yet to do. She relaxed, slowing her breath with each exhale. She drifted further into the realm of sleep and dreams, though somewhere in that in-between, she thought a hand grazed her forehead. The hand brushed hair out of her eyes and flattened against her cheek.

Juniper didn't mind it. She fell into the best sleep she'd had in months.

CHAPTER TWENTY-EIGHT

The Galamond mountains had not been kind. Reid and Ison had trekked over the rugged, barren landscape, seeking a way through the endless expanse of rocks. They managed to head northwest, but every pass, valley, and rock looked identical to those they'd already seen. If Reid didn't know any better, he would say they'd gone in circles.

Ison knew a trick with magic to tell the direction. He carved a rune into sand, dirt, or snow—the rune resembled a compass, and its glowing arrow always pointed north.

Again, magic helped them.

Reid kept his mouth shut about it. Ison's magic had been invaluable during this...setback. If Reid had fallen alone, he would have died after wandering through the mountains until he starved, got eaten, or fell from one of the countless cliffs and bluffs.

Reid took the lead, aiming their trek toward the flattest ground. As they wound up the side of a valley, he noticed old cobbles nearly buried in the hard-packed dirt. He glanced behind them, at the trail they had followed up the valley's side. By the gods...a *road*. An ancient road. Reid followed it up and out of the valley, and sure enough, the old cobbled road wound through the rugged terrain, even through the rock in places. Maybe they were not yet doomed. Their conversation had been minimal, nothing more than verbal warnings of loose rocks.

The weather changed between snow and sleet, and the bleakness of it all had long since sank into Reid's bones. Every bend, every incline—rocks, rocks, and more rocks. Frigid air, frozen ground, scraggy brush, prickly trees. Galamond was proving to be a horrible, miserable place.

They hadn't run into anything they couldn't handle. A few wolves howled in the distance, hearty and stubborn goats jumped over the loose rocks, and Reid thought he spotted the pale hide of something that resembled pictures of mosscats—he would rather not run into one of those.

Reid spotted countless ruins in the mountains. From ancient settlements and foundations to archways and placed stones. History traced the first people to Galamond, but little was known about the ancient civilizations that had dotted the mountains.

Finally, legs burning from the trek and lungs aching from the cold, they stumbled across a village tucked into a shallow valley. Lean-to shacks and stone buildings dotted the space between pines. Smoke puffed from each chimney. Somewhere, an ax thunked, echoing off the trees. Ison let out a shuddering breath of relief.

Reid had never seen such a beautiful sight. "Bala's blessing," he breathed.

"Do you think they're friendly?" Ison whispered.

Reid hadn't heard the mage approach. He had grown irritated with the mage's unnatural grace, even when walking on loose rocks with cold feet.

"I don't care," Reid said. "If they're cannibals, we'll rid the world of them and take what supplies we can."

"That's a ruthless approach, squire."

Reid did not miss the spite in the mage's voice. "I value my safety over theirs at the moment," he spat back. He had to save Adrian. And to do that, first he had to save himself.

Reid started toward the village with Ison a step behind. He felt the crackle of the air as Ison readied his magic—it irritated Reid, but he also felt more confident walking into an unknown settlement with a magical guard around him.

The village was old. The buildings were made of perfectly fitting stones, no two quite the same shape. The roofs were wood and vaulted to keep the snow from piling. They passed between two buildings, and Reid spotted runes on many of the stones—Reid knew some but not all.

"I've never seen some of these runes," Ison whispered.

Reid's unease doubled. Ison knew more about runes than Reid did, and yet the mage didn't know them? That meant these runes were not those the Marca taught or among those Ison had picked up in the Undercity. They might be dangerous.

They wandered through the village for a while before Reid saw people. He spotted a man and two young boys—twins, likely—by a woodpile. The man chopped wood. The two boys carried the slabs to the woodpile and stacked them.

At last, Reid found what he had been looking for: an inn. A sign hung from thick iron brackets, laden with fresh snow and ice, with the word curved in a heavy script. Reid opened the door, as heavy and hard to move as the thick wood implied. Inside, a burning hearth welcomed him. A pot of stew boiled over the fire, filling the air with spices and steam. A bear-skin rug adorned the stone floor by the hearth. In the traditional Galamond style, the main room was divided into a sitting area and a kitchen. Iron bars hung over the kitchen, holding all manner of dented and scarred pots and pans and utensils.

At the kitchen counter, a middle-aged couple played a game of cards. At the sound of the door, they paused and turned to meet their guests. Both looked at Reid with wide eyes and slightly parted lips, as if guests were the last thing they expected to have come through the door.

"I saw the sign." Reid swallowed nervously. He would rather not fight his way out of the village, but he would if he had to. "The inn."

"Yes!" The man stood looking pleasantly surprised. "This is an inn! Welcome, welcome! What do you need? One room or two? Something warm to eat? Something spiced to warm your throat? The stew is nearly ready."

"All of those things, please," Ison said.

❋

An hour later, Ison and Reid had been escorted to separate rooms. The rooms were nothing fancy—a simple bed, washing basin, and clean water. Reid asked for nothing more. After a quick wash, Ison and Reid joined the couple—married since sixteen, they said proudly—for a dinner of warm stew and spiced ale.

They had stumbled into the village of Denegar, one of the oldest settlements in Galamond. Once people had lived in the mountains, but over the centuries, the resources had dwindled, and many had relocated to the south and east of the vast country, where the climate better suited a variety of crops and livestock.

"We get few travelers these days," said the innkeeper's wife. "Especially this close to winter."

"We survive well enough," said the innkeeper, a rugged man who used to hunt in the wilds of the mountains. "Too old and stubborn to pack up and find somewhere else."

After the meal, the innkeeper went to the tavern to see about a game of cards, and the innkeeper's wife had errands to run. Neither would be gone long, they said.

Reid and Ison sat alone in front of the hearth.

"They trust us in their home?" Ison's brows rose.

"Either they are hiding their plans to kill us, or they are genuinely trusting," said Reid. "I'm inclined to think them trusting. We might be the first visitors they've had in quite some time."

By the way they both doted on the visitors, it might have been years since the last guest.

"We still have a chance," Reid said, if only to break the silence. "We resupply here, rest, and head out. These people will know a way northwest."

Ison picked at a scuff on his boot.

Reid had a thought. Ison had nowhere to go, no one to hide behind. "What happened during the Demon Crisis?"

Ison's gray eyes, lit by the hearth, turned toward Reid. A subtle panic reflected there, and his shoulders hunched. "I don't know what you mean."

"Juniper mentioned that you had your own reasons for wanting revenge on Nexon." Reid said the name quietly.

Ison focused on Reid, a cautious fire burning behind his eyes. Reid hadn't seen the expression on the mage's face before, and he didn't like it. It held something wild, something cold.

"What did she tell you?"

Ison's low voice crawled along Reid's skin, and he wanted to draw his blade, though he doubted it would do much against Ison's wind magic. Instead, he steadied himself, readying a ward should he need one.

"She let it slip," Reid said. "She mentioned that she wanted revenge for all that Nexon had done to her, and she said you had just as much right to revenge."

Ison held Reid's stare for a long moment, the flames flickering. "She didn't tell you what happened? What I did?" Ison's voice barely spoke above the crackling of the fire.

"She didn't." Reid felt the quiver in the magic seed—apprehension or a warning? "She said it was not hers to tell."

Ison fell silent. The caution dropped from his face, and guilt replaced it. "I suppose it doesn't matter now. I can't return to the castle, and the knights are already cursing my name." Ison's gaze drifted to the hearth, and a coldness came over his face. "Nexon was behind the missing servants. He used them to create those abominations."

Reid held his face firm. A part of him had already accepted it, ever since he had seen the servant girl's eyes on one of those monsters. He had told Knight Commander Fowler, who told Reid to keep his worries to himself, that the Order would investigate. Knowing now what he didn't know then, he doubted Fowler had looked much further.

"Nexon didn't demean himself with the drudge work." Darkness claimed Ison's expression, and something hollow took over his eyes, his voice. "The wechun performed the ritual, but he forced me to gather his human subjects."

"You...?" Reid gasped. Ison had been stealing the servants from the castle?

"He can...get into your head," Ison explained. "I didn't notice for a long time. It started as a voice in my mind, and then I experienced blackouts. I had days where I couldn't remember what I was doing or where I'd gone. My head ached, my body felt like it hadn't slept in weeks, and then, before Juniper defeated the wechun, I started to remember bits and pieces. Mason knew something was wrong, and he warded me in my chambers more than once. Without the wechun, something broke, and I could remember more and more. Eventually, I could remember everything."

"Everything?" Reid asked.

"The ritual required blood," Ison said, his voice distant. "In the catacombs below the castle, there was a rune carved into the floor. It needed to be filled with blood. Several...bodies' worth."

Reid didn't dare ask. He saw the answer written on Ison's face, the blankness, the haunted daze. Ison had killed those people, drained their blood, and then they had become those monsters.

And Clara had been among those missing. The realization struck hard. Ison had killed her, the girl he'd been seeing.

Reid swallowed. "Nexon was in your mind?"

"Josephine taught me how to block him." Ison looked up from the hearth to meet Reid's gaze. "I haven't heard his voice since we fled the castle. But, to answer your question, I have plenty of reasons to seek revenge on Nexon."

Reid didn't know what to say. Ison had been involved, just as he'd suspected. The entire time. Every missing servant had been taken by Ison, his will or not.

"I told Juniper everything," Ison said quietly. "She was the only one who knew. That's why I sought her out. Because I could talk to her. Not because I wanted to take her from you."

"It wouldn't have bothered me if you had," Reid said quickly.

Ison let out a half laugh. "Yes, that's why you slammed the chamber door and glared at me when I slept in her bed."

"I did no such thing," Reid said, though he remembered doing so. "I would not be so petty."

Silence pressed in again.

"She said your name, you know," Ison said after a while, so quietly that Reid thought he'd misheard.

Reid blinked. "What?"

"Juniper," Ison clarified. "When we..." He motioned with his hand. Words failed him, and he glanced sheepishly at Reid.

So they had taken their relationship a step further. In the very bed Juniper had shared with Reid. The idea of Ison with Juniper in that way sent his blood boiling, and he wanted to shove the mage out into the snow and let him freeze to death. He had suspected, but now that he knew, it felt worse. He clenched his fists without realizing it, and when Ison swallowed and glanced at the squire's curled fists, he released them.

"That doesn't matter now." Reid wished he could believe it.

"We didn't..." Ison paused for words. "We didn't make love. Not like that. We didn't have that kind of relationship. We don't have that kind of love for each other. It was a release. But, when she did, it was your name on her lips, not mine."

Reid had no response. The boiling rage in his chest turned slippery. Something dangerously like pride swelled in his chest to know that Juniper's mind had been on him during those intimate moments with another man.

"After what happened with Clara, something broke," Ison said, his voice thin. "And then..."

"And then what?"

Ison blinked, like he hadn't meant to speak aloud. His face warmed, and he shook his head, jostling his head of curls. "And then nothing."

Reid leaned forward, narrowing his eyes at the mage.

"What?" Ison shrank inward. "It doesn't concern you."

"Then why the secret?"

"It's not a secret." Emotion cracked Ison's voice. He cleared his throat. "It's just...private. And confusing. And none of your business."

"You met someone?"

Ison's blush surged into a fiery heat in his ashen cheeks.

"You did," Reid confirmed. Despite his feelings a moment ago, this turn lifted Reid's spirits. "An Undercity mage, I take it? Is she part of that guild—Josephine's?"

Ison cleared his throat, his face burning. "He is not."

Reid raised his brows. "And it is confusing?"

"Not in the way you think," Ison said. "I've been with men. It's...everything else. I didn't think I would ever feel anything for anyone again. It was hard enough to feel something for Clara to begin with. I've never been... I've never found it easy to fall in love. But...I think...there's something there." Ison put a hand to his chest.

"I can't say it's been hard to fall in love," Reid admitted. Though he would rather keep the information to himself, Ison had shared personal information. It was only fair. "I've found it easy, which is a problem in itself. Last year, I fell in love with a lord's daughter, Nanette. At the time, I thought her the most beautiful creature I'd ever seen."

"Brown hair?" Ison asked, and Reid nodded. "I remember her. I remember seeing you together once."

"She batted her eyelashes at me, and I was in love. When she left me, I was devastated. I swore I would never fall in love again." Reid chuckled. "You know how well that turned out."

"I think, between the two, Juniper was the better choice."

Reid agreed, but he wouldn't admit that. "I tried my best not to feel anything toward her, but she made it difficult." With her wit, her eyes, and her teasing.

The fire crackled, bathing them in its warmth and light.

"What is your plan from here, squire?"

"We continue northwest." Reid wished Isaac would have told them more of the quest. He knew the direction and that the plant grew on the edges of the realm—presumably far into the Dolomin Mountains.

The door to the inn opened, and the fur-laden figures of the innkeeper and his wife appeared through the darkness, snow swirling in the air behind them. The snowfall obscured the street beyond in a grayish blur.

"Ah, I didn't know if you'd still be up or not," said the innkeeper. "I thought maybe you two had called it a night after all that traveling on foot."

"Madness," chimed his wife.

"I hate to ask this of you, but could you give directions?" Reid asked.

"Of course," said the innkeeper. "I've got maps by the dozens."

"He does." Her tone indicated disapproval with all those maps. "He'd have more if I'd let him."

The innkeeper retrieved several maps of Galamond and the surrounding areas. He spread them over the large dining table. A few old trails led north and northwest, though few villages remained that far north. Those that did were like Denegar, old and rugged and closed off to the rest of the world. Reid didn't explain why they wanted to go that way, and the innkeeper never asked.

Until he did.

"Few people come up this way anymore," said the innkeeper. "Fewer go farther."

"This isn't something I am supposed to boast about," said Reid, "but I am on a king's quest to earn my knighthood."

The innkeeper's wife's eyes brightened, and her husband stood a little straighter.

"Well, in that case, it's been an honor to put a roof over your head this night," said the innkeeper.

Reid bowed his head. "Thank you."

"This route north is old and narrow, used centuries ago by pilgrims and traveling merchants." The innkeeper returned to his maps with new vigor and respect. "I haven't traveled north in nearly a decade. I've no reason to, but when I last did, this path had been destroyed by a landslide. This way goes around, but it is a safer road."

"Thank you for the advice," Reid said.

The four of them stood around the map for hours, talking, planning, and memorizing the trail. Reid drank in every word of advice the innkeeper could give, and he hoped Ison was doing the same.

CHAPTER TWENTY-NINE

Juniper felt remarkably better in the morning. She washed with lukewarm water and dressed in clothes gifted by Roslyn—thick wools and fur-lined leathers made for function and warmth, not style. A servant guided Juniper to the dining hall where Roslyn and Fynilli were seated. The grand table had been set for three, though it could have sat twenty. A hearth burned on the far side of the room, flickering golden light over the table.

"Good morning." Roslyn wore her hair up in a twisted braid. A black fur collar hugged her neck. "I hope you're hungry."

"Yes," Juniper said and meant it.

Breakfast came on simple silver platters: roasted mutton, eggs, fatty sausages, and muffins. Juniper ate greedily, though her appetite lessened quickly. She wasn't able to eat the plate she had filled.

Roslyn ate plenty, without stopping to mind her manners or use her fork properly or keep her elbows off the table. Wouldn't Reid love to know.

At the thought of him, out there in places unknown, with her magic, something tugged—her magic kernel, she realized, tugging for the three others. If she followed that tug, would it lead her to them?

Juniper sipped the hot tea, a bold blend that warmed her insides.

"You said you were a mage." Fynilli's eyes flickered to Juniper over the rim of her teacup.

"Yes." Only now did Juniper realize the danger of telling these two strangers everything. Her heart thumped—had she made a grave mistake?

"And you successfully gave a kernel of your magic to your friend?"

"Yes. Three of them."

Fynilli choked on her tea—it dribbled down her chin and down the side of the cup. She set it down and brought a napkin to her face.

Juniper feared she had said something wrong. She glanced at Roslyn, but she looked just as confused by Fynilli's reaction.

"You took *three* kernels of magic from yourself?" Fynilli pinned Juniper down with her wide eyes.

"Yes," Juniper said again. "One to Reid, one to Penet, and one to Ison."

"And you still retain enough for yourself?" she said, a bit breathless.

Juniper hesitated to answer. She hadn't been able to use her magic since. Not really.

Fynilli hummed during Juniper's silence. "I assume that means you didn't."

"I wasn't thinking about myself at the time," Juniper said. "I thought I would return, not be captured by slavers. I wanted them to survive. Was that wrong of me?"

"No." Fynilli shook her head. "There is nothing wrong with wanting to protect your friends, but...how does your magic feel now?"

Juniper felt her magic. It stirred after her warm meal and long nap, though it still dwindled. Fynilli eyed her as though she already knew the answer, so Juniper answered honestly, "It feels small. It's there, but not what it's supposed to be."

"That you can move around at all is astounding," Fynilli said. "I've rarely met a mage who could divide their magic, let alone into four pieces."

"Is that why you were so out of it when I found you?" Roslyn asked.

"She shouldn't have been able to move." Fynilli stared at Juniper like she struggled to see her clearly. "Taking one's magic from oneself is like removing a sense, a piece of the soul, and often leaves the mage bedridden and ill until it is returned."

"I haven't felt *good*," Juniper acknowledged. And she had felt sick, but she had attributed some of that to the slavers and the cold.

Fynilli leaned onto the table. "I am a mage. I've known many mages in my lifetime, of every element. Of those, I've only met one who could pull more than one kernel and be all right."

Juniper swallowed. The older woman's dark tone shadowed the room. "What does that mean, that I can do it?"

Fynilli didn't answer for a while. Her dark stare bore into Juniper's. Then, she asked, "Is Thimble your family name?"

"No."

"What is?"

"I don't remember."

Fynilli frowned.

"I-I was kidnapped by bandits and sold in the Undercity of Rusdasin," Juniper explained in a small voice. "I don't remember anything beyond my first name. I can't even remember my parents' faces."

Only honeysuckle and lavender growing outside her bedroom window.

Fynilli searched Juniper's eyes. "It's very likely you've got Iluvin blood and the magic to go along with it."

"I'm Iluvin?" Juniper gawked at the notion. She remembered Ison saying something about how all mages descended from the Iluvin. "But I thought they died out a thousand years ago?"

"Not all," Fynilli said. "The Iluvin may no longer be a proud people, but their bloodlines still exist, maybe to the far reaches of the world and back again."

Juniper looked down at her hands. She imagined her bright blue magic ribboning around her fingers. Her, Iluvin? All the stories of the powerful Iluvin and their impossible magic—could it be true? She had learned so fast. Her magic well had deepened so much. Could her magic be a portion of that old magic? The magic of the world when dragons flew overhead, when stars could grant wishes, when trees would sing when no one could hear, when spirits and sprites wandered the deepest woods—the very idea sent a spark tingling down her spine.

"So what does it mean?" Roslyn asked. "To be Iluvin?"

Fynilli shrugged. "It might mean something; it might mean nothing. The bloodlines have been watered down over the last one thousand years, and anything is possible. But magic has its own laws and logic that people can't hope to understand." She leaned back in her chair and regarded Juniper thoughtfully. "Some say the element a mage possesses comes from the Iluvin family blood that runs thickest. That is why I asked your surname, though I suppose names change over the years."

Juniper clutched her teacup. She didn't see how this piece of knowledge about herself changed anything, but she felt like it should.

"In the old ways of the Iluvin," Fynilli started, her voice weary from memories. "When a couple married, they took the more prominent name. If one had a gifted name, that was the surname the couple took. Of course, like most else of the Iluvin, the tradition has fallen to history's dusty pages."

"Gifted name?" Juniper repeated. It sounded familiar. Mason had told her about the Iluvin, but it felt like a lifetime ago.

"Five gifted names, for the five Iluvin families," Fynilli explained.

"The five families gifted with magic," Juniper added. The story clicked into her mind. She could almost hear Mason's somber voice telling it.

"Yes." Fynilli adjusted herself in the chair, a motion Juniper had seen older people do when they collected their thoughts. "You claim Nexon is behind the uprisings in both Duvane and Collatia."

"His followers mentioned that he was an Iluvin mage." Juniper didn't dare mention that they thought him an archmage. "He had powers to speak directly into their minds. He could control them, to an extent."

Fynilli inhaled, her breathing controlled. "It takes a powerful mage to break into another's mind, more power yet to take over one's mind." She traced the handle of her teacup. Thoughts churned behind her eyes. "I so hoped Nexon's return to be hogwash."

"What do you know of his return?" Juniper's voice was no more than a whisper.

"Only that it was prophesied shortly after his downfall and widely ignored," said the older woman. "Nexon was gone, and no one wanted to think about him anymore. They all believed him dead and gone at last, his reign of terror ended. And when the celebrations came to an end, the Order of the Knighthood began. With the Order's increasing power, people forgot about Nexon."

"How do you know these things?" Was Galamond less strict with knowledge about the Iluvin? She knew the kingdom was strict about their mages.

Fynilli fixed a gaze on Juniper that reminded her of how Mason would sometimes look at her, like he knew something but didn't want to tell her. "Much knowledge has been lost in the years since the Order took it upon itself to rid the world of the Iluvin and all they were," she said flatly. "Some of that knowledge and history has been carefully preserved and passed down without the Order catching wind, through bedtime stories and campfire tales."

"And you think it's really him? Nexon?"

"The evidence supports it. What I've gathered on my own, what I've heard elsewhere, and now what you've told me. It would be foolish to ignore the signs."

Juniper swallowed. Her throat had gone dry—she gulped her warm tea. Fynilli had opened a door to knowledge—she knew more than any library Juniper could find. "Do you know about the second part of the prophecy?"

The older mage nodded mournfully. "Nexon will rise again to power, but the princess who returns shall defeat him. Or something along those lines."

Roslyn leaned onto the table. She glanced between Fynilli and Juniper. "Who is that?"

"No one knows." Fynilli shook her head. "The prophecy was made a thousand years ago."

Fynilli and Juniper glanced at Roslyn. Her brown eyes moved rapidly between them, then she shook her head. "What? You think it's me?" She laughed and waved the idea away. "I'm not a princess."

"But you are with the prince," Fynilli said. "Close to a princess. The translation might not mean a legal princess, but a girl of royal blood."

"No. I don't have royal blood. I am royal by marriage. I am the king's niece, but my blood is the queen's. Should I marry a prince, I would be a duchess until he becomes a king and I become a queen. I won't ever be a princess."

"We thought it might be Myrisha Balendin," Juniper said. "Her brother, King Crespin, is thinking about giving her the crown."

"And she will return," Roslyn added.

Fynilli nodded. "She is a likely candidate, considering Collatia's history, or maybe her daughter. Suspicious how few princesses there have been in the past few hundred years, wouldn't you think? Or how many have died so young."

"Several," Roslyn said.

Juniper shook her head. "I don't follow the royal lines."

"My uncle had two daughters," Roslyn said darkly. "Both died in infancy. Before their first birthday. The worst funerals I've ever had to sit through."

"The king of Janti has lost five daughters," Fynilli said, "over his many wives."

"And the Collatian civil war killed King Balendin's daughters," Roslyn added.

"You think Nexon has been killing princesses?" Juniper's stomach twisted at the thought. "Because he knows one of them might rise against him should he reclaim power?"

"He has been reclaiming power for years now." Fynilli glanced at the door where the servants had come and gone. "And making sure his biggest threat never appears."

Juniper repressed a shiver. Nexon had been crawling his way back to power for decades, maybe even centuries. What if they were too late?

"So..." Roslyn started, tapping her short fingernails on the table. "In order to stop Nexon, we have to find this princess who will return, but what can she do against him?"

"No one knows that either." Fynilli shrugged. "The prophecy was given a thousand years ago in a tongue no longer spoken, and I'm not sure every detail remains."

"And you're going after this guy?" Roslyn asked Juniper.

"I have to do something," Juniper said.

"I've met Myrisha," Roslyn said. "She's smart. If you can get an audience with her, she will listen to you. If I send word ahead and confirm you and your story aren't a product of madness, she might listen harder."

"But before that," Juniper said, "I have to find Boxel's Grace and save Adrian's life."

"About that," Fynilli started, "what do you know about it?"

"It can cure any illness, and it's located at the end of the realm. The herbalist we were traveling with had this old book with hundreds of plants I'd never heard of. Boxel's Grace was one of them. It's supposed to be somewhere north of Galamond. I don't know exactly where."

The wrinkles between Fynilli's eyes multiplied.

Roslyn stilled. "I know of where you speak," she whispered. She drew her arms in closer. "It is not a place meant for mortals."

Roslyn paused, and Fynilli motioned for the younger woman to continue.

"My grandmother told me stories of pilgrims who journeyed to the end of the world. Many did not return. There used to be a group of nomads whose elders went there to die. They saw the journey as the final test of their life in this world and the way into the next," Roslyn said, her voice solemn. "She called it the Garden of the Gods. It rests on the crown of the world, a place mortals should not tread. Legends say it is guarded by ancient beasts, holds a treasure trove greater than any king and knowledge unknown. The entrance is through the ruins of an ancient city whose name has fallen to time."

Juniper swallowed. Roslyn spoke with reverence of this place, a place Juniper planned on trampling through. Not that she had never defiled a temple, but she would rather not anger the gods any more than she already had. "Have you been there?" Juniper asked.

Roslyn's dark brows came together. "No. I know this land. I've climbed to the top of the tallest trees, swam in the deepest lakes, and conquered the mountains, but I have not gone to the Garden of the Gods. I know my place is not there."

Juniper sighed and leaned back in the chair. "Then how do I know it's really there and not some folktale?"

161

"If you thought it a folktale, you wouldn't have come all this way and nearly died for it." Roslyn pointed at Juniper. She held herself like a queen, her shoulders straight, her back poised, but she also held herself like a warrior, arms loose and ready to fling a hidden dagger in any direction. "I haven't seen the ruins myself because I respect the legends warning me to stay away. Nomads don't journey up there anymore, but adventurers and treasure hunters go up the mountain every year. None return."

Juniper folded her hands together under the table. What happened to those adventurers and treasure hunters? Eaten by the guardian beasts? Trapped in a cave-in? Fallen off the edge of the world?

The kitchen door opened, and their conversation fell silent. Two servants appeared and quickly took away the cooled teapot. "More tea, my lady?"

"I would love another cup." Roslyn's smile was wide and kind.

"Yes, my lady." The girl curtsied without jostling the dishes.

In a few moments, a fresh pot of tea was set on the table. Roslyn quickly made herself a cup and sipped it, humming. None of them spoke until both servants returned to the kitchens.

"That girl is one of the refugees who have come into Galamond in the past few weeks." Roslyn eyed the kitchen door. "More and more are coming over the border. The border towns have grown. I admit, when I first saw you, I assumed you were another refugee. They've gotten lost in the woods, and well, you know, bears and wolves and frozen rivers."

"They are seeking a warm hearth and a safe place to sleep," Fynilli said. "Not unlike the days of Nexon's reign, when the world wasn't safe for anyone, mage or not."

Refugees from burned villages, fleeing from apostates with all they could carry. Stones fell into Juniper's stomach.

Fynilli looked into her tea with a distant expression. "Something is happening, and it is stirring the apostates who have remained hidden for so long. When I was young, I wandered the northern countryside of Duvane with several others. We were what the Order considered apostates, but we never burned anything or hurt anyone. We protected each other, nothing more. Duvane has become a dangerous place for mages of late."

"Nexon's followers have congregated in the northern part of Collatia," Juniper said.

Fynilli nodded. "That is where he started before, where he gathered followers and started his campaign against the world." She met Juniper's eye. "Trouble is indeed brewing."

Juniper thought back to Josephine's dire warning of an incoming darkness.

"Nexon is working faster than anyone thought." Fynilli tipped her teacup to Juniper. "You need to get this plant and heal your prince as quickly as you can. Nexon must be stopped."

"Ison and I planned on going together," she said, only reminding herself they were gone. "I have to find them first."

"If you're all going after this plant, there is a chance you'll find each other on the way." Roslyn's smile widened.

And Juniper could feel the kernels of magic tugging her own. She knew she could follow that tug straight to them. Juniper leaned forward, elbows on the table. "I feel better after telling all this to you. Now, if something were to happen to me, the information won't be lost forever."

Fynilli stared into the hearth fire. "I will write letters to a few old friends, spread the word about Nexon as much as I can and hope they do the same. We might be few, but we are still here." She sighed and looked far older. "We all knew it was only a matter of time before he gathered himself back together again. I just always hoped I would be gone before then."

Juniper held her gaze on the older mage until she returned it. "You knew?"

Fynilli gave Juniper a grandmotherly smile. "Yes, we knew. It doesn't seem as long ago as it was, and I often forget how old I really am."

Juniper studied Fynilli's wrinkled skin, silver hair, and wizened eyes. She could have been seventy or eighty. "How old..." Juniper stopped herself before the words came out.

Fynilli chuckled at Juniper's hesitation. "Let's see... If I'm right, I'll be one thousand and forty-two next spring."

Juniper almost dropped her teacup, and Roslyn choked—coughing, she set the cup down and wiped her mouth on a napkin.

"What?" Juniper asked. "You... How?"

Fynilli laughed. "I'm Iluvin," she answered softly, a secret. "One of the few left from before the war."

The older woman had both Juniper and Roslyn's undivided attention. Juniper had never met anyone that old, never thought she would, and sitting at a table with someone who had seen so much of history, who knew so much that had been lost, her limbs turned to lead and her tongue turned to sand.

Fynilli conceded and said, "I don't remember the world before Nexon. He was a general who went to war and never really came back. His ambition got the better of him. He wanted power, all of it. When it became clear he must be stopped before he tore the world apart, I joined the movement to undermine him." Her eyes grew misty and distant. "We met in basements and root cellars. We formed an alliance with the growing band of monks who would become the Order of the Knighthood, thinking we could defeat Nexon and bring back balance to the world. You see how that alliance turned out." Fynilli chuckled. "The Order took our execution blades and turned them into weapons against magic."

"Mage's Bane?" Juniper blurted. "That's Iluvin?"

Fynilli nodded grimly. "It was a ceremonial death sentence for those who broke the tenets of magic." Juniper started to ask, and Fynilli added, "Those who used their magic to harm, kill, or torment."

"I thought the Order invented it?" Roslyn asked.

Fynilli harrumphed. "I wouldn't believe a word the Order says of their history," she said bitterly. "What began as an earnest hope to rid the world of Nexon became a force against all mages. The Order destroyed the Iluvin and their knowledge. Thousands of years of culture, gone."

Roslyn gawked at Fynilli. "Why did I never know any of this? Why didn't you tell me?"

"Because one doesn't brag about being Iluvin when the Order hunts down apostates like deer," Fynilli said.

Juniper understood. She had kept her magic hidden as long as she could. "You were there when Nexon fell?"

"I was on the battlefield when we heard the news of Nexon's defeat. How glorious it seemed." Her eyes misted. "I saw the light. It rose like a sunrise, raw power like I had never imagined." She took a deep sigh.

"What happened?" Juniper asked. "History glosses over the actual defeat."

"Another part of our history the Order wishes to purge from existence." Fynilli muttered. "Nexon met his end when his fellow archmages turned against him."

"Archmages?" Roslyn and Juniper said in unison.

"They're real?" Juniper added.

"They are very real," Fynilli said. "The archmages' betrayal is the only reason Nexon was defeated. They knew he had to be stopped."

"How?" Juniper whispered.

"I don't know." Fynilli shook her head and took a sip of her tea. "An archmage isn't like a normal mage. They're..." She stumbled for the right words. Her boney fingers searched the air for them. "They're harder to get rid of. Their magic is considerable. And Nexon built a revolution around himself so that he was never exposed. A blade to the heart would kill him just as easily as any other, but he... They say he took measures to guard his life. I don't don't know more than what the legends say, and they say the archmages banded together in order to defeat him. How and why they did it was never explained. It was kept secret." Fynilli caught Roslyn's intent stare. "Don't look at me like that, I'm not an archmage."

Juniper's heart thumped. Could the answer to defeating Nexon exist with the archmages? And if the Archmage of Fire existed within the Collatian court, it gave them another reason to seek out Myrisha's help.

"If you're Iluvin," Roslyn started, eyeing Fynilli suspiciously, "Then you are from one of those five houses?"

Fynilli nodded. "I belong to the Balendin line, the same as the former king of Collatia. He was a distant relative of mine."

"We need to find the archmages," Juniper whispered. "If they know how to defeat Nexon, they could help us do it again."

Fynilli chuckled. "Finding Boxel's Grace will prove easier than finding an archmage. The archmages hide their identity as such. The laws of inheritance do not always make sense, and once an archmage dies, it might take a decade for the next to emerge. They could be anywhere in the world, any age, any race."

Juniper slumped and rubbed her face. She kept adding tasks, and each one seemed bigger and more impossible than the last.

"What about the Collation court?" Roslyn whispered.

Fynilli nodded but didn't say anything.

"The Archmage of Fire," Juniper whispered.

Fynilli's brows rose.

"I heard...from someone else."

"Then he might be your best bet," Fynilli said.

"Are you sure you're not an archmage?" Roslyn asked, squinting at Fynilli.

Fynilli smiled. "I am very sure. The Balendins were gifted with the element of water, and though I am a powerful mage by modern standards, I am not the archmage." Her brows came together. "Juniper, your magic is ice, you say. A branch of water." She smiled. "Maybe we are distantly related too. I wouldn't be surprised."

Juniper's heart lurched. "You're a water mage?"

Fynilli nodded. She lifted her tea from her cup, ribboning it around the air like a dozen thin snakes. The tea fluttered around the room in the form of butterflies, and each fluttered back into the teacup without a single splash.

"I am fine with having you as a relative." Juniper sipped her tea. When she got her magic back, she would try that butterfly trick. "I'm sure we would get along just fine."

Fynilli tipped her tea to Juniper. "In Iluvin tradition, all mages of a certain element were considered family. Because of our water magic, we would have been adopted into the Balendin house, if we hadn't been born there."

How many more members of the Balendin house existed out there? Wandering the world in secret from the Order? Juniper swirled her tea, the idea both mesmerizing and stressful. Did her parents know about their Iluvin heritage? Would they have explained it to her when she was old enough to understand?

"It's bad luck to look glum so early in the morning." Roslyn nudged Juniper's arm.

"And we've got a long ride ahead of us," Fynilli said. "Rest up, the both of you. You will need your strength and wits for what is to come."

CHAPTER THIRTY

Reid woke to a steady beating in his chest, a pulse—Juniper's magic. It pulsed in time with his heart. It tugged him westward, toward Juniper, or so he imagined.

Lying in his warm bed, everything felt possible. He had the map of the mountains in his head. He could finish this quest, save Adrian, find Juniper, and give her magic back to her. He would then become a knight.

The innkeeper and his wife had breakfast ready and supplies gathered for them. The townspeople were thrilled to have a soon-to-be knight passing through their little town, and when they had asked for supplies, plenty had been given. Reid didn't know what to say. He fumbled over his gratitude.

He'd not forget the name of this little town. Sir Sandpiper, renowned knight of the Order, would not have survived his quest without the generosity of the little village of Denegar.

They ate, washed up, and readied their packs. It seemed the entire village had come out to bid them farewell. Men, women, and children lined the narrow street leading from the eastern side of the village to the western side, connecting the two ancient roads. The people waved and cheered, and Reid felt like a real knight going out to defeat a menace, to save people.

Reid and Ison started the incline of the western road, the ancient steps that would take them into the mountains—they did not make it to the top of the stairs. The screams reached them first, followed by the thudding and booming.

"What's that?" Ison stammered, sliding on the snowy stairs to turn around.

From where they stood, they could see over the homes and buildings. On the eastern side of Denegar, ice and water crashed, snow came alive, wind sliced through stone, and rock destroyed.

"Magic," Ison breathed.

"Apostates," Reid growled.

"They followed us," Ison said, and Reid knew it was true.

"And they waited until we'd come to a village to attack." Reid started down into the village to put an end to the apostates before lives were lost. "To do the most damage."

Ison didn't hesitate to follow behind.

They collided with the apostates near the middle of town, in the square. The people, thankfully, had fled for safer ground. Reid met the first apostate's blast of air with a ward, and just like he had done with Juniper, he thrust that burst of magic back on the mage. The apostate let out a wail of pain and collapsed. Reid left him there and took on the next.

He repeated his ward's rebound when he could, though he relied more on his sword. Beside him, Ison fought with slices of gray wind, pushing apostates into stone walls, knocking them out but never killing them outright.

And now Reid understood why Ison hesitated to kill—his time spent under Nexon's mind control. He didn't want to kill anyone.

Reid rebounded ice magic onto an apostate, and she let out a gasp of pain. He moved on to the next, but something struck him in the back—hard enough to knock the breath from his throat. His first thought was that Ison had betrayed him, but he found Ison defending him, sending the apostate who'd struck him into a stone building with enough force to leave blood behind.

The earth loosened underneath them, and then they were falling—the earth had opened to a pit, trapping them and a portion of a building inside.

For a moment, silence rang. Reid regained his footing, and Ison groaned as he stumbled to his feet.

Figures appeared at the edge of the pit, looking down. Reid knew in that moment what it felt like to be a mouse trapped between a cat's paws.

Arrows of sharpened air and ice and stone struck at them relentlessly. Reid had his ward and Ison had his magic. The air and ice and stone hit his ward, but it held. Ison's shield of wind protected him and flung the projectiles into the earthen walls. Reid and Ison stood back to back. They were outnumbered fifteen to two, and Reid knew his ward wouldn't hold up for much longer. Sweat lined Ison's brow, and each hit on his wind-shield knocked the air from his chest.

"This can't go on." Each word Reid uttered was strained. An arrow of ice slammed into his ward, right above his heart.

"Then do what I tell you," Ison gasped, his voice raw.

Reid felt a tingle in the air, an intense floral scent underlined with metallic—natural magic and unnatural magic. The wind picked up around them, the grayish color underlined with pale blue. Ison was gathering his magic, and to Reid's disbelief and horror, Juniper's.

"I follow your lead," Reid conceded.

Gray and blue swirled around them, funneling dirt and debris upward. It caught the magic arrows and carried them along the currents. Faster and faster the wind moved, whistling higher and higher.

The apostates readied. Each had raw magic twisting around their hands, in shades of blue, green, red, purple, and colors Reid had never seen. The raw magic stained the air like a flower garden.

"Get down!" Ison screamed.

Reid dropped to the ground.

The magic in the air shattered and crested, and Reid heard it smack into arms and legs and chests and necks, breaking and tearing and ripping. The wind scraped against the side of the pit, flinging rocks and bodies like leaves. Reid remained flat on the ground, even as tiny bits of stone pelted his back. His cloak whipped every which way, shifting as the wind moved.

And then it stopped.

The wind died all at once. Bodies thumped on the stone ground, dozens of them, all limp and lifeless. Reid looked up in time to see Ison fall onto his knees, gasping for breath. Sweat glistened on his brow, and his arms shook.

All the apostates surrounding the pit were gone.

Reid pushed himself onto his hands and knees. He heard scattered fighting above.

"Are you okay?" Ison asked between gasps. He had paled considerably.

"I'm fine." Reid jumped to his feet and pulled Ison onto his. "We need to get out of this pit."

"Here!" called someone from the surface. A bearded man with shoulders like an ox threw a rope into the pit.

Ison wobbled, and Reid lifted the skinny mage and threw him over his shoulder—Ison didn't object. Reid climbed, carrying them both out of the pit, albeit awkwardly. The scene on the other side startled him. Townspeople had returned, bearing swords and shields. The few remaining apostates were now dead or dying. Dead apostates circled the lip of the pit, those Ison's magical attack had killed.

"Is that one all right?" a woman holding a short sword asked of Ison.

"He needs rest," Reid explained quickly. He stood Ison on his feet, but he wobbled too much to let him stand on his own.

"This way," said a familiar voice—the innkeeper. He held a bloodied sword in one hand, and he motioned to Reid with the other. "Lucky we've got some warm beds and leftovers."

Reid guided Ison toward the inn, and he heard the whispers going around. The apostates had attacked after they had showed up. And they had left the village a mess—a crater had swallowed the square and a few homes, and everywhere he looked, he saw damage. How would he explain this?

By the time they returned to the inn, the fighting had subsided. The townspeople had managed to finish off the remaining apostates. Reid helped Ison into a bed. They couldn't travel with Ison in such a state, so Reid left him to rest and went with the innkeeper to inspect the damage. As they surveyed broken walls and iced-over doors, even more guilt weighed on Reid's shoulders. The apostates had followed them here. He had led them to these people.

He took comfort in knowing those apostates were now dead, thanks to Ison.

The townspeople started to gather the bodies. Reid steeled himself. These were the apostates the Order warned against, not apostates like Ison and Juniper. These apostates used magic to harm. Ison had used his to defend.

And Reid understood what Juniper had meant.

He didn't know what it meant for himself, a squire, to be questioning the Marca or the Order. Maybe, when he was a knight with sway over the council, he could make changes to the Marca. Make it a place mages wanted to go.

It was yet another dream on his list, but he had time to think on it. First, he had to save Adrian and become a knight. But before even that, he had to help these people.

Chapter Thirty-One

After breakfast and tea, Juniper and Roslyn packed for their journey. Roslyn talked about the northern parts of Galamond, the dangers of hungry bears and packs of wolves and the rare mosscat.

"Though mosscats generally leave us alone." Roslyn was going through the closets of the house. Juniper sat on the bed of the main bedroom—the one Roslyn had commandeered for her own. "They're crazy smart, mosscats."

"No bandits?" Juniper asked.

"Only incredibly foolish bandits would travel this far north." Roslyn winked at Juniper. "Let alone mess with me."

Yes, Juniper liked Roslyn. Adrian had been right.

Fynilli oversaw the servants and stable hands as they readied a covered sleigh and two horses. As their supplies were packed into the trunk, Roslyn explained how the horses were a special Galamond breed—their coats were thicker, more woolly than their southern cousins, their legs were shorter but thicker, and their tolerance for the cold was high.

"They're as smart as any other horse, though," Roslyn said quietly, behind her hand, as though the horses might overhear.

The sleigh had the oddest shape. It looked like an upside down boat. The wooden sides were long and slightly curved, made to protect the driver from the cold winds and also to guide the winds and snow along. The runners curved at the front and the back into decorative knots. According to Roslyn, the snow didn't pile on the sleigh's angled roof, it slid right off the polished sides.

Standing outside, waiting for the servants to pack the sleigh, Juniper got her first glimpse of the town. The buildings were stone and wood with vaulted roofs and puffing chimneys. A layer of snow covered the stone roads, and a fresh layer floated from the overcast sky. In every direction, the snowy pines stretched into the gray-white nothingness. In the far north, she thought she could see the outline of distant mountains, stretching nearly to the sky.

That's where they were headed. The edge of the realm.

Her skin prickled with the unknown. Anything could be lurking beyond humanity's reach.

The inside of the sleigh was smaller than Juniper anticipated, though she imagined the thick walls protected from the cold. The three of them climbed inside, Fynilli and Roslyn on one side, Juniper on the other. With their furs and leathers, the space felt smaller still. The sleigh set off at a good pace, gliding along the snowy path.

They passed the time with talk, and though the destination worried her, Juniper enjoyed the ride. She and Roslyn spoke about Adrian, about how Roslyn had met him, and Juniper's adventure into the castle.

It took two days to arrive in Bushue, a village so similar to Oriel, Juniper thought they'd made a circle. The mountains to the north loomed closer and clearer than before, piercing the clouds.

They rested and shared a warm meal at the king's house—a smaller version of the house in Oriel. The servants happily relayed news and happenings to Roslyn. When they boarded the sleigh the next morning, Roslyn jotted down what the people had told her into a leather-bound journal.

"When I go out into the kingdom, people tell me things, I write them down, and I take them back to my father or to my uncle," Roslyn explained. "There are no steady lines of communication between provinces, especially between these outlying towns and the royal city. It's not the most effective, but it works."

Their journey north slowed due to a snowstorm. Bits of ice pelted the side of the sleigh, but the horses kept going.

"There's not much else this far north," Roslyn said. "A few little villages, but nothing more than a few hundred people."

With no windows in the sleigh, the few glimpses Juniper had of the countryside came during their brief stops in those small villages to water the horses and themselves. Mountains rose on every horizon, and the clouds swirled with snow. The people were as sturdy as the mountains, undeterred by the cold and bundled in well-used furs.

Finally, they reached a tiny village nestled in a grove of ancient pines. Roslyn climbed out of the sleigh first, followed by Juniper. The pines grew thicker than most houses and taller than any trees Juniper had ever seen. She craned her neck to see the top but couldn't. They seemed to reach the clouds. The village was laden with snow and built to withstand the worst of it. The roofs were sharply pitched, the chimneys puffed smoke that vanished through the pines, and Juniper could see trapdoors on every roof.

"Welcome to Halsig," Roslyn said. "The last settlement to the north."

"Why are there trap doors on the roofs?"

"So if the snow piles to the roof, the people can still get out," Roslyn said simply.

The idea of snow piling that high daunted Juniper, but as fluffy white flakes began to fall in earnest, she understood. By the time they found the small inn, secured their horses in the stable, and gotten a room big enough for the three of them, the snow had accumulated halfway to her knees. There was no king's house in Halsig because it would never get used. Roslyn didn't seem upset by it. They sat in the inn and talked to the villagers who had come to share a meal and speak with Lady Roslyn.

Like the people in Oriel and Bushue, the people of Halsig told Roslyn about the town and its people, and she remembered it all to write down later.

No one asked about Juniper or Fynilli, beyond that they traveled with Lady Roslyn. The crowd chatted and laughed, and the entire inn glowed with a certain kind of merriment, the kind that came from a warm hearth and a cold night. Roslyn sat listening to a few woodsmen talk of the surrounding wilderness, and Fynilli leaned over to whisper to Juniper.

"Meals are traditionally shared in Galamond," she said. "To eat alone is considered a form of shame."

"I've eaten plenty of meals alone," Juniper said.

"As have I," Fynilli said.

"How did they do it? Your people?" She didn't want to say Iluvin in case someone overheard. She didn't know how these people felt about magic, and she didn't want to find out.

"The midday meal was always shared," Fynilli explained. "The early hours of the day were considered sacred, a time for reflection and silence. Many meditated before the day started."

"I've never been a morning person," Juniper admitted. "I suppose that comes from a lifetime of spending my nights thieving and spending my mornings sleeping."

Fynilli offered a glare of disapproval. After a moment, she said, "My people were strict when it came to the law. If you were caught red-handed, you would have faced death."

"The higher the risk, the more fun it is," Juniper said, and she meant it.

Fynilli frowned.

"I always loved coming back to the keep to see everyone's faces when I pulled off the impossible heist or the job no one thought I could do."

"You seem to make doing the impossible a habit."

"How so?"

"You have set your sights on a plant which might not exist that grows in the harshest corner of the world. Next you plan to take on an enemy who intends to conquer the realm and who has once before."

Juniper considered it. "I suppose I do."

❄

Throughout the meal, Juniper felt her kernel of magic shiver and tug. If she focused, she could feel movement on the other end of the thread. Her friends were coming. They would meet again, find Boxel's Grace, and return to Rusdasin as heroes. Or Reid would. Rusdasin would never see her as a hero.

After dinner, they returned to their hearth-warmed room. Roslyn and Juniper shared the larger bed while Fynilli took the smaller one. Juniper didn't mind. She liked having a friend, and this way she and Roslyn could still whisper without waking Fynilli.

"Did your father really blindfold you and leave you in the woods for your sixteenth birthday?" Juniper whispered.

Roslyn chuckled. "He did. Adrian told you that story?"

"Just that part."

"My father told me he had a surprise for me and I couldn't see it. He blindfolded me, and we rode out. I kept thinking about what it could be, maybe a fine horse or a new dress or a house or something worth having in the woods. Then we got to the woods, and he took the blindfold and...nothing. We were in the middle of the woods." Roslyn's eyes glittered like fresh ink in the muted hearth light. "He handed me a knife and told me I had three days to find my way back home."

"That's it? He didn't offer you a prize for incentive?"

"Surviving was his idea of incentive," Roslyn said. "He isn't the most nurturing of human beings. That's Mother's role, but she never objected to Father's ideas. He thought this would be a prime experience for me, and he was a great father for allowing me the chance. Regardless, I followed the stars and used the knife he gave me to set traps for game. I slept under the pines, in shallow caves, and made it back in two and a half days. Then Father took me to the dressmaker in town."

Juniper still thought it a feat. "I don't see how anyone can survive out there for that long."

"You got caught in a blizzard," Roslyn explained. "Storms out here can last for weeks. I lucked out and had clear nights. I don't want to think what might have happened if it had stormed. But tell me about the Undercity. Adrian only mentioned it. What is it? What happens there? Who lives there?"

Juniper told Roslyn about the Undercity, everything she wanted to know.

Talking like this, whispering through the darkness, it reminded her of the days when she and Amery would stay up and talk about anything and everything while the keep slept around them. It made her feel like a girl again, without the world on her shoulders.

"Do you have anyone?" Roslyn asked after a short silence.

"What do you mean?"

"Anyone waiting for you, a lover?"

Juniper's silence weighed. "No."

Roslyn turned her head toward her, the blink of her eyes the only movement. "You hesitated. Do you?"

"I did, but I don't anymore," Juniper said. Saying it out loud still hurt. It pinched that heartbroken wound. "It's complicated."

Roslyn rolled onto her side, facing her. "What happened?"

"Do you really want to talk about boys?"

"Isn't that a hot topic for girls these days?"

Juniper smiled. "He... I met him while I was at the castle."

"Oh?" Roslyn's tone held her smile.

"He was—I mean, he is—a squire."

"Oh." Roslyn's smile faded.

"And I'm a mage. He didn't know at first. He found out, and hated me for it."

"What happened to him?"

Juniper chuckled. "He got sent on a quest to retrieve Boxel's Grace."

Roslyn blinked. "Reid?"

Juniper nodded. Realizing Roslyn couldn't see it, she said, "Yes."

"I've never met him, but Adrian talked about him a good deal and mentioned him in his letters. They're good friends." Roslyn paused, chewing on the words. "From what I've heard, he seems like a good man."

"He is," Juniper said, her voice small. "One of the best I've ever met.

Honorable to a fault, loyal to the Order and his friends, and his sense of humor shows it."

Roslyn hummed. "I'm sorry it didn't work out. Love is great when it works, but it feels like pins in the chest when it doesn't. I fell in love a few years ago with a boy from the royal city. He worked for my uncle, a lord's son. He was charming and handsome, but it was a show. He was a rotten human being to the core, and he tossed me aside when a girl with higher status came along. I didn't see his ugly side until then, and I felt foolish for it. I was too absorbed in his attention because someone was paying attention to me and I wanted to feel loved.

"Because of him, when I met Adrian, I thought him the same. I pushed his flirtations aside, but he persisted. He was beyond sweet, but I thought it a ruse." Roslyn giggled. "He won me over in the end."

"Adrian doesn't have an ugly side."

Roslyn inhaled and released it slowly—the sigh of a girl in love. "The point of that story was that each heartbreak sets you up for the next, and each prepares you for the real thing." She turned her head toward Juniper. "Yours will come along. At least, that's what Mother said."

Juniper didn't answer, mostly because she didn't believe it.

Chapter Thirty-Two

Breakfast in Galamond, unlike dinner, was quiet. The crowd was somber, but Juniper didn't complain. She would rather drink her tea without commotion. The three of them sat at a table by themselves. A few villagers had come for a meal, but the air remained subdued.

The innkeeper added a log to the hearth, sending a wave of embers swirling into the air.

They spent the day gathering information. No one else had passed through Halsig, which meant they had arrived before the others. Juniper couldn't imagine just waiting around for them to show, so she took to wandering through the small town.

According to an old woman whose son ran the smithy, nomads once passed through on their way to the summit—called the Crown—an ancient and sacred place. No maps of the Crown existed. The old woman drew a map in the snow with her walking stick, not of the Crown, but of the mountain trail that wound up the Dolomin Mountains.

Juniper memorized the map, the words the old woman said, and when Roslyn went to visit with the elders in town, she wandered through the village. People shoveled snow from the streets, chopped wood, and hauled water. Juniper found a quiet place just outside the village and dusted the snow from a fallen pine. She concentrated, feeling her magic, feeble and trembling. She commanded the snow into a perfect ball at her feet. She released her breath. That single task had taken much of her energy.

"Wow," came a small squeak of a voice.

Juniper turned. Standing behind her was a little boy, no older than six. His heavy clothes made his limbs puffy and hard to move, yet he shuffled to where Juniper sat. He looked at the snowball with wide eyes.

Within those eyes, she saw fear. And wonder.

"Do you want to make a snowman?" Juniper asked.

He looked at the ball, then her. He nodded.

Juniper gathered snow again and added it to the snowball she had made, forming the base. The little boy stood in wonder, but he didn't step closer. Juniper set a second ball on the first, then the head.

"There, the body is done," she said. "We need stones for the eyes and mouth. Do you know where we could find stones?"

He started through the trees, and Juniper followed. He led her to a narrow stream with ice at its edges. Along the bank, the two of them gathered little dark stones. Juniper picked the boy up to let him place the eyes, the nose, and the mouth.

"There," Juniper said. "Do you think he needs a name?"

The boy nodded.

"What do you think about Herald?"

The boy shook his head.

"Gerald?"

Smiling, the boy shook his head faster.

"...Carl?"

The boy laughed. "It's a girl," he said, his voice small and dry.

"Oh!" Juniper said, pretending embarrassment. "Geraldine?"

The boy giggled, then nodded.

Juniper and the boy walked back into the village, where a woman met them, looking a bit frantic. "Oh!" The woman placed her hand over her heart at the sight of the boy. "I turned around, and you were gone."

"My apologies," Juniper said. "I didn't realize he was missing."

The woman waved off her concern. "I went to have Merle hammer out a few buttons, and he wandered off." She motioned for the boy's hand, and he placed his tiny glove in hers. Kindly, she asked the boy, "What were you two doing that was more important than buttons?"

The woman started to lean up, then the boy squeaked, "We made a snowman, but it's a girl."

The woman blinked at the boy like he'd said something horrible.

"Her name is Geraldine," added Juniper.

"Is it now?" said the woman, her face locked in blank surprise.

"Is there something wrong?" Juniper asked.

"Oh, no, no. Nothing at all. Let's take a look at Geraldine, shall we?" She flashed Juniper a smile that did not hide her surprise.

The boy tugged her through the village toward the snowman. Juniper remained behind.

"I'll be damned," came a gruff voice.

Juniper turned to see the blacksmith standing in the door of his smithy, apron burned and stained. A maul rested over his shoulders. Unlike most others, he wore a heavy woolen tunic that left his upper arms bare.

Soot smeared and spotted almost every inch of him. His coal-dark eyes followed the boy and the woman.

"Did I do something wrong?" Juniper asked.

The blacksmith blinked, and his bushy blond brows rose. "Gods no. That boy there? He and his parents went to visit his father's family down south. We don't know what happened, but about a month later, a merchant shows up with the boy. Says his parents were dead. The boy hasn't said a word since."

Juniper blinked after the woman and the boy. They'd vanished from sight.

"His aunt tried everything, but I guess you had something she didn't." The blacksmith shrugged and started back into his smithy.

Juniper and her companions spent two days in Halsig, waiting on the others. Juniper spent her time helping around the village. It helped take her mind off her lack of magic. It felt like a hole in her chest, one she desperately needed to fill. She could feel the strings that tied her kernels of magic together, and she felt those strings shorten as the others came closer. It was a strange feeling. Although she felt strings, she couldn't tell them apart.

During dinner on the second day, a villager burst into the inn. "We've got three strangers arriving. Travelers by the look. You got enough?"

"I've got plenty," said the innkeeper, who looked thrilled at the prospect of so many visitors.

Juniper's heart jumped up into her throat. She had felt the pulsing of her magic grow, and she had hoped it meant the others were close. Three strangers. Reid, Ison, and Penet. And her heart plummeted into her gut. Had they not found Henry and Isaac?

The door to the inn opened, and Juniper jumped to her feet, nearly tripping. Roslyn stood with her. Fynilli remained seated, though she looked grave. Juniper couldn't take her eyes off the door. The pulsing of her magic had grown into a maddening beat.

Isaac entered the inn first, his face rosy from cold. Snow dusted his cloak. His eyes found hers across the inn, and though his eyes widened, he didn't look surprised to see her. Three strangers—two remained unknown. A dark-skinned young man she didn't recognize followed Isaac inside—Henry Julian, likely. Her heart began to race, and then the final traveler entered.

It was Penet. His eyes met Juniper's. He stopped dead in his tracks and went white as a ghost.

Juniper crossed the room without feeling her feet move. She stopped in front of Penet, who looked nearly sick. "Where are they?" she breathed.

Henry stepped closer to Penet, hand resting casually on the pommel of his blade. He looked her up and down. "Look at that," Henry said in a voice that would have otherwise been well-humored. "I half expected you to be a myth."

Juniper didn't take her eyes off Penet. His cheeks flushed.

She said again, louder and more firmly, "Where are they?"

Penet bit his lip.

"Where are Reid and Ison?" she begged.

Penet didn't answer. His terror only worsened her own. A firm hand landed on her shoulder. Isaac appeared at her side, pulling her attention from Penet.

And it was Isaac's grim expression that made her stomach fall into her knees. He gave her shoulder a gentle squeeze. "After a warm meal and something to drink," he said, his voice dry and hoarse, "we will tell you the story."

Juniper started to protest, but Roslyn appeared on her other side. Her hands folded around Juniper's arm.

"That sounds like a fair deal," Roslyn said to Isaac.

❄

After the meal—which took too long, for Juniper's insides quivered and her hands shook—Juniper and Roslyn retreated to the mens' room at the inn. Fynilli did not join them. She gave no reason, but Juniper suspected it had everything to do with the Order.

"Lady Derean." Isaac bowed his head. "It is an honor to finally meet you. I am Sir Isaac Pinul of the Order of the Knighthood."

"Pleasure," said Roslyn, her tone crisp and short. "But save the formalities for later."

Isaac did not hold in his surprise at her brashness.

"Roslyn knows everything," Juniper added.

"I thought this was supposed to be a secret quest?" Henry plopped down on one of the beds.

"Where are Reid and Ison?" Juniper repeated. The question had rattled around in her mind since they had refused to tell her the first time. She clenched her fists in her tunic.

Silence thickened enough to suffocate.

Isaac stepped closer to Juniper, his grim expression set. "While traveling through the mountains, we crossed a narrow pass overlooking a valley." Isaac's eyes hardened. His throat bobbed as he swallowed. "The pass crumbled under our feet. Reid and Ison did not make it across."

Juniper felt the color drain from her face.

"They went with the landside," Isaac said. "We could not get to them. It was too far below."

Juniper felt the floor shift under her feet, jutting sideways. Roslyn grabbed her arm and held her steady, though the room still wobbled.

"There is little chance they survived," said Isaac. "Even if the fall somehow didn't kill them, the beasts of the mountains would have. I am sorry."

Penet said something else, but she didn't hear it. The world wobbled dangerously, and she felt her breakfast coming back up. She started to lean forward, and someone pushed her back onto one of the beds. Juniper buried her head in her hands and squeezed her eyes shut.

No. No. No. It couldn't be possible. Not Reid. Not Ison.

Warm hands graced her shoulders, but she couldn't hear what they mumbled. It all faded behind the gushing of blood through her ears and the tremors that wracked her body.

Roslyn helped Juniper into their room. Fynilli spoke, but her words jumbled. Juniper collapsed onto the bed, and the sobs started. She buried her face in the pillow, and a warm hand rested on the center of her back, warm and comforting. Roslyn didn't speak. She didn't demand an explanation. She remained—a presence should Juniper need one.

Juniper had never been more thankful for silence—she couldn't speak if she wanted to. Words were lost to her mind, her heart, her mouth.

Reid and Ison, gone. Both of them, in a heartbeat.

And she hadn't been able to do anything.

CHAPTER THIRTY-THREE

Amery disentangled herself from Maddox and washed up in her private bathing room—another thing she refused to share. The mages could have the rest of the manor, but her bedroom and her bathing room were hers. And currently, Maddox's. Amery dressed as quietly as she could. As she tied up her boots, Maddox sighed and rolled onto his back. The silken sheets shifted over his bare shoulders, but he did not wake.

Dawn hadn't yet broken. Most of the mages were sleeping. Somber breathing filled the manor. The pale light of a low burning lantern shaded her bedroom, but most of it remained in shadow.

Amery had scouts on every side of the manor every hour of the day. They would not be caught off guard. Since Captain Tinnly had demonstrated his distrust of Nera, Amery didn't trust him. Not that she had to begin with.

She meandered through the house, her footsteps as light as a cat's. Dim dawn light filtered through the windows, illuminating the gathering dust motes. The house reeked of magic now, florals and tangy metallics. She found Xavier in the kitchen, hoisting himself up on the doorway.

"Why here, of all places?" Amery asked.

"It's quiet," Xavier said shortly.

He had healed well, considering. According to the healer, his cut hadn't been very deep. The poison had knocked him down for a few days, and he had hated it. Josephine ended up drugging his food to get him to sleep through his recovery—or else he would have driven the healers mad and reopened his wounds.

Amery waited. Finally, Xavier dropped to the floor, sweat shimmering on his brow and along his neck.

"I'm going on a little scouting mission," Amery said. "Want to tag along?"

Xavier considered it. "Is it a real mission or an excuse to get away from your new beau?"

She didn't miss the slight bitterness in his words. Thanks to their new living space, her affair with Maddox was no longer a secret. Especially since he slept in her room.

182

"You can sleep in the middle if you'd like," Amery said. "Or I'll sleep in the lounge, and you can have my place."

Xavier growled at her.

"Now come on, I want to be gone before people wake up," Amery snapped. She started toward the larder, and Xavier followed.

They were in the tunnel, Amery's lantern illuminating their path, when Xavier spoke again. "It's not that you're sleeping with him. It's that I didn't know."

"Ah," Amery said. "You're mad you didn't see the signs? You didn't miss anything. I'm just good at keeping secrets."

He huffed. "What are we scouting?"

"I want to see what chaos has consumed the Undercity." She said the word lightly. Of course, Xavier caught what she hadn't said.

"And?"

Amery hesitated to voice the second. "I also want to see where that monster came from."

"Why?"

Amery didn't have a good reason why. She just did. Those monsters were vile and fascinating in the worst way.

"Juniper said Nexon made several of those monsters." A note of fear leaked into Xavier's words. "I'd rather not run into any more of those things."

"I've got my dagger." Amery patted her side. She kept the Mage's Bane blade on her person at all times. She had looked into procuring another blade or two, but the knights kept their Mage's Bane with them or locked up, and the Order was harder to break into than the tightest bank vault. Ridiculously hard, but not impossible.

Juniper would have been able to do it. While Amery considered herself talented, she was not Juniper.

They reached the fork—one tunnel led to Josephine's, and the other led to the Dual Fangs' keep. The tunnel entrances had been hidden, but Amery would rather not run into any City Watch.

"Which way?" Amery asked. Xavier knew sneaking better than she.

"Josephine's," he said.

The tunnel to Josephine's led into a storeroom, to the false back of a cabinet. Xavier stalked to the false back and listened, while Amery stayed out of sight with the lantern. He deemed it safe, opened the false panel, and stepped through. Amery reached into her pocket and pulled out a crystal Josephine had given her a few days earlier. A rune inscribed on the crystal to make it glow when it touched skin. Josephine had called it a mage stone. As Amery closed her fingers around it, a soft yellowish white glow emitted from the stone. Unlike the lantern, she could drop the stone in her pocket and douse the light, then touch it again to rekindle it. Easier for sneaking through a darkened Undercity. She set the dark lantern on the ground just inside the tunnel and followed Xavier through.

Without the mages, the magelights no longer glowed. The Undercity had gone dark. Amery's mage stone served as their only light. She kept her fist around it, keeping their light to a minimum.

Josephine's keep felt haunted without the mages and their chatter and magic practice. Xavier crept through the darkened halls to the front door, and if the keep had been unsettling, it was nothing compared to the rest of the Undercity.

It felt like a cavern, lonesome and empty. The usual sounds of life had gone, leaving a deathly chill in its place. The space felt too large and too small at once, and Amery did not care for it. And the smell. The dank mineral-thick air reeked of blood and death. A smattering of voices came from the direction of the market, and as Xavier and Amery crept through the dark streets, they saw that the City Watch had set up their command center at the fountain—the heart of the Undercity. Dozens of candles burned, lighting their camp.

Sneaking around the City Watch camp was easy with so many shadows. Xavier led them into the outskirts of the Undercity, to the smaller, rundown homes.

"This is it." He gestured to an unremarkable house, voice dark.

He let himself in, and Amery followed close behind. Inside, she let the mage stone glow brighter. Xavier led her into the back room, where a woven rug adorned the floor. Xavier lifted it. Someone or something had carved a hole in the ground. It angled for easy climbing and vanished into darkness.

"Oh, that looks inviting," Amery whispered. "You first."

"Why me?"

"Because you have magic," she said firmly.

Xavier growled his annoyance and summoned twin daggers of charcoal magic. He started into the hole first, and Amery and her glowing stone followed a step behind. She held the stone with one hand and gripped her Mage's Bane hilt with the other. The tunnel angled down, down, down, and ended not in a sewer but in a chamber.

"What is this?" Xavier whispered.

Amery stretched her fingers out, letting the stone's light flood the room. They stood in an ancient chamber. The ceiling domed, and five hallways stretched into darkness, their archways carved with delicate swirls and runes.

"Jun mentioned ruins," Amery whispered. She didn't want to speak too loudly in this strange place.

Xavier crept around the chamber and paused by the fourth hallway. He motioned to the floor. "This way."

The dust had been disturbed by claws. Xavier and Amery shared a glance. Neither wanted to meet another monster in these cramped dark ruins.

They followed the hall and the claw marks in the dust. The ruins were silent. The hall opened into a large empty chamber. A few steps in, the light spread over the chamber, and they realized it was not empty.

There, carved into the floor, was a rune. It was more complicated than any rune Amery had ever seen, lines and whorls that curved and bent. It was a maddening pattern to follow. Scattered on the edges of the chamber were bones, human by the looks of the skulls and ribs. Several of those bones looked fresh. A few looked old, darkened sinew and tendons.

Xavier knelt by the rune, drawing her attention away from the bones. She saw what he saw—the rune had been stained red.

"Blood," she whispered.

Xavier used the pommel of his dagger to scratch at the trench. Blood flaked. "It's dry."

Xavier glanced up at her, and she knew they had arrived at the same conclusion. That monster had been made here, likely by the apostate, Nexon.

"What do you think this means?" Amery whispered.

Xavier didn't answer at first. He looked around the chamber and made a slow lap, staying away from the rune and the bones. "I think whoever was here isn't here any longer. Or they haven't been here since that monster joined the City Watch invasion."

"We should get back," Amery said, mostly because she didn't want to be here anymore.

Xavier didn't object, and the two of them started back toward the Undercity. They snuck past the City Watch with ease. Their patrols carried obvious torches, visible a dozen streets away in the dark, and Amery and Xavier stole back into the tunnels.

Amery didn't like the implication that Nexon was still making those monsters. She knew what went into one—Ison had told them. But why? With the prince poisoned, he didn't need a monster to harm him. And, she reminded herself, the monster had not gone to the castle. It had gone to the Undercity. The only reason she could think of was to cause panic. As good a reason as any madman, she supposed.

Still, Josephine needed to know.

CHAPTER THIRTY-FOUR

Juniper spent the next day in bed, refusing to talk to anyone. Roslyn brought her tea and sat with her for a while. She didn't say anything, and for that, Juniper was thankful. She couldn't fathom it, the endless pain in her chest that dulled into a gripping ache.

Gone. Just like that.

She spent the day in a daze, retreating into the nothingness, away from anything and everything. If she didn't feel at all, she couldn't feel pain or loss or anger.

She could feel the kernel of magic inside Penet, so close to her, it had calmed. A thread linked her to it, to him, and if she focused, she could feel the other two, but they were weak. She didn't know how to take the kernel back from Penet. She didn't know if it would hurt him or not or if he knew what she had done. If she took it now, in front of the others, would they think it black magic?

Roslyn returned, but she didn't bring tea. "Sir Pinul wants to know if you are up to joining us for dinner," she asked carefully. "He wants to talk about the journey ahead."

The journey ahead. To the edge of the realm. To save Adrian.

Juniper gathered her strength and pushed herself to a sitting position. Roslyn stood dutifully at the bedside, but she stood like a queen, not a nursemaid. She held her hands gracefully in front of her, her shoulders straight and unmoving, her expression kind but stern.

"I'll go," Juniper said, the first words she had spoken that day.

She washed and found the others around a table in the main room. At her arrival, the conversation hushed, and she did her best to ignore it. She sat down beside Penet, but the silence remained.

"We need to plan our final move," Isaac said to Juniper.

Juniper told them about the old woman who had drawn her a map and the old nomad road that would take them there. It was not a long journey, but it wasn't an easy one. She told them what Roslyn had told her about the edge of the world being a sacred place. Isaac was undeterred. Sacred place or no, they would attempt it.

They ate, drank, and returned to their rooms for one last comfortable night. They would set out in the morning. Juniper didn't sleep. The night came and went in fitful tosses and turns.

Morning came under a pale blue sky and puffy clouds.

"Be safe." Roslyn's eyes drifted to the looming mountain, to where the Garden of the Gods supposedly lay. She and Fynilli would remain in Halsig.

"We will return." Juniper promised Roslyn. She held her hand out to the other girl. "We will save Adrian."

Roslyn knocked Juniper's hand aside and embraced her tightly. Juniper hugged her back.

Juniper secured the latch on her satchel and climbed onto a horse with Penet. There was no other horse to spare, and the travelers only had their own. Penet's hand landed on her waist, a steady weight.

Roslyn stood on the inn's step and waved.

Isaac led the way through the pine forest, steadily north, toward the looming mountains.

"You don't have to mourn alone," Penet said after a time.

She kept silent. She feared that if she spoke, it would be a sob. Her tears would likely freeze to her skin in this weather.

"We will mourn once we return." Penet lifted his hand from her waist to hold the reins. "Together. We will mourn those lost."

She tightened her gloved fingers into fists. She didn't want to think about Reid or Ison or anything but the quest ahead.

So she didn't.

❄

The trek north became treacherous. The snow drifted twenty feet in some places, burying entire trees where the pines didn't block the wind. The gusts seeped between the seams of their furs and leathers and wools. The path wound through the pines and around rocks and rose steadily higher and higher until Juniper could look back and see the dots of the houses of Halsig, the silvery smoke nearly the same color as the snow.

The mountain path rose and fell and twisted and turned and dipped. Higher still they climbed until the air thinned and the clouds swirled above their heads. The wind howled against the rocks, sounding like a thousand different voices of warning. The pines became fewer and fewer. The cold persisted.

They reached the peak of one mountain, and Juniper's breath left her in a gasp that Penet soon mirrored. Before them, mountains stretched to the horizon, as far as she could see, rising higher into the clouds, their peaks vanishing on the other side. To the horizon, all was rock and ice.

The edge of the world.

Isaac led the way down the first mountain and toward the next. Penet followed behind, and Henry came after. They made their way slowly through the mountains, riding steadily higher and higher until Juniper could reach up and touch the bottom of the clouds. She had never touched clouds before, and she had always imagined them like steam. These clouds were not steam—they were frigid, like air packed with ice. She felt the ice in the air, hovering in the sky, the clouds. Her seed of magic responded. She imagined herself commanding the skies, swirling the clouds together into an impenetrable ice storm.

If she had all of her magic, could she?

The path straightened, but it rose up and up—it vanished into the clouds along with the mountain they climbed.

Isaac and his horse went first, and Juniper held her breath as he vanished through the clouds. Yet his horse's hooves still clomped on the stone.

She blew out a breath as she and Penet approached the cloud ceiling. A thousand tiny pinpricks of ice kissed her face, and she squeezed her eyes shut until the sensation passed.

When she opened them, the sight took her breath away.

The sky above them was priceless blue, and it stretched all around them. Below them, a sea of clouds swirled with the motion of the horses. The mountains rose above the clouds, rising to ice-capped peaks.

"Gods," Penet breathed. His voice carried strangely on this side of the clouds.

It felt like too much sound and too quiet at the same time, and she understood Roslyn's desire to remain in the world of the living. For this world truly felt like another. A world reserved for the gods and the dead. The end of the human realm.

The horses climbed higher along the mountains, leaving the sea of roiling clouds below. Juniper couldn't take it in fast enough, the sky, the clouds, the mountains. It felt beyond otherworldly. She was glad she didn't ride alone. Penet reminded her she hadn't crossed into the world of the dead just yet.

Isaac led the way through the mountains, around boulders that did not look naturally made—their spherical shape was too perfect to have been formed by nature, and their placement at the turns in the path were too coincidental. Remnants of the nomad's path that ushered humans to the otherworld. The path wound through the peaks, through winding open stretches where the wind threatened to sweep them off the mountain, and under ancient archways of perfectly placed stones.

"Those could only have been placed by magic," Penet whispered as they passed under an archway.

That meant mages once lived here, or they had once carved this road from the mountain thousands of years ago. The age of it chilled her more than the frigid wind coming down from the ice caps.

They trekked for the better part of the day, and as the light started to fade from the sky, Isaac called for camp. They found a little nook in the side of the mountain, next to a clear stream that had long ago carved its way through the rock, and silently set up camp.

Juniper couldn't keep her eyes off the sky. The sun pulled the pale blue to the west, streaking purples, pinks, and yellows across the sky like she had never seen. Of all the sunsets she had witnessed, none could compare to the beauty of this one.

Within the nook, they had no need for tents and bundled themselves in furs and wool. They set their bedrolls close to fit within the cramped space, and Juniper could feel the breathing of Penet on one side and Isaac on the other. Henry snored slightly.

She slept little. The sun never truly set, and the world remained in a dreamy and terrifying perpetual twilight.

When the sun brightened the other side of the sky, they set out again. The sunrise mirrored the sunset. Blossom pink, buttery yellow, and lilac streaked the sky, growing brighter with every heartbeat. The stars blinked out one by one. The mountaintops were strangely absent of sound and life, although more than once, Juniper thought she heard a strange call on the wind, a roar unlike anything she had ever heard, distant and close all at once. Each time, Penet's breath hitched. He heard it too.

The wind, she told herself—the wind whistling through the crevasses.

Her mind drifted to the beasts Roslyn had warned her about, the legendary beasts guarding the garden. Would they have to fight for the plant? Reid had been the best fighter among them, and without him to watch her back, she felt vulnerable. Of course, she hadn't seen Penet or Henry fight. They had received the same training as Reid.

The kernel of magic within Penet tugged at her own. She would find the time to take back her magic from Penet. Traveling over narrow mountain roads over unknown heights was not the time.

If she followed the other threads, would it lead her to Reid's body? The thought sent a shiver down her back and heat to her eyes. Penet's hand moved around her middle, securing her against him.

The mountain road rose and curved around peaks and bluffs, sculpted rocks and magicked formations, each larger than the last. Among the carvings, ruins appeared, abandoned thousands of years ago, carved with faded runes and forgotten calligraphy and glyphs.

The road slowly widened. They passed through a tunnel carved from the mountain, covering them entirely in shadow. Before them, the only proof of an end was a pinprick of light. They walked on, hooves echoing against the stone. The tunnel opened up to a grand archway, and through it, a ruined city that time had long forgotten.

The stone ground smoothed into a circular courtyard, walled by stone pillars and a wall of perfectly laid stones. At the far side of the courtyard, wide stairs led up to the forgotten city. On either side of the stairs, clear water flowed through channels around the courtyard and vanished into small holes in the ground. Juniper could hear the trickle as the water flowed down.

What people had once called this place home? This stone city nestled in the highest of the mountains?

Penet steered his horse toward the stairs, but halfway across the courtyard, his horse shrieked and jumped back. Penet gasped and clutched the reins in one hand and Juniper with the other. A heartbeat later, Henry's horse gave the same objection—the horses would go no further.

"We are on foot from here," Isaac announced, his voice louder and soft in the strange silence.

"Just leave the horses here?" Henry asked.

"Doesn't this look familiar?" Isaac slid off the saddle. He guided his horse to the side of the courtyard, between the pillars. "This is an ancient stable."

Juniper blinked—she could see it. The pillars, the walls, the water trough, the remains of a roof. She slid from the saddle and stood while the others tied off their horses and gathered what they needed from the saddlebags. Juniper glanced up to the city. How long had it been since humans dared enter?

She started up the stairs slowly. Juniper walked through one of the few remaining archways—the stones had been carved with runes, some of which looked vaguely familiar. They were not the simple runes taught by the Marca, but the old runes, complicated and expertly carved.

191

They looked similar to the runes carved in the ruins below Castle Bradburn. Were the people who once called this ruin home connected to the people who had once lived in that ruin?

The others caught up with her, and together they started into the forgotten city. Most of the buildings were one or two rooms and constructed with stones fitting perfectly together. Juniper didn't see any mortar, only stone. They might have been homes. Each had narrow holes for windows and a cold hearth. Every building she looked into was empty. No sign of the life that had once existed here, no remains of treasure hunters or adventurers.

Only stone and ghosts.

CHAPTER THIRTY-FIVE

Their echoing footsteps made it sound as if an army walked behind them. Her breathing sounded far too loud, felt too warm on her lips. She doubted even she could be silent in this place, as skilled a thief she was. By the cautious, worried looks on the others' faces, they felt it too.

Juniper didn't see anything she would call a garden. She assumed the Garden of the Gods would be thriving with plants. What if it wasn't?

Ahead, a mountain rose. The rockface loomed over the city. She assumed that to be their destination. She saw nothing else remotely interesting in the forgotten city. If she were designing the Crown of the World, she would make it as obvious and glorious as possible.

Finally, they came to what once had been a plaza. An long-dry old fountain stood at the intersection of four streets.

"That way looks suspect." Penet nodded across the plaza. The street directly across from them seemed to lead onward to the mountain.

This close, they could see that something had been built high into the rockface. What looked to be a path snaked from the temple, down the mountainside, and out of sight.

"A temple?" whispered Henry.

"There is one way to find out," said Isaac.

Juniper didn't dare speak. She didn't want to hear her own voice in this strange air. She followed a step behind Isaac. Penet walked beside her, as any honorable and dutiful squire would. He would make a fine knight too.

Each of them walked with a hand on their sword. Juniper kept hers on her dagger. Just because her magic dwindled didn't mean she would go down without a fight. She had been fighting without magic nearly her entire life. She'd just have to do it again.

And she didn't need her magic to feel the things moving about on the other side of the plaza. They were not alone. Her instincts screamed it at her. Things were moving, always just out of sight, always gone by the time her eyes moved. They were being watched and followed, she knew it.

She detected movement ahead at the same time Penet did, but she saw nothing there. Penet gave a sharp intake of breath as though he had seen something, but he didn't say anything. Maybe, like her, things moved just out of sight.

The houses on this side of the city were larger and more elaborate than those near the entrance. Higher society. Juniper was looking at a two story stone house with what looked like a waterwheel on its roof when Isaac stopped dead in his tracks.

Penet gasped and halted, and Juniper's attention snapped. It didn't take her long to see why.

"Gods," Penet gasped. His hand tightened on his sword.

Up ahead, peeking out at them from a doorway, was a white and gray dire wolf. Her heart tumbled into her throat and stayed there. The wolf blinked, its black eyes wide and unrelenting.

"I don't think it likes us in its home," Henry whispered.

"What is—" breathed Penet.

"Dire wolf," Juniper answered.

"Shh," said Isaac.

Juniper sucked in her breath. It couldn't possibly be the same dire wolf she had rescued, who had saved her from those slavers, could it? The dire wolf took a step into the street, its massive body filling the entire doorway. Its paws made little sound. Its eyes met hers.

It was the same wolf. Somehow, she knew it.

Behind it, a street down, another dire wolf appeared, this one tawny. Its black eyes settled on them. Further down the street, two more appeared, shades of brown and gray and white. All watched the intruders.

Isaac took a step back, and Juniper fixed her eyes on the white dire wolf. Pleading.

The wolf tilted his head, cocking his ears, intelligent gaze pinned on Juniper. For a long moment, they studied one another. Then the wolf lifted its snout to the sky and let out a howl—the sound shattered the silence.

The wolves all returned the howl, the sound the same and yet different. It filled the mountain top with its cadence.

"What does that mean?" Henry asked, panicked.

Penet started to pull his sword out, but Juniper grabbed his wrist. "No," she whispered.

And the wolves went silent once more. Even the wind went quiet.

The wolves vanished one-by-one until only the white and gray wolf remained. It blinked at Juniper but, unlike the other wolves, walked into the street and ran toward the mountain. *This way*, it seemed to say.

Juniper started to follow the wolf at a run.

The others started after her.

"Are we sure about this plan?" came Henry's gasping breath. "Following the wolf that can eat us in two bites?"

"Give yourself some credit," Penet said. "With your big head, you'd be at least three bites."

Juniper didn't catch what Henry said next. She wasn't paying attention to them. She kept her eyes on the speck of white. She kept running, even as her side threatened to tear open, even as her lungs squeezed with the cold, thin air, even as her legs burned and her throat felt like fire. At last, the road ended. The dire wolf sat in front of a tall, narrow set of stairs that led further up the mountain, through a series of archways—most of which had fallen.

The wolf blinked and tilted his head as if to say, *Here you go.* But his look came with a warning.

"Thank you," Juniper said aloud.

The dire wolf stood and started back toward the ruins. As it passed, the others froze. The wolf made no acknowledgment that anyone else was even there.

When it had gone from their sight, Henry put a hand over his heart. "By far the most terrifying part of the trip."

Juniper caught her breath before she started up the stairs.

"That was an interesting trick," Isaac said. He walked behind her, the squires following.

"No trick." Juniper glanced over her shoulder to see him. "Dire wolves are deadly smart."

"First time you've encountered one?"

She hesitated before answering, "No. Yours?"

"No," he answered. "They are interesting creatures, to say the least. Have impeccable timing and remarkable memory. Like their distant cousin, the dog, they are loyal to a fault but are wise enough to know where their true loyalties lie."

"I saved a dire wolf from a bear trap," Juniper explained. "Before we were separated." When Reid and Ison had been there.

"Likely that wolf considers itself in your debt."

"It has already paid me back in full," she said.

"Is that so?"

"A dire wolf saved me from those slavers. Killed them and let me escape."

"Fascinating."

"When did you see one?" Juniper needed to keep the conversation away from herself, away from memories she didn't want to visit right now.

"I had been a knight only a few months." Isaac paused to climb over the fallen stones of an archway. "I served under King Balendin for a time before the civil war. As his connection to the Order. While escorting Queen Lenore, we came across a dire wolf and three pups. They had stopped at a river for a drink, and we stopped to watch. The wolf mother knew we were there, and I was worried she would think us a threat, but the queen assured me dire wolves could sense the threat of a person, and as long as we did not threaten her or her pups, she would leave us be. She warned me dire wolves have a wicked memory, and if a human crossed them, that human would be a marked man."

"And what happened?"

"We watch the pups drink from the river," Isaac said. "The wolf mother and her pups vanished into the forest. The thick forests of Collatia are home to a great number of dire wolves, though their numbers have dwindled over the past century."

"I like my story better," Juniper said. "More exciting."

Isaac chuckled. "That it was, though I don't envy you."

Juniper gratefully climbed the last step. They arrived in a stone courtyard. Stone pots held dry packed dirt that might have once held flowers or other greenery. Before them, carved into the mountain, was a temple. It stood as tall as a castle, towers etched from the stone, two massive stone doors carved in the center. On either side of the doors stood twin dragon statues, their skin carefully and skillfully carved with scales along their sides and backs, leathery skin on their stomachs, and folded wings. Unlike the ruins around them, the dragons looked as though they had been carved the day before.

Penet and Henry arrived at the top, both panting.

"Is this it?" asked Henry. "It doesn't look like a garden."

Juniper took a few steps closer to the doors. Isaac followed behind her.

The still air shifted—she felt it before she heard it: crumbling, shifting stone. Juniper froze, and movement caught her eye.

The twin dragons were *moving*.

Their stone wings flexed out, shedding dust. Their long necks shifted and bent. Their stony eyes blinked, and in the place of stone, eyes appeared. The dragon on the right had bright green eyes, and his twin on the left had bright blue eyes. Those twin gazes narrowed at Juniper in frightening unison.

"Another comes," said the blue-eyed dragon in a voice like thunder.

"Another journeys," said the green-eyed dragon in a voice like a crashing wave.

"To the end of the realm," said the blue-eyed dragon.

"To the edge of the world," said the green-eyed dragon.

The dragons took mirrored steps forward, off their stone pedestals and into the courtyard. They bent their heads to see the intruders. Their massive bodies blocked the way forward. Juniper caught a whiff of smoke, like molten metal—dragon's breath.

"Who comes to seek," said the blue-eyed dragon.

"Who comes to pillage," said the green-eyed dragon.

"Who comes," said the dragons in unison.

"To learn?"

"To steal?"

"To explore?"

"To take?"

"To explain?"

"Who comes?" asked the dragons together, their voices merging into an otherworldly crash.

No one spoke—the dragons were looking at her. The silence felt deadly. She glanced sideways at Isaac, who had paled several shades. He met her eye and nodded. With his encouragement, she stepped forward.

The dragons bent closer toward her, their eyes as large as her entire body. "Who comes?" they hissed.

"Juniper Thimble," she announced. Her name in the silence felt like a marking, a curse.

The dragons bent closer still—their stony snouts large enough to swallow her whole—and she could feel the heat of their smoky breath on her skin. The dragons sniffed in unison.

"Juniper," said the blue-eyed dragon.

"Thimble," said the green-eyed dragon.

The dragons looked at her with an intensity that made her bones shake. Silence thickened, and she feared herself not good enough—like the dire wolves, these dragons could sense far beyond what humans could. What did they sense about her?

"Enter," said the blue-eyed dragon.

"Juniper Thimble," said the green-eyed dragon.

The dragons stepped aside, moving their muscular tails out from in front of the great stone doors. Juniper started up the steps, and as she did

197

so, the great doors began to open. The dragons moved behind her, and she heard the thunderous voice of the blue-eyed dragon say, "Only she may enter."

She turned to see Isaac, Penet, and Henry at the bottom of the steps, blocked by the dragons. The dragons said no more, only glared.

Juniper met Isaac's worried gaze. "I'll be all right," Juniper said to him.

Isaac nodded, though he didn't look happy about letting her continue on alone.

Juniper turned her back and climbed the steps to the doors. The opened doors revealed an arched tunnel. At the far end, light shone. Juniper grabbed the strap of her satchel, took a deep breath, and continued toward the Crown.

CHAPTER THIRTY-SIX

Reid had little chance to rest. He helped rebuild from dawn to dusk, wearing himself out beyond exhaustion so when he collapsed into his bed at the inn, he did not dream. When the work paused, his mind drifted to the incessant tugging in his chest. That kernel of magic refused him silence or peace.

Ison rested. That blast of ice and wind had emptied his magic stores, and the mage could barely stay awake the day after, and those that followed he spent in an exhausted daze. He slept through the rebuilding—which irritated Reid.

And then there was no more rebuilding to be done. Reid had done enough, they said when he offered to chop wood or patch roofs or shovel snow.

And then he couldn't *not* notice the kernel of magic. It tugged him northwest. Toward Juniper, toward where the others might also be.

So the morning he returned to the inn—after being turned away from everyone he asked for work—and he saw Ison standing by the hearth, he said, "We leave at once."

Ison blinked and turned his head toward him as though he hadn't understood. "Right now?"

"Lunch will be ready in an hour or so," chimed the innkeeper.

Reid inhaled and released it. "Fine, after lunch. In the meantime, we prepare to travel."

Ison had not objected, though he looked like he might. Two hours later, Reid and Ison climbed the rocky mountain path out of the village. Reid led the way with Ison a few steps behind.

Once the village was out of sight, Reid said, "Those apostates followed us."

"I can't argue with that," Ison said quietly.

"How do you think they found us?"

Ison didn't answer.

Reid let the question sink in, let his unspoken answer lay in the frigid air.

"You think I had something to do with it?" Ison's quiet voice was tight with anger.

"We saw no one in the valley, no villages, no waystations. And yet a group of apostates found us."

"I did not lead them to us," Ison defended.

Reid spun and faced the mage. In the cold, his ashy complexion had turned pale. The tip of his nose, his chin, and his cheeks were rosy from the wind. Shadows darkened his eyes.

"You said Nexon used you, got into your mind, and knew your thoughts," Reid said lowly but loud enough to be heard over the wind.

Ison's calm expression turned. "And you think Nexon somehow knew our location through me? I haven't heard his voice since I fled the castle. While in the Undercity, I learned mental resistance to keep him and others out—something the Marca never even mentioned was possible. Almost like they want mages to be weak-minded and weak-willed."

"Magic that alters the mind is forbidden," Reid said firmly.

"As it should be," Ison agreed. "I alter no mind. I strengthen the walls around my own."

"What's to stop you from controlling mine?"

"Common decency for one," Ison snapped. He started forward along the path. "And for another, I don't know how. I didn't learn that sort of magic. What's to stop you from running me through? The same thing!"

The wind picked up, hissing through the mountains and sparse pines. The sound was a ghostly, terrifying harbinger of what lurked in these inhospitable lands. Over the wind, Reid thought he heard howling.

"We need to keep moving." Ison's tone was clipped. "We have to find a safe place to camp before dark."

Reid agreed, and as Ison started along the barely-there path, he followed. He kept his eyes open and his ears trained for howls and growls, and he kept one hand on the hilt of his blade. He would not be taken by surprise.

CHAPTER THIRTY-SEVEN

The light on the other side of the tunnel brightened with each step. Juniper heard the doors close behind her. Her heart thumped in a quick panic—what if she couldn't get back out again? Regardless, she kept walking. At last, Juniper stepped into the Crown. Her eyes adjusted, and through the blinding glare, she spotted green—vibrant and healthy green. Blinking away the sting, her jaw dropped.

The sight stole her breath.

Greenery took over the mountaintop. Oaks, maples, plum, birch—every tree imaginable grew impossibly tall, boughs lush and ringing with birdsong. Two bluebirds fluttered above her head and vanished into the boughs of an oak. She spotted trees she had never seen before, thick with leaves as small as her fingernail and larger than her entire body. Grasses and bushes grew thick with berries. Herbs grew like weeds: basil, rosemary, thyme, mint, lavender, all mixing together in her nose.

It was so warm! Juniper shed her winter wools and furs and dropped them into the grass beside the archway. Wearing nothing but her tunic, trousers, and her satchel, she started through the garden. Mossy grass softened her footsteps.

After the harrowing journey here, the air smelled sweeter than any summer air she had inhaled.

"Take only what you seek," said a calm, ghostly voice.

Juniper spun around, and at first she saw nothing, but then her gaze settled on a pair of eyes staring back at her. They belonged to a creature with green scales. It had blended in so well, she hadn't seen it. The creature stepped out of the verdant bushes, and Juniper held in her gasp. A dragonling, as green as summer. It had small horns of gold and matching talons, and plates lined its spine. It was about the size of a dog.

"Take only what you seek," said the voice again.

The dragonling *spoke*. Juniper blinked, unsure if what she heard was real or not, and then the dragonling turned and vanished between two blueberry bushes.

She sought Boxel's Grace, and she would take only Boxel's Grace.

Juniper watched the bushes, but the dragonling didn't return. A grassy path wound through the garden, and she followed it at a slow pace. She wanted to see everything, and with each step, she spotted something new and unknown: bushes with multicolored leaves, trees whose branches curled in on themselves, and flowers in shades she had never before imagined. It was the most beautiful place she had ever dreamed of. The grassy path led her through archways made of tree roots, under and over little brooks and streams, past golden sundials, brass fountains, bejeweled walkways, copper and ironwork benches and birdbaths, and more plants than she thought possible to exist.

A garden crafted by the gods, indeed. Planted by Boxel, God of the Harvest. Tended to by Bala, Goddess of Nature. A gathering place for the gods, unfit for mortal feet and eyes.

The garden path led her to a grand pavilion made entirely out of white marble. A dozen pillars held up the domed roof, each adorned with gemstones as large as her hand. Rubies, emeralds, diamonds, topaz—even colors she had never seen before, each catching the sun and glowing with light. Juniper took a cautious step into the pavilion. Her footsteps echoed, and the sound itself felt like an intrusion.

The dome of the pavilion was dotted with stars—she blinked—no, what she thought were stars were diamonds, thousands of them, big and small. Rather than dark stone for the night sky, the diamonds were set against sapphires and onyx.

The wealth of the world, contained in a single pavilion. Juniper turned in a circle, taking as much of the sight in as she could—she would want to tell the others all that she had seen.

Around the pavilion, piles of gold bars and coins from every era and land. A horde of treasure, a treasure to rival every kingdom in the realm twice over—emeralds, sapphires, rubies—as if they had been left by the mad architect who had erected this pavilion. She spotted crowns among the treasure, of silver, gold, and steel, encrusted with every gemstone imaginable, some without any.

The gods' treasury.

Despite the dragonling's warning, the thief inside of her squirmed with the absurd splendor. A few of those gems, and she would be set for life—a few of those gems, and she wouldn't have to worry about gold once this quest ended. She could ditch the others, find a place in the Undercity to wait out Nexon's storm, and—

No, she couldn't do that.

Things would never go back to the way they were.

She would never be the thief she had once been. The Undercity, if it still existed, would never accept her back. She would be an outlaw until the end of her days, to criminals and the Watch.

And without Reid or Ison, she didn't know what she would do after this quest ended.

Juniper swallowed her instincts to take whatever she could fit in her pockets. She hadn't come for gold or gems, and she couldn't carry much back. She had limited room in her pack, and food took priority. She would have to carry them all the way back to Rusdasin to a black market dealer.

No. It wasn't worth the trouble.

Juniper turned her back on the gemstone pavilion and continued to the other side, to another part of the vast garden. The greenery continued, seemingly endless as the cloud ocean. Juniper trailed her fingers along the silken fronds of weeping ferns, looking at the long, straight leaves.

A meow stopped her cold.

She brought her hands in close to her sides.

Standing in the center of the path was a cat. It was the strangest cat she had ever seen, long and lean with a pale purple coat. It blinked—its large yellow eyes did not blink in unison. It looked at her as though it had never seen a human. Knowing this place, it might not have.

The animals in this garden were not normal animals. They inhabited the gods' land, and like the dragonling and dire wolf, the cat had abnormally intelligent eyes that seemed to spear through her.

Juniper clutched the strap of her satchel and took a chance. She knelt in front of the cat.

It held itself proud, still as stone, yet its chest gently rose and fell. No fear shone in its eyes. If anything, it looked at her with cautious curiosity.

"Can you help me?" Juniper asked the cat.

One of its ears twitched, as if hearing something behind it.

"I'm looking for Boxel's Grace," she said. "One of my dear friends is sick and needs it. My entire kingdom needs him. He's the future king, you see, and I know he will be the best king we've ever had."

The cat's other ear twitched. It blinked at her, and then it started down the path. Its purple tail swayed behind it, a ribbon of sleek fur that shimmered like silver. Juniper didn't hesitate to follow. The cat led her off the path, between bushes with berries of red, blue, and black. It slipped through flower beds with ease, and Juniper carefully tiptoed around the flowers using the stones dotting the ground, some almost too far apart.

Flowers with chartreuse blossoms grew around the stones. They tinted the air with an overpowering sweetness.

The cat stopped in a small clearing. It waited for her to jump into the clearing from the last stone, and then it vanished into the thin trees forming a wall around the small clearing.

Juniper started to call after it, but then she realized where the cat had led her.

In the middle of the clearing, in the circle of sunlight, grew half a dozen white flowers.

Boxel's Grace. It looked just like the picture in the book.

Juniper couldn't believe it. She'd found it. She'd done it.

She tiptoed into the clearing, trying to steady her racing heart, then knelt at the end of the flower patch. Her hands fumbled with the clasp of her satchel and took out a glass vial and small gardening shears. Carefully, as if she were about to cut into live flesh, she clipped one of the stalks. She lifted the fallen flower into the vial, the green flesh of the stem warm under her touch.

Corking the vial, she felt eyes on her.

Through the thin trees, she spotted the wide eyes of the cat. It blinked, one eye closing a little faster than the other.

Juniper gently tucked the vial of Boxel's Grace in a strip of cotton and tucked it into the satchel. She had what she needed to save Adrian and the kingdom. She wouldn't let Nexon take him too.

She carefully navigated her way over the flower bed's stepping stones. On the other side, she glanced both ways down the grassy path. They looked identical. The trees grew on both sides, shading the path.

Which way had she come?

A meow came from behind her, and the cat came nimbly from between two glossy blue tulips. It blinked at her once, then started down the path to her left. Juniper followed. The cat jaunted around the path, this way and that, until the trees opened and the flowers thinned.

The cat led to her a temple of white stone. A well-kept temple.

The arched doorway let her see inside, and it gave her a fierce chill. It was a grand hall of gold and ivory, with alcoves along both sides. In each alcove was a statue.

The gods. All of them.

Juniper felt remarkably small. Insignificant. She took a step into the temple. Her footsteps echoed. The sunlight filtered in from somewhere unseen and glinted off the gold and ivory, making the space glow. The statues looked the same as those in the temples scattered throughout Rusdasin, only larger and grander, carved with exquisite detail. The flowers along Bala's robes had texture along their petals and veins on the leaves. The chicory sprig looked like it had been dipped in gold.

Juniper saw Boxel and his wheat stalk, Rappa and his sword, Espone and her quill, and finally, she came to Blugo. He stood tall and proud in his furs, the strands etched into the gold. Ivory snowflakes lined his robes, each different than any other.

None of the statues had offering plates at their feet.

Whoever had built this temple had not intended for offerings to be made. Who? Who built this place? Who lived in the ruins below? So many questions without answers.

If she could give no offering, she did the only other thing she knew to do. She knelt onto her knees and placed her hands flat on the floor in front of Blugo's golden feet. "Thank you," she said. She meant it, though it still felt silly to kneel at the feet of a statue.

"I wouldn't be here if not for you. I know I've done horrible things. I've lied and cheated and stolen and killed. I thought I was surviving, doing whatever I could to get by and protect myself. I know now that I wasn't doing anyone any favors. I don't know what I'll do when this is all said and done, if I'm still alive. I will hold myself to my word about the Janti slavers, somehow. Before that, I will stop Nexon. Even if I don't know how. Please, Blugo, watch over us as we make our return to Rusdasin. Help us to save Adrian and Duvane from whatever Nexon has in store." She started to stand, then quickly added, "I promise to stop by the temples more and treat the priestesses and priests with more respect."

A chime sounded, a faint bell. Juniper stood and looked for the source, and with every moment that passed, she thought she imagined it.

A bird, she thought.

Juniper meandered to the other side of the temple. At the far end, a narrower hall—but no less grand—contained the lesser gods. Rather than gold and ivory, the lesser gods were carved expertly from marble. She passed Bera, Goddess of Shadow, the hood of her robes pulled over her eyes; Hiada, the Dark God, carved bones under his bare feet; Meryda, Goddess of the Seas, her robes carved with seaweed and waves; and a god whose name Juniper didn't know. He had been carved with a friendly smile, grapevines along his robes, and a goblet in his hand.

To her surprise, there were another half a dozen gods and goddesses she hadn't heard of. A god had robes covered in clover. A goddess had a snake curled around her shoulders. A god held what looked like a coconut.

Who were these gods? Another thing the Order had cleansed from the world?

Juniper came to a massive circular room, benches carved from the same marble curved around the room. A great number of people would have been able to gather here. Off the side, a balcony overlooked a sprawling garden of colored stone—gemstones, she realized—arranged in a mural of the sun, moon, and stars. The sun rose to the top of the mural, gold and topaz bright as pure sunlight. At the bottom of the mural, onyx and diamond shaped like bones, hundreds of bones, human and not.

Juniper stared at the mural—it looked familiar, but she knew she'd never seen it before.

And then she remembered: one of the runes on the court magician's desk. It had shown the sky, stars among bones.

A piece of the ancient world.

Juniper started back through the temple. Enough gawking. Her friends were waiting on her. Adrian was waiting on her. She had trampled through this world meant for gods with her worthless human feet long enough.

On the stairs to the temple sat the cat. It watched her like it knew, like it had heard her prayer. It tilted his head expectantly.

"Can you show me the way back to the big doors? The way out?"

The cat blinked rapidly.

"I know, this is a lovely place." Juniper patted her satchel. "But I have friends depending on me."

The cat started off down the grassy path, and Juniper followed. The cat took her through parts of the garden she hadn't seen before. She couldn't take in the godly scenery fast enough. She wanted to memorize every last detail.

If the nomads of ages past had come here to die, where had they done it? Just layed down among the flowers and never rose again? To inhale the sweet scents of the garden as her last breath didn't sound so bad.

The cat led her back to the arched tunnel. Her warm clothes were not in the pile she'd left them in. Someone, or something, had folded them neatly and left them in the middle of the courtyard. She glanced back but saw no one among the garden. Juniper sat her satchel on the ground as she pulled her furs and wools and leathers back on.

As an afterthought, she took Boxel's Grace out of her satchel and secured it in her tunic's pocket. If anyone wanted it, they would have to kill her first.

Dressed for the frigid air of the Dolomin Mountains, Juniper took a deep breath of the sweet summer air.

The cat meowed.

"I'd rather stay here and see everything there is," Juniper said to the cat. "But I have to go. Maybe one day, I'll come back to see you. You can show me around again."

The cat blinked, one eye and then the other.

"Goodbye," Juniper said to the cat.

It remained seated as Juniper started back through the arched tunnel. The sweet smells faded to the stark cold of the mineral-rich stones. The sunlight faded, the temperature dropped, and she continued forward in the dark. The tunnel seemed endless, but then stone began to grind against stone, and the massive doors started to open. Amber light poured through, and with it came a chilled wind.

The dragons stood guard on the other side, seemingly returned to stone. They did not move or breathe as she started down the stairs. The doors ground to a close behind her, and Juniper only glanced back once.

The world looked as it had before—the forgotten city surrounded by an ocean of clouds—only the sun had set and doused the world in dark gold and twilight shadows.

The others were not waiting for her at the bottom of the stairs.

"Isaac?" Juniper asked the still air.

No response.

Silence pressed in all around her. She walked through the ruined village, but she didn't see any sign of the others. Her footsteps echoed. Juniper looked down every alley and in every stony building. The air felt different, lighter somehow. Or had the garden tuned her senses?

She came to the entrance of the city and spotted three familiar tents and a smoldering campfire. As she approached, movement shifted in one of the tents, and Isaac's head popped through the door.

He blinked at her, and then sleep vanished from his face and he stumbled through the tent's door. "Juniper?" He rushed to her. "Thank the gods you're alive." He looked to her satchel. "Did you find it?"

"I did." She patted her satchel. Let them all think she carried it separately.

Penet and Henry fumbled out of their tents, both bleary eyed and mussed.

"Could you not wait for me to return?" Juniper said lightheartedly, nodding to the tents.

Isaac's brows came together. "What do you mean? You've been gone for three days. We waited until we could barely stand."

Juniper gasped. "Three days?"

"The guardians mentioned that time moves differently here." Penet pushed his messy hair out of his face. "They warned us that you might be gone longer than you intended."

"I was." She looked at the smoldering campfire. She caught the scents of a cooked meal. "It doesn't feel like it's been more than a few hours."

"And I feel like it's the middle of the night." Henry yawned. "Can we wait a few more hours? I'll travel better if I'm awake."

"He whines less too," said Penet.

"Fine." Isaac nodded to them. "Go back to sleep. We travel as soon as we're able. Juniper, if you require rest, you can sleep in my tent." Isaac looked exhausted.

"No, but thank you," she said. "I feel wide awake."

Isaac gave her a moment to change her mind, and when she didn't, he returned to his tent. Juniper sat by the remains of the fire. She closed her eyes. If she focused, she could feel the warmth of the sunlight and smell the sweet summer scents of the garden. She could still feel the warmth radiating through her being, almost like magic.

CHAPTER THIRTY-EIGHT

Juniper didn't know how long she sat by the ashy remains of the fire, watching the plums and ambers of the sky shift. A gentle glow in the east signaled the approach of day.

Three days. She had spent three days wandering that garden.

She heard rustling behind her and then footsteps. Penet sat beside her. He looked much more awake than he had earlier. The thread between them went taut. Her magic reached out to the kernel tucked inside him. The need to take it back spiked with such sudden ferocity that it stole her breath. She sucked her next in quickly.

"How was it on the other side?" he asked quietly, as to not disturb the others.

"Amazing," she said. "Everything was in full bloom. There was so much to look at, plants and flowers and trees." She started to tell him about the temple, but something about it didn't feel right on her tongue.

"Did you meet anyone? Was anyone else inside?"

"I didn't see any people, but I met a cat. He showed me the way to the herbs and helped me find my way out again."

Penet's brows rose, and a kind smile stretched across his lips. "Really? That sounds incredible. I wish I could have gone in, if just to see what it looked like."

"It was aptly named," she said. "A garden fit for the gods and likewise unfit for unworthy human feet."

Penet scooted a little closer, closer than he normally would have. She didn't chide him for it. Maybe she should have. She cast her eyes back to the warming east, where the plum and amber were brightening into pink and gold. She glanced back to find Penet's eyes on her neck. At once, his gaze flickered to meet hers. He flushed a deep red and turned his head away.

He cleared his throat. "And you have the herb?" He glanced at her satchel.

"Yes."

Penet's gaze lingered on the satchel with a hunger she hadn't seen on him. She fought the urge to put her hand over where the vial rested in her tunic's pocket.

"Can I see it?" Desperation wormed into his words. In her hesitation, he lifted his hungry gaze to her.

"When we get back to the village," she said. "I'll show everyone."

Penet looked like he might argue, but he didn't. He pursed his lips closed and swallowed. After a while, he nodded.

Silence fell between them, thicker than it had been before. She tried to think of something to say to shatter it, but Penet beat her to it.

"I'm sorry about what happened to Reid and Ison." He set his hand on her shoulder. "I keep thinking that I should have done something. I should have seen the loose rocks first, but I didn't. I-I keep thinking that I could have stopped it from happening."

"I doubt it's your fault," Juniper said. "A landslide is hardly anyone's fault." Though she wished it could be so she could tear them apart, starting with their nonessential insides. Make them feel the hollowness she did.

"I know you and Reid...you know," Penet started. He motioned forward with his hand.

Juniper sighed. "I think the entire castle knew by the time I left."

Penet didn't deny it. "What will you do after this?"

"I don't know," she said. "Stop Nexon any way I can."

"I-I know it might not be much," Penet started, his cheeks warming, "But I can help you find somewhere to stay."

He sounded too much like Reid in that moment, offering her an alternative to her future. Despite how it prodded at her chest, she smiled. "Thank you, Penet." She meant it. He would make a fine knight someday. As Reid would have. "First, we worry about returning the herb to Adrian, and then the rest of the world."

"You're intent on returning it?"

"It is what Reid would have done," Juniper said. "I can do this for him. Complete his task and save his best friend, his kingdom. And I refuse to lose Adrian too."

Penet nodded, understanding in his eyes. "You're noble, for a thief."

She half laughed.

Penet mirrored her smile. And then his hand reached for hers. "Juniper," he whispered, and his touch and her name on his breath caught her off-guard. In the next moment, his lips were against hers.

The shock wore off quickly, and Juniper pulled her mouth from his.

Never had a more awkward moment existed, not that Juniper could think of. Penet's cheeks burned red, and she felt her own face heat. They both looked away.

"I-I'm sorry," Penet mumbled.

Before she could fathom a response, a loud yawn came from the tents. A moment later, Henry crawled out. Juniper had never been more happy to see him.

"Breakfast ready?" he asked as he came to the old fire.

"Breakfast?" Juniper's brows rose in mock sincerity. "And what would the squire like? Warm porridge? Sausages? I'm afraid we're in short supply of both."

Henry blinked at her, then rolled his eyes. "Right, you've not been here. You got to go play in the garden while we waited and waited and tried not to lose our minds. Anyway, every morning there would be food waiting on the ground. Flatbread and fruits and vegetables."

"You're joking," Juniper said.

"He's not." Isaac climbed out of his tent and to his feet. He stretched his arms above his head. "And, by the looks of it, our mysterious friends did not forget us this morning."

He nodded toward the stairs to the ruined city, where a platter had been set on the bottom step, piled with flatbread, grapes, apples, peppers, and carrots. A jug set on the stair above. Oats had been brought for the horses. Juniper at once looked to the top of the stairs, but she saw no one and no thing.

How had she missed that?

Isaac and Henry retrieved the gifts, but Juniper kept looking. And there—movement on the far left side. Two eyes peeked over the top stair, barely visible among the stone. Two eyes, a small head, and a small body. Then another appeared beside it. Two somethings. They blinked and then vanished into the ruins.

How many creatures called this place home?

"Juniper," came Isaac's voice.

She stole her gaze from where the mysterious little things had vanished and met the knight's. She saw that knowing look—he suspected she had seen what none of them had, but he didn't pressure her to explain. He offered her an apple, and she took it. They had eaten so much dried venison, her mouth watered thinking about biting into the fruit.

She chewed the apple slowly. Never had she had a fruit with such flavor! Had it been grown in the garden? She wouldn't be surprised.

The others ate in silence, and when Juniper glanced up from her apple, she found Penet watching her. Their eyes met, and she felt something like dread pull her stomach down. She looked away first.

That was not an obstacle she wanted to have or think about.

She finished the rest of her breakfast without looking up.

❄

After eating their fill and packing the rest of the food, they struck camp and started out of the mountaintop ruins. A weary cloud hung over them, and as if in response, the sky dulled. Juniper felt elation at finding the herb, but the idea of the long ride back to Rusdasin filled her with dread.

They had a long, long way to go before she cleared her name and saved Adrian. A very long way to go.

Juniper rode with Penet. He had offered, and she didn't want to refuse in front of the others. Besides, she would have felt awkward riding with Henry or Isaac. Penet was... She didn't know. He was Penet, stable and unassuming.

They spoke little as they navigated the mountaintop. The cloud sea rolled beneath them, gentle waves of white and gray. Juniper thought she heard the rolling of thunder more than once. Did they ride above a storm?

They camped near the same place they had before, and by the time the tents had been erected, Juniper's exhaustion pulled at her limbs. She crawled into the furs and wools and barely remembered closing her eyes.

She woke to Isaac's voice coming from outside. "Time to go," he said.

Juniper rolled out of bed to find the others nearly ready. "Why didn't you wake me sooner?"

Isaac grinned. "I tried."

She hurriedly readied while the other waited; then they started again along the mountain path. Juniper tried to find the time to extract her kernel of magic from Penet, but she didn't want to encourage anything more than friendship between them, though he spoke to her any chance he got. While her magic did not feel as tightly squeezed and starved as it had—she thought his presence might have something to do with it—she wanted it back.

Finally, they came to where the path dipped below the clouds, to the other side of the world, to where the mortals ruled.

Juniper held her breath as Penet guided the horse toward the clouds, and his hand around her tightened slightly. He held her to his chest as the hooves sank into the clouds, the legs, the body, their feet—and she shut her eyes as the cold cloud kissed her face. The icy air engulfed them. She cracked her eyes open. Gray surrounded them, so thick she could barely see the horse's dark mane in front of her. If not for Penet holding onto her, she might have thought herself falling.

The clouds lifted, and they re-entered the land of mortals.

The Dolomin Mountains stretched all around them, gray and sharp and covered in fresh snow. The steely clouds spit snow and sleet, and frigid wind seared through the seams of her wools. Her breath puffed from her lips. Penet shuddered and tucked her as close as he could. They trekked along the path, through the snowstorm, and just when Juniper thought herself nearly freezing to death, Isaac called for them to camp.

The day faded, and soon their campfire was the only light. Beyond the cavern mouth, the world was silvery and cold. By morning, the snowstorm had abated and left the path covered with powdery snow. Isaac deemed the path too dangerous to go on horseback, and they led the horses. Juniper took the lead, feeling through the snow with her dwindling magic for hidden ice or loose stones. It made the trek torturously slow. The snow did not start again, and the worst of it seemed to have been higher in the mountains.

Down, down, down, they traveled. Juniper did her best to ignore Penet, though his continued stares made it difficult. It was midafternoon when at last Halsig appeared through the sprawling pine forest. Juniper released a breath of relief. Smoke billowed from the chimneys, snow had been shoveled from the main roads, and the smell of woodsmoke and pine needles warmed the air.

At the inn, Juniper went straight for the burning hearth and sat down on the floor in front of it.

"You're back!" The shrill call came a moment before two arms fastened around Juniper's shoulders, nearly knocking her to the floor.

"Roslyn?" Juniper asked, for all she could see was black hair.

The girl leaned away, her brown eyes wide and thrilled. "I was starting to worry. Well? What happened? Did you get it?"

"In due time, my lady." Isaac sat down at one of the tables. "Perhaps over something warm to drink?"

"Tea!" came the innkeeper's voice as she trotted into the kitchens. "Coming up!"

To avoid being overheard, they retreated into Roslyn's room. Fynilli joined them, looking none too happy about having so many members of the Order in her presence. Juniper sat before the hearth, marveling at the heat of the fire on her skin and the warmth of the teacup in her hand.

Isaac told them about their journey through the Dolomin Mountains, the strangeness of the other side, the dire wolves, and the dragon guardians. Roslyn remained stone still, taking in the story with curious eyes. Fynilli's expression remained stoic. And then it came to the part when Juniper walked through the stone doors, Isaac fell silent.

With the hearth warming her outside and the tea warming her insides, Juniper told them what she had seen in the Garden of the Gods. She told them of the plants and trees and warmth, the dragonling that warned her only to take what she sought, the cat that guided her, and the marvelous and humbling temple.

While she spoke, no one said a word.

When she finished, silence settled.

"It is a good thing you chose to tell us here rather than where the entire village could hear you," Fynilli said at last, warning on each word. "Word would spread about the girl whom the gods deemed worthy to set foot into their land. It would bring much unwanted attention."

"But you've got it?" Roslyn asked, her voice wispy.

"Yes," Juniper nodded.

All eyes turned to her. The attention prickled against her skin. She would have to prove it to them sooner or later. She reached into her tunic and pulled out the cotton-wrapped vial holding Boxel's Grace for them all to see. The flower looked as though she had just cut it, the petals still vibrant and full, the leaves lush and green.

"By the gods," breathed Isaac.

Roslyn's eyes widened, and she placed a hand over her mouth.

Juniper tucked it back into her tunic. She wouldn't let it out of her sight. Not something as important as this.

A knock came to the door, and the kind voice of the innkeeper rang on the other side, "Dinner will be ready in an hour. I've got rooms ready for you, if you'd like to rest first."

"Rest sounds fantastic." Henry stood. "Not that I don't find this conversation stimulating, but I am exhausted."

"I agree," said Isaac. "We'll talk more after dinner."

Juniper remained in Roslyn's room while the men filed out. Fynilli meandered to the door, her footsteps light and soundless, and shut it behind them. Deftly, she slid the deadbolt into place. Other doors in the hall opened and closed.

"Is that truly what happened?" asked Fynilli. "Did you leave anything out?"

Juniper shook her head. "No."

Fynilli held her gaze, as if waiting for her to change her answer. She didn't.

Juniper glanced between Roslyn and Fynilli. "Did I miss something?"

"Visitors came while you were gone," Roslyn said. "Strange folk. Said they heard rumors of travelers going to the edge of the realm or something like that. But I overheard them talking about an heir."

Juniper blinked. "An heir?"

"You mentioned your friends thought their quest was a ruse to hide Bradburn's secret heir," Fynilli said.

"And either someone thinks the rumor is true, or they know the rumor is true." Juniper's stomach tightened. "Where are these visitors?"

"Gone," Roslyn said. "Left two days ago."

Juniper chalked up the pitting in her stomach to hunger. A good meal would settle her nerves. That was it. Maybe the rumors of Bradburn's secret heir had spread. Maybe they were true. Her head hurt too much to think about it. With Reid gone, it didn't matter anyway.

"Isaac is right." Juniper sat down on the edge of the larger bed. "I'm too exhausted to think clearly. Wake me up when dinner is ready."

CHAPTER THIRTY-NINE

Dinner at the inn turned out to be the most crowded meal yet. Everyone in the village clamored to get a look at the returned squires. It took the pressure off Juniper, at least, to know they were more interested in the soon-to-be knights than her. It also kept Boxel's Grace safe—she thought about leaving it in her room but refused. It rested safely in her pocket.

When she and Roslyn returned to their room that evening, that decision turned out to be the right one. Juniper's satchel had been resting against the right side of the dresser, but now it rested against the middle. *Someone* had moved it.

As Roslyn combed out her hair, Juniper went to her satchel. "Someone's gone through my belongings." She pointed to the satchel. "They tried to put things back in order, but it's not the same.

"Are you sure?"

"Very sure." Juniper had arranged her satchel with purpose, memorizing the location of everything she put inside it. She had a limited amount of space, and she knew each and every item she carried, what pocket they went into, and someone had jostled the items around. "Someone was looking for something. When we went to dinner—that's the only time we left the room."

"The herb." Roslyn narrowed her eyes at the back of the door. "But who? The only people who know are us."

"The entire village knew where we were going," Juniper felt foolish. This was why Reid had kept it a secret from the others. "And who knows how many other people knew squires were heading this far north. It wouldn't take much to put the pieces together: squires questing in the far north, sick prince."

"Well, that leaves most of the village," Roslyn said. "Except for you and I, because you would not go through your things, and I desperately want to see Adrian alive and well again."

"I doubt the men would," Juniper said.

Isaac had no reason to, and he was too loyal to King Bradburn. Henry... She didn't know him well enough. She thought of the way Penet had stared at her satchel, the hunger in his eyes. But their knighthood rested on Adrian's recovery.

"It doesn't matter," Roslyn said. "You've had it with you the whole time, right?"

Juniper nodded.

"Maybe someone in the village caught wind and thought they could steal it for a sick relative or a payout," Roslyn suggested. "Either way, keep it on your person."

That night, the girls pushed the dresser in front of the door. Just in case. Juniper kept the herb on her person as she crawled into bed.

Someone had gone through her things. *Her* things. She hated the lingering feeling of invasion. A voice in the back of her mind whispered it was poetic justice she should be the victim of a thief.

✳

The next morning, they set off for Oriel. Juniper, Roslyn, and Fynilli rode in the sleigh, while Henry, Penet, and Isaac rode behind on horseback. Juniper gladly relaxed her legs after riding for so long, and this way, she didn't have to deal with Penet. She napped on and off, and the weather allowed a quick ride to Oriel, then Easley. From Easley, they would head south on the White Road. It would take them all the way to Rusdasin.

Easley, while not a large city, was larger than Oriel and much larger than Halsig. The royal house was a small mansion, enough for all of them to stay in their own room. A doorman took their outerwear, and another escorted them into the hearth room for tea.

When the servants offered her a warm bath, Juniper couldn't pass it up. While they prepared it, she sat by the hearth in her room, soaking in the heat. A servant returned faster than Juniper expected and led her to a stone-floored room with a smaller hearth. A stone bath had been carved from the same stone as the floor, and steam rose from the water within, curling toward the wooden ceiling.

"Anything else, miss?" asked the round-faced servant.

"No." Juniper started to undress, and the servant retreated into a narrow hall whose door blended in so well with the paneling of the wall, Juniper hadn't noticed. A servant's passage. Which explained why the main halls had been free of servants, yet they moved about the house like ghosts.

Juniper submerged in the bath. At once, the warm water began soothing the ache in her bones and the worry in her mind. She scrubbed the grime from hair and rubbed it with a pine-smelling tonic, like the snowy forests that surrounded them. She twisted her clean hair up and out the way and reclined against the curved edge of the bath.

Oh, what a luxury a warm bath had become—though it paled in comparison to her claw-foot bath at Castle Bradburn or the salts and oils they'd stocked in her bathing room.

She took a deep breath of the steamy air, and in that moment before she exhaled, she heard it.

Whispers.

She held her breath.

"The other girl is bathing in there," whispered a voice. From the servants' passage.

"Who do you think she is?"

"She rode in the sleigh with Lady Roslyn."

Juniper released her breath slowly, as to not alert them.

"Do you think it's her? She's the only one we don't know."

"Maybe. She doesn't look it, though, does she?"

"Well what do you think the heir is supposed to look like? She can't very well be the prince's twin without everyone knowing it."

Juniper bit her lip to keep from drawing a quick breath.

"What are you two doing?" came an older, quick and harsh voice.

The two servant girls shared a sharp intake of breath.

"Get back to work," said the older voice. "The water in the boiler is ready, and Lady Roslyn would like a bath too."

Two sets of feet quickly padded away.

How utterly absurd. They truly thought her the secret heir? Simply because they didn't know her?

Juniper finished her soak, dried and dressed, and sat while one of the servants braided her hair into a dozen tiny braids and twisted them together in a neat bun.

"Thank you, it looks lovely," Juniper said, admiring the handiwork in the gold-framed hand mirror.

"My pleasure, miss," said the servant.

The servant had been one of the two in the passage suspecting her of being the secret heir. The girl scanned Juniper's face, no doubt trying to find something regal in it. Wouldn't she be disappointed.

After naps and baths and fresh sets of clothes, they met in the hearth room for dinner. Fynilli did not join them. She had gone into town to find a courier. Roslyn mentioned she had letters to send, but in the presence of the men, she didn't elaborate. Juniper assumed those letters were to other Iluvin mages, telling them about Nexon.

The hearth burned warm and bright, and Juniper looked forward to her warm bed for a long night's rest. She would be sleeping on the hard ground for the next several nights, and if she immediately headed east to find Nexon's followers, she might not sleep in a warm bed for a long, long while.

The thought of going against Nexon without Ison struck her heart with a slicing pain of sadness. She had kept him and Reid mostly out of her thoughts for her own good, but when her vigilance slipped, the grief of their loss hit her again, always catching her off-guard.

Juniper slumped against the velvet-padded chair and sipped her herbal tea as the others played a game of cards. Roslyn had requested herbal tea, suggesting they needed something to ease them into sleep after their harrowing journey.

"Juniper," Isaac asked lowly, to keep her name silent. "What will you do once you reach the city?"

"I don't know if I will go that far," Juniper admitted.

Roslyn looked up from her fresh cup of tea with sorrowful, confused eyes. "What do you mean?"

"I have...important business elsewhere." Juniper didn't want the servants carrying the gossip of her vengeance with Nexon anywhere else.

"It is a dangerous journey to be made alone," Isaac said.

"I don't have much of a choice," Juniper said a bit bitterly. "Ison was supposed to go with me."

Silence fell over the table, and a part of Juniper felt satisfied with the guilt that came over Isaac, Henry, and Penet.

"I have friends in other places in the city," Juniper said, thinking of the Undercity mages, both Bois's guild of disbanded Dual Fangs and Josephine's guild. She might find allies willing to go into Nexon's territory.

And as she thought of the Undercity, a fist knocked the air out of her lungs.

Xavier.

How was she supposed to tell him that Ison wasn't coming back?

"Maybe," Isaac started, his finger tapping the side of his teacup. "Maybe it would be better if you did not go alone."

"Are you volunteering yourself?"

Isaac inhaled and glanced at the kitchen door. "I suggest you consult the king before making any brash decisions."

Consult the king? The thought had crossed her mind, but it had mostly been fantasy. She hadn't actually thought the king would listen to her. But with Isaac to back her up, she might gain an audience. And with the king of Duvane on her side, she would have a better chance at striking against Nexon.

Of course, this all assumed she wouldn't be cut down the moment the Royal Guard saw her, or the Order, or the City Watch, or Maddox. Too many people wanted her dead.

Regardless of that, the king needed to know about Nexon.

"Return with us," Isaac said. "I will see that you make it through the city safely." There was a promise in his words.

She opened her mouth to say something, but the kitchen door opened. She pursed her lips tightly—the servant noticed. The servant set a fresh pot of herbal tea on the table, lingered while arranging it, and casually glided back to the kitchen door. As the door opened, several young servant girls jumped back from the door—they had been crouched by the seam, listening.

The door closed.

Penet chuckled. He leaned forward onto the table and whispered, "It would seem that the secret part of our secret quest hasn't been kept a secret after all." He nodded toward the kitchen door. "They're all gossiping about the secret heir."

Henry scoffed, glancing quickly toward the kitchen door.

"Isaac," Juniper started, and she met the knight's stoic, guilt-lined eyes. "Do you think the king will listen to me?"

He hesitated, then nodded. "Yes."

"Why?" The question had been on her tongue for some time. "Why would he listen to me? By all reason, he should be hunting me down for execution, not agreeing to listen to me." She stared into her tea. The king had never made sense in that regard. "Why let me wander around his castle?"

Why hadn't he sent his men to hunt her down? If he wanted her dead, he would have done so. Isaac would have carried out the king's order.

"He requested that you be brought in alive," Isaac answered.

"Again, why?"

Isaac laced his fingers together and released a long, slow sigh. "I suppose it wouldn't hurt to tell you, with what we might be facing in the future."

Juniper blinked. Henry and Penet exchanged confused glances with each other.

"Tell us what?" Henry whispered. "Is there something else you've kept from us? Another hurdle before this quest ends?"

"Not a hurdle, not for the quest at least," Isaac said softly. "It was more of a...surprise hurdle. For everyone, the king included."

Everyone sitting at the table fell silent. Isaac glanced over his shoulder at the kitchen door.

"I think this might be a conversation best had elsewhere," Roslyn added kindly to the knight, and he nodded.

The five of them stood. They had not made it halfway across the hall when Fynilli entered, her fur-lined cloak and silver hair spotted with snowflakes. After depositing her outerwear in the hall closet, the older woman joined their procession. Roslyn led them down to her room, closed the thick wooden doors behind them, and secured the deadbolt. She then walked into her private bathing room, checked the servants passage, placed a bucket against the door—to alert them if someone opened it—and shut the bathing room door.

"There," she whispered. "There's no servants' door directly into the bedroom. We should be fine to speak quietly here."

"Thank you," Isaac said.

They gathered around the hearth.

"The old story of the secret heir has a kernel of truth," Isaac started. The older knight held every pair of eyes.

"There *is* a secret heir?" Henry asked, eyes wide.

Isaac bent forward, elbows on his knees, and everyone leaned in closer. "Yes, but the story is not the one you've heard."

Henry and Penet shared a knowing glance.

"Years ago, when I was a young knight, fresh to the Order, I served as a liaison between King Bradburn and King Balendin." Isaac met Juniper's eyes, and she remembered the story of his ride through the woods with the queen. "I served as liaison until the civil war took the king and his family from this world. Before his death, King Balendin asked a favor of King Bradburn."

The silence in the room could have been sliced with a butter knife. Penet eyed the knight without blinking, the firelight making his eyes appear lighter, almost icy. Henry stared just as hungrily, and Roslyn listened with the attentiveness of a curious child, eager for the rest of the story.

"King Balendin suspected the worst might happen to him and his family," continued Isaac. "He asked Kind Bradburn to take in his newborn child for safekeeping."

Juniper's next breath came quick, and she heard others do the same.

Roslyn mouthed, *Adrian?*

Isaac's eyes took on a faraway look, and he glanced at Juniper. He wore mourning in his eyes, for the king and queen he had served, for their children that he had known.

"What happened?" Penet asked, his husky whisper low, impatient.

Isaac glanced at the hearth. "I delivered the child to King Bradburn, traveling under the cover of night with the infant's wet nurse. We hadn't yet made it across the border when the king was murdered by his own brother. I wouldn't know until I reached Castle Bradburn."

The silence thickened, heavier and heavier, until she thought it might break.

"Reid is the son of the dead king of Collatia?" Henry's eyebrows rose.

"No," Isaac said at once. "Reid is the son of his father, nephew to the captain."

"Then...what happened to the heir?" Roslyn asked.

Isaac continued, "I took the infant straight to the king's chambers. That's when the king told me of what had happened in Collatia. Had we waited another day, we would not have been able to cross the border. We knew we had to hide the child. The rebels would not rest knowing the heir to the throne still lived.

"It happened that the royal herbalist had had a child not a week prior, a sickly child. The night before we arrived, the child died in its sleep," Isaac said with a heavy sigh. "At the king's behest, I delivered the Balendin heir to the herbalist with the king's task of raising it as her own. The Royal Greenhouses were close enough to the castle that he could keep an eye on the child without being obvious."

Juniper's heart stopped. Isaac looked at her again, *knowing*. She couldn't gather the strength to draw breath, or move, or blink. Something hard and cold had grabbed her heart and squeezed tight, pulling it down into her stomach at the same time it pulled it into her throat, filling her insides with something airless and heavy.

"It was a task I fear the poor woman resented," Isaac continued, eyes on Juniper. "Thank the gods the wet nurse stayed, or I'm sure the herbalist would have let the child die in spite."

And her *tutor*...the kind woman whose round face she remembered more than either of her parents. Her *tutor*, who had taught her to hide her magic. For her safety. To remain hidden.

"She buried her own child in the gardens of the Royal Greenhouses." Isaac's voice was low and full of regret. "I stood beside the wet nurse, who held the child, as the herbalist buried her child without a funeral, because no one could know the child had died."

"There's a child buried in the Royal Greenhouses?" Henry's face twisted in horror and sorrow.

"Underneath the juniper tree," Juniper whispered.

And realization squeezed her breath from her throat.

Every eye in the room shifted to her.

"Yes," Isaac answered.

The few memories she had of her mother were of her crying at the scraggly tree in the corner of the garden, on her knees, her face buried, asking, *Why, why, why?*

She had been mourning her child—the child Juniper had been sent to replace.

Chapter Forty

Silence pressed in against her ears. Blood rushed, smothering the sounds of the fire, of the others' whispering. Her vision blackened, and she leaned forward and steadied herself by flattening both hands on the hearth-warmed floor. She felt the worn grain of the wood, smoothed by thousands of feet.

"Juniper?" someone—Fynilli—asked. A hand touched Juniper's shoulder.

She sat up and forced herself to meet Isaac's gaze. "What was her name?" Juniper asked, her whisper as shaky as the rest of her.

"Isolde." Isaac's tone was warm and mournful. "Isolde Balendin, Princess of Collatia, second daughter and fifth child of King Sebastian Balendin."

Roslyn seemed to understand the meaning of his words, of his story. She grabbed Juniper's hand and squeezed it. Juniper managed to squeeze back. Fynilli had gone very still and very pale.

"By the gods," Henry breathed, his dark eyes pinned on her like he was seeing her for the first time. "He's talking about you, isn't he?"

Juniper bit her lip—her stunned silence was her answer.

"Damn," Henry said, his astonishment making way for his good humor. "First a thief, then an assassin, then an apostate, and now a princess. You move fast."

Juniper tried to mimic Henry's smile, but her lips wouldn't move.

"But if you're the only living child of King Sebastian..." Penet's eyes widened with surprise and something else, something she couldn't quite glean. It must have been the firelight shading his eyes and pulling shadows across his face. A hunger—the same hunger she had seen on the mountaintop. "That would make you the rightful ruler of Collatia, the rightful queen."

Those words stabbed and prodded deep into the soft tissue between her bones.

"Penet is correct," Isaac said. "However, since the people believe Isolde died with her parents, claiming your title and birthright would be a fight. Proving it would be a problem in itself."

Juniper waited for Isaac to add the punchline, to deliver the last bit of his story that would prove that he couldn't possibly be talking about her, she couldn't be this long-lost princess to a kingdom she'd never been to, she had panicked over nothing—but Isaac remained stoic.

"No," she gasped. She shook her head. The entire idea of claiming *her crown* or *her kingdom* made her sick and dizzy. Impossible. Ridiculous. "I don't want that. I don't want any of it. I'm not a princess. I'm not a queen. I'm not... I don't want to be."

Roslyn's hand gave hers a gentle squeeze—a reminder that she was there.

"Isolde," Penet started, his eyes wide.

Juniper glared daggers at him, and he sucked in his next breath, and whatever he'd been about to say.

"My name is Juniper," she spat. She inhaled, solidified her voice, and said again, firmly, "My name is *Juniper.*"

Her last name might not be Thimble, but she was Juniper.

Penet swallowed, he blinked, and then he nodded. "Juniper," he corrected, his voice small.

Silence fell, thick and heavy.

"This is a lot to take in for one night," came Roslyn's chime. "I suggest we sleep on it and meet back up in the morning when we've had time to rest."

"I agree," said Isaac.

Roslyn stood and tugged Juniper to her feet. The others bid Juniper goodnight and left. Juniper couldn't find the words to speak. Fynilli closed the door behind them. Footsteps in the hall faded as the others went to their rooms.

"Stay in here for the night," Roslyn said to Juniper. "The bed is large enough for five anyway." She proceeded to crawl to the opposite side.

Juniper went face-first into one of the many pillows. She felt like tearing the silk sheets apart and setting the whole place on fire, like throwing things, like drowning herself in the bathtub, and like running into the freezing night and letting the cold take away the confusion, the rage, the...everything else. She felt like sleeping until the world righted itself, until Isaac made sense of his story and she found solid evidence that he wasn't talking about her.

Roslyn patted Juniper's back, a soothing and motherly motion. "You're not all right."

Juniper rolled onto her side, facing Roslyn. "No, I'm not all right. First Reid and Ison, and now this nonsense. I don't even know who I am anymore."

Fynilli frowned. "What do you mean you don't know who you are? You're still you, no matter what your name is or what people call you. Nothing about you changes."

Juniper rolled over and sat up. "So supposedly being a princess and heir to a kingdom doesn't change anything?"

Roslyn shrugged. "Unless you're intent on reclaiming that throne, not really. You can still do what you want," she said, then her voice lowered. "But don't you see what this means?"

"That I've learned humility by living in the bottoms of society rather than arrogance and greed by having everything handed to me?" she deadpanned.

"Jun, if you are indeed a princess by birth," Roslyn started, then motioned her hand between them.

Understanding came like a cold wind around her lungs. "Then I am one of the few remaining princesses," Juniper whispered.

"And you can *return*," Fynilli stood by the closed door, arms crossed, face grim.

For the second time that night, Juniper's heart stopped.

The princess who returns—the one capable of stopping Nexon.

"This changes things," Fynilli whispered. "Once Nexon or his followers catch wind of your existence, he will not stop until you are dead. This cannot wait. I must return to the royal city at once. I know other Iluvin survivors and others who have kept their knowledge in hidden libraries. There is research to be done and more letters to write. My lady, it has been a pleasure traveling with you."

Roslyn wasn't smiling. Her eyes had gone watery. "I understand, Fynilli. Safe travels, friend. I will try to write as soon as I am able."

"I wish you all the luck in saving your prince." Fynilli pressed a kiss to Roslyn's temple, then left.

Roslyn got up to lock the bedroom door.

Juniper groaned in frustration and collapsed face-first into the pillow. She didn't want to think about any of this, her name, Nexon, or anything else. She wanted to get the herb back to Adrian and see what was left of the Undercity—if anything remained at all.

"But this means that King Bradburn knew who you were." Roslyn scooted underneath the covers beside Juniper.

She'd forgotten about that bit of information. He had known who and what she was. For how long?

"But what am I supposed to do about it?"

"I wish I knew what to tell you." Roslyn sighed dramatically and pulled the blankets to her chin. "It is a hard life to be saddled with power. People expect the world from you, but generally, all you can do is give them pretty words and a nice smile and try to make horrible things sound normal and acceptable."

"Your people love you," Juniper said.

Roslyn shrugged. "They like me because I have little impact on the decisions my father makes or the decisions my uncle makes. They don't blame me for anything, so they like me. The king is often stressed because the duty of protecting and providing for the people falls on him, or so the people want to think, when in reality, the people are what keeps the kingdom going. My uncle just keeps the laws in order to keep the people safe in the process."

"I've never thought of it like that," Juniper said.

Roslyn gave her a motherly smile. "Besides, if you marched into the Collatian throne room and demanded the crown, they'd likely have you thrown in jail. Myrisha is a sweet soul, but her brother... Let's say he's a general at heart. He would demand proof."

"I demand proof." Juniper pressed the heels of her hands into her eyes. "It doesn't matter. Myrisha can have the crown. I don't want it. I don't want to rule people. I don't want to be a princess. I just...I want to be me and live peacefully without people hunting me down or having to steal for my supper or kill people while they sleep."

"You know," Roslyn said, "if you can prove your lineage, the Collatian crown might adopt you anyway and let you live as a princess. You'd be a political figure, nothing more, but living in luxury wouldn't be bad. You'd have to say nice things to people when prompted and maybe marry a duke or a lord or some other important figure, maybe a general or captain."

Juniper snorted her displeasure. "I'd rather stay a thief than become some lord's lapdog."

Roslyn poked Juniper's side. "Not all of them are horrible. My father is quite a nice man. Maybe you could find a nice Galamondian lord and we could be neighbors! It would be nice to have someone around I like."

"You don't have friends here?"

"None that I'd share a bed with."

"Then I am honored to be bedfellows."

"You know, I've only shared a bed with one other person. Adrian." She winked.

Juniper giggled at the admission, though she wasn't surprised. Then, her smile faded. "You know, if you marry Adrian, you'll live in Rusdasin."

"Oh..." Roslyn's voice and smile deflated. "That is true, I suppose."

Juniper detected doubt and rolled onto her side. "You don't think you will?"

Roslyn pulled her bottom lip between her teeth. "It's not that I don't think he wouldn't be in favor of our marriage, but his parents...I don't think they like the idea of me. I'm a heathen in their sophisticated eyes, you know."

Juniper huffed. "If Adrian wants to marry you and you want to marry him, his mother's opinion doesn't matter," she said firmly. "He will be king one day, and his mother isn't royal by blood."

"She is still his mother," Roslyn muttered.

"She didn't like me either."

Roslyn laughed; then her smile faded. Her brows came together. "Wait, was that when you were supposed to be me?"

"It might have been."

Roslyn groaned dramatically, saying, "That means she hates me!" She threw an arm over her eyes and sighed.

Juniper laughed, and the feeling lifted something heavy from her chest. Like her lungs hadn't gotten enough air, and now they had plenty.

Roslyn dropped her arm back onto the bed. "But wherever you end up, Jun, I'd like our futures to be intertwined more than just through letters. Adrian too. I love my kingdom, but gods be damned if it's not boring as hell up here. I hate talking to Adrian through letters and being so far from everything else. It's so isolated up here, and sometimes when I'm out in the woods, I feel like the only person left in the world. I don't really like that feeling. I like my alone time, but I like knowing there are others out there. I like knowing I'm not alone."

Those words rang over and over in Juniper's mind. She liked knowing she wasn't alone too. All those days spent following targets in Rusdasin, spying potential marks, hiding in shadows—she knew she could go back to the Undercity, to Amery and Xavier, where she didn't have to hide and steal.

"I understand," Juniper whispered. "Does your father know you intend to leave?"

Roslyn gave her a mischievous smile. "He'll find out when I send him a wedding invitation." Both girls laughed. "He wants me to marry the nephew of some lord on the other side of the kingdom. I've only met the man once, and while he's nice...he's just...he's not..." She sighed. "He's not Adrian."

"Few others compare to the dear prince." Juniper had never met anyone like Adrian and probably wouldn't again.

The girls talked into the night about wedding plans, ways to steal Roslyn into Duvane, and ways to surprise everyone about her marriage to the prince. As they talked, the hearth burned low, snow whipped against the thick walls of the house, and Juniper's panic subsided. They talked until Roslyn's eyes fluttered closed, and she fell into a deep sleep.

Juniper did not fall asleep.

She lay awake, thinking of Roslyn and Adrian, and then her own predicament returned.

Princess. She could hardly believe it, but the story added up. It felt unreal, and a part of her desperately wanted it to be a lie, but then a smaller part of her entertained the idea. She thought of her time spent in Castle Bradburn, getting measured for silk and velvet dresses, the extravagant tonics and bath salts, the food, the servants—was that how she would have grown up had she not been stolen as a child?

She released a slow sigh.

And then...those people who found her in the woods that day, the smell they carried with them, the smell Nexon's monsters had shared. Had those people been Collatian rebels looking for her? Hunting down the remaining member of the royal family? Drenched in the same black magic?

She remembered that day in bits and pieces. After waking up in high spirits, she had gone outside in her bare feet and nightdress. She'd run through the garden and into the surrounding woods. They had been so alive with spring, birds and bugs and bees scurrying and chittering. And then the horrible smell, and hands—she remembered visceral fear. She knew, even as a child, the strangers in the woods were bad. They intended her harm.

Had her magic been warning her even then?

She had gotten away somehow. She'd run—right into the bandits who had sold her in the Undercity.

Gods, if they had only known.

Juniper wished she had paid more attention to her history lessons. She knew only the basics about Collatia, its royal family, and its civil war.

Sleep felt far away. Resigned, Juniper slipped out of the bed. Quietly, sleek as a thief, she laced her boots and grabbed her fur-lined cloak. Sneaking through the royal house came naturally, easing around doorways, listening for footsteps and breaths, the creak of servant doors.

She knew where she wanted to go. She had seen it on their approach. On the back of the king's house, an elegant and sturdy stone balcony overlooked a frozen lake that stretched on for several leagues. She let herself onto the balcony. A biting wind greeted her. Her pitiful magic called to the night, to the moonlight, to the vast frozen wasteland.

In the darkness, she couldn't see the other side of the lake, only a blur where the ice met the dreary night sky. Clouds gathered along the horizon, but at the crown of the sky, stars glittered and silver moonlight shone down on Galamond. The moonlight touched every fluttering snowflake, every spike of ice, and the entire world glittered as if made of diamonds.

As beautiful as it was deadly.

Ice. Like the ice that should be flowing through her blood, her bones. Juniper leaned onto the thick stone railing, carved with hand-sized snowflakes and straight-sided whorls. She would have to get her magic back from Penet soon. She missed being able to shoot ice from her fingertips.

Curious, she called to her magic. A few flurries came, but no more than she'd been able to summon when she'd first started training with Mason Hobbs.

The door to the house creaked open, no more than a sigh on the night's gentle breeze. Thinking Roslyn had followed her, Juniper kept her flurries in her hand, letting the tiny flakes of ice twirl around one another.

But the figure that came to stand beside her stood taller and wider than Roslyn, and as he leaned against the railing, his sandy hair caught the moonlight. "Can't sleep either?" asked Penet.

"No." Juniper felt his eyes on her hand, and she let her magic fade. "I've got a lot on my mind."

"I can imagine," he said. "I might not be able to relate, but I can imagine."

Juniper didn't turn to face him. She didn't want to see the emotions exposed in his eyes. She didn't want to give him another opportunity to kiss her—but a small part of her wanted to.

"My mother always said girls could think about a dozen things, where boys could only think about one thing at a time." He chuckled softly. "If that's true, I can't imagine thinking about so many things all at once."

She smiled. He was trying to help.

"I've never seen so much ice and snow. Not in the Rusdasin winters. It's beautiful." Penet stepped closer. "But dangerous. Not unlike you."

Despite herself, she blushed.

"I am sorry for what happened to Reid," Penet said. "I know there was something more between you. I'm sorry for what happened to Ison too. Despite being an apostate, he seemed all right. It's...never easy to lose a friend, and you lost two at once."

"You lost a friend too," she whispered. She hadn't realized it until then—Penet and Reid had been friends. And not that long ago, Reid had asked Penet to stand guard outside her chambers in his absence. "Thank you. He might be gone, but I've still got a piece of him." She put her hand to her chest, over where those threads tugged at her magic, connecting her to Reid and Ison. The threads still pulsed, or so she thought—the thread between her and Penet pulsed louder and stronger. She would need to follow those threads to her kernels of magic, but the thought of going to where they had died sent a wave of nausea down her spine.

Penet shifted his body toward her and held out his hand. He stood straight as an arrow, shoulders square, expression stoic and serious as death—like a knight, like Reid. A lump caught in her throat.

Juniper placed her hand into Penet's. The cold air slipped underneath her cloak.

Penet drew her closer and placed a lingering kiss against her knuckles, and said, breath where his lips had been, "Princess."

She laughed, her breath puffed between them.

Penet released her hand and held his arms open, a smile warming his stoic expression. Maybe it was the cold or their shared grief, but Juniper stepped into Penet's offered embrace. She closed her arms around his narrow middle, and he closed his arms loosely around her shoulders. She rested her head against his shoulder. Unlike her, he hadn't yet removed his leather armor. His warm breath puffed against her temple in time with his heart. For a moment, she let herself pretend Reid held her, not Penet.

She felt the thread between them go taut. The kernel in Penet called to her, wanted back, needed her—as she thought about retracting it, her thoughts were cut short by the sigh of steel.

Her magic quivered in warning—she shoved herself away from Penet just as something sharp sliced through her cloak and through her skin. Heat tumbled from the wound, gushing with the blood that splattered onto the stone balcony.

Juniper stumbled into the railing. Moonlight glinted on the bloodied dagger in Penet's hand.

Chapter Forty-One

Penet straightened—his stoic expression became murderous. He adjusted the dagger in his hand, her blood fresh in the moonlight.

"What are you doing?" Juniper pressed her hand against her bleeding side, anger and shock erupting from inside her. "Why?"

"He told me to kill you, but he didn't say why." Penet focused on her with a deadly calm she had seen so often in Reid. Intent. His voice chilled her—confused, angry, and scared. "I never asked why."

Her blood turned cold. Penet had betrayed them. Penet.

He took a controlled step toward her, and she took a step back. Penet had come armed. Two daggers, one he held, one in the sheath. His sword hung at his side. Juniper reached deep inside for what remained of her magic. There wasn't much.

It would have to be enough.

But she needed time to pull it out.

"Who?" she demanded. "Who wants me dead?"

"Because you're in the way, *Princess*." Penet spat the title with bitterness so unlike him, it unnerved her.

It took a shuddering moment for those words to sink in.

"The princess who returns," she whispered.

Penet's glare narrowed. He started to speak, bitterness twisting his pleasant features. And then his eyes shifted. They clouded with dark smoke.

"Penet?" she gasped.

His face blanked of expression. His bitterness faded, his brow smoothed. He blinked, and the smoke cleared. Where his brown eyes had been, icy blue eyes appeared. Those cruel eyes met hers, and a feverish shiver ran down her spine and into her toes. She had seen those very eyes on Ison in the Death Chamber, the night Nexon had possessed him.

"You," she snarled.

"Yes, that's right." The cold and ancient voice did not belong to Penet, yet she heard the squire's pleasant tone within it. He looked her up and down, hate twisting his features with every heartbeat. "I knew you would be trouble the moment I saw you, you little bitch. I should have killed you when I had the chance, but you just keep slipping through my fingers, don't you?"

"Nexon," she whispered.

His eyes never left hers. He barely blinked. Penet grinned, a horrible, wicked smile, full of ancient cruelty and bubbling rage. Directed at her. This close to him, she felt her resolve waver. Fear crept up her spine. Her feeble magic wavered.

"What have you done to Penet?"

"This fool?" Nexon motioned to Penet's body with the dagger. "He didn't take much convincing. All he needed was someone to tell him he could be more, he could be better, rather than always living in the shadow of the other squires. He's quite jealous of Sandpiper, did you know? Did you gather that much?" He chuckled. "A seed of jealousy can grow into something ugly when properly nurtured."

And Nexon had been messing with Penet the whole time, just as he had been messing with Ison.

"Why Penet? Why not me? Or Henry? Or Isaac?"

Nexon shrugged. "Some minds are easier to break into than others. A weakness of will." He frowned at her. "I tried to talk to you first, but you put up too much resistance. Of them all, this fool was the easiest target, and beggars can't be choosers. With Ison keeping me out, I had to look elsewhere for helpers."

Bile rose in Juniper's throat. He had tried to talk to her? He had tried to get into her mind?

"And you've been listening to everything," she said.

"And trying to deter this foolish quest," he spat. "It wasn't hard to have the squires followed, though I hadn't counted on you and Ison joining the fun. I admit, it has kept things interesting."

Juniper curled her hands into fists.

"Nothing so far has been hard," he taunted, icy blue eyes glittering. Nexon's wickedness and pride twisted Penet's kind face into something hideous. "Telling my followers to wait in the forest, follow your friends, or in the case of this fool, starting a landslide. Of those I've used, it is rare I find someone so weak-willed I can use my magic through them."

She lost her breath. "You killed them," Juniper whispered. Her heart skipped a beat.

"They were in my way." He took a step closer, moving with unnatural, predatory grace. "And you are still in my way, little princess. I always

234

wondered if you had slipped through my hands, but it doesn't matter. My time has come again, and I will not be stopped by the likes of you. It won't be long before this entire realm is mine again."

"Not while I'm here," she said.

Nexon laughed. He tossed the dagger aside and withdrew Penet's sword. She had been pulling out the residual magic deep within her. As Nexon came at her, she gathered her ice into a shield. Steel smacked into her ice. It cracked, knocking her back into the stone railing. Her shield shattered, and Nexon came at her. She ducked to the ground as the sword sliced through the air—barely missing her.

"Not so skilled with steel?" Juniper taunted.

Nexon seethed as he adjusted the blade. She predicted the path he would swing and prepared a dodge, but something hard smacked into her back. Her breath rushed out of her throat, and she fell forward—a piece of the stone railing thumped on the ground.

"I don't need steel," he said, arrogance in every word. Because he had *magic*. Earth magic.

Juniper jumped back to her feet.

Nexon lifted his empty hand, and pieces of the railing chipped away. They flew at her, one by one. Juniper dodged with quick footwork and brought up a shield of ice. Not fast enough. One stone struck her shoulder, another struck her thigh, and one struck her arm. Nexon cycled the stones around her, striking her until her remaining ice shattered.

The stones halted in midair.

"Missing something, little princess?" Nexon patted his chest. "I can feel your magic. Right here."

He tossed his steel sword aside and reached his hand toward the railing closest to him. To her horror, the ice began to move. It did not move elegantly, but it listened to Nexon's command. It rose and molded into a lumpy arrow. He shot it at her—she twisted to the side. The blunt arrow thumped into her upper arm and clattered to the ground.

Juniper called to the ice. It wobbled but did not come.

"How much longer do you have, princess?" Nexon came closer, his steps leisurely and controlled. "Your magic must be weak. You're missing a seed, hmm?"

He brought the stones together to form a sword. Juniper stumbled to her feet—he noticed and laughed. "Feeling low?"

Juniper gathered what pitiful magic she had left. Barely any at all. Nexon lunged with his stone sword. She brought a shield in front of it.

Stone smashed into her ice, and had she more magic, she would have turned the stone so cold it could burn.

But her ice cracked.

Nexon's stone smashed into her ice again. Pieces of her shield tumbled to the ground.

"You won't leave here alive," seethed the cold, ancient voice.

The stone sword came down again, shattering the ice. The impact thrust her backward, knocking her breath from her chest.

"I will not be stopped," Nexon seethed. "Not by you or anyone. You know how long I've been waiting for this? Do you know how long I've been planning this? Centuries. All the pieces are coming together. You will not stand in my way."

He raised his stone sword. Juniper's magic wobbled and failed. She staggered to her feet, desperate to get out of the way of his attack.

He brought the stone sword down, and she didn't have enough time.

She brought her hand up to take the worst of the attack—a shadow moved in front of her, blocking the moonlight, and then a crash—stone on steel.

"You?" Nexon spat, surprise in his tone.

Juniper opened her eyes. Someone stood in front of her, steel sword against Nexon's stone blade. Though he wore a tattered cloak, scratched leathers, and matted furs, there was no mistaking the man who stood steel to stone with Nexon, who had jumped in to save her—*Reid*.

CHAPTER FORTY-TWO

Juniper couldn't believe her eyes. Reid stood in front of her—sword braced against Nexon's stone, warrior eyes fierce, snow frosting his hair. A healing cut ran down his left cheek, and a bruise darkened his jaw and vanished under his woolen cowl. His leather armor was stained with blood. His breath puffed out of his mouth like an angry dragon, ready to devour Penet in white-hot flames.

Juniper didn't have the time or presence of mind to ask how or why—he was alive, and she didn't care about the details. And by the fury on his features, he had overheard Nexon. He had overheard the monster of a man speaking through Penet, bragging about possessing the young squire.

Nexon's surprise vanished as quickly as it appeared. Instead, he grinned that ugly grin of his, twisting Penet's face. "You survived after all," Nexon said, arrogance in every word. "You're more bothersome than I thought."

"Get out." Reid's knuckles turned white on his sword hilt. "Let Penet be."

His voice sent a wave of relief through her bones. She thought she'd never hear it again.

Nexon laughed. "Why? He's a prime candidate for control. He barely fought back."

"Get out, or I will end you both."

"You won't kill me," Nexon said proudly. "You won't kill this boy, not your dear friend. He looks up to you, didn't you know? You're quite the idol in his eyes."

Nexon's icy blue eyes drifted over Reid's shoulder to where Juniper sat, crouched against the railing. Reid didn't move. He didn't fall for the bait. He held his focus on Nexon.

"He thought he could wedge in now that you were dead, or so we all thought." Nexon narrowed his eyes maliciously at Juniper. "He thought about her, you know. Quite a lot."

Juniper felt numb. Penet had thought about *her*?

Reid didn't rise to the bait.

"He thought you were dead." Nexon slid his icy eyes to Reid. "He kissed her. Invited her into his tent. Invited her to live with him now that you were gone. He would be a knight, and he could protect her from the Order, he thought."

Reid seethed, and Juniper wished she could see his face.

Nexon laughed. The stone sword wiggled, tiny bits of dust falling from the seams between the stones. "Your timing couldn't have been better, squire. A moment more, and your little princess would have lost her head. Without her magic, she's useless, it seems. Not the skillful thief I assumed, just a worthless waste of—"

Reid attacked. He slammed his steel into Nexon's stone with an ear splitting clack. Nexon stumbled back a step. They fought back and forth. Reid's skill with a blade greatly outmatched Nexon's, but she could see the squire was holding back. He didn't want to hurt Penet.

Juniper struggled to her hands and knees. Nexon's words rang in her mind, *worthless, useless.* Without her magic, she was.

No, she thought as she crawled toward Penet's discarded sword. She was Juniper Thimble, master thief, ice mage, and apparently a princess. She had trained for years with steel, trading blows with Maddox, with Xavier, and with Reid. She would not be bested because she couldn't throw ice arrows at her opponent.

Her fingers fastened around the hilt of Penet's sword, and she forced herself to her feet. Reid had knocked Nexon back to the railing, chips all along the stone sword. Reid wore nothing but determination.

Nexon was smiling. He knew Reid held back.

Juniper adjusted the sword for attack, her heart trembling.

And then—

Reid's sword hit the stone, and the stone grabbed onto his sword, yanking it from his grip. A stone dislodged from the railing and slammed into Reid's side, knocking him off his feet and into the railing. Bones cracked.

"Reid!" she screamed, the sound tearing up her throat.

Nexon laughed, and without thinking, Juniper charged at him. Nexon readied to grab her sword too, but she feinted and struck at his side, leaving a bloodied gash along the weak spot in the armor.

Nexon cried out in surprise or pain—she didn't care.

"You won't—" he started.

"I won't what? Kill the puppet you've chosen? Kill a boy I barely know? Kill the boy who's been spying on us? Who betrayed us? Who tried to kill us more than once?" She mustered the old Juniper, the heartless thief, and threaded animosity into a throaty growl. "I've killed for less."

And she swung. He readied himself for a feint, but she aimed higher—for the throat.

Nexon stumbled back, his icy eyes filled with surprise, but she pretended it was fear. Fear of her, just like her targets who never thought an Undercity rat would challenge them.

She'd show him.

She heard Reid move behind her, and as she feinted, as Nexon moved to block her attack, Reid came from behind. With a warrior's cry, Reid thrust his sword through the back of Penet's armor, straight through the heart.

Nexon cried out—the painful scream became solely Penet's.

The icy blue eyes vanished, replaced with Penet's brown. Those eyes met Juniper's. Pain, fear, and remorse looked back at her.

"Penet?" Her voice came out weak.

Reid withdrew his blade, the sound tearing apart Juniper's heart, and lowered Penet to the ground.

Penet looked to Reid. "You're alive."

"I am," Reid said, nodding.

Penet tried to smile. "I'm glad. I'm sorry, Reid. He...he made me. I-I didn't know... I didn't want... I-I'm sorry."

"It's Nexon's fault," Juniper added. "Not yours, Penet."

Penet looked to her, relief in his eyes.

"And we will end him for this," Reid promised. "For all he's done."

"See that you do." Penet lost strength with every word. "Because...you... He thinks...you can."

Juniper and Reid remained by Penet as the light left his eyes.

She felt it the moment it happened. The kernel of her magic within him returned. Its warmth surged into her dwindling, quivering supply of magic and filled her like a drink of warm tea. A soft moan escaped her lips.

"Jun," Reid said, his voice soft. "Are you all right?"

She met his honey-brown eyes. "Yes, but you are not. I heard bones snap."

He didn't deny it.

She stood on shaky legs. "We need to get you inside and call for a healer. Before you die a second time."

She wouldn't be able to handle that.

Reid closed Penet's eyes and stood. He wobbled, pain on his face, and she rushed to catch him before he fell. Reid put an arm around her shoulders, and she helped him to the door he had left open in his rush. The commotion had stirred most of the house, and as Juniper and Reid stumbled into the hearth room, servants scrambled to rebuild the fire.

Footsteps came from the hall, and Juniper's heart thudded hard at the sight of Ison, in the same mismatched furs and leathers as Reid. Roslyn, Isaac, and Henry hurried into the room, all wearing their night clothes. Isaac had the sense to grab his sword, at least. At the sight of Reid, Henry let out a whoop of excitement. Juniper helped Reid into a chair by the fire.

"Reid?" Isaac knelt beside him. "What happened?"

"A healer," Juniper demanded. "He needs a healer."

"I'll send word." Roslyn marched into the kitchen with all the authority of a queen. Juniper heard her send one of the servants for a healer, another for a pot of tea, and one to prepare rooms for two more guests.

Juniper met Ison's gaze. He looked like he hadn't slept in days. He offered her a kind smile of greeting, but Juniper pulled him into an embrace. He hugged her back. The kernel of her magic within him hummed at the proximity.

"I thought you both were gone," she said.

"Sorry about that," Ison said, his calm, pleasant voice soothing.

The front door opened, and a servant entered. Snow fluttered through the air behind her. "The healer won't be here until morning, my lady," she said to Roslyn. "He's gone out to the country on a call."

Roslyn huffed. "Thank you," she said to the servant. To Reid, she asked, "Will you be all right until morning?"

Reid nodded, though he couldn't very well hide the discomfort in his face. "A few bruises," he said.

"I heard those bruises crack." Juniper met his stubborn gaze with her own. "You should be lying down."

Reid started to protest, but Isaac refused to hear it. "She's right, Reid." He helped Reid to his feet and to the nearest bedroom, the one Isaac had been staying in.

"Can you tell how much damage is done?" Reid asked Ison, much to Juniper's surprise.

Ison pushed past Henry into the bedroom. He hovered his hands over Reid's middle, his steely eyes lost in concentration. His pale gray magic glowed on his palms, searching for injuries underneath.

After a long moment, Ison said, "Nothing broken beyond repair. A few fractured ribs, maybe. I don't feel any internal bleeding. Nothing life threatening, if you take it easy."

"You'll rest until the healer arrives," Isaac commanded.

"Fine." Reid lay back against the pillow.

"All right, now the fun part." Henry leaned against the doorframe. "What the hell happened?"

Reid and Ison took turns explaining what happened since they had gone over the cliffside. As they explained their journey through the mountains, Juniper realized something had happened between the two of them. Reid no longer glared at Ison, and Ison did not look at Reid with coldness or caution. More than once during the story, Reid winced in pain. He tried to hide it but couldn't.

"We arrived here, and the innkeeper said a group of squires was staying in the king's house. I heard voices coming from the balcony." Reid looked at Juniper. His words vanished, but his hesitation did not come from his injuries—regret chilled his eyes. He did not want to talk about the death of his friend.

"Nexon got to Penet," Juniper said for him.

Reid nodded in gratitude.

Disbelief sucked the air out of the room.

"What?" gasped Henry.

Isaac looked between Reid and Juniper, the shock written on his face. "Penet? A traitor?"

"He'd been feeding Nexon information," Juniper said.

"Where we were, where we were going, and why," added Reid.

"Everything said in front of Penet was said in front of Nexon." Her stomach felt like a giant stone just thinking about it.

The knight rubbed his face. "I never would have suspected him."

"I wouldn't have either," Reid said. "Had I not heard him with my own ears, I would not have believed it. I heard him speak with a voice that wasn't his own and eyes that were not his. He was possessed."

Ison paled. He looked down into tea.

"Nexon convinced Penet that killing us was the right thing," Juniper said. "Nexon wanted us gone, all of us, and he wanted this quest to fail."

"That explained why Penet was so insistent on there being another reason for the quest." Henry rolled his head over his shoulders. "I shouldn't have told him about the secret heir thing."

"You couldn't have known," Isaac said. "Nexon convinced him."

"He doesn't convince." Ison didn't lift his eyes from his tea. "He commands and coerces. If you don't obey, he takes over. He forces you to do what he wants anyway."

Ison glanced up at Reid, then Juniper. She waited for the suspicious stares, the needling questions, but they did not come. Reid didn't look at all bothered by what Ison had just revealed. Had Ison told Reid what had happened to him?

"We have what we came for." Isaac nodded toward Juniper.

Reid's sullen expression turned hopeful.

"But," continued Isaac, "we will talk about this in the morning. You two" —he motioned to Reid and Ison— "need your rest and a good meal."

"The rooms will be ready," Roslyn added.

"Reid, take this room," Isaac said firmly.

Isaac gave Roslyn a quick bow, then headed to another room. Henry followed.

"I've sent for fresh clothes for the two of you," Roslyn added. "Unless you're hard-set on those outfits."

"Thank you..." Reid paused, waiting for Roslyn to introduce herself.

Juniper grinned. "Reid, this is Roslyn."

Reid blinked once at the girl; then understanding dawned. To Juniper's surprise, he laughed, then cringed at the pain in his middle.

"Remember how Adrian said I'd like her?" Juniper nudged his arm. "Turns out I do."

"Oh, tell him the part where I saved your ass from freezing to death." Roslyn waved her on.

Reid let out a smaller laugh, then glanced Ison. "I apologize for thinking you the traitor."

Ison shook his head. "It's all right. I would have suspected me too."

"Enough of all this talk." Roslyn barely covered a large yawn. "We're all due for a long nap."

No one argued. Ison retreated from the room, then Roslyn. Juniper lingered in the door. She glanced at Reid, who watched her. Pain twisted his features.

If only she had learned some sort of healing. For right now, her kernel of magic would have to do. It had healed him once. It could do it twice.

"I'm glad you're alive," Juniper whispered.

"I feel the same," Reid whispered, pain laced in his words. "We will speak in the morning. You need your rest, and so do I."

"You're right." She left, shutting the door behind her.

CHAPTER FORTY-THREE

The following morning, they remained in the king's house in Easley. Roslyn requested they all get a check-up from the healer, just in case, and a good meal—Ison and Reid especially, because they had been wandering through the stark wilderness for too long, eating strange game and roots.

The healer arrived midmorning, and his gruff voice filled the house like smoke. Juniper and Roslyn had been sitting in front of the hearthfire, sipping tea, when he arrived, his patched wool cloak a maze of colors and patterns, the fur at the collar matted. His beard reached his chest and eyebrows grew wild. He looked as mad as anyone could.

Juniper did not mind staying another day. While the healer made his rounds—going to Reid first—Juniper went into town with Roslyn. They spoke with shopkeepers, weavers, farmers, lumber workers, and all manner of people, gathering information for Roslyn's book. When they returned to the king's house, the healer was ready for them. It didn't take long. The wound Nexon had inflicted hadn't been deep, and the healer patched it up within a few moments, during which she squirmed under the itch of knitting skin.

Juniper was headed back to the hearth room to see the others when one of the servants found her.

"Your presence is requested, miss." The servant bowed quickly. "By Squire Sandpiper."

Juniper went straight to his room, heart flipping over and over. She braced herself on the other side of his door, took several deep breaths, and knocked.

"Enter," came Reid's calm, healthy, articulate voice.

Juniper opened the door. Reid was sitting up in bed. He'd had a wash. The dirt and grime were gone. He wore a fresh tunic. A fire roared in the hearth, glowing against his bronze skin.

"You asked for me?"

He patted the bed. "I did. I wanted to talk to you first."

She sat on the bed, a short distance from his hand.

"Ison and I found our way here because of you." He put his hand over his chest. "Because of this piece of magic you put inside me."

She paled. She felt the string between them go taut, and she knew he felt the same. She curled her fingers into her fists. "Are you upset?" Her voice came out small.

He hesitated, his eyes searching hers, always unreadable. "I should be. But your magic saved me. Again."

"I couldn't let you die," she whispered. "I couldn't let any of you die."

"You gave one to Ison too," he said. "And Penet."

She nodded. "It was to help you heal, though, if I had known Penet would try to kill me later, I wouldn't have given him one."

"What happened to the magic you gave him?"

"It returned to me when he died" She put a hand over her chest where her magic resided. "I felt it come back."

"Ison said giving us kernels of magic likely weakened you." Reid's honey-brown eyes searched her again. This time, she saw the scrutiny.

"It did." She didn't give him any further detail. "But you three lived, so I consider the risk worth it."

Silence hung in the space between them.

"What happened in the woods that day?" Reid asked. "Why didn't you come back?"

She tried to give him an innocent smile, but it didn't work on him. "I was attacked by slavers and hauled north. They intended to cross into Janti and sell me, but with the help of a dire wolf, I got away. I went north because I knew you would be going north, and I thought we'd meet up again. But a storm blew in, and I nearly froze to death. That's when Roslyn came out of the storm like a wraith."

"And saved your ass from freezing to death." His brows came together. "A dire wolf? Are you sure?"

Juniper told him about the wolf she had saved from a bear trap, the wolf that had come to her rescue after she prayed to Blugo, and the dire wolves that had appeared in the forgotten city in the clouds.

Reid's eyes remained on her face, taking in her words, the same surprise Isaac had worn.

As her story came to a close, the silence returned. Reid's surprised expression didn't change or soften.

"So..." she started. "How are you holding up? Feeling all right? Any of that strange wilderness food fighting to come back up?"

A small smile came over his lips. "Ison inspected everything we ate."

"You trusted his judgment?"

244

"He ate what I ate," Reid said. "So, yes. Despite him being a mage, I am glad I was stuck with him. His magic was invaluable out there."

"I'm glad you didn't kill each other."

"We thought about it, or I did." Reid glanced at the fire. "I only assume that he did as well." The fire warmed his honey-brown eyes like liquid flame.

"What are you thinking about?" she asked.

"Penet." His brow creased, and a mournful sorrow came over his face. "I thought him a friend, a brother-in-arms, a fellow squire. We took lessons together. I trusted him, and he betrayed us to Nexon. Though I had to kill him, I regret it. If I had known Penet had been seduced by power and greed, maybe I could have persuaded him otherwise, saved him before it was too late."

"Don't blame yourself for Penet's corruption," Juniper said.

"I don't. I blame myself for not seeing it sooner. Had I been a moment later to the balcony, he would have killed you."

She offered him a smile. "But you arrived right on time!"

Reid didn't smile back. His frown deepened.

She wanted to say something to help. Damn Reid and his refusal to let anyone else take any blame. "Some people are more susceptible to corruption than others. Some people are quicker to pick up gambling or drinking or drugs. Not all men have your steadfast duty and sense of honor."

A smile picked at the corners of his lips, and warmth came to his cheeks.

"Before you arrived," Juniper started, "Nexon admitted to having tried to get into your mind, as well as mine, and Henry's, and Isaac's. Penet was the weakest of mind among us, so he was the one Nexon chose."

"He tried to break into my mind?"

"You look about as disgusted at the idea as I did," Juniper said. "But yes. Since we were too hard to break into, he went for Penet. Ison learned mental resistance while in the Undercity, and Nexon had a harder time getting to him."

"Gods," Reid breathed, running his hand through his hair.

It had gotten a little longer since she'd last seen him, and longer since she had first met him. He caught her staring, and she quickly moved her eyes anywhere else—they settled on a folded piece of parchment on the bedside. The parchment was faded and worn at the edges and seams, from being unfolded and folded so many times.

"I carried it with me." Reid handed it to her.

Juniper blinked at him, then took the parchment. Carefully, she unfolded the worn edges. And her heart fell into her knees.

It was the letter she'd sent him. Faded and worn from being carried.

"You kept it." Pressure pushed against her eyes, but she held it back.

"I did." Reid pulled the letter from her hands, folded it, and returned it to the bedside table. He reached for her, and she didn't move. His hand cupped her cheek, warm and calloused but gentle. "When the news came you'd been killed, I couldn't think straight. All I could think about was you, how I pushed you away, and if I hadn't, you wouldn't have run. I kept thinking what I could have done differently, of all the things that could have happened that would have left you at the castle with me."

"But I'm an apostate." Her voice quivered.

"You are." His thumb moved across her cheekbone.

"And you are soon to become a knight."

"I am."

Tears pushed hard against her eyes, forcing her to squeeze them shut. Reid's hand remained solid against her cheek. "Reid," she started, her voice thinned by the tears she refused to cry. "We can't be anything more than we are now."

"And what are we now, Juniper?"

Her name on his lips did her in. The first tear started down her cheek. It vanished into the warmth of his hand. She opened her eyes and found a familiar comfort in the honey-brown of his, steady and stoic.

"Reid," she started, but her words failed her.

"What will you do after this?" he asked.

"Save Adrian," she said. "He comes first. Then I have to do something about Nexon. What, I don't know. But something. The king needs to know all that's happened, and there's an archmage supposedly loyal to the Balendin crown. If anyone knows more about Nexon, it will be him."

Reid removed his hand from her cheek. A part of her felt relieved, but the other part wanted his hand back.

"But if I go back to Rusdasin, I'll be killed before I get through the castle gates," Juniper said. "Too many people want me dead. The City Watch. The Royal Guard. The Order. I can't...I can't go back. Not anymore."

Reid nodded again. He beheld her with a curious gaze. "Of course, with you being a princess now, you might have more pull with the king."

Juniper sighed. "Who told you?"

"Isaac came by this morning," Reid said. "By the grim look on his face, I thought it worse news."

Under his curious stare, her cheeks heated. "It doesn't seem real. I'm not sure I believe the story."

"Why would Isaac lie?"

"I don't know."

"Isaac told me the king suspected who you were, and that's why he assigned him to you. Isaac served in the Balendin court before the war." Reid searched her face. "According to Isaac, you look remarkably like your mother."

She scoffed at the notion. Her mother, a queen.

"It's a bit of a step up from a lady." A smile snuck across his lips.

She half laughed.

"To think what could have been if Collatia hadn't fallen into civil war." Reid's smile widened. "You would be the unmarried princess, a prize. They might have tried to marry you to Adrian."

"Why not marry me off to a handsome young knight?" As the words left her lips, the impossibility of that marriage stung worse than it had in a while.

Reid's smile turned tragic. "Who knows?"

Silence fell between them, thicker than before.

"Do you want your magic back?" Reid lifted a brow at her.

She hadn't forgotten. She could feel the thread between them, drawn taut at his proximity. She leaned closer and held her hand over his chest. It didn't take more than a heartbeat to find her kernel of magic. It hummed as she came closer, as she drew it out of Reid. Extracting it felt like pulling something out of sand.

Reid gave a small sigh as it left his body, and it entered hers like a cool breeze. And her magic grew, filling her where before she had felt only emptiness. She would have to retrieve the last from Ison.

"Juniper," he said. "There is something else I wanted to tell you, although it's not as dire as it was last night."

"What is it?" Juniper's stomach clenched.

"It's about your parents," he said. "Or, more specifically, the couple running the Royal Greenhouses who were supposed to raise you. I went there with Graison and met them, I saw honeysuckle and lavender growing underneath a window, and I thought…"

"You thought right, apparently." She twisted her fingers together. "I barely remember anything from then. I remember a garden, but not their faces or where. I suppose I know for certain now."

"Will you go back?"

"For what?"

"To see them."

Juniper let out a bitter chuckle. "I don't think so. Now that I know the truth, that I was just a child sent to replace their own, I don't think I could face them. Certainly not the woman I thought was my mother. I always thought she hated me, and I guess I know why. I remember her husband more, and the woman I always thought was my tutor."

Reid leaned forward, elbows on his thighs. "Do you remember what happened?"

"Oh, I remember that day just fine." She bit back the familiar feelings of guilt and shame. "I wandered too far and thought the men in the woods were knights, come to take me to the Marca and lock me up. I was afraid. I ran from them and ran straight into the bandits."

And was then sold in the Undercity.

Juniper slumped forward onto her knees. Reid didn't say a word. She could hear the clatter of voices and the commotion of food and drink in the hearth room.

She wanted to say something more, if only to hear the softness in his voice. She wanted to tell him she still felt for him, but she knew the words would only hurt them both in the long run. Their destinies pointed them in opposite directions, and anything they tried would be strained and difficult.

And yet, when Reid's hand found hers, when his fingers interlaced with hers, she did not pull away.

A burst of laughter came from the hearth room, but it sounded a world away.

"Are you feeling up to dinner?" Juniper asked.

Reid considered it.

"You could use a good meal," Juniper teased. She leaned forward and examined his upper arms. "You've lost weight. You're simply wasting away!"

"Fine, fine." Reid swatted her hands away. "Let me put my boots on."

CHAPTER FORTY-FOUR

At dawn the following morning, they set off toward the southern horizon. The skies were clear and crystalline blue. The wind carried woodsmoke and the scent of pines through the city. Juniper took a deep breath of it as she climbed into the saddle. The forests stretched on forever south, divided by White Road. Beside her, Roslyn rode a midnight black horse. She wore matching black fur around her neck, the same color as her hair.

Roslyn had declined a coach. It would draw too much attention, she'd told them.

"Ready for Rusdasin?" Juniper's breath puffed in the air.

Roslyn gave Juniper a knowing, wicked smile. "I think the better questions is if Rusdasin is ready for me?"

Juniper grinned back.

As they rode, they spoke little, mostly to keep the cold air from getting inside their bodies. They rode most of the day, stopping for a midday meal and rest, and then for the night as twilight inked across the clear sky. Roslyn found them a safe clearing nestled between rocks and trees, perfect cover from the road and the cold night winds.

"Do you have a plan?" Roslyn asked Juniper as the sun reached the midmorning mark the following morning. "About Nexon?"

Isaac's head twitched. He was listening. The others likely were too.

"First, we inform the king," Juniper said. "Then see if there is indeed an archmage working for the Collatian crown."

Roslyn gave her a particular look. "You know, that is technically *you*."

"It is legally and technically Crespin Balendin until he hands the crown to his sister," Juniper corrected. "But if there is an archmage there, it's a good place to start looking for answers. He might know where the other archmages are too."

"You intend to gather the archmages against him?" Isaac asked without turning around.

"They defeated him a thousand years ago," Juniper said matter-of-factly. "We could use an archmage on our side. They are the only ones who know how, and they might be the only ones who can defeat him now."

"There is also the matter of his followers in the northern parts of Collatia," Ison added.

"And that." Juniper nodded.

"I've been thinking about that," Ison said. "I could go there with a few mages from the Undercity. Nexon will be watching for you now, and the mages who used to follow him might know how to get in."

"Is that safe?" Juniper turned to see Ison's face.

He wore no humor or fear. Only steady resolve. "Of course not," Ison said. "It's a horrible idea, and we will all likely be killed. But it's a plan."

"I'm sure Xavier would agree to go." Juniper delighted in watching Ison's face turn a bright pink.

Reid glanced curiously at Ison. Ison had told him about Xavier? She felt a pinch of jealousy at their bonding, then reminded herself she had found Roslyn. She had made a friend along this journey too.

The rest of the day went by smoothly, and that night, Juniper found the chance to retrieve her kernel of magic from Ison. She went to refill the canteens and volunteered him to help her carry them. When she explained the need to get him alone from the others, he understood. Juniper placed her hand over Ison's chest and drew her magic back to herself. A sigh escaped her lips—whole again.

"You know, splitting your magic into three is beyond remarkable." Ison held the canteens while she pulled clean water from the stream, an effortless task with all her magic.

She marveled at the feeling she had sorely missed. "Can't you?"

"No." He corked one canteen and uncorked the next. "I've never heard of anyone splitting it that much."

"Fynilli said it might be because I'm an Iluvin descendant." She snaked water into the canteen.

Ison didn't look surprised. "I suppose that makes as much sense as anything."

"Do you really intend to go north without me?"

"I didn't say you couldn't go," Ison said. "But Nexon knows your face. He'll be looking for you, Princess." Ison nodded to her. "He's been killing off princesses, remember? One of them is supposed to be able to defeat him, and he's worried it might be you."

"Because I'm ever so capable." She remembered Penet's dying words. Nexon thought she could. "And he knows your face too."

"Regardless," Ison said, "it's safest if you don't go to the hub of his followers. I'll take a small team and infiltrate it, see what we can learn, if we can sabotage anything."

"And I will see if I can recruit this archmage." Juniper snaked clean water into the last canteen.

"And we kick Nexon's ass." Ison corked the canteen.

They started back toward camp.

"So...*Princess*," Ison started.

"Stop." Juniper laughed and gave him a friendly shove on the shoulder.

They spent the evening around the fire, listening to Roslyn tell another wild story of the north. Juniper listened to her friend, but she also listened to her magic. Now that she had all of it, it responded to the ice in the air. It felt the darkness around them and pulled toward it.

And she felt, underneath it all, a dangerous drop of hope forming. They had a plan, they had possibilities, and they had a chance.

❄

After journeying another full day, the next evening, Juniper once again volunteered to fetch clean water for their canteens. No one objected. She took them all and headed to a nearby stream. The stream emptied into a lake. A waterfall cascaded down a rock face into sapphire water. From her angle, she could see a shadow in the rock. Curious, she navigated her way along the bank to the waterfall.

The waterfall was hiding a cave. With her night sight, Juniper walked inside.

No animals waited inside. It wasn't a deep cave. Terraced pools lined the cavern, fed by a waterfall high on the back wall. Water streamed from pool to pool until it formed a single stream flowing into the lake outside. Moonlight slipped inside through the roof of the cave, between the tree roots and hanging moss, and created a maze of silver streaks on the floor. In her night sight, the water glistened in shades of indigo and silver. The sound of trickling water echoed incessantly.

The water had smoothed the sides of each pool where it flowed. Water couldn't be held back, not even by solid stone. It would carve its own way through, no matter how long it took. Days, decades, centuries.

She felt power within the water, flowing through the pools, constant and steady.

She set the canteens on a smooth rock beside one of the pools. She opened the first canteen and pulled clean water from the pool to fill it. She proceeded to do so with the others.

She felt his presence before she heard his footsteps. "A princess should not walk alone at night," Reid said, his voice soft yet strong.

She capped the last of the canteens and turned. Reid stood just within the dappling moonlight, hair and eyes tinged with silver and blue. Oh, the look of those eyes on her again with favor, with kindness—her bones felt like water, yet stronger than ever before.

"You don't think I can handle myself?" She summoned a ribbon of water and formed it into a snake. It snapped its fangs at him.

Reid smiled as he swatted away the water snake. "I have no doubt that you are more than capable. More so than any woman I've met." He paused, and a subtle confusion came over his face. She recognized it. He didn't know the words to say what he wanted to say.

And her elation broke apart. "But...?" she started for him.

He swallowed and took a step closer. "But the thought of you going out alone into the night again terrified me enough that I couldn't let you go alone." He took another step closer. "I told you I would protect you, and I will uphold that promise."

Those words tingled over her skin. She knew what she wanted to say, what she wanted to do, but she knew what she wanted would only be temporary.

"I've thought about what I would say over the past several days," Reid started. "No, I've thought about it since the night you defeated the wechun." He inhaled. "I have regrets. I regret pushing you away after I saw your magic. I shouldn't have. I should have kept you close. I regret not being there when the knights came for you. I could have diffused the situation. You wouldn't have run. Neither you nor Ison would have fled for your lives. I regret not stopping Adrian from drinking the poisoned wine. I regret thinking you would have done such a thing. I regret letting you go."

Each word fell like a hammer into her stomach.

"I regret not telling you sooner," Juniper whispered. She took a step toward Reid, her legs wooden. "I regret not letting you take me in the woods."

The subtle emotions on his face softened. She took another step toward him and then another until she stood within arm's reach. As much as she wanted to, she did not reach for him.

"Reid," she whispered. "Look at me. You know who I am and what I've done. I'm no princess. I'm a fraud, a killer, a thief, a liar. And an apostate. You said it yourself, there can't be anything more between us." And those words ripped something out of her chest.

Reid cupped her cheek. His thumb moved across her cheekbone, her nose, her lips. "I don't care what you've done. There is no changing who you are or what you've done. The past is set in stone, but the future is not. It can be changed for the better. I don't know what the future will hold for you or for me."

"But—"

He pressed a finger against her lips. "I don't care about anyone else," he whispered. "I don't care what anyone says about you, Juniper. I want you with me. I don't care what name you call yourself or who your father was. I care about you, the real you, the girl I met, the girl I fell in love with." He stroked her cheek.

Her bones turned to molten metal, and his words sank into that dark abyss she had always protected herself with. She felt far too much at once, like she could fall through the cavern floor or float through the ceiling. Reid, her Reid, the brave and honorable soul she had met and fallen in love with, had returned to her.

"I've thought about you since that first night," Reid whispered. "I couldn't imagine anyone else but you. I didn't want anyone else. If I couldn't have you, I didn't want anyone."

"I thought about you." Her voice quivered. "When you wouldn't look at me, I wanted to drown myself. I didn't want to live in a world where you hated me."

"Juniper," he whispered, a plea. He struggled before continuing. "I hated not being able to look at you, because I couldn't hate you. I shouldn't have pushed you away. I shouldn't have let you go. Mage or not."

She leaned into his hand, and then he wrapped his arms around her. She pressed her forehead against his jaw and said, "Gods, Reid, keep talking like that, I might fall in love with you."

He chuckled into her hair, his breath warm tingling against her scalp. His lips met her temple, her ear, her jaw, her neck—he nudged his lips against the sensitive spot underneath her ear, and a gasp escaped her throat. He hugged her closer, and she held onto him. With every kiss he laid against her skin, she doubted her ability to let him go again.

He trailed kisses up her neck, along her jaw, and to her lips. Then pulled away.

Juniper blinked at him.

"What?" Reid asked, his voice husky. "We're in an icy cave. The moment I unbuckle my belt, the cold is going to ruin it."

She didn't feel like inviting the cold onto her private bits either. Biting her lip, she grinned at him. "It doesn't have to be cold."

He raised a brow.

She slipped out of his arms and sauntered to one of the pools. She dipped her hand into the water. Indeed, while not freezing, the water was too cold for her liking. She urged her magic into the water, warming it, warmer and warmer, until it began to steam. Reid chuckled as the steam rolled along the walls and ceiling, fogging the cavern, heating the cool air. Steam rose from every pool and waterfall.

Reid's eyes darkened with desire.

"Is it too cold now?" Juniper shucked her cloak onto the floor, followed by her jacket.

He met her mouth with his own. She unclasped his cloak and shoved it from his shoulders, unbuckled his jacket and pulled it down his arms. They pulled and tugged and unbuckled each other until not a stitch remained between them. She gasped at the feeling of his skin against hers, the skin she remembered, the skin she'd dreamed of, the body she had tasted so briefly.

They tumbled to the smooth cavern floor, a tangle of lips and limbs. Her magic felt him, felt his presence, felt his being. If he noticed her magic spreading through the air, keeping it warm, stroking his back, he didn't show it. She curled her magic around them, around him, and she felt something within him react. It drew her closer. Something inside of him embraced her in return, something she couldn't begin to describe—wholeness, safety, pleasure—and nothing in the world mattered. No war, no royalty, no ancient mage, no sick prince.

Reid let out a soft moan as it enveloped the two of them. He felt it too.

This, Juniper decided, was how she wanted to stay forever.

She hit her release. A surge went through her expended magic, a tidal wave of power, and the waterfalls and pools turned to clear blue ice. Reid collapsed onto the floor beside her, holding her closer than she thought humanly possible. His molten eyes followed the frozen waterfalls to the cavern ceiling, where the moonlight speckled through the ice, making it seem as though the moonlight too had frozen solid.

"Gods," Reid said, eyes on the ice. He turned to her.

She grinned, the residual happiness warming her more than the humid hair. She leaned closer and placed a kiss on his cheek.

It might have been temporary, but in that moment, Juniper couldn't think of anywhere she would rather be. She could pretend she and Reid might have more nights like this, they could be together sometime, somewhere, and forget the future looming with the unknown and impossible.

CHAPTER FORTY-FIVE

The rest of the journey south didn't seem as long as the one north, at least not to Juniper. They did not run into bandits, apostates, or dire wolves. No one attacked their camp in the middle of the night, and the weather was mild. Bala had finally conceded to Boxel, and the rolling hills and fields of northern Duvane had faded into the browns of late autumn. The air had turned chilly, though it seemed warm in comparison to the extremes of the Dolomin Mountains. Most trees had lost their leaves, and rain had left the ground a mush of faded reds and oranges.

At long last, Rusdasin came into view against the midday horizon. Juniper never thought she would return to this city, and yet she rode toward it. It left a bittersweet taste on her tongue.

As they came closer, she pulled up her hood, as did Ison. They were still wanted apostates, despite her supposed death at the hands of Captain Tinnly.

They rode on, and the city grew. The castle sharpened into towers and turrets and rooftop courtyards. As they rode through the outskirts, Juniper's stomach knotted itself. She wanted to turn back and head straight toward Collatia. That, too, turned her stomach to knots.

She rode beside Reid as they made their way toward the castle.

"It's all right," Reid said as they paused to let a coach pass in front of them.

"I'm fine," she said.

"Your hands are shaking."

Indeed they were. She tightened her grip on the reins, turning her knuckles white. Reid didn't understand. She rode through a city where the majority of the population wanted her dead.

They did not ride far before Ison left them.

"This is where I leave you." Ison glanced toward the Marca, hidden by the buildings on either side of them. "I will see you again, Juniper."

"I will make sure of it," Juniper said.

Ison smiled; then he peeled away from the others. Juniper blinked, and he and his horse vanished down the shadows of an alley.

The crowd grew thicker with every block closer to the castle gates. People stopped to gawk and point and whisper. Shoppers clogged doorways and window displays to get a look at the strange procession.

"I've rarely seen Rusdasin so cheerful," Juniper said as a group of children jumped up and down to see them.

"Squires returning from a quest are not a common sight." Isaac waved to the people with a kind smile. "Becoming a knight is a grand affair."

"And rumor has it," started Reid, "thanks to a secret source, the City Watch has spent the last few weeks cleaning up the dreaded Undercity."

Juniper feigned shock and placed a hand over her heart. "Is that so? Well, I do hope that source informed the nice people of the Undercity to stay indoors."

"I hear she did," Reid added.

Juniper caught Reid's stare, and it brought warmth to her cheeks. They hadn't had much time alone since that night in the cave, only a few sparse touches during meals or when they stopped to rest.

"It looks amazing!" Roslyn beamed. She looked down every street and waved to the people who might one day be her people. And the people waved back as though they knew it.

They turned onto Royal Avenue, and to Juniper's horror, the sidewalks were thick with onlookers. As they rode toward the towering castle gates, riotous cheers made any conversation impossible. The Watch had come out, keeping people from the streets.

Juniper kept her head down. Reid and Roslyn rode on either side of her and slightly ahead, blocking her from immediate view. Reid, sitting like a knight with his handsome scowl and broad shoulders, captured the attention on her right. Roslyn waved and smiled like a queen, stealing the attention from her left. Gods bless the both of them. Henry rode behind her, and Isaac led the party toward the gates. With every clop of the hooves against the street, her heart raced faster. So many things could go wrong between here and the gates, between the gates and the front steps, between the front steps and the throne room.

A mixture of City Watch and Royal Guard stood outside the castle gates. They recognized Isaac, Reid, and Henry. Juniper felt eyes on her, studying, scrutinizing, but they did not demand her identity. The gates opened with a shrieking squeal of iron, and they trotted through. The castle loomed ahead, its towers and turrets shading the front garden. Her stomach threatened to send her last meal back up.

Captain Sandpiper stood on the front steps. Pride beamed across his features as his nephew came closer. Royal Guard gathered outside, all watching, all armed. Juniper spotted several in silver armor, armed with Mage's Bane.

Isaac dismounted first, and at once, a stable hand rushed forward to take the reins. Reid and Henry followed, and Juniper dismounted and handed the reins to the waiting stable hand. Somewhere between the front gate and the steps, her heart had started to skip every other beat. Roslyn appeared at her side and gave her a gentle nudge.

"Welcome back." Captain Sandpiper stepped forward to shake Isaac's hand, then Henry's, and then Reid's. The captain looked as though he wanted to embrace his nephew, but he maintained his professional demeanor. His gaze slid to Juniper, then quickly to Roslyn. Any disgust or confusion he felt was kept hidden underneath his stoic expression.

"Captain Sandpiper," Isaac said quickly. "It is imperative that we see the king at once."

The captain's features tightened at that, and he gave Juniper one last suspicious glance before he led them into the castle. The grand front doors closed behind them, swallowing them in the gloom of Castle Bradburn.

Isaac stepped closer to the captain and added, "It would be beneficial if we met with the king with as little audience as possible."

Captain Sandpiper frowned but nodded. He led them through the castle and up several staircases and finally to a lounge with few windows. The red and gold seating angled around a coffee table, a small fire burned in the hearth, and it smelled of dust and linseed oil. The walls were the same gray stone. The windows were the same leaded glass.

"I will inform His Majesty." The captain vanished into the corridor.

Isaac released a sigh of relief. "That was easier than I feared it would be." He looked at Juniper.

She nodded. "I'm alive, so it went better than I feared."

Henry plopped in one of the dainty chairs, but Juniper meandered to a window. It overlooked a courtyard below. The courtyard's trees were barren, once-green bushes dull brown, and the grass dead. A pair of servants raked the last of the fallen leaves.

Odd. During her stay at the castle, she'd never once seen anyone tending to the courtyards.

The door to the lounge opened, footsteps stormed inside, and she turned, thinking to see the familiar face of the king.

It was not the king.

Henry jumped to his feet. Reid tensed and straightened his shoulders. Isaac looked as though he'd swallowed something rotten.

Knight Commander Fowler marched into the room, flanked by two scowling knights in silver armor. The owl and chain on the breastplate caught the light and sent it flashing over Juniper's face.

"You've returned," Fowler said, his tone drawling, his frown steady.

"Only just this moment, Knight Commander." Isaac gave a respectful bow of his head. "We must speak with the king at once, I'm afraid."

"You belong to the Order," snapped Fowler. "You should have come to see me immediately."

Juniper saw the flinch in Isaac, subtle, but there. He did not agree with the knight commander, and neither did she.

Fowler glared at Reid, then Henry. His angry, bitter gaze paused only a moment on Roslyn before resting on Juniper. His scowl deepened. "What is this?" Fowler spat. "You bring back guests?"

"Sir," Isaac said, "this is Lady Roslyn Derean and her guest."

"She requested to return with us," Reid added.

"I don't care what she requested," Fowler spat, his eyes lingering on Juniper. "It is not your duty to escort whores around the continent at their whim."

Roslyn started at that, and Juniper felt even more like smacking the old man. She opened her mouth to correct him, to remind him that Roslyn very well could be his future queen. Roslyn took a small step closer, a glare of warning to stay silent.

"Sir," started Isaac, but Fowler ignored him, stepping closer to Juniper.

He squinted, further tightening the wrinkles around his eyes. In a swift motion, Fowler ripped the hood from Juniper's head. She yelped in surprise.

"I knew it!" Fowler spat. A hand gripped her arm and yanked, and she tumbled to the floor at the old man's feet. "You've been fooled. This is no guest, but a vile creature—Juniper Thimble. You should've been dead months ago, you roach. Now you will get the death you deserve."

She heard swords being unsheathed. She stumbled onto her knees as one of the knights came forward, Mage's Bane drawn. The sunlight caught the dark blade, the feathered red, the horrible death for any mage.

"Knight Commander," Isaac started.

"Sir!" Reid called.

"Silence! You are defending an apostate? Have you lost your minds? This is why the Order exists! To eradicate her type from the world. To keep her kind from rampaging through the streets."

"But you don't understand," Isaac tried again, but Fowler spun and glared at him.

"I don't understand? Sir Pinul, you are a knight of the Order, and therefore, you answer to me. My order is that this apostate is to die. As a knight, you must obey my orders."

Isaac looked as though he had never seen Fowler before.

"She returned willingly." Reid stepped closer to Juniper. "She has information for the king."

Fowler turned his deadly stare to Reid. "What madness has gotten into you, Reid? I thought you would be among the greatest of your generation."

The blow stung, she knew, but as the Mage's Bane sword came closer, she didn't care.

Before another word could be said, the door to the lounge burst open. King Bradburn marched inside, Captain Sandpiper on his heels. "What in Bala's name is going on?" King Bradburn demanded, his commanding voice filling the room.

Juniper had never been more glad to hear his voice.

"This is an apostate," Fowler said. "The apostate who poisoned your son."

"She did no such thing." King Bradburn squared off to Fowler, tone imperious. "Release her at once."

The knight hesitated.

"I commanded you to release her," King Bradburn said. "Do you deny an order from your king?"

A tense moment passed. The knight hesitated. Deny an order from his commander or his king?

The knight released Juniper. She scrambled backward. Small, strong hands pulled her to her feet, and Roslyn put an arm around her shoulders.

"This monster deserves the Bane," said Fowler.

"I will hear what they have to say before I let the heads roll, Knight Commander." King Bradburn's voice had an uncanny edge to it when he said the old man's title.

"These squires—"

"Have returned from a quest that I sent them on," said the king. "And I wish to speak with them. You will have them soon enough."

Fowler looked as though his head might just pop from anger. He shouted commands to his knights and stormed out of the lounge. His knights followed. The air in the lounge felt thick as water.

King Bradburn turned to Isaac. "Was the quest a success?"

"Yes, Your Majesty."

Relief settled into the king's features. That relief did not fade as he took in the others in the room. His gaze lingered on Roslyn, then settled on Juniper. "Explain your numbers," he said to no one in particular.

They sat around the lounge and took turns explaining to the king all that had happened. The king never flinched, not even as they told him about Nexon, what had happened to Penet, and what Nexon yet planned to do. When the story ended, the king took a deep breath and rubbed his eyes.

"Lady Derean," the king started, "my son is not in the best of health, but I will not limit your visits. Would you like to see him?"

"Yes." Roslyn did not hide the desperation in her voice.

"I will have one of my men escort you." Captain Sandpiper motioned toward the door. A few of his men stood in the corridor, and with a quick order, one of them led Roslyn toward the Royal Chambers.

"I am glad to see the three of you alive," the king said to Isaac, Reid, and Henry. "I will inform Knight Commander Fowler of your good deeds, and your knighthood ceremonies will be planned." Then his eyes fell on Juniper. "But you."

"Your Majesty," Reid interrupted, bringing the king's attention to him. "We could not have completed this quest without Juniper's help. She saved us more than once."

"It was her the gods allowed in the garden," Isaac reminded the king. "She obtained the herb."

Henry, without a hint of joking, said, "Juniper proved herself invaluable on this quest, Your Majesty."

"I can attest that she proved herself loyal to the crown and loyal to her friends," Isaac added.

Juniper's heart threatened to beat out of her chest. Never had anyone stood up for her, not in front of Maddox, not in front of the Watch, and now three squires and a knight defended her in front of the king of Duvane.

She met the king's hazel eyes. He did not look surprised. If anything, he looked wary and worried. "Are these things true?" he asked her, his voice quiet. "Did you assist?"

"Yes." Her voice shook. "Your Majesty."

For a long moment, the king considered her. "I would grant you a pardon in a heartbeat; however, Fowler knows of your presence. No doubt half the Order knows by now, as well as anyone in the castle."

And the reality of those words hit her hard.

"Majesty," Reid started, but the king held up his hand.

"I will take this to the council and argue on your behalf, but I alone cannot grant you a pardon from being an apostate," the king said grimly.

"Fowler will have her killed," Isaac said, his breath short.

"Not if I forbid it," the king said. He returned his stare to Juniper. "I ask that you give the herb to me. I will see that it is given to the royal healer at once."

Juniper carefully pulled the glass vial from her pocket, still wrapped in cotton, and set it into the king's hand.

His fingers curled around the vial as if it might shatter. "Until this matter is resolved, you are a guest of the castle," the king said to Juniper. "But I must place you under house arrest."

Juniper nodded, though her stomach quivered. Coming back had been a horrible, horrible idea.

"Rest," said the king. "You have earned it. Captain, escort Juniper to the guest wing. Make sure someone is outside her door at all times."

She caught the tone of his voice. The guard would not be just to keep her in, but to keep others out.

The captain did not look happy. She didn't like the idea of leaving the others, but she had her magic back. She could defend herself if she needed to.

The captain led her through the castle and to a quiet wing with tall, narrow windows. Her guest room held a moderate bed of blue and gold covers, a thick rug of the same colors, a writing desk, a wardrobe, and a small sitting area.

"It's not as nice as my room in the Royal Chambers," Juniper muttered to the captain.

"You're lucky you've got a room at all." Captain Sandpiper glared at her. "Fowler wanted you dead."

"Is that any different from anyone else?"

Captain Sandpiper didn't smile. He stepped closer, hand on his pommel. "The king can only protect you to an extent," he whispered. "If the knight commander wants you dead, you are in danger."

"And I'm assuming you'd rather me be dead?"

He didn't answer, confirming her suspicions. He still found her deplorable.

"There will be a guard positioned outside your room at all times." Captain Sandpiper headed for the door. "If you need anything, let my men know. Do not leave your room. Do not invite anyone in."

She scoffed. "I can't have friends over?"

Captain Sandpiper frowned. "Do not invite strangers into your room. Do not invite anyone that you do not wholly trust into your room."

She understood his meaning.

He stood a moment longer, his face twisted with dislike for all she had done in her thieving career and for what she had done to his nephew. The captain turned on his heel and left her to her rooms.

Juniper made a slow lap around her new prison cell. Through the windows, she spotted the stables where their Galamondian horses were resting. As she stood there, she spotted specks of silver through the other windows of the castle. Knights. Patrolling the corridors, even the grounds. Waiting for her.

A horrible feeling settled into her bones. She didn't have an easy way out of this one. She could only hope that the king would help her, that her good deeds on the quest would be enough to sway the council.

And yet that feeling didn't go away.

CHAPTER FORTY-SIX

Roslyn cried when she saw Adrian lying as still as stone. His skin pale, his hair limp and listless, the protruding bones in his face and neck and hands... She remembered Adrian being strong, vibrant, and full of joy. To see him so lifeless, so close to the veil, it felt like a knife through her chest, continually twisting. She sat beside the bed while the young healer worked, keeping the poison from spreading to Adrian's heart and lungs and mind.

Castle Bradburn looked just like Adrian had described it, only with more windows. And the courtyards! She had never seen so many. She imagined how lovely they would look in summer's bloom. She would make Adrian take her to see every single one.

Because he would live.

At last, the royal healer and a wide-eyed man entered. The royal healer held a vial of bright white liquid that appeared to glow from within. Roslyn knew at once it was the potion made from Boxel's Grace.

The royal healer replaced the young healer at the bedside. Using her magic, she lifted the potion into a thin stream and sent it between Adrian's lips. The royal healer wove the potion down his throat and into his bloodstream. "That ought to do it." The royal healer hovered her hands over Adrian's chest, eyes focused, hands glowing bright green.

Roslyn's skin prickled. After all this time, all their letters, she had come so close to him. She refused to lose him.

The royal healer straightened. The green glow on her hands faded.

For a long while, Adrian did not move. Roslyn's knees trembled, and her heart inched up her throat with each beat. Roslyn feared they hadn't done it right.

Adrian took a deep breath. And another. Waking up.

Roslyn leaned onto the bedside, hands itching to touch him, but she held herself back. She instead whispered, "Adrian?"

His lips parted, already losing their deathly paleness. He took another deep breath, and then his hazel eyes flickered open. His unfocused and glassy eyes stared at the ceiling. With every breath, that gaze sharpened.

"Adrian?"

His gaze dropped to Roslyn, and she pulled her bottom lip between her teeth. Tears pushed against her eyes.

What if he didn't recognize her? Fear tugged on her lungs. Juniper could have been mistaken about his feelings for her. He might not want her here at all.

Adrian blinked once, twice. With every heartbeat, color returned to his skin. His clearing eyes searched her, and his smile stretched wide. Although weaker than she remembered, it was no less genuine. "I saw you in my dreams," Adrian said, his voice dry and weak. "Am I dead?"

Roslyn giggled, a sound only Adrian had ever been able to entice out of her. Her face heated, and her smile widened. "No," she said. "You're not dead. And you're not sleeping anymore."

"You're here?" Adrian asked. "You're really here? Roslyn?"

She brushed the hair out of his face. "I am."

Adrian blinked. Disbelief warmed his face. He pulled a shaky hand out from under the blankets and reached for her.

She caught his hand between hers and held it. "I hear you've had quite the summer," she said. "I want to hear all about it, but first, you need something for that throat. You sound like a wounded crow."

A laugh escaped his lips.

Roslyn sent the order for tea, and the servants did not hesitate to follow it. Quicker than she expected, a tray of tea and cookies arrived. After a cup of tea, his servants helped him into the bathing room. Roslyn stood outside the door, just in case. If any of those servants turned on him, she would twist their heads off their shoulders.

Finally, Adrian returned to the bedroom in a fresh tunic and trousers. He leaned heavily on one of the sturdier servants. Adrian and Roslyn sank into the soft cushions by the hearth, and over tea, he told her about the Demon Crisis and all that he hadn't been able to put into letters. Roslyn had heard much of it from Juniper, but she didn't stop him. She loved the sound of his voice, like summer. It spoke to something deeper within her, and she wanted to listen to it for the rest of her life.

Then she told him about the last few months. Her life hadn't been nearly as exciting as his, not with the early snow and poor hunting. She arrived at the part where she saved Juniper from a snowstorm.

At that, Adrian's eyes widened. "You met Juniper?"

Roslyn nodded. "I like her."

His smile lit up his entire face. "I knew you would."

Roslyn told him about the rest of the journey, as much as she could while being cautious of listening ears. Adrian drank in every word.

"You're incredible," Adrian said at last. "Frighteningly so."

She shrugged.

"Roslyn..." Her name on his lips sent a shiver down her spine. "Stay here with me."

Her entire body tingled with those words. "Adrian," she started.

"I know this isn't as romantic as it should be, but I fear that I might not get another chance," he said. "If I blink, I fear you'll be gone when I open my eyes. I want you to stay here with me, forever."

She lost her breath. She never thought she would hear those words. "I can imagine my father's face."

He smiled. "I think he'll get used to it when you sign your letters as Duchess Roslyn Bradburn."

She sucked in her breath. "Adrian?"

"Marry me," he said. "I never want to be away from you again."

She couldn't help herself. She abandoned her tea and flung her arms around Adrian's neck. How often had she dreamed of this?

Adrian's arms folded around her. "We'll have a dinner tonight to announce the news," he said into her ear, "though we should tell my father separately so he's not surprised. He hates being surprised in front of others."

"I'm sure he will be thrilled to see you," Roslyn said.

Adrian lifted their intertwined hands and kissed her knuckles, then pulled her closer for a kiss on the lips. "But we can hold off telling him a few moments longer. I'd rather spend as long as I can with you."

She giggled against his lips. Oh, she could get used to those lips.

CHAPTER FORTY-SEVEN

Ison guided his horse through alleys and down side streets, keeping his head down. He heard people shouting about the returning squires—women yelled at one another across alleys and from apartment windows, washing hanging between them. People rushed to Royal Avenue to catch a glimpse of the squires returning from their harrowing quest. The air had turned giddy.

Ison rode toward one of the few Undercity entrances he knew about. All the while, he thought about the others. If Juniper had turned the Undercity over to the City Watch, what would he find? If the others had gotten out, where were they now? Had they even made it out?

He paused alongside a canal. The entrance was through an iron-gated door under the narrow, rundown bridge. The door couldn't be seen from the road, but Xavier had taken him to see it once.

Down below, the water rushed along the stone-walled canal. Unlike the crystalline waters of the northern rivers, the water in Rusdasin was muddy brown and filled with debris and gods knew what else.

"Thinking of taking a swim?" came a low voice from a shadowed alley. The speaker was lean and tall and wore dark leathers and a hood. But Ison didn't need to see his face to know him. His voice had sent something warm through his chest. Something he hadn't felt in a long time. Maybe ever.

Xavier looked up, his blue-gray eyes unchanged.

Ison searched his mind for something to say, something witty and smart. But he had nothing. His back ached from riding so long, he'd run out of water leagues ago, and he hadn't slept well for several weeks.

Xavier seemed to realize it. He stepped out of the alley and climbed onto the back of Ison's horse without a word. Bringing his arms around Ison, he took the reins. Xavier guided the horse along the canal, toward the castle. It loomed in the distance, towers and turrets just visible over the city.

"You smell terrible," Xavier said after a block.

"My apologies," Ison said. "I haven't had the amenities for washing."

They rode another block in silence, and Ison felt the air turn awkward. The last time they had seen each other, Xavier had kissed him. What should he say? Ison had never been good with these sorts of things.

They rode alongside the canal and into the small stables beside a grand yet modest manor. Pointed ironwork lined the dormers and window boxes, the small yard was brown with autumn, and the leaded windows were adorned with dark shutters. Beautiful and foreboding.

Xavier led Ison along a walkway and through a side door into the manor.

"Where are we?" Ison whispered as they entered a mudroom full of shoes, boots and slippers alike.

Xavier opened the interior door to the house, and a murmur of voices flooded into the mudroom. Ison blinked curiously at the assassin. Xavier didn't say a word, only nodded for Ison to enter first.

Ison hesitated.

"I'll explain, but first, you need a bath," Xavier said.

"That is agreeable," Ison conceded.

Xavier led him down a corridor and to a well-used bathing room. A tub had been curtained off from the rest of the room, and while Ison washed, Xavier leaned against the vanity and explained how they had escaped the Undercity's scourge via underground tunnels built by the earth mages. The house serving as their headquarters belonged to Amery. She had graciously allowed them to stay. Some of the mages had found their own residences in town, but those with an interest in defeating Nexon had remained, including most of those from Bois's keep and several from Josephine's.

When Xavier's story came to an end, Ison started to speak. He told him everything, including his plan to head into the northern parts of Collatia and sneak into Nexon's camp. At that, Xavier went silent.

In a heartbeat, the curtain flew to the side. Ison jumped. He hadn't even heard Xavier move.

"Are you fucking mad?" Xavier growled. "You want to march into Nexon's camp without more of a plan than that?"

"I thought I would ask some of his ex-followers for tips," Ison admitted in a quiet voice.

Xavier's scowl deepened. "That's a horrible idea. You'll be eaten alive by those maniacs. You'd be a fool to walk in there without backup or an alternate plan in case your barely-there idea goes horribly wrong. Gods only know what they're doing over there."

Ison didn't have anything to say. He thought of how both of them should be embarrassed, but neither were. Xavier continued to glare at him.

"Do you have a better idea?" Ison finally asked.

"No," Xavier said. "Which is why I'm going with you."

"Even if it gets us both killed?"

"That's why I'm going." Xavier crossed his arms. "To make sure you don't get yourself killed. When do we leave?"

Ison didn't have an answer.

Footsteps sounded in the corridor, and a voice called, "Xavier? One of the scouts said you brought back a friend."

It took Ison a moment to place her voice—Amery.

"It's Ison," Xavier said.

"Oh? What are you both doing in there? This is a communal bathing room. None of that, please. There're plenty of bedrooms."

At that, Xavier's brows rose, and his smirk vanished. Ison chuckled. It would take a lot more to embarrass a Marca mage.

"We're talking," Xavier spat.

"Is that what you're calling it?" she said back, her voice lithe with amusement. "Do you need any pointers?"

"No!" Xavier's voice cracked.

Ison laughed harder. Xavier stomped back toward the vanity. On the other side of the door, Amery's light cadence of laughter floated down the hall as she walked away.

CHAPTER FORTY-EIGHT

Juniper woke and lay in bed until the misty blue light of dawn turned buttery and warm.

House arrest. Her reward for saving the crown prince, for risking her life for his yet again—this time of her own free will—was endless days in this dreadful room. Locked up because of her magic, because the damn knight commander had found her first.

She decided she did not like the bitter old man one bit. She'd envisioned his death a hundred different ways while waiting in this...cell.

The windows were narrow, but they weren't sealed. She'd opened one the evening before to gauge how hard it would be to escape. Hard, but not impossible. She could scale the walls and slip into the Royal Grounds. She had delivered the herb to the king and told him about Nexon. She had done her part in the game. Any reasonable thief would have left on the first night, rather than wait out what could be a death sentence.

Rusdasin thought her a ruthless criminal, and she doubted a few words from the king would change that. The council would be no different.

The king wouldn't let the council condemn her to death, would he?

That morning, pacing by the window, she made her decision. She would wait. If the council sentenced her to death or imprisonment or anything horrible, she would escape. No cell could hold her. The king knew it. The Order knew it. The captain knew it. Placing her under house arrest had likely been a trial—to see if she could follow the rules.

She could play along for a while.

To pass the time, she practiced her magic. She sat in the middle of the room and created snowflakes the size of her hand, each more intricate than the last. Oh, she had missed the feeling of her magic! She weaved tendrils of ice around and around, creating rune-like snowflakes that glittered in the sunlight and did not melt.

She was so caught up, she didn't hear the footsteps in the hall or the key sliding into her door.

A shadow fell across the snowflake.

Captain Sandpiper stood above her, his black and gold doublet immaculate. "The council is ready for you," he said grimly.

The snowflake vanished, and she stood.

The captain regarded her without feeling, and she felt even more like a prisoner. "Are you ready?" he asked.

She glanced at the simple jade dress she wore—one of the few remaining in her dressing room from when she had been pretending to be Roslyn that spring. Donning a dull shawl, she followed the captain into the corridor. She didn't remember much about the walk—aside from the number of knights in the castle. They were everywhere. Even the fearless captain seemed on edge.

The council chamber was a square room of black and gold tiles laid to resemble the sun. The council sat on tiered seating around the room, all grim faces and black robes, all staring down at Juniper with indifference. Small windows ran along the top of the stone walls, letting in a miniscule amount of sunlight. Torches lined the walls, their flickering light pulleing shadows across the room.

King Bradburn sat in a box reserved for him. Beside him sat Isaac and a younger man—his advisor, Ron Hendle. Isaac looked dire. His Majesty looked grim. Ron wasn't looking at her at all. He was talking to Knight Commander Fowler, who looked like he had just heard good news. His eyes met hers, that smile stretched imperceptibly, and she felt a shiver run over her skin.

What did he know?

"Juniper Thimble," came an older, grave voice. A councilwoman stood. Unlike the other members, her black robes were accented with silver. Her graying hair was twisted up into a severe bun, and her dark eyes glared down her nose at Juniper. "You have been brought before the council." Aside from the older woman's voice, the chamber was silent. "You stand accused of theft, murder, forgery, and a grand number of things that would take too long to list. You have been accused of the attempted assassination of Prince Adrian Bradburn. You have been accused of faking your own death to escape retribution for your crimes."

The councilwoman paused, and the silence turned deadly. Juniper folded her hands together in front of her to hide their shaking.

"Of these things," the councilwoman said, "His Majesty, King Bentley Bradburn, has acquitted you."

Juniper released a breath she didn't know she had been holding. Her knees threatened to give out but somehow held. The king had acquitted her of her crimes. She wanted to turn to him, but she couldn't move. If she tried, she might collapse onto the floor.

Captain Sandpiper shifted from his place behind her. A reminder of his presence.

"The council agrees that your acts of crime are deplorable. You should be given an execution befitting your lifestyle and status as an apostate: Mage's Bane," said the councilwoman, and Juniper felt her bones turn to sand. "However, we have heard from several sources of your deeds of bravery, sacrifice, and selflessness. We have heard accounts of your loyalty to the crown. Because of this, the council has approved the king's decision."

Juniper bit her lip. She didn't care how it made her look in front of the council.

"However," came the councilwoman's grave voice, "for being an apostate, there is no king's pardon. Under the laws of the Order, a mage cannot be turned free."

Juniper sucked in her next breath.

"Tomorrow morning," said the councilwoman, "you will join the mages in the Marca and begin working toward redemption."

A gavel struck wood with a sharp clatter, finalizing the council's decision. The room's still air became a murmur.

Juniper couldn't feel anything. The world didn't seem real. A hand touched her elbow, and she didn't have the will to pull away.

"Don't look so glum," came Captain Sandpiper's voice, an older version of Reid's. "The king argued for a good two hours to save your life." The captain guided her out of the room and into the corridor. Toward her guest room. "Reid, Henry, and Sir Pinul argued on your behalf as well." He added lowly, "Fowler argued vehemently against you."

She didn't have the voice to speak. Her heart felt as though it might tumble out of her mouth at any given moment. Captain Sandpiper led her through the doors and into her guest room. She took a breath and started toward her bed, only then realizing they had not walked into her room.

They had walked into the court magician's chambers. Mason Hobbs stood at his grand rosewood desk, looking as grim as the councilwoman. He wore robes of deep plum, secured with a golden cord around his middle. His gaunt face seemed thinner than she remembered, and his silver hair longer.

"The king will be along shortly," the captain said to Mason.

"Juniper, come sit." Mason gestured to one of the armchairs angled in front of his desk. She obliged and sank into the one closest to her. "Take a breath."

She took several. His desk looked the same, carved with runes and whorls, and she found the one with stars and bones she had recalled in the gods' temple. The stars in the sky, the bones underneath. The strange grandfather clock ticked away, but she didn't know if it actually told the time. It had a dozen hands in different metals, lengths, and shapes. Mason's study smelled the same, like hundreds of herbs and minerals, exotic and familiar. The air had a gentle energy to it—magic.

"They're sending me to the Marca," she said after a while, her voice weak.

"I know," he said softly, apology in every word. "It is better than what the knight commander wanted. He wanted you executed immediately by Mage's Bane. The king outright refused him, and it has caused tension."

Movement. Someone came to stand beside the chair, and in a blink, she found honey-brown eyes looking into her own. Something inside her calmed.

"Reid?"

His hand grasped her shoulder, steady and strong.

"We must hurry this along," came the voice of King Bradburn. He strode into the room. "We haven't much time. Captain?"

"Your Majesty." Captain Sandpiper marched across the sitting room and into the corridor.

Mason's gaze fell on Juniper. "The king tells me you plan to move against Nexon," he said quietly, his wizened voice sharp as any blade. "You plan to seek out the archmage serving the Balendin crown?"

"Though I don't know how I will be able to from inside the Marca," she said softly.

Mason moved around his desk and knelt in front of Juniper. He grabbed her hand and held it tight. "Juniper," he said, his voice urgent. "It has come to my attention that you spoke to a certain mage regarding the Iluvin and Nexon. I need to know what this mage told you. Exactly what she told you."

Fynilli. She had written to several of her Iluvin contacts. Juniper blinked at Mason, and understanding loosened the edges of her dread. Mason had been one of those contacts?

"What did she tell you?" he asked again, softer.

Mason Hobbs was Iluvin. Of course he was. His power, his knowledge—it seemed obvious now.

"She told me that Nexon had done something to protect himself, and only the other archmages had been able to defeat him. No one knows how

273

they did it. The archmage in Collatia might know," Juniper whispered. "Nexon has been returning to power since his demise, killing princesses because he fears one might return to stop him."

Mason remained quiet for a long moment, his piercing eyes searching hers. Thoughts churned behind those eyes, too quickly for her to grasp. Did that come with age? At long last, Mason turned his attention to the king. "It would seem she knows more than I anticipated," Mason said.

"It is yours to explain, Mason," said the king, his tone reserved, almost nervous, and that made Juniper worried—what could make King Bradburn nervous?

Reid squeezed her shoulder, and she sought out the steadiness of his eyes. He looked not at her but at the king, worry pushing through his stoic indifference.

Mason returned to the other side of his desk. He sat. Leaning onto his desk, he folded his bony fingers together. "I didn't realize you would become such a part of the castle," he said to Juniper. "If I had known, I might have done things differently. But, what has been done is done. First, I don't know what Nexon did to himself or what the archmages of the past did to him, but whatever they did, they did not kill him. They weakened him. It is my understanding he ended up in Bradburn Castle, looking for something."

"You knew it was him?" Juniper breathed.

"Not at first." Mason shook his head. "It was the presence of the wechun that gave his identity away. Luckily, he did not know I knew."

"And you..." Juniper paused.

"I am an archmage," Mason answered.

The beat of silence that followed made the hair on her arms rise.

Mason Hobbs, an archmage? Of the energy element, Juniper reminded herself. It made sense. Ison had commented on Mason's remarkable power.

"Then you know how to defeat him," Juniper blurted, hope worming its way back into her voice.

Mason looked down at his hands. "I was but a boy when Nexon fell from power. My uncle was archmage then. I came into the position two decades later, when my uncle passed. I can't tell you how it happened. My uncle never spoke about it."

And that hope withered and turned to ash.

"Does Nexon know you're here?" Reid asked.

"I suspect he does," Mason said. "It would be foolish to assume he didn't. I suspected his presence, so I assume he suspected mine. Only he hides his face. I do not hide my own."

"He's still hiding in the castle," Juniper whispered. "Using his powers of earth to move between walls and floors without being detected."

Mason nodded grimly. "The archmages are of equal power. Alone, I would not be strong enough to face Nexon. If other archmages were to stand with me, we would be enough. The archmages are well hidden. Delmont Thacket is the Archmage of Fire. He is in Collatia, working alongside the Balendin throne. Nexon is the Archmage of Earth, and I am the Archmage of Energy. I haven't the slightest knowledge about the Archmages of Air or Water. They could be anywhere."

"Would this Delmont know where they were?" Juniper asked.

"It is possible," Mason said. "He is safe in Collatia. He might have connections to the others."

"We need to see him," Juniper said.

"We need to get you to safety," Mason said. "Fowler is out for your blood."

"Tomorrow, the Order will take you to the Marca," the king reminded her.

And that dwindling sense of hope fell.

Reid squeezed her shoulder and asked, "Isn't there something we can do?"

"I can conscript mages into service," King Bradburn explained. "In the coming weeks, King Crespin will step down as king and crown his sister. It would be wise to strengthen the alliance with Myrisha. It is common to send ambassadors when a new head wears the crown." To Juniper, he said, "Seeing that Squire Sandpiper and yourself work well together, it would not be unwise to send the two of you."

Juniper blinked at the king, the man who had enslaved her, treated her as a pawn to keep his son alive, and now who planned to help her escape the Marca.

A knock sounded on the door. A beat passed, then a knock came again, twice.

"We are out of time," King Bradburn said. "Juniper, Reid." He nodded to them a farewell, and then he swept out of the door.

Captain Sandpiper appeared and motioned for Juniper. "You need to return to your room before your absence is noticed."

She stood and paused to meet Reid's eyes. They didn't have time for words.

Captain Sandpiper pulled her by the arm, out of the court magician's chambers, through the corridor, up a servants' passage, and into the guest wing. The Royal Guards standing on either side of the door didn't so much as blink as the captain ushered her inside and closed the door.

Juniper stood alone in her guest room, her temporary prison cell. Her stomach twisted and churned.

Tomorrow morning, the Order would come to take her to the Marca.

She hadn't gotten to say goodbye to Reid or ask about Adrian or see Roslyn.

She took a deep breath. There wasn't anything to be done now. She could only wait and hope the king's plan worked.

If not, she could always blast her way out of the Marca and find her own way into Collatia, like she and Ison had planned.

Either way, she would get to Collatia. She would find the archmages. She would stop Nexon. With or without the blessing of the Order.

Coming Summer 2023

Nightmares in the Ice

Stars and Bones Book IV

Acknowledgments

When I set out to write what would be the first draft of *Thief in the Castle*, I never dreamed I'd make it this far. This book did not come about without help. First and foremost, I have to thank Mom and Dad for believing in my dream of being a writer. I don't deserve the support and enthusiasm I've received.

My force of friends who put up with my overly enthused talk of fictional characters and the worlds they inhabited. Laurel, you have been invaluable during my writing journey so far. Travis, you never shied away from that nerdier side of me and listened to my world-building rants. I'm lucky to have you.

This book would never have come about had it not been for the amazing team at Authors 4 Authors. Renee, Rebecca, Kari, and Brandi, thank you for giving Juniper a chance and believing in me. I don't know where I'd be without you.

And most importantly, the reader. Thank you, each and every one of you.

ABOUT THE AUTHOR

Beatrice B. Morgan lives in southern Illinois. When she isn't reading or writing, she is most likely playing a video game. She is a night owl, caffeine addict, yoga enthusiast, dog person, hopeless romantic, optimistic, and a shameless Ravenclaw.

Follow her online:

www.bbmorgan.com
Twitter: @BBMorgan_W
Facebook: @BBMorganBooks

Also by Beatrice B. Morgan
Hard as Stone

Seventeen-year-old Raven Thane wants an adventure...and she's going to get one. Just not the way that she expected. Bored and disinterested with a routine life in her remote underground community, she fails to notice a thief during her turn at guard duty. Zander, a charming sharpshooter, tasks her with helping him retrieve the mysterious stolen item. Posing as a couple on the road, they'll face deadly automatons and Gray Elite soldiers, entangle themselves in a complicated world of spies and freedom fighters, and hide secrets of their own. Can Raven fix her mistake and prove herself more than a simple country girl? Or will she create even more chaos?

books2read.com/hardstone

Authors 4 Authors Publishing

A publishing company for authors, run by authors, blending the best of traditional and independent publishing

We specialize in speculative fiction: science fiction, fantasy, paranormal, and romance. Get lost in another world!

Check out our collection at https://books2read.com/rl/a4a or visit Authors4AuthorsPublishing.com/books

For updates, scan the QR code or visit our website to join our semi-monthly newsletter!

Want more female-led fantasy? We recommend:

Exile
by Melion Traverse

After killing a paladin in revenge for her family, Squire Bryn is cast out by order of the god Avgorath himself. Now she seeks atonement with the father of the dead paladin. But machinations far greater than a disgraced squire are at play. Unicorn riders—believed to be only legend—ride through the land. A young sorcerer needs help in finding his father, and a mystery brews that could hold the fate of two worlds.

books2read.com/exile